The Throne of the North

Path of the Ranger, Book 18

Pedro Urvi

COMMUNITY:
Mail: pedrourvi@hotmail.com
Facebook: https://www.facebook.com/PedroUrviAuthor/
My Website: http://pedrourvi.com
Twitter: https://twitter.com/PedroUrvi

Translation by:
Christy Cox

Edited by:
Mallory Brandon Bingham

DEDICATION

To my good friend Guiller.

Thank you for all your support since day one.

Other Series by Pedro Urvi

THE ILENIAN ENIGMA

This series takes place several years after the Path of the Ranger Series. It has different protagonists. Lasgol joins the adventure in the second book of the series. He is a secondary character in this one, but he plays an important role, and he is alone…

THE SECRET OF THE GOLDEN GODS

This series takes place three thousand years before the Path of the Ranger Series

Different protagonists, same world, one destiny.

MAP

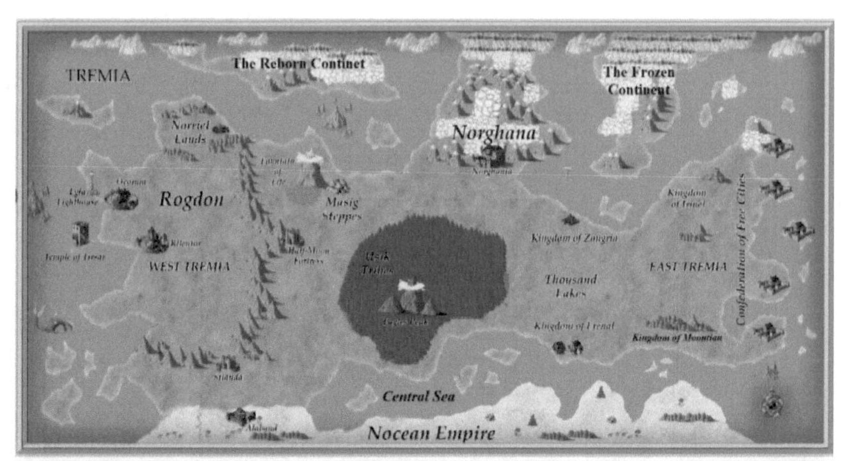
TREMIA
The Reborn Continet
The Frozen Continent
Norriel Lands
Norghana
Rogdon
Masig Steppes
Kingdom of Zangria
Kingdom of Irinel
WEST TREMIA
EAST TREMIA
Thousand Lakes
Kingdom of Moontian
Confederation of Free Cities
Central Sea
Nocean Empire

Coperne Island
Nocean Empire
Wahalatan
Salansamur
Tanwalha
Zenut
Jibalalfajr
Wahazarqa
Madinatalmusa
Almadinat
Albahrwalin
Kabiramadina
Cinders Island
South Tremia

Chapter 1

Gondabar was looking at the maps he had spread on the top of his large desk. The biggest one, which took up the whole center, showed the mid-south deserts of the continent. Due to its size it was covering a piece of another map that lay on the lower left side of the desk, which showed the whole south of Tremia. It was also hiding part of the map displayed at the top right, which showed the northern part of Central Tremia.

The leader of the Rangers looked dispirited and weak. The former was no doubt due to the gravity of the situation the kingdom found itself in, as well as all of Tremia. The latter was because of his health, which was not improving, even under the care of the Healer Edwina, which was not a good omen.

He looked up and stared at the room with the look of someone who had forgotten where he was. He saw Raner beside him, also studying the maps closely. On the other side of the desk stood the Snow Panthers, who had been summoned to discuss the state of the kingdom, and the new discoveries and dangers.

"Thank you for coming so swiftly," Gondabar told them.

"When our leader calls, we come at once," Ingrid replied.

"We are happy that our leader is able to enjoy his freedom and his own rooms," Lasgol said.

Gondabar twisted his mouth in what looked like a slight smile.

"You can be sure I am even happier about that."

"It was such an injustice," Nilsa said, unable to disguise the anger she felt.

"An irreparable attack to your honor," Astrid added with contained fury.

Gondabar raised his right hand.

"I appreciate your sincere support and loyalty. But it's no good to regret past injustices. We must overcome them and keep working toward a better future. What's already happened can't be changed, we can only learn from it and strive for a better tomorrow."

"One can always seek revenge. It doesn't change the past, but it can bring joy to the future," Viggo commented in the usual caustic tone of his amoral comments.

Raner stiffened when he heard.

"Nothing will be done about this," he said firmly. "None of you will do anything about it. That's an order. Understood?"

"Understood, sir," Ingrid promised.

"You must never judge the King or get in his way. No matter what his designs are. You're here to protect and serve him, not to question him. Never forget that," Gondabar admonished them, pointing a finger at each of the Panthers.

"We understand that the King's designs are above our personal opinions and wishes. We serve the crown and Norghana with honor and patriotism, sir," Egil said. "But we all think that what happened is an ignominy."

Lasgol threw a sidelong glance at Egil. The words he had just uttered sounded correct, yet he noticed Egil had made no mention of the king at all. He was not the only one to notice—Viggo was flashing one of his dangerous smiles.

"The matter is closed then," Raner concluded.

"Let's focus on what's important now," said Gondabar. With his bony index finger, he pointed at a city on the map, one in the middle of the deserts.

"It's here, right? In Salansamur?" he said without looking up from the map.

"That's right, sir," Lasgol confirmed.

"At the end of the Amsaljibal Mountains."

"Those mountains are now known as the Cursed Mountains," Raner said as he stared at the maps beside Gondabar.

"From what I understood from the desert dwellers, the whole area is cursed," Lasgol explained.

"Then we can assume that the Noceans know something's happening there," Gondabar said. "They must have investigated, Malotas is a ruthless emperor. He'd never let one of his main cities vanish from his empire like that."

"The fact that they know something is happening doesn't mean they're going to do anything about it," Raner said as he bent over the desk to take a better look at the map.

"Perhaps they already have and the result wasn't at all satisfactory," said Egil.

"That might be, indeed," Gondabar nodded heavily. "Anyway, I think we should make sure the Nocean Emperor knows what is inside that mountain."

"And whether he's going to do anything about it," Raner added, folding his arms over his chest.

"Most likely he'll have news that something's going on and will have sent someone to find out what it is," Ingrid said. "That would be the most reasonable thing to do. No ruler would let an important city become a ghost town without investigating the cause."

"Isn't the Nocean Empire immense? And isn't it always involved in inner wars? Perhaps he hasn't even given any attention to this matter," Nilsa said thoughtfully.

"True. Emperor Malotas has conquered the whole south of Tremia and formed a large empire. But he's having difficulty keeping it unified. Rebellions are constant in the desert lands," Gondabar told them.

"We should inform the Noceans. They might already know what's happening, but if not they should be warned. After all, it's their territory. Perhaps then they will take action. They have the most powerful army on the continent," Raner said.

"They're going to need it against the reptilian monsters the Immortal Dragon has," Lasgol added.

"Informing them and verifying whether they know about the trouble or not would be an interesting option," Egil commented. "In any case, it doesn't ensure that the Nocean forces will act."

"Emperor Malotas will act without a doubt," Ingrid said with conviction. "There's a dragon with an army enslaving his subjects. It's what honor dictates."

Viggo smiled, making a face.

"I'm always telling you that you shouldn't assume others will act according to your values and code of honor, least of all a foreign emperor only interested in conquering more land and power."

"From what I've heard some Rangers and soldiers comment, the Nocean Emperor is quite ruthless and bloodthirsty…" Gerd said.

"Yeah, he has that reputation, I've also heard the same thing," Nilsa confirmed.

"Perhaps they give him a bad name because he's misunderstood. Most of the conquering leaders are," Viggo said with irony. "They only want to conquer and collect riches and increase their power. If in order to gain this they have to shed a little blood, what else can they do? There's nothing wrong in that, they're misunderstood and people judge them too harshly. That's my opinion, of course."

"Don't speak non…" Ingrid had to hold back when she saw that Gondabar and Raner were looking at her. "You know perfectly well that his bad reputation has been earned with the atrocities he's committed," she finished saying, instead of what she had intended to.

"Ingrid's right," Nilsa joined in.

"In any case, it would be an intelligent strategy to get the Nocean Empire to intervene in the situation with this Immortal Dragon," Egil argued. "We must consider that, for us or any kingdom in northern Tremia, trying to get to the bottom of the problem would be very complicated. That is if we even managed to obtain the royal approval for such a campaign."

Gondabar nodded repeatedly.

"King Thoran will never approve sending forces to a Nocean territory, least of all now that we're about to enter a war against the Kingdom of Erenal."

"And least of all if we tell his majesty the reason. He would lock us all up or hang us," Raner added. "We have recent and clear evidence of that," he commented, looking at Gondabar.

They all nodded and bowed their heads in thought. Gondabar had already suffered the consequences of trying to persuade the King of the existence of Dergha-Sho-Blaska. Trying again without any other evidence than Lasgol's testimony would be condemned to failure. And the punishment would be merciless, without a doubt.

"Exactly, we can't go to the King," Egil said in agreement. "He won't listen to us and we can't let him lock us up or execute us as an example which, on the other hand, I find very likely. We have to try a more subtle approach."

"What do you have in mind?" Gondabar asked him, and from the look on his face he already guessed Egil was planning something.

"We must force Malotas and his armies to be the ones to take back the city and Cursed Mountains," Egil explained. "Sending Norghanian troops or our allies of the Kingdom of Irinel to the deserts is something I don't see feasible. First, because we wouldn't manage to persuade the monarchs of either kingdom, and secondly, because even if we did find a way to persuade them, the Nocean Empire would take it as an aggression and we'd have another war on our hands, which is not in our best interests at all."

"Especially now that we've just started a war with Erenal," Gondabar said, nodding.

"It's a good strategy, but I can't see how we're going to persuade Emperor Malotas to send troops there to face the Immortal Dragon and his army of monstrous reptiles, not even mentioning lesser dragons," Gondabar commented, shaking his head.

"Unfortunately, we can't send a contingent of Rangers to fight them either. It would be a suicide mission—they would be destroyed," Raner concluded.

"They would tear us to shreds, I can swear to that," Lasgol said, nodding emphatically.

"Is his army so formidable?" Gondabar asked. "Not that I doubt what you've told us in full detail. I just want to make sure I understand the situation correctly, to be able to act accordingly."

Lasgol nodded, snorting.

"Formidable and numerous. Even without their leader, we'd need a great army to defeat them. In fact, I don't even know whether our own army would be able to," Lasgol said with a shrug and a grimace.

"Which leads us back to my idea of forcing the Nocean Emperor to act," Egil insisted. "He has thousands of seasoned desert warriors. He's in his own environment, and he also has powerful sorcerers and warlocks at his disposal."

"That's not going to be easy," Ingrid said, making a face.

"I never said it would be. What I'm saying is that that's our best asset against the dragon and his hosts right now," said Egil.

"I agree with you," said Gondabar. "We'll need a plan to convince Malotas and his armies to go there and stand up against the Immortal Dragon."

"I bet the know-it-all is already thinking of something," said Viggo, patting Egil's shoulder.

"Don't put pressure on him. This is a complicated and dangerous situation. You can't trick an emperor and his armies just like that," Ingrid replied.

"If anyone can do it, it would be Egil," Gerd said in a proud tone.

"I'm already thinking about it," Egil said with a shy smile.

"You see? The wise guy is already on it. We've got nothing to worry about," Viggo said, waving aside the matter nonchalantly.

"Very well, it's agreed. Egil will tell us his plan when he has one," Gondabar said to Egil, looking into his eyes.

"I'm already on it," Egil confirmed.

"There's another matter we must discuss and which I believe is of the utmost importance," Lasgol said in a serious tone and with a look on his face that meant he considered it of the utmost importance.

"Go on, Lasgol, tell us what it is that you deem crucial and must be discussed," Gondabar said encouragingly with a wave of his hand.

"Well, you see, in this last adventure I was able to confirm that Aodh's Bow is truly a weapon that can kill dragons. Thanks to the magical bow, we were able to defeat the lesser dragon. Its magic allows the arrows to pierce the unbelievably tough armor of a dragon's scales, which normally resist any physical harm."

"The magic of the bow makes the arrows capable of piercing through the dragon's scales?" Raner asked, greatly interested.

"That's right," Lasgol confirmed. He reached for the magic bow he carried slung over his shoulder and showed it to all of them.

"A beautiful bow," Gondabar said admiringly.

"And with the power to kill a dragon," Lasgol added.

"Even Dergha-Sho-Blaska?" Raner asked. "It's one thing that you were able to kill a lesser dragon with that weapon, and a very different one that you'd be able to kill such a mighty dragon."

Lasgol considered the matter for a moment.

"With this bow I was able to wound Dergha-Sho-Blaska and kill Saki-Erki-Luzen. On both occasions, the bow was able to pierce through the dragon scales, so I'm convinced it was created to that end. Furthermore, when you use it against any other target it behaves like a regular bow. Its magic only activates when you attack a dragon or a Drakonian, to be precise, which is what I believe happens."

"This information is monumental," Egil said, "it means that this weapon has a specific goal: killing Drakonians. The fact that you've already killed a lesser dragon with it proves it."

"Well, that's great news for us," Nilsa said, clapping her hands with glee.

"But, that doesn't prove that we can kill Dergha-Sho-Blaska with this bow," Astrid said, crossing her arms. "It only suggests that it might be possible, although Lasgol was not successful when he stood up to him, and it nearly cost him his life," Astrid finished her sentence by looking at Lasgol with concern.

"True. What else have you found out about the bow that might help us?" Ingrid asked.

"The bow is a weapon of power," Lasgol explained. "It possesses magic that will pierce the nearly indestructible scales of a dragon's skin. When I fought the Immortal Dragon I didn't know how the weapon worked or its potential. Now I know it better. When I shot at the Immortal Dragon, I didn't do it using the full power of the bow, I realize this now. That's why I didn't manage to seriously wound him. But, after fighting the lesser dragon and other reptilian creatures, I've discovered that the bow can be a lot deadlier than what I managed to make it do initially."

"What do you mean by deadlier?" Viggo asked, raising an eyebrow.

"I've discovered that, in order to make the bow reach its full potential, I have to use my magic to interact with its magic. This way, I make the power much greater. My magic is a lot more powerful since I repaired the bridge, which has empowered the shots I can deliver with this bow. I can also use my skills jointly with those of the bow."

"That's fascinating!" Egil cried excitedly.

"And it gives us an advantage and an opportunity against the Immortal Dragon," Raner said.

"I wouldn't call it an advantage. Rather a small chance," Gerd said, not looking too sure that they could kill the great dragon with the bow.

"In any case, we should find more weapons that have the capacity to slay dragons," said Ingrid. "That way we could fight him."

"That's an excellent idea," Raner said.

"It certainly is," Gondabar agreed. "But, I don't think it will be at all easy to obtain them."

Egil sighed.

"It will be complicated. They're either lost or in foreign lands. Besides, we don't have much information about them. On the other hand, that was the case of Aodh's Bow, and we did find it. We shouldn't give up on the possibility of finding them."

"Very well, it's decided then, you will be tasked with finding these weapons," Gondabar told them.

"You don't have much time. The war is about to begin, and when it does, you'll be summoned to serve the King," Raner told them. "It's going to be a long, difficult campaign. The King of Erenal is seeking support and alliances with kingdoms that share common interests. If he succeeds, the war will become a nightmare for all."

"That would complicate things," said Lasgol.

"Quite a lot," Viggo added.

"Not to mention that we're still in charge of the Queen's protection," Astrid added. "How are we going to get rid of that obligation?" she asked, looking at Raner and Gondabar.

"I'll see what I can do," Gondabar said thoughtfully. "I can't guarantee that I'll free you from that duty, but I'll try."

"We should also keep an eye on the cursed city and mountains in case anything new or unexpected happens," Raner said.

"Yes, that too," Gondabar nodded. "It's not going to be easy, we'll have to find a way to do that… some kind of undercover surveillance…." The leader of the Rangers looked to the end of the room while he turned the problem over in his mind.

"It sounds like we have a lot to do and great obstacles to overcome," Gerd said, snorting.

"Isn't that always the case?" Nilsa said with a nervous giggle.

Gerd smiled.

"Indeed."

"Go now and let Raner and I plan everything we've talked about. Egil, start working on that plan for the Nocean Emperor and get all possible information about the weapons. It's important that we find them, and fast. We don't know when we're going to need them, but I have the awful feeling it's going to be sooner rather than later," Gondabar told them.

Egil nodded, "I'll get started immediately."

"We'll do it," Lasgol said with conviction.

They left the room, and although they tried to maintain their optimism, the looks on the Panthers' faces showed deep trouble, more than usual.

Chapter 2

The following morning, Lasgol was getting ready to go and check on Camu and Ona. It worried him to leave them alone for too long, more so now with everything that was going on and considering that they were hiding Dergha-Sho-Blaska's Silver Pearls.

"So, you're going to see the bug and the kitty?" Viggo asked him, raising both eyebrows.

"Yep, I'll give them your regards, you know how much they love you for calling them that," Lasgol replied with sarcasm.

"They all adore me—bugs, animals, men, and women. My personal magnetism and charisma are greater than the forests of the Usik."

"So is your ego!" Ingrid chided while she checked both her weapons sitting on her bed.

"You know what they say about fish ..." Nilsa said as she folded her clean clothes to put in the chest at the foot of her bed.

"It's delicious grilled?" Viggo said, pretending he did not know the saying.

"It gets caught by a worm, you idiot," Nilsa said, closing the chest.

"To kill me you'd need a couple of armies," Viggo replied nonchalantly, wiping imaginary dust off his shoulder.

"He's having one of his glory days..." Ingrid warned the others.

Nilsa and Gerd made horrified faces.

"You said that in order to return from the desert, you took the portal in the Pearl in the Mountains of Blood. How did you find the Desher Tumaini tribe?" Nilsa asked.

"Yeah, how are our good friends with the tan skin and baffling ruby eyes?" Viggo asked.

Lasgol nodded. "I was glad to see them again. Tor Nassor welcomed us and treated us well. He sends greetings."

"A good chief and leader, he's a good, wise man," said Egil admiringly. "Does he still think Camu is a Hor, a descendant of the Gods?"

"He's convinced. Him and the whole tribe, more so now that

they've seen him use the Pearl to come back."

"I can imagine," Egil nodded. "Have they had any more trouble with the city of Jafarika, their people and the Abyss?"

"No, but the Sand Dragon is still active, and they're always on the alert."

"If they want me to, I'll deal with that ugly giant worm from the depths of the deserts again," Vigo said.

"You stay put. The last time you almost didn't make it out alive," Ingrid told him.

"Were they aware of what's going on in Salansamur?" Egil asked, curious.

Lasgol shook his head.

"They weren't. The distance to the red mountains of the cursed city is great, and the Desher Tumaini barely leave their own mountains. They don't go into the deserts. I told them what I had found out. Tor Nassor was intrigued by my story. He identified the dragon I killed as a Minor Hor. I told him about Dergha-Sho-Blaska and that interested him even more. According to him, he's an Evil Hor."

"We all agree on that," said Gerd.

"I told him he might use the Portal, and that if he did they should all flee at once or else they'd end up enslaved or dead," Lasgol said. "He promised they'd do that."

"Dergha-Sho-Blaska had better not use that Portal and appear in their mountains..." Nilsa said wishfully.

"Let's hope for the best," said Astrid.

Lasgol was thoughtful for a moment.

"I didn't want to mention it, since Gondabar and Raner didn't bring it up either, but we have to find a container like the one Eicewald had, and one that's more powerful if possible, to store the pearls and free poor Camu of that constant danger."

"And Ona, who's also with him," added Astrid.

"Yes, this has to be a priority for us. Our leaders are more concerned with the imminent danger of the war with Erenal than the Immortal Dragon and his armies," Egil commented. "Yet, it's crucial that we prevent Dergha-Sho-Blaska from recovering the Pearls and continue with his plans for conquest."

"I fully agree," said Ingrid, putting aside the axe she was sharpening. "The container has to be a priority. We must prevent the dragon from carrying out his plans."

"Do we know where to get such a container?" Gerd asked, scratching his head.

"I bet we haven't a clue and, as usual, the weirdo will get us in a terrible mess trying to find it," Viggo said with his usual irony.

"Don't be a bird of ill omen," Ingrid chided.

"He's not going to get us into any trouble," Nilsa said, rejecting the idea.

"D'you want to bet?" Viggo dared them with a big, confident smile.

"We should consult with someone who has vast experience in magical matters," Egil mused out loud.

"I'm afraid that won't be possible with Maldreck and his Ice Magi," Viggo said sarcastically while he played with his throwing knife.

"That's true. I'm not Maldreck's favorite person right now. By the way, what do you know of him and his intentions? I'm asking because I guess he survived the wreck in the Utla and must have come back."

"Yes, he has. He's back in his Tower. We haven't seen much of him since then. He accompanied Thoran and his nobles along with the other Ice Magi when they left to fight against Zangria. He must be back in his Tower of the Ice Magi by now," Nilsa said.

"It appears our dear friend the treacherous mage likes water a lot, and he manages pretty well in it," Viggo said mockingly.

Nilsa could not help chucking, and Gerd laughed out loud.

"We should take him seriously, he's a dangerous snake," Astrid warned them.

"Yeah, a water snake, or rather an eel," Viggo said, and again Nilsa and Gerd laughed, filling the room with mirth.

Astrid was shaking her head with her arms crossed over her chest.

"We can't go to Maldreck, and we can't count on the other Ice Magi for the same reason," said Egil. "With this I don't mean to imply that all the Magi are like Maldreck, but it's more than likely they'd inform him of any interesting piece of news that has to do with magic. Some Rangers seeking a container to suppress an object's power is something they'd tell him, without a doubt."

"Besides, we have an added problem with Maldreck. He not only knows of the existence of the Pearls and was studying them during the voyage, but he also knows of the existence of Camu. He was spying on Eicewald, and I'm afraid Maldreck followed him to the Forest of the Green Ogre where he was teaching us. He knows Camu is a magical Creature of the Ice," Lasgol told them.

"That's not good," Ingrid said, shaking her head and hanging her axe from her waist. She started pacing around the room, making a face.

"It's a risk and a danger," Astrid agreed. "We'd better be very alert to the movements of the leader of the Ice Magi. I bet he's planning something."

"Astrid's right," Egil said. "We must be very aware of Maldreck's movements in the shadows. He knows of the existence of the Silver Pearls and Camu. He knows they are both unique and powerful. It's likely his present interest is only for the Objects of Power, but we can't dismiss the fact that he might want something from Camu."

"The thing is that this poisonous toad is very sneaky," Viggo said, throwing his knife at the window frame.

"Not more than you are," Nilsa said scornfully.

"Sneaky or poisonous?" Viggo asked with a comic grin.

"Both, and very much so," the redhead retorted.

Viggo smiled, satisfied, as if the barbed words the redhead threw at him were the best compliments.

"How are we going to watch him?" Gerd asked, wrinkling his nose as if he thought it was not an easy task.

"The best of us at spying is me," Astrid said. "So it'll be me who watches him," she volunteered.

Lasgol looked at her with concern.

"It makes sense. That's how it must be," Ingrid agreed, nodding.

"You know, if you need anything…" Viggo offered. "We, of Expertise, must help each other."

"I'll keep that in mind. Although you're extremely good at having targets die accidentally."

"That's what being the best Assassin in Norghana and part of Tremia means," he smiled.

"If the Magi give you any trouble, you'd better call me," said Nilsa. "I have a few improvements in my anti-magi arrows that I think will work well."

"Let's hope I don't need either, but thanks anyway," Astrid said courteously.

"Do you have anyone in mind who we might consult about the magic container?" Lasgol asked Egil, turning toward his friend.

Egil thought for a moment.

"There's a Mage in Rogdon, a wise man in the magic arts known as Mirkos the Erudite. He lives in a tower filled with tomes of knowledge, and he's known to instruct young people with the Gift he takes on as pupils. He's very well respected and loved in Rogdon. King Solin appreciates him greatly and often consults him. I believe he might be able to help us with our problem."

"Do you want us to go to Rogdon to speak to this Mirkos the Erudite?" Lasgol asked.

Egil nodded.

"It's the best option I can think of right now. I don't know whether he'll help us, but he has a very good reputation regarding his knowledge and character. We lose nothing by trying."

"Then that's what we'll do," Lasgol said.

"Remember, he's a powerful Mage of the Four Elements and a defender of the Kingdom of Rogdon. I don't think his King will get involved in the war with Erenal, but keep it in mind, just in case," Egil advised him.

"I will. I don't want him to receive me with a ball of fire straight at my face," Lasgol joked, making light of it.

"Knowing you, I bet he welcomes you with a shower of burning meteorites," Viggo laughed, as he moved his hand like objects falling from the sky on Lasgol.

"Don't pay any attention to him," Astrid waved Viggo aside. "I bet you can get him to help us, and perhaps he'll even teach you something."

"That would be very good, indeed," Lasgol cheered up a bit. He sat on his bed to study a map of Rogdon he had taken out of his chest. Since the adventure in the deserts, he had found a new respect for maps. They saved lives.

"I wish I could go with you," Astrid said softly, sitting beside him on the bed.

"Me too, I'd like you to come with me. I don't like going away without you," he replied, looking into her green eyes, losing himself in their depth.

"Unfortunately, we have to look after Queen Heulyn," Astrid sighed.

"How's she been doing lately?" Lasgol asked out of curiosity.

"You'll be surprised to hear this, but although she's still as obnoxious as ever, haughty, bossy, and yells at everyone else, with us she's much less so," Viggo said.

Lasgol's eyes opened wide.

"Seriously?"

Astrid nodded, looking as if she also had trouble believing it.

"Seriously. I never thought I'd say this, but I believe she no longer hates us to death and that she might even like us a teeny bit," Astrid said, showing the tip of her little finger.

"That much?" Lasgol laughed.

"It's something, and in this case, it's a lot," Nilsa joined her.

"Let's hope Gondabar finds a way to get us off her personal protection," Ingrid said hopefully.

Viggo made a sign meaning he did not believe that would ever happen, and he threw his knife at the middle of the upper frame of the other window.

"Our dear old leader doesn't have much influence on the King. I'd say that if he's not careful, Thoran might still hang him from his toes," he said as he got up to fetch his weapon.

"Rather, he doesn't have the King's approval for actions that aren't related to royal protection or the war with Erenal, and her allies," Egil corrected him with half a smile.

"We have to help him as much as we can. It pains me to see him like that. He's a good man," Nilsa said sadly, "a great man and leader. The Rangers owe him a lot, and the kingdom even more so."

"We all agree on that," Ingrid said.

Suddenly, there was a knock on the door.

They all turned toward it.

Nilsa jumped up and opened it with her usual celerity.

"Royal Eagles, you are requested downstairs," a Ranger on duty told them.

"Downstairs, in Gondabar's study?" Nilsa asked.

"No, downstairs in front of the Tower."

The Panthers exchanged puzzled looks.

"We'll be down right away," Ingrid said from inside the room.

Chapter 3

They went downstairs and left the Tower fast, as the Rangers always did whether there was an emergency or not. They met with a scene that puzzled them. Before the main building of the castle they saw Queen Heulyn on horseback. Valeria was with her, as usual, as well as Aidan and the other two Druids. In front of them was an escort of Norghanian soldiers on horseback. Behind the Queen was her escort of Irinel soldiers.

"Where's the Queen going?" Nilsa asked, widening her eyes.

"That's a very good question…." Ingrid was watching the scene with her head to one side.

"Does she want us to go with her?" Gerd wondered out loud.

"We'll soon find out," Lasgol said, seeing Valeria signaling them to join the retinue.

"It looks like we're wanted," Viggo said.

The group approached the retinue, which seemed ready to leave.

Queen Heulyn, escorted by Valeria and Aidan, came toward them.

"Your Majesty, do you require our company?" Ingrid asked as they stopped right in front of them.

The Queen remained silent. She motioned Valeria to speak in her place. She wanted to keep appearances before the people.

"Her Majesty must leave for Irinel at once," Valeria informed them.

Their surprise was obvious.

"Bad news from the kingdom?" Egil asked in a concerned tone.

Valeria looked at the Queen for confirmation.

Heulyn gave a curt nod.

"The Queen's mother in Irinel is very sick. She's requested to see her daughter. King Thoran has allowed the journey, even if the times are not the best for traveling."

"We are very sorry, Your Majesty," Egil said.

"We hope she soon recovers," Nilsa added.

"King Thoran has also allowed the Healer to come with us to help cure the Queen of Irinel," Valeria said and indicated a rider coming from the stables.

They all recognized her. It was Edwina. She nodded to them as she passed them by and the Panthers nodded back in respect and appreciation. The Healer took her place with the Druids in the center of the retinue.

"I'm sure the Queen will soon recover with the wisdom and power of the Healer," Lasgol said in an optimistic tone.

"Our Healing Druids are already looking after the Queen of Irinel, and we expect a prompt recovery," Aidan said.

"No doubt Edwina's help will be welcome," Valeria said.

"No doubt. All help to save the Queen's life is welcome," Aidan nodded.

"What does our Queen want the Royal Eagles to do?" Ingrid asked.

They all looked at Heulyn and then at Valeria, awaiting orders.

"You'll stay here and wait for Her Majesty's return," Valeria told them. "She doesn't need you for this journey to Irinel."

Lasgol had to hold back a snort of relief. For a moment he had taken for granted that they would have to accompany her, which would spoil all their plans. By the look on Astrid's face, he had not been the only one.

"Then that's what we'll do," Ingrid confirmed.

"We wish Her Majesty a good journey and a swift return," Egil said with a small bow.

Lasgol and Astrid exchanged a look. No one wanted the Druid Queen to come back soon, but Egil knew what they should say in such a circumstance.

The Queen nodded and gave them a look that for a moment almost seemed to be friendly, even respectful. Then she lifted her chin, put on her usual pose of pride, and gazed around her as if everyone should kiss the hem of her dress. A moment later, she indicated for Valeria and Aidan to return to the retinue with a wave of her hand.

The preparations for the journey finished and the Queen's retinue set off at an order of the officer in command. They headed to the gate, which was already open and with the portcullis raised. King Thoran did not come out to see his Queen off, nor did Orten or Maldreck. Not even the court nobles at the castle. Lasgol found that strange. They did not seem to care too much, or at all.

The Panthers watched the Queen leave, and looks of relief began to appear on their faces.

"It looks like we're finally going to have some peace," Nilsa said in a shrill voice and shaking her arms, as if she was really getting rid of some weight.

They all heard Gerd's snort.

"You don't say!"

"I thought you were getting along better with her," Lasgol said as he watched the last members of the Queen's escort crossing the gate into the city.

"A little better, but not that much," Astrid said, winking at him with a playful smile.

"We're already like flesh and blood, inseparable best friends," Viggo said, nodding hard. "My love for her is as big as the Eternal Mountains."

"Yeah, you'd waste no time in pushing her off the summit of those mountains, which is totally different," Ingrid corrected him.

"Ahh, you know me so well, my quarrelsome blondie," Viggo replied, smiling at her with loving eyes.

Ingrid showed him her fist and threw him a kiss.

"Way too well."

"I'm glad we're free of the Druid Queen and her personal bodyguard, especially the latter," Astrid said with a frown.

"Valeria has been good to us and can be a good ally," Nilsa said, defending her.

"The fact that you have a friendly agreement with her doesn't mean she won't betray you in the end," Astrid told her, jabbing her finger at her. "Remember that."

"Don't you worry, I'm watchful and I don't forget the past," Nilsa said in a more serious tone than was usual in her.

Astrid nodded, convinced by Nilsa's reply.

"I don't think Valeria will betray us this time, but you're right, we can't trust her," Gerd commented.

"I didn't know that old Gondabar was capable of such a trick to rid us of the Druid Queen's whip," Viggo said jokingly.

"The Queen's illness isn't Gondabar's doing," Nilsa snapped, unable to believe such an outrageous accusation.

"If you say so … I only know that our beloved leader was going to try and free us of our obligations, and look what's happened …"

"Don't be such a blockhead. This has been a turn of fate in our favor, a bit of good luck we sorely needed. We'll have a little peace and freedom until the Queen's back," Ingrid said.

"Both are welcome," Astrid said, nodding.

"It would be very interesting to know what kind of illness afflicts the Queen's mother in Irinel …" Egil said thoughtfully. "It might have some significance in the events that are going to develop in the near future."

"Gondabar can help us with that, whether he had something to do with it or not," said Viggo.

"Yeah, he could find out in the court circuits," Nilsa said. "He has contacts, and this kind of thing is always a matter for gossip at the court."

"King Thoran must know what the problem is," Lasgol said. "King Kendrick must have told him, which is why he didn't oppose the Queen's journey."

"Which leads us to assume it's likely something serious," said Egil.

"I don't see why this is so important," Gerd said blankly. "The Queen of Irinel is old and she might die. If she does, nothing will change in Irinel, will it? King Kendrick will continue ruling and there's also his son, Prince Kylian, the heir to the throne."

"I agree with the big guy. Why do you find this significant at all, Egil?" Viggo asked, turning to him.

"Certain events, such as what might happen, although I hope and wish it doesn't, might trigger a series of unexpected events of great importance."

"You mean that if the Queen of Irinel dies, it will cause undesirable effects?" Ingrid asked, frowning.

"That's what I'm afraid of."

"For instance?" Lasgol asked. The conversation intrigued and interested him, since he could not foresee what might happen.

Egil smiled lightly.

"For instance… King Kendrick, broken by grief, might return to Irinel and stay there, mourning his loss. He might even withdraw his armies from the fight against Erenal until he recovers."

"Thoran wouldn't like that at all," Ingrid commented.

"It might also be that Kendrick would not mind getting rid of his wife at last, after putting up with her all this time… he might even celebrate it," Viggo said with an evil smile.

"Viggo…" Ingrid began.

"I didn't say anything," he said, raising his hands. "But honestly, knowing their daughter…"

"He's right, in a way," Gerd said, looking toward the gate through which the retinue had gone out.

"We should plan what we're going to do now," said Lasgol. "We have some precious time which we can't afford to waste."

"Let's go somewhere discreet where we can talk," Astrid suggested. "You never know who might be listening," she commented, looking toward the Tower of the Ice Magi.

"Let's get away from the castle, go with Ona and Camu and talk it over calmly," Egil said.

Nilsa clapped her hands, delighted. "Wonderful!"

"Yeah, that's a great idea, I need to get out of the castle and breathe the forest air," said Gerd eagerly.

"It'll be good for all of us, to go out and breathe the fresh air," Astrid nodded.

"Did you leave them at the Shelter when you came back through the White Pearl above the Lair?" Gerd asked

"We stayed a couple of days at the Shelter, yes, but I didn't leave them there."

"How so?" Viggo asked.

"Gisli offered to take them to the secret valley within the Shelter. In his opinion they'd be safe there and well hidden."

"Good idea," Gerd said firmly.

"But you said you didn't leave them there, why?" Nilsa said.

"Sigrid and Annika didn't think it was such a good idea after consulting with Enduald and Galdason. Once she told them everything that had happened to me, both magi saw the danger of the Silver Pearls being in the Shelter."

"In case Dergha-Sho-Blaska sensed them?" Ingrid asked, wrinkling her nose. "How?"

"Enduald and Galdason reasoned that with the Objects of Power being so near a White Pearl, a portal, the Pearls' essence might be transported through it. They thought it might be dangerous. According to their studies and findings, they believe that the White Pearl and the portal it creates are not only designed for bodies to travel through but also for power, the magical auras of people and objects."

"Camu was capable of tracing Drakonian magic in the portal," Egil said, thinking. "It all makes sense. The portal must be like an open door, and magic can cross it and be felt on the other side."

"But the portal is shut, isn't it?" Gerd asked.

"It is now, but don't forget that we came through it to the Shelter. We don't know how long the traces might remain. That's what Enduald and Galdason told us," said Lasgol.

"It's good that they're so cautious. That way we'll avoid unpleasant surprises, like Dergha-Sho-Blaska appearing at the Shelter," said Astrid.

"Without a doubt, caution and vigilance are the best approaches in this situation. It would be catastrophic if the Immortal Dragon found the Shelter by following the trace of power left by the Silver Pearls," Egil said.

"Let's hope that never happens," Nilsa said, looking horrified.

"They have a system to alert and evacuate the Shelter," Lasgol said. "When the Pearl is activated and the portal starts forming, an alarm sets off that Enduald has created and everyone escapes from the Lair."

"Clever, how does this alarm work?" Gerd asked.

"He's enchanted a metal rod which he stuck right in front of the Pearl. When the portal activates, it produces an energy the rod picks up and it begins to vibrate strongly with a shrill whistle. You can hear it from half a league away."

"Excellent idea. Nothing like having an enchanter capable of charming objects as an ally at the Shelter," Egil smiled.

"We tested it. Camu opened the Portal and it worked perfectly. The Lair was emptied in the blink of an eye."

"I would've liked to be there to see everyone running. I bet it was a spectacle," Viggo said acidly.

"In any case, Loke is watching the Pearl day and night, so if it activates they'll know instantly."

"Loke has good hearing and better instincts," said Astrid.

"The people of the Masig usually do," Nilsa nodded, "or so it is said among the Ranger Specialists."

"How's Engla? Has she fully recovered?" Ingrid asked.

"Almost. It's taking her longer than Gerd, but she's a lot better.

She still has some side effects though …"

"Like me, right?" Gerd said, looking down at his hip.

"Yeah, like you, but she's very well."

"Like Gerd," Nilsa said, putting her hand on his wide shoulder.

Gerd smiled.

"I manage, which is a great deal."

"You informed everyone of what had happened, didn't you?" Ingrid asked.

"That's right. The Mother Specialist, the Elder Specialists, Enduald, and Galdason. They know what's going on and the danger we're all in," Lasgol confirmed.

"Good. The more everyone knows, the better," Egil said. "Less chances of misunderstandings and mistakes or delays if we need to act swiftly and precisely."

"Then you left the Shelter with the Silver Pearls?" Gerd asked.

Lasgol nodded.

"It was the best course."

"Where did you hide them then?" Nilsa asked him.

Lasgol sighed.

"In a place Sigrid suggested. One so deep it will prevent the trace of the pearls from being detected from the outside."

"And where's that?" Viggo asked, raising an eyebrow and looking suspicious.

"In the Gray Chasm," Lasgol replied.

"That name doesn't sound good at all," Viggo shook his head.

"Is it very far?" Ingrid asked. "I don't remember having heard of the existence of that place."

"It's a hidden, obscure place, one of the secret places of the Rangers. Only the Elder Specialists and some locals from a nearby village know of its existence, from what they told me. It's three days away on horseback, to the southeast," he nodded in that direction.

"In that case, we'd better start out as soon as possible," Astrid said.

"Yeah, we'd better. Come, let's get going," Ingrid said.

Chapter 4

They left the Tower of the Rangers with their traveling backpacks and weapons to go to the Gray Chasm. They had explained the situation to Gondabar and Raner and they had given the Panthers the go ahead to act now that they had the time and the occasion. They urged the Panthers to leave the city quickly, before the King gave them another mission once he found out they were free of service. Luckily, Thoran and Orten were too busy with their preparations for war to notice them.

Gerd and Viggo had already gone to the stables to fetch their mounts. Ingrid and Nilsa stopped to talk to Molak, whom they found chatting with Kol and Haines.

"You're leaving?" Molak asked, widening his eyes.

"The Royal Eagles must fly away?" Kol asked, eying Nilsa and smiling at her seductively.

Nilsa smiled back.

"We never stop for more than a moment."

"We must deal with an important… matter…" Ingrid replied, looking at Molak.

"Oh, important, but you don't need me," Molak said, disappointed.

"Not for this mission," Ingrid replied, indicating by her look that it was not an official mission.

"Oh, I see," Molak nodded. "It's a Snow Panther matter."

"That's right," Ingrid confirmed.

"We have some time now that the Queen is on her way to Irinel," Nilsa told him.

"You'd better be back soon. There's rumor that the alliances are nearly finalized. Once they are, we're all going to the front," Haines warned them.

"Where did you get that information?" Nilsa asked him.

"Haines is so ugly that the ladies of the court always ignore him, so he hears conversations he shouldn't," Kol said jokingly.

"I'm not that ugly. I have many hidden qualities," Haines said defensively.

"Sure, well hidden," Kol said, raising both eyebrows.

"I hear important things because I pay attention, not like you, who does nothing but ogle all the passing maidens and ladies of the court."

Kol turned white.

"Me? No way. How can you say that?" he replied defensively and shaking his hands, looking at Nilsa.

"I believe him," the redhead said, glancing at Kol through narrowed eyes.

"I swear it's not like that," Kol said, shaking his hands.

"Sure…" Nilsa was relentless.

"The orders we have from Raner are to protect King Thoran," Molak said.

"Now that you're a Royal Ranger, your life's going to drastically change," Ingrid warned him.

"I'd rather continue with the Royal Eagles, but now that Lasgol's back you don't need me," Molak said regretfully.

"Not right now, but don't go very far, because things are constantly changing," Ingrid said.

"Well, if I'm not around it's going to make a certain someone very happy…" Molak said, looking into Ingrid's eyes.

"Well…" she started to say.

"You just forget about Viggo, he's like a toothache, everyone knows that," Nilsa said.

While Nilsa and Ingrid were talking to Molak and the Royal Rangers, Lasgol and Egil went to the stables. They were crossing the bailey when they heard a voice they both recognized at once.

"Rangers, a moment!" they heard.

Lasgol and Egil stopped at once and turned toward the voice.

Maldreck and two Ice Magi were coming toward them from the Tower of the Magi.

"They must've seen us…" Lasgol whispered to Egil.

"Remember that you've done nothing wrong," Egil whispered back.

They waited for the Magi to reach them. They wore their usual pure-white robes, as white as their hair and beards. They carried staves, also white, crowned with a large crystalline jewel. The Magi were impressive and terrifying.

"I see you're back, Lasgol, and that you look well," Maldreck greeted him in a suspicious tone, ignoring Egil entirely.

"Leader of the Ice Magi," Lasgol greeted him with a slight bow of his head. "I feel well, thanks for your concern."

"I thought that river monster would've finished you off. I see you were able to survive, not like many of those on board."

"I was lucky I was able to hold onto a piece of the floating wreckage."

"Yes, so was I."

"I am glad to see you are fine."

"You wouldn't happen to know what became of the Objects of Power that were in the chest…" Maldreck looked into Lasgol's eyes inquisitively.

"I seem to remember that the river snake swallowed them."

"Are you sure?" Maldreck's gaze fixed on Lasgol's eyes like ice daggers.

"Everything happened so fast… there was so much chaos during the attack…. But yes, I'm sure. The monster swallowed the chest with the Objects of Power."

Maldreck was silent while he continued staring at Lasgol, as if he wanted to extract the truth by digging inside his head with the ice daggers.

"Very convenient for you."

Lasgol wanted to say something negative, but he held back. He would not get anywhere by antagonizing the leader of the Ice Magi any further. He was a poisonous ice snake, and the less dealings and confrontation they had with him, the better.

"I lost the objects Eicewald asked me to keep safe. I feel terribly bad for having failed him."

"Sure…" Maldreck looked at him condescendingly and with loathing. "You and your friends had better stay away from Objects of Power and magic creatures. Matters of magic must be dealt with by Magi, not Rangers."

"I'm a special Ranger…" Lasgol said defensively.

"I know you are. I can read you like an open book. I have the power of a great mage, don't you ever forget that. I can pick up your insignificant aura of power," he said, drawing a circle with his staff over Lasgol's head, which made both him and Egil throw their heads back. "The fact that you have the Gift doesn't make you a Mage, not even close."

The two Ice Magi accompanying Maldreck studied Lasgol from head to toe with interest.

"He might join us," one of them said.

Lasgol looked at Egil, who looked back at him.

"It's too late for this conversation. He's too old. He couldn't become an Ice Mage now," Maldreck replied.

"Our leader is wise," said the other one, accepting his master's verdict.

The Ice Mage who had suggested that Lasgol join them had to accept the decision. He bowed his head.

"Our leader knows what's best."

"This is my last warning. If I find you or your friends with Objects of Power or creatures of power, I'll send you to an ice dungeon head first."

"We're Royal Rangers in the service of the King," Lasgol replied, which was a way of telling him he could not touch them.

"That won't save you. In everything regarding magic, I'm the highest authority in the Kingdom. What I say is law. Consider yourself warned," he said with rage and loathing. He turned around and left the way he had come. The two Ice Magi followed him.

Lasgol and Egil watched them leave.

"Very pleasant, as always," Egil commented, amused.

"He's dangerous. If he can he'll lock us up, or something even worse," Lasgol said, feeling troubled. "He knows I have the Gift, and Camu too. He's a dangerous enemy and we must be very careful, or we'll have a serious problem."

"He's dangerous and has decided to be our enemy, which makes him arrogant and not very intelligent. He would've gotten more from us with a little more subtlety."

"I guess that's something."

"It is. The worst enemy is the one we don't know or don't see coming."

"I don't doubt that. But this one does worry me. He's ambitious and won't stop for anything in order to get what he wants."

"Yeah, you're right about that. Too much ambition makes people dangerous. He could make serious trouble for us. We'll have to tread very carefully," said Egil.

"Let's go. We'd better avoid any more unpleasant or troublesome encounters."

Egil made a wishful face, and they went on to the stables where Astrid, Gerd, and Viggo were already waiting with the horses all ready.

Ingrid and Nilsa wasted no time in joining the others, and they set off. They left the Royal Castle and rode along the main roads of the capital. The joyful festive days of the royal wedding were far behind them, and now they could see anxiety and fear in the looks and faces of the citizens. Men and women, whether soldiers, miners, farmers, merchants, or artisans, they all knew that dreaded war was coming. It was like a gray shadow falling over the city and its people with every passing day. When at last war was declared the shadow would change hue, shifting from gray to a darker shade, which would finally be tainted with the dark red of blood, shed by all the Norghanians wounded or dead.

The Panthers could see the effects of that shadow over the city and the citizens who tried to maintain a semblance of normalcy but failed. Everyone seemed busy with their daily tasks, but there was no laughter or joy except among the children, who continued playing, unaware of what was going on around them and the political climate of Tremia. The innocence of the youngest kids, their innate joy and happiness, was the only thing the coming war did not seem to affect.

As they crossed the city they were already seeing large numbers of soldiers patrolling and on leave, but when they left through the south gate they met with the whole Snow Army camped south of the capital. Thousands of tents as white as the peaks of the highest snow-covered mountains formed a snowy sea. Luckily the army had left a wide corridor from the gate of the wall that crossed the whole camp and they did not run into the soldiers because it was kept clear, like a long bridge over the camp. A multitude of carts and riders were traveling in both directions, most of them traders and transports of supplies coming and going to and from the capital.

They left the city behind, and in the distance they saw the Thunder Army camped to the east, the Blizzard Army camped to the west, and the Invincibles of the Ice to the north, each with their identifying tents and banners. Thoran had his armies close and ready to act, which only increased the certainty that war would happen sooner rather than later. The only ones not present were the Nobles of the West with their forces; Thoran had already sent them to the border with Zangria. The situation in the neighboring country was calm, but Thoran did not trust this calm and maintained the pressure. On the side of the Kingdom of Irinel, Prince Kylian was also waiting on the border with Zangria to the northeast, while his father, King Kendrick, had gone back to Irinel to be with his sick wife and to consolidate alliances before entering the war with the Kingdom of Erenal.

They made the journey to the Gray Chasm at a good pace, cheered at being all together and in the forests and plains of the south part of the realm. There was nothing like leaving the huge city of stone and regaining contact with nature to cheer a Ranger's soul. Gerd had a permanent smile on his face. Being back in nature and seeing the wildlife was like a healing balm for the giant. Of all the Panthers, Gerd was the one who suffered the most from having to serve within four walls. He loved nature and wildlife in particular, and being unable to spend time among animals in their natural habitat made him terribly sad.

Unlike the rest of his partners who could use their specializations in the missions assigned to them, Gerd had not had much chance, or rather none at all. A Beast Master was most useful when immersed in nature, like forests, mountains, and rivers, not inside a castle in the middle of a city. There were few animals for him to interact with, apart from the usual horses, donkeys, mules, and oxen, which he already knew intimately and which did not provide any excitement. Nor did pets like dogs, cats, or some exotic birds. They did not require a specialist like him and did not raise his interest.

He spent time with the royal hounds and the great mastiffs the court nobles kept for boar and bear hunting. These did provide some satisfaction, since he enjoyed training them. Because he was a Wildlife Specialist he was allowed access to them, access which was restricted, since they were valuable animals and the nobles and the king did not let anyone bother them. Egil had recommended that Gerd study Gondabar's tomes, as well as others in the King's Library whenever he could not be outside and was forced to remain indoors. It was not what Gerd most enjoyed, but it helped him pass the time, and he also learned things that might be useful someday. The good thing about spending so much time with Egil was that the good habits rubbed off, especially those of reading and studying.

During the journey, Gerd had the chance to enjoy the wildlife of the southern part of the realm, and he could not be happier. In the evenings he watched the night predators, especially birds, of which owls were his favorites. They crossed paths with a couple of red-furred foxes that delighted Gerd. He considered them clever, playful, and nice. Well, as long as you were not a farmer with hens and rabbits; in that case, they were not so adorable. They also came across several deer and even a large, solitary wolf. It was odd to see one like that, which made Gerd want to study it. Unfortunately, he could not, since they had to keep going.

Lasgol led them to the Chasm, which was hidden by some rocks that looked as if they had fallen from the small mountain behind them. They dismounted and tethered their horses to a lonely oak a few paces away.

"Wow, it's hard to find, even if it's quite large," Nilsa commented from a rock she had climbed up on.

"It looks as if it's been hidden on purpose," Gerd said from the rock in front.

"Yeah, it's interesting that the hole is at the bottom between those huge fallen boulders," Ingrid agreed from the top of one of them.

"It gets even more interesting," Lasgol told them as he approached the round hole the size of the base of a house.

Viggo bent over the hole to look inside.

"It's pitch black. It doesn't look like anything more than a huge hole."

Egil came closer and looked inside, dropping a stone in. He put his finger to his lips and they all waited for a long moment.

"We haven't heard the rock hit the bottom. It's very deep," said Astrid.

Egil nodded.

"It seems that way."

"How are we going to get down there?" Nilsa asked.

"We don't have enough rope, that's for sure," Gerd commented.

"We're not going down," Lasgol told them.

"I don't get it, did not you say the Pearls are down there?" Ingrid said, baffled.

"They are. They're in a cave you can access once you reach the bottom of the chasm. From what we've calculated, it's over a thousand paces deep."

"That's very deep. I'm not going down," Viggo crossed his arms.

You go down, they all got Camu's message.

"What...?" Viggo turned around.

All of a sudden, Camu appeared, flying using his Drakonian Flight skill. His silver wings shone brightly against the clouded sky. Without hesitation he headed toward Viggo, whose eyes opened wide. Camu kicked Viggo with his back legs, and he fell backward into the chasm.

"What!" Viggo cried, trying unsuccessfully to keep his balance.

"Camu, don't!" Ingrid cried with a horrified look and reached out to try and grab Viggo, but she could not. He was too far away.

Chapter 5

Viggo was falling backwards into the black chasm.

"Viggo!" Gerd cried out in terror.

Nilsa screamed and put her hands to her head.

Astrid was about to jump to grab him, but Lasgol stopped her by taking hold of her arm.

"Don't worry," he whispered.

Viggo continued falling into the chasm. But for some reason he did not fall—he remained hanging in the middle of the great abyss. He was hanging from Camu's back legs, which were clinging to his torso as if Camu were a giant eagle carrying a black sheep.

"By the Ice Gods!" Astrid cried.

"Camu, what are you doing?" Ingrid demanded as she watched with wide eyes how the man she loved was hanging from Camu's back legs while he hovered over the great black hole, flapping his large wings like a giant silver humming bird.

"Put me doooooown!!!" Viggo shouted, staring at the hole under his body.

Very well, I put down, Camu messaged to all.

"This is going to be fun," Lasgol whispered to Astrid without letting go of her arm to keep her calm.

Astrid stared at him, terrified.

"Are you sure?"

"It's all right," Lasgol promised.

Camu started going down into the chasm, carrying Viggo.

"Noooooo! Not into the abyyyyyyss!" Viggo was shouting as Camu went down and the darkness of the chasm swallowed them. A moment later, they had vanished. Not even the silver aura that surrounded Camu's wings and body could break through the darkness of their descent into the depth of the chasm.

Not move, can fall, Camu messaged to Viggo.

"What do you mean fall! Take me back!"

We go down to bottom.

"Up! Not the bottom, you brainless bug!"

While Viggo's shouts came up and reached his friends, the two of them traveled down further into the abyss.

"Lasgol, tell me he's going to be all right," Ingrid urged him.

"Don't worry, he'll be fine," Lasgol said, smiling.

"Are you sure? It looks very dark down there, and it's so deep," Gerd said, looking down into the darkness of the chasm with a look of terror on his face.

They were all staring in the direction of Viggo's shouting, but the darkness did not let them see anything.

"That's fantastic," Egil said, sounding delighted.

"Fantastic? My heart almost jumped out of my mouth!" Ingrid cried.

"If he makes it all the way down, it will have been most amusing," Nilsa said.

Ingrid glared at her.

Nilsa shrugged and jumped onto another boulder.

"Awesome and astonishing," Astrid commented.

"Since when can our dear friend do that?" Egil asked, very interested.

Lasgol smiled at him.

"We're now practicing our magic every day, and it's led to some surprising results. Camu has managed to control his flapping, and he can fly like a hummingbird for periods of time that will continue to increase with practice. He still has trouble landing when he comes down fast. That's why he's developed this Hummingbird Flight skill. Instead of gliding to land, he stops in mid-flight and goes up or down vertically."

"Fascinating," Egil commented, looking impressed. "Our friend is intelligent and resourceful. Very well thought out."

"When we arrived here at the chasm, we were faced with a new problem: we couldn't go down such a distance without rope. So Camu started going down part of the way and coming up again until he mastered the flight and his magic energy to go down to the very bottom and come back up. When he managed to do it easily, it occurred to him that he could take Ona and me down with him."

"Isn't that crazy!" Nilsa said, unable to believe it.

"We practiced for a whole day outside, and Camu was able to take me up and down without any problem. It appears that his magic is growing in power."

"Magic? Isn't he holding the weight with his own strength?" Gerd asked.

"No. We've discovered that the skill he has to cling to any surface and hold his own weight is really a magical skill. As his magic power grows, he can carry heavier loads and lift them with the power of his Hummingbird Flight."

"Fantastic and fascinating!" cried Egil, who could not stop smiling with such a magical development.

I much incredible, Camu's message reached them as he appeared from the chasm and remained hovering above the dark void.

"You really are," Astrid told him.

Much handsome too.

"We don't know that for sure, since we haven't met any other Drakonians to compare you to," Nilsa told him.

"Is Viggo okay?" Ingrid asked, uneasy.

Viggo shouting bottom of chasm.

"But is he all right?" Ingrid asked, worried.

Head no, rest yes.

Nilsa burst out laughing, and Gerd joined her. Lasgol and Egil smiled and Astrid covered her mouth to muffle a guffaw.

"He's with Ona and the Pearls in the great inner cave," Lasgol explained.

"What a scare..." Ingrid muttered under her breath, shaking her head.

Who next? Camu messaged.

"Are we all going to go down?" Nilsa asked blankly.

"It's quite the experience," Lasgol told them. "One you'll remember, I promise. It's worth it."

"Without a doubt. A vital experience I can't afford to pass up. Take me down, Camu," Egil volunteered.

Egil light, easy, Camu messaged.

"If you turn around, he'll grab you by the back and the descent will be better," Lasgol recommended.

"Awesome," Egil replied, delighted, and turned his back to Camu to facilitate the grasp.

We go down, Camu messaged, and clinging onto Egil's back with his hind legs, he lifted him easily and then the pair prepared to enter the abyss.

"I see it and I still can't believe it..." Gerd said, sitting by the edge with his legs crossed.

"I'm still not over the fright," Ingrid snorted. "Can't we behave more like any other normal group?"

"We?" Nilsa asked rhetorically. "Impossible. Look at who we are," she smiled at Ingrid.

"Yeah… I was afraid you'd say that… but I can dream, right?"

Nilsa shrugged and smiled.

"Are we all going down? Will Camu be able to take all of us?" Astrid asked Lasgol.

"I think he can do half of us, the smallest people. Then he might need to rest and restore his energy."

"Okay, then we'll do two shifts," Astrid said.

"I'd better go in the second shift, once he's rested," Gerd said. "I weigh twice as much as any of you."

"More like three times," Nilsa told him.

"Yeah, three of him," Gerd had to admit, blushing.

"That sounds good," Lasgol agreed. "Nilsa and Astrid, you'll be next. The three of us will wait for the next shift," he told Ingrid and Gerd.

"Good," said Ingrid, "We'll need torches, it's very dark."

"I'll help you," Nilsa offered, and they both set to work making a couple of torches with what they carried in their saddlebags.

Camu took the first group down and, as Lasgol had predicted, he began to run out of energy. They did not want to risk it, so they let Camu sleep to recover.

Ingrid, Lasgol, and Gerd camped beside the chasm while their friends rested in the depths of the cave.

The following morning, full of strength, Camu came up for them.

Now I have energy.

"Let's go down then," Lasgol told him.

Who first?

"I will," Gerd said.

Much brave.

"Not really, if I go last I'll be thinking about it the whole time. I'd better go down first, then the torture will be over."

"Very wise," said Ingrid.

Lasgol patted Gerd on the shoulder.

"Everything'll be fine, you'll see."

Camu clung to Gerd's back, and before going down he did a couple of tests going up and down on firm land to see whether he could hold Gerd's weight.

You eat too much.

"Isn't it that you don't have enough magic strength?" Gerd said defensively.

Both things, Camu admitted.

"Can you manage?" Lasgol asked him.

Yes can, much long no. Gerd weigh like ox.

"Don't exaggerate!" Gerd cried, offended.

Yes be, you know.

"I'm a big person, there's nothing I can do about it."

Eat less? Camu suggested.

"I have to feed this huge body," Gerd said, pointing his fingers at his own torso.

"All right. Take him down fast," Lasgol told Camu.

Okay.

"Not too fast either!" cried Gerd when Camu was already beginning to go down.

I make nosedive.

"What do you mean by nosedive?" Gerd cried, beside himself with fear.

Go down at once.

"Nooooo! No nosedives! You're craaaazy!"

No nosedive, be joke, Camu's message reached them all, along with a feeling of laughter.

Ingrid and Lasgol burst into loud laughter.

Gerd was so scared that he went down without being able to say another word.

A while later, Lasgol came down last with Camu into the depths of the dark abyss.

He had already made the flight with his friend before, but even so, he was still impressed by the feeling of emptiness he felt at the pit of his stomach as they went down into the great chasm in the midst of complete darkness. It was like descending toward the center of the earth where a monster of darkness waited to devour their souls.

The way down seemed endless, but suddenly Lasgol's feet touched ground.

We're here, Camu messaged him.

Wonderful.

Once they were at the bottom he heard Ingrid and Gerd, who

were already inside a tunnel going north. Ingrid had lit a torch and was illuminating the rocky entrance to the cave.

Let's go, Camu messaged as he landed.

They went down a long natural tunnel that headed from the hole into the depth of the rock that surrounded them entirely.

"Are we going into the heart of a mountain?" Gerd asked.

"I couldn't tell you, big guy. I only know that we're going through the depths of the earth to a large cavern."

"This is all natural," Ingrid commented, feeling the walls and inspecting them in the light of the torch.

"It is. I don't think any human has ever been down here. It's too deep," Lasgol said.

"Been here, perhaps, but survived? Impossible," Gerd said, looking at the rocky passage that could fit three people. Camu had enough space, so he walked happily behind the group.

"We're so deep that cries for help would never be heard from above," Ingrid commented.

"Most likely," said Gerd.

Cries no hear above.

"How do you know?" Gerd asked him.

Viggo shout a lot. Above no hear.

They all laughed out loud, including Ingrid.

"A very valid method to measure distance. Egil will surely approve," Ingrid said, laughing.

"Let's use Viggo as a measure for chasms from now on," Gerd said.

Much funny.

They went on along the tunnel until they saw light. It was the large cavern.

Inside, their friends were waiting, and with them Ona, who came to welcome them with a loving chirp.

"Ona, good," Lasgol welcomed her, crouching and opening his arms.

Ona put her front paws on his shoulders and rubbed her head against Lasgol's.

"It's nice to all be together again," said Gerd when Ona came over to greet him the same way she had done with Lasgol.

"It is, very nice," said Ingrid. "Unfortunately, we have a lot to do. Let's get started."

Chapter 6

Lasgol used his *Guiding Light* skill and created a spot of light in front of him. Then he pointed at the wall on his right and the light went to it and stayed hovering against the rock. He created a second and a third light and sent them to the other walls so the end of the cavern was pretty well lit. Then he used his *Fire Creating* skill and started the fire his companions had prepared with branches, twigs, and other vegetation that had fallen to the bottom of the abyss, which was not much but did the trick.

"This way we'll be more comfortable," he told his friends as he sat before the fire.

"You're becoming a full-fledged mage!" Gerd said, surprised.

"I wouldn't say that much, let's just say I'm learning things…"

"Fantastic things!" Egil said, going to each of the lights to check them.

"Where are the Pearls?" Astrid asked suddenly, looking around.

Pearls here, Camu messaged.

"Here? Where?" asked Nilsa, also looking around and seeing nothing.

"We buried them," Lasgol said and pointed to where Ona was resting, almost against the back wall of the cavern. "As deep as we were able."

"Excellent idea!" Egil said approvingly.

"The problem is that they're not in a magic container. We buried them in a leather sack," Lasgol said, ruefully.

"Dergha-Sho-Blaska isn't going to find them down here. We're in the heart of the earth, and you've buried them deep. It's impossible," Viggo said, waving his hands.

"Unfortunately, magic can be felt from great distances and depths, if it's powerful," Lasgol explained.

"And if the one seeking is mighty," Astrid added.

"Exactly," Lasgol said.

They all sat around the fire.

"Sigrid and Annika told you they'd be safe here," Nilsa said.

"That's what they believe, because of the great depth and because magic has trouble going through solid rock. But Enduald and

Galdason couldn't swear to it. Yet, it's the best idea they could come up with. That doesn't mean that this place is infallible though," Lasgol replied.

"I find it difficult to accept that the power of the Pearls can go through all the rock we have above us," Gerd said, pointing at the upper part of the cavern.

"I have the feeling this is a safe, secure place," Astrid said, looking toward the entrance of the cavern.

Much safe, Camu messaged in agreement.

"Let's hope it's enough. But just in case, I want to find a container. We have to prevent Dergha-Sho-Blaska from finding them," Lasgol said.

"That would be the wisest and most prudent thing to do," Egil agreed.

"I'll make sure of that," Lasgol said.

"Very well. So, now that we know the Pearls are relatively safe, what's the plan?" Ingrid asked, looking at Egil.

"We'll have to divide and conquer," Egil smiled.

"Dividing is never good," Nilsa said, looking sad.

"I know, but we have too much ground to cover and very little time. The Queen or the war might make us go back at any moment," Egil said.

Good. Our first priority is finding the weapons capable of killing dragons and their reptilian creations," Ingrid said.

"If I remember correctly, there was a knife among those weapons which I'd be interested in having..." Viggo commented, raising an eyebrow.

"You and me both," Astrid said quickly and gave him a look that meant she was also interested in the weapon.

"Yes, 'Sansen's Knife,'" Egil said. "It's said you can tear out the heart of a dragon to eat it and obtain its power."

"I like the idea of obtaining its power," Viggo said, beaming.

"I do too," Astrid followed, refusing to drop the matter of the weapon.

"There's no need for competition regarding the knife," Egil interceded. "While I was gathering additional information about these weapons in order to find them more easily, I came across another one."

"Another one? What's that?" Astrid asked eagerly.

"The Gauntlet of Liriana Luna," Egil said.

"What makes this gauntlet special? Why would it interest me more than a knife?" Astrid asked.

"Well, from what I found out, this is a very special gauntlet. When a woman puts it on, and it can only be a woman, the gauntlet flashes in gold and on its surface there appears a long blade, so sharp and strong it can penetrate the scales of a dragon. They say that young Liriana was able to avenge the death of her beloved with this weapon."

"Her beloved?" Nilsa was interested.

"According to legend, Liriana's lover, Duncan Esparagen, stood up to a dragon to save the people of his kingdom. Liriana begged him not to fight the dragon—it was suicide. But Duncan was a knight, a defender of the realm, and had sworn to protect the weak. The dragon tore him to shreds. Broken with pain, Liriana spent years seeking revenge. In the end, she found a gauntlet in the hands of a sisterhood of warriors, the Fighters of the New Sun. She joined them and learned to fight. She never revealed her true intention, which was no other than to steal the gauntlet the sisterhood was keeping and which they considered sacred. It took her a long time to organize it, but she finally managed to steal the sacred gauntlet and escape."

"And what happened then?" Gerd asked, spellbound by the story.

"Liriana searched for the dragon until she found him."

"She faced the dragon?" Nilsa asked.

"She did something more intelligent. She waited until the dragon hibernated, and when he did she used the gauntlet to kill him."

"Clever girl," Viggo said, nodding hard.

"Well, a happy ending after all," said Nilsa.

"Not entirely," Egil replied.

"Why's that?" Gerd asked.

"The Fighters of the New Sun found her and killed her for stealing the sacred gauntlet."

"That's terrible!" Nilsa cried, upset.

"I'll take the gauntlet," Astrid said confidently. "Those fake warriors will learn what a real warrior is."

Lasgol felt that might be dangerous and gave Astrid a troubled look. She noticed but looked back confidently, gesturing to him not to worry.

"I prefer 'Gim's Double Death', a two-headed war axe believed to be capable of cutting through the neck of a dragon and killing him," Gerd said, nodding hard.

"Logical that you should prefer that, since you're a strong brute," Viggo mocked him.

"You come with your little knife and you'll see what I do with my great axe," Gerd threatened him.

"Remember, it's for dragons and Drakonians and such," Viggo told him, smiling.

"Yeah..." Gerd threw him a look that said "don't mess with me."

"The axe is a good choice," Ingrid joined in. "But I'd rather use the sword you mentioned..."

"'Neil's Dragon-killer,' a golden sword capable of piercing through the scales of a dragon," Egil reminded them.

"Yeah that one, it would come in handy. Besides, I believe that out of all of us I'm the best sword wielder."

"Only you and Egil have been trained with the sword, so absolutely," Nilsa said.

"My sword art isn't very exact," Egil commented.

"I bet it's better than you imply. You're a noble, and you're smart. I'm sure you learned as a child," Gerd told him.

"Yeah, but I preferred books. Besides, my arm wasn't very strong then."

"I'll take the sword then," said Ingrid. "My aunt taught me, and although it's been ages since I've used one, I hope I haven't lost 'my touch.'"

"I bet you'll pick it back up fast," Viggo encouraged her.

"What else is there besides Aodh's Bow, which we already have?" asked Nilsa.

"There's 'Antior's Beam,' a javelin that pierces any shield and protection, including the scales of a dragon," said Egil.

"I'll take that one," said Nilsa, "after all, it's the closest to a bow."

"In that case, I believe we each have our own task," Egil said. "Viggo will go for Sansen's Knife, Astrid for Liriana Luna's Gauntlet, Gerd for Gim's Double Death, Ingrid for Neils' Dragon-killer and Nilsa for Antior's Beam."

"Great, I like the plan. Weapons are always good to have, magical ones even more so," Ingrid said, and the others nodded.

"To make your jobs easier, I have something for you," Egil said as he searched in his traveling rucksack.

"Are you going to give us bags filled with gold?" Viggo asked, looking excited.

"Something better," Egil replied as he continued searching in his heavy sack. Egil's rucksack was always the biggest and heaviest. Not because he carried extra weapons or supplies, but because he always carried tomes to study and his famous notebooks where he wrote down everything he found of interest, which was a lot.

"He's going to give us some tome of study, you'll see…" Nilsa commented with a wave that implied it would be something difficult to learn.

"Better than that," Egil replied without stopping his search.

"Better than a tome of study?' Gerd raised an eyebrow. "There's nothing better than a tome of study for you."

"Yes, there is. A summarized tome of study with all the vital information in it: one of my summarized notebooks," he said, proudly showing one to the group.

"Aahhhh… that's what I thought," Gerd nodded.

"You and everyone else," Nilsa joined him.

"This is the summary of Neils' Dragon-killer," he said, rising to hand it to Ingrid. "Here's everything I could find out about the subject."

Ingrid took the notebook and opened it. There were Egil's notes and several drawings of the weapon, even a description of the area of Tremia where it was supposed it might be found.

"That's amazing. You're incredible," Ingrid congratulated him, very impressed.

"I thought you could use some help," said Egil, waving the matter aside.

"Are there notebooks for everyone?" Gerd asked, hoping the answer would be "yes."

"Irrefutable, my dear friend," Egil replied as he started handing notebooks to each one of them.

"You leave me speechless," Viggo said, leafing through his notebook.

"And that's really saying something!" Nilsa teased him.

Viggo smiled.

"Hold on tight to that notebook. I bet you accidentally drop it in the fire."

Nilsa made a face.

"Not a chance," she said, but just in case she held it firmly with both hands.

"This is fabulous," Astrid said. "You're a genius, Egil," and she went over to him and kissed him on the forehead.

"Thanks… not really…" Egil replied, waving the praise aside.

Egil much smart, Camu messaged to all, along with a feeling of respect toward Egil.

Ona chirped once.

"We'll have to preserve his brain for posterity or something," Viggo burst out.

"Don't say stupid things," Ingrid snapped.

"Well, just make sure I'm dead, and well dead, first," Egil said, laughing.

"No way! Don't talk about death, that's asking for trouble," Nilsa said with a grimace.

For a moment they all studied the notebooks Egil had given them, fascinated and happy. They knew the books would make their tasks easier.

"At the end you have a summary in one or two paragraphs of what's most significant," Egil told them.

"It couldn't be any other way," Gerd said, beaming.

"A summary of a summary. You deserve a statue!" Ingrid said.

"I think we're ready to start searching," said Ingrid.

"Hmmmm, from what I see, I have to go all the way east to the city of Galdar, where Tremia ends at the Eastern Sea."

"I also have to go to the eastern coast, based on the final conclusions here," Ingrid said, leafing through the notebook. "It's very far away. It'll take us a long time to go and come back."

"Not if Camu takes you through the Eastern Portal," Lasgol told them.

I take.

"Is that the Portal you used to go to the Kingdom of Moontian?" Ingrid asked.

"The same one. It'll leave you not far from the eastern coast. Then Camu can come back and join me in Rogdon."

"Sounds good," Gerd said eagerly.

Good plan, Camu messaged.

"But how do we come back after we find the weapons?" Ingrid asked.

"That's a good question..." Lasgol was thoughtful, seeking an answer.

Egil already had one.

"Take owls with you. Once you're done, release them and they'll come back here. Then Camu will go and fetch you."

Better plan.

"That's that then."

"I'll join you on the journey east," Viggo said unwillingly.

"Why's that?" Ingrid asked him. "I'm delighted you're coming, but where do you have to go?"

"It's not very clear, well honestly, not at all. It says it must be between Erenal, Zangria, and Moontian, where the Aribai River splits in three."

Egil shrugged.

"It's all I could find out," he apologized.

"My weapon is all the way in the opposite direction, to the west... so I have the same problem. How do I get there fast? Is there a Portal to the west?"

Not know, Camu messaged.

"We don't know it yet, but if there's one east, there should be one west, logically," Lasgol commented.

"Camu could see whether he finds one and take you there," Egil told Gerd. "I also think it's logical that there's one west."

"Let's hope there is," Gerd said gloomily.

"What about you, Astrid?" Nilsa asked her.

"I'm going somewhere we're all familiar with but which isn't a good idea to visit right now."

They all turned to look at her, curious.

"Where's that?" Lasgol asked, concerned.

"Erenal."

"Wow..." Lasgol became really worried.

"You're going to have a blast," Nilsa said, shaking her hand.

"Yeah, that's the feeling I have. Nothing like going to enemy territory for a visit at the start of a war," Astrid replied ironically.

"Especially if you're a spy by profession and from the enemy kingdom," Viggo said sarcastically.

"Precisely..." Astrid snorted.

"You'll make it. We all will. I'm sure," Ingrid said encouragingly.

"What about you two? No notebook or weapon for you to

retrieve?" Gerd asked Lasgol and Egil.

Lasgol nodded.

"I have to go and see Mage Mirkos in Rogdon to find a container for the Silver Pearls."

"And I must deal with some business that has to do with the war and the throne..." Egil said in a secretive tone.

They all looked at him, intrigued.

"The Western League?" Ingrid said.

Egil nodded.

"They're worried."

"I don't blame them. The King has sent them to the front while his own armies are at the capital. That doesn't look good," Nilsa said, shaking her head.

"Besides the fact that if Norghana and her allies defeat Erenal, Thoran will become stronger," Ingrid said.

"It looks as if we're going to be very busy," Gerd commented. "Will you manage without me, Egil?"

"What other option do I have?" he said with a shrug.

"Perhaps you could get help from other trusted Rangers, like Molak," Ingrid suggested.

"Captain Fantastic? I wouldn't recommend him at all," Viggo wagged his finger. "That one's straighter than a Rogdonian spear. He wouldn't agree with your methods."

"You know, he's somewhat right," Gerd said.

"Molak has always behaved properly," Nilsa said defensively.

"Sure, wait until Egil asks him to betray the King a couple of times in a single week," Viggo grinned ironically.

"Don't worry, I'll manage," Egil assured them.

"We're your friends, we do worry," said Lasgol. "You take too many risks, and there are many who want to see you dead, both your political rivals and some of your allies of the West."

"Very true, but what would life be without a little excitement?" Egil smiled.

"We wouldn't know what to do with ourselves," said Astrid.

"I can't stay still. I'd have a fit if I didn't have something to do," Nilsa said as she twisted one of her red curls around her finger.

"But we also have to consider that too much action might be dangerous..." Ingrid warned.

"I don't think we'll be inactive for a long time. We have too many concerns and more which will no doubt appear at the most inopportune moment," Egil said, smiling. "But you don't need to worry. We just need to focus on our priorities. We each have a mission. That's what matters now. If each of us manages to be successful and complete the mission, we'll have a much better chance of achieving our goals."

"Very true!" Ingrid said, nodding emphatically.

"I absolutely agree," Astrid joined her.

"Remind me of those goals again, please," Viggo said.

Egil looked at him and smiled.

"First, finish off Dergha-Sho-Blaska and frustrate his plans to enslave the continent."

"And second?" Gerd asked.

"Second, get back the Throne of the North," Egil said firmly.

"That's the throne of Norghana, isn't it?" Nilsa said.

"That's right. In times of old it was known as the Throne of the North, before the kingdoms and countries were settled and the borders we have now drawn," Egil confirmed.

"Sounds easy, piece of cake," Viggo said, stretching his arms and back as if he were warming up before entering the action.

"Very easy," Gerd nodded with eyes widened and a look on his face that said exactly the opposite.

"No matter how impossible both goals appear to be, we must try and achieve them," Lasgol said, trying to cheer them up. "As Egil says, let's focus on our specific missions. Let's each do our job and our goals will be closer."

We can, Camu messaged with confidence, and Ona joined him with a growl.

"Then it's decided," Ingrid stated.

"Let's get out of here and get started," Astrid joined her.

"May luck be with us," said Gerd.

"And the Ice Gods," Nilsa added.

Chapter 7

Astrid and Lasgol were riding together to the south. Their paths were joined for the time being, but they would soon have to part ways, and they both knew this. Lasgol would have to veer west to Rogdon and Astrid would be continuing south, to Erenal. So, they were enjoying every moment of their time together, since they were both well aware of how precious and scarce the time they could enjoy together was.

At nightfall, they camped and sat by the fire they had built.

"Come closer," Astrid said with a sweet smile.

Lasgol returned the smile and moved until they were both sitting shoulder to shoulder in front of the fire.

"Is this better?" he asked, putting his arm around her back to hold her by the waist, firmly but lovingly.

"Much better," she smiled with a look of happiness on her face.

They were both happy when they were together, and there was no way they could hide the fact. As Nilsa used to say, "they oozed love and happiness." It was also true that Viggo always said that "seeing them like that made his stomach turn," which Astrid and Lasgol considered a compliment. They could not help but look at each other lovingly or keep others from noticing their happiness. They spent too much time apart, which was becoming increasingly common, and that made their reunions and every moment they spent together precious. And not only lovely, but also invaluable, since no matter how much they wished it was the case, they could never spend as much time together as they wanted to.

"Don't you feel that the moments we spend together, like this, are becoming rarer every time?" Lasgol asked, looking into her eyes.

"Why are they rare?" she teased him with a big smile.

"I mean they're fewer."

"I know, but I like to tease you."

"You mean laugh at me."

"I mean laugh *with* you."

"Thank goodness," Lasgol smiled.

"And yeah, I agree that they're rare. We're always in the middle of complicated situations, missions or adventures that separate us," she nodded, and her intense green eyes dulled a little. "When we're not together, I worry terribly about you."

"Same here."

"I can't stop thinking that if something bad happened to you… I'd die," Astrid looked at him with a look of anguish quite uncharacteristic of someone like her who always approached life with a fierce gaze and without fear in her heart.

"And what would I do if anything bad happened to you?" Lasgol sighed as if there was a hole in the middle of his chest and the air escaped through it.

"If anything bad happens to me, you need to live your life. Don't weep for my absence. Go on with your life."

"I couldn't… nothing would be the same… nothing would make sense any more. I couldn't," Lasgol shook his head, waving aside the idea and casting it out of his mind.

"It would, and you know it. You'd still have to save Norghana and Tremia from destruction and evil."

"The others can do that. I wouldn't be able to even lift my bow," he replied, touching Aodh's Bow beside him.

"I know you'd suffer for my loss, but you must promise me that you'll go on with your life."

"I don't want to promise you anything, because I don't want it to happen. I feel like we're asking for bad luck," Lasgol raised his hand to the sky and wagged his finger to indicate he was not.

"Promise me," Astrid told him seriously.

Lasgol heaved a deep sigh.

"Fine, you win. I promise, but only so we don't keep talking about this."

"Okay, we won't talk about it again."

"Thank you," Lasgol snorted.

"Besides, I've always told you that you were born for something much more important than chasing after criminals for the King. You have a destiny of gigantic importance. I know it, and I can see it more and more clearly every day. Heed my words—one day you'll save Norghana and all of Tremia. I know it, I can feel it in here," she said, putting her fist to her heart.

"You have the wrong hero. I already have enough to deal with just surviving all the trouble we get into."

"And don't you think that being in all this trouble is for a reason?"

"I hope you're not getting that from Viggo. It isn't my fault," Lasgol shrugged.

"I know it's not. But don't you think that making Egil King and defeating Dergha-Sho-Blaska and his plans to enslave Tremia won't lead you to saving Norghana and Tremia? Because I certainly do."

"I doubt they'll lead me that far, and we're all in up to our necks in this. Everyone equally, not just me."

"But you're the most special."

"Only in your eyes," Lasgol said, smiling gently.

Astrid could not help herself and kissed him passionately.

"What I'm saying is that if you're in trouble, it's because you have a much more important destiny than you think. It's time you started believing it."

"You are my destiny."

Astrid was left speechless.

"You're wonderful," she said, moved, and she took his face in her hands. "You're good of heart, brave, honorable, and also very handsome. What have I done to be so lucky that you love me back?"

"I'll keep the latter," Lasgol smiled, not believing for a moment he was handsome.

Astrid kissed him again.

"You're somewhat melancholic this evening."

"Perhaps, maybe, yeah…"

"I wasn't aware I had that effect on you."

"It's not you, dopey," she said, elbowing him gently. "Being together alone again makes me think about our lives, about how we're living them, about what they'll be like in the future," Astrid remained thoughtful, gazing at the stars.

"Things aren't turning out the way I thought they would. I always thought that, both of us being Rangers, we'd share a thousand and one adventures together and we'd be inseparable, that we'd live everything together."

"That's because you're a dreamer," Astrid kissed his cheek lovingly.

"I've come to realize that a Ranger's life, and more so ours, with all the problems we always have to face, is very different from what I had planned when I first met you at the Camp."

"You mean when you fell at my feet hopelessly in love with me at the Camp."

"I didn't fall at your feet..."

"You didn't?" Astrid said with disbelief.

"Well, maybe a little," Lasgol admitted, blushing a little.

"I see I can still make you blush, that's good. Don't ever stop doing it."

"I'll try, although I don't know how."

"By simply being you," Astrid said, smiling

"That I can do," Lasgol replied with a laugh.

"Real life, or rather adult life, is never like you dream about it when you're younger," Astrid told him. "You can't do everything you dreamed about because of the circumstances you have to live with, and these change from one person to another."

Lasgol nodded.

"Yeah, I can see that. The years at the Camp went by in the blink of an eye. Just like those at the Shelter, and now they're flying past. I feel that in no time we'll be…"

"Old?"

"Older."

Astrid nodded.

"We'll be older, yes. We're almost there."

"Yeah, I can feel it."

"And what do you want to do once we reach that point?" Astrid looked at him with curiosity.

"Hmmmm, that's a good question," Lasgol said, looking up at the moon and the stars. "I'd like to have a family."

Astrid's eyes widened.

"A family? Don't you want to go on being a Ranger and save the kingdom and the world?"

Lasgol thought about it.

"Yes, I want both. Something like my parents had: a family and fighting for the kingdom and the greater good."

"That does you credit. It's a beautiful wish."

"If it's what you want too, of course, otherwise…" Lasgol looked at Astrid with pleading eyes.

Astrid smiled at him from the bottom of her heart.

"That's what I want too."

"That makes me very happy," Lasgol smiled with bright eyes.

"Me too," Astrid smiled back.

"Have you thought about us having children…?"

"To be honest, I have. It makes me feel strange, but I have to admit that I have thought about it. One day, I'd like to have children."

"With me, I hope …"

"Of course with you, halfwit!"

"Well, that's a relief," Lasgol snorted, joking.

"Girl or boy?" Astrid wanted to know.

"I have no preference. I'd be delighted with whatever comes, one or the other."

"I knew you'd say that," she replied, smiling.

"And you? What would you like?"

"A girl, of course."

"Of course?"

"Girls are a lot more empathic and intelligent."

Lasgol laughed.

"I'm not going to go against you on this. I'll be delighted with a girl."

"But because it's you, and I know that you want it, we'll have two, a girl and boy," Astrid said, smiling tenderly.

"That would be spectacular."

"But only after you save Norghana and Tremia."

"Absolutely, only then."

Lasgol laughed.

"I'm touched to the core that we've talked about all this. We should do so more often. It gives me strength and certainty to face the future."

"Whenever you want. It does me good as well."

They kissed and embraced for a long while.

"When do you think we'll get to that moment in life?" Lasgol asked her.

"A lot sooner than you think. Our lives fly at the speed of a hawk chasing after its prey."

"Yeah, I have the same feeling."

"But whatever happens, we'll be together. Promise me."

"Together, always, I promise."

They both enjoyed that moment of happiness as if it were their last.

With dawn, the moment to go their separate ways arrived. Lasgol had to continue to Rogdon and Astrid to Erenal.

"I don't want to be apart," Astrid told Lasgol, and she hugged him hard as if she might lose him.

"We'll be back together soon," Lasgol promised, although he was really not sure at all that might be so.

"Be very careful."

"I'm just going to visit a mage of great renown and ask for his help. My mission is the least dangerous of all. It's you who should be careful. You don't know what you might come across."

"I'll manage, don't you worry."

"I know you can manage, but even so, you might encounter a high number of enemies."

"They won't even see me," Astrid winked at him. "Don't be too trusting. That mage might be very respectable, but you know that all of them have a special interest in Objects of Power."

"You're worried he might be greedy? He's a Royal Mage. King Solin of Rogdon has him as a defender of the realm."

"That may be true, but he might be greedy in terms of magic. We have the best example in Norghana. Maldreck is the leader of the Ice Magi and serves the King."

"That's true," Lasgol had to admit.

"Don't be fooled by the mage's appearance and his reputation. They all seek magical power, don't forget that."

"You're right. I'll be careful."

They kissed with a bitter farewell kiss. Neither of them wanted to part—they wanted to stay together, become full adults, start a family, and live happily. Unfortunately, all those wishes would have to wait. Today they had to do their duty. They had to go on their separate missions. The lives of countless people depended on it.

They would not fail them.

They parted and proceeded on to their destinations.

Chapter 8

Beside the White Pearl at the Shelter, Camu, Ona, Nilsa, Ingrid, and Viggo were getting ready to begin their journey east. Egil was waiting off to the side—he was not going on this journey. He would have to wait for Camu and Ona to return to take him west. On the other side of the Pearl, Loke, Galdason, and Enduald watched carefully. Enduald was holding two metal rods with gloved hands that were a head taller than him and which were emitting orange flashes. Galdason had a large metal dish, and by the markings engraved and several little holes in it, it looked like some kind of measuring device.

Sigrid and the four Elder Specialists arrived from the Lair.

"Mother Specialist, Elders," Ingrid greeted them.

"Greetings to all," Sigrid said. "Camu, you may become visible. There's no-one around, we are alone," said Sigrid, who had been informed Camu was with the group.

I let see.

Camu became visible and with him Ona, whom he had been keeping camouflaged.

"Hello to both!" Gisli said cheerfully.

"You look wonderful," Annika said.

I much wonderful always.

Ona chirped once.

Gisli approached them with swift strides and stroked them both with a great smile.

"We have been reflecting about your intention of going after the weapons to fight the great Immortal Dragon," Sigrid said, addressing the whole group, but with her gaze fixed on Egil.

"Do you approve?" Nilsa asked, a little nervous that it might not be so.

"After talking about it thoroughly, we believe it is the right decision given the situation we are facing," Sigrid nodded. "Gondabar has been keeping us informed of everything, as well as Dolbarar at the Camp. The owls and pigeons haven't had a rest in a while. They go between the Shelter, the capital, and the Camp constantly, carrying messages back and forth."

"We are very worried with everything you have found out in the deserts," Annika commented.

"This is going down the drain fast," Ivar joined her with a troubled look on his face.

"An army is only needed for one thing," Engla commented.

"For war," Ingrid stated.

"That's right. What you've discovered indicates that the Immortal Dragon and his hosts will soon attack," Engla continued with a frown.

"We must prepare for the possibility of what might happen," Gisli said. "Those weapons will help us against the great dragon and the lesser ones."

"That is our hope, yes," Egil said, nodding.

"I wish you good luck. Find the weapons and bring them back," Sigrid said, crossing her arms over her chest and looking at her brother. "Enduald is an Enchanter, as you already know. He will be able to study those weapons and see what enchantments, spells, and power they have."

"That's our hope, indeed," Egil said, nodding.

"It will be a great pleasure for me to be able to study those weapons. They intrigue me. When we studied Aodh's Bow after Lasgol found it, we found out the weapon was authentic. It was over three thousand years old. Our theory is," she said, looking at Galdason, "that it was created by the Gods who were supposed to live during that time. The weapon had strong traces of their magic. We could not understand the working of the spells or the magic, but we did identify their origin."

"Exactly," Galdason intervened. "The bow was created with the magic of the Gods who fought the dragons. We believe it was specifically created to fight them. Unfortunately, we were unable to fully understand the bow's magic and the way it worked. We would need to study other similar weapons to see whether we can unveil its secrets."

"As long as they work it's good enough for me. The why is irrelevant," Viggo said, shrugging.

"We must understand how the power of those weapons works, the spells they have," Enduald corrected him.

"Why is it necessary?" Nilsa asked. She did not see the use either.

"Because it can help us understand how to defeat the dragons," Enduald explained.

"And also because it's a mystery, and mysteries exist to be discovered and solved," said Galdason. "If we understand how the magic in these weapons works, we can make them more powerful, even replicate them."

"Replicating them would be good," Ingrid said eagerly. "The more weapons the Rangers have like that, the better."

"That is what we think as well," Sigrid said. "Bring them back so Enduald and Galdason can analyze them, and we might have a positive surprise."

"I don't mean to be a bird of ill omen, but it might also be a negative one," Viggo commented.

"What do you mean by negative?" Engla asked.

"It might be that once we analyze them we'll find out that not only can they not be replicated, but that in order to use them we would need to have the Gift. What would we do then?"

The Elder Specialists exchanged worried looks. Sigrid motioned for her brother to speak.

"That fear is not only yours. We feel the same way. Enchanted weapons, as a rule, do not need the wielder to have the Gift. But some of them might be deadly for whoever wields them, precisely because of this fact. More than one noble and even some kings have gone crazy after using an enchanted sword or crown without having the Gift."

"That's not good news for us..." said Nilsa.

"Not good at all," Ingrid joined her.

"For now, we know that Lasgol has Aodh's Bow and his magic works against the dragons. It hasn't had any negative effects on him, although our friend does have the Gift," Egil said. "Maybe the Gift is necessary to use these weapons, maybe not. It could also be that, even if the weapons require their wielders to have the Gift, we might find a way to get around this need or its negative effects. In any case, we won't know until we find them and study them."

Bow magic no Drakonian, Camu messaged.

"That is what we believe too. We have to study the weapons and see what we discover. It is imperative," Galdason insisted.

"You bring them back and I'll study them in my workshop," Enduald said.

"We have to find them first and see whether they really exist," said Ingrid. "There might be some that are only imaginary."

"That's true, although we have reasons for optimism. Lasgol found the bow, and not only does it exist, but he has already been able to ascertain that its magic works against dragons," Egil said.

"We're good at being optimistic," Viggo joked.

"Sure, you in particular," Engla said.

Viggo smiled.

Open portal now? Camu messaged.

Ingrid looked around.

"Don't worry. I've called all the contenders back. They're inside the Lair studying tomes of knowledge," Sigrid said. "They won't come out until I tell them."

"Then we can open it," Ingrid said.

"One moment," Enduald said, raising his hand. "We need to place the measuring rods."

"Very well, do it then."

Enduald took one of the rods and planted it deep five paces to the north of the Pearl. Then he walked around to the south and planted the second rod just as deep. Galdason placed a ball that looked made of glass on the tip of the first rod and then did the same with the second. They both put a spell on the rods and the balls at their tips. The rest watched the preparations for the measurements.

"There we are, done," Enduald told Sigrid.

"Good, now you can go ahead. All of us here know the secret of the White Pearl, so there are no obstacles," Sigrid told Ingrid.

"Okay, Camu, open the Portal."

"One more thing," Loke said, and he brought a ladder to help them up to the Pearl.

"Good idea!" Nilsa said, clapping her hands.

"I thought it would be easier this way."

"Absolutely," Ingrid replied with a smile.

I open, Camu warned, and he shut his eyes to concentrate. He gave off a silver flash. This was followed by two more. He started sending silver pulses to the great object using the correct rhythm and cadence. The Pearl awoke with a great silver flash. A moment later, the Portal began to take shape above it. Three silvery circles were formed: the first one, which was the same size as the Pearl, the second, which was larger and oval in shape; and the third one, which transformed into a huge silver sphere. The great sphere gradually stabilized and remained formed as if it were filled with liquid silver.

Portal open, Camu messaged.

"Wonderful. Look for the eastern rune," Egil told him. "You remember it, don't you?"

I much memory. Remember.

For a moment, they all watched how Camu interacted with the energy of the open Portal. It was as if his energy and that of the Portal were talking.

Have rune already.

"Well done, Camu," Egil congratulated him.

"Those of us heading east, up we go," Ingrid said.

"I've brought you new potions which I hope will be of use," Annika said, handing them a leather bag.

"Yes, please! I hate the negative effects of crossing the Portal," Viggo cried and wasted no time in taking one of the potions from the bag and downing it in one gulp.

"We're really grateful. The effects are honestly quite terrible," Nilsa said.

"I hope these'll help. I can only guess at the effect from what you've told me, so the potions may not be as effective as I'd hope"

You cross and see, Camu suggested.

"Thank you, Camu, it is a good idea, but for now we've decided not to experiment with the Portal, only study it and measure it," Annika replied.

Crossing be studying.

"True, but I don't think it's a good idea until we better understand the way it works," Sigrid said. "We have had bad experiences with magic that have made us more cautious than we used to be," the Mother Specialist said, looking at Engla out of the corner of her eye.

I understand.

"Later on when we have a better understanding of what we face," Galdason commented as he climbed the ladder and placed the measuring dish in the Portal. "Camu, bring this dish back, it's an energy catcher."

No problems, I bring back.

Ingrid, Nilsa, and Viggo went into the Portal, followed by Ona and Camu. They vanished at once.

A while later, the Portal vanished and the Pearl looked the same as always.

They waited for Camu's return so he could take Egil on his mission to the west. They were all talking about the weapons and how to get the most advantages from them as they stood or sat around the Pearl. Enduald and Galdason were not particularly optimistic—deciphering the mysteries of such an ancient and powerful magic was not something that would be done easily. But they were prepared to try with all their good will and effort.

"How's Gerd? Engla asked Egil, sitting beside him.

"He's doing well. A lot better, Ma'am."

"Has he managed to recover completely, or does he still have some side effects?"

"He still has to deal with some lingering effects, but he has learned to live with them. He has a good spirit and a great heart."

"He does indeed. I have the same problems. I am glad he's taking it so well. I'm finding it difficult to adjust to the idea of being impaired. Yet, I know that life is not fair and we sometimes have to suffer. Complaining to the skies is of no use, the Ice Gods aren't listening. It's best to go on with our life and face it, regardless of what comes our way."

"Gerd faces it with a good attitude, he's an example of will power," Egil said.

"You are lucky to have such a friend. You'll need his strength, both physical and his strong will. He's going to get you out of more than one mess."

Egil nodded.

"We know, Ma'am."

Suddenly, the Portal began to open. The circles took shape, and after a moment the great silver sphere formed above the Pearl. The Portal was majestic and shone with silver hues that held everyone watching spellbound.

"They're coming back," said Sigrid.

Enduald and Galdason were manipulating the two rods they had planted south and north of the Pearl. As the Portal was forming, creating the great silver sphere above the White Pearl, currents of energy jumped from the Portal to the two rods. It looked like a storm brewing and releasing bolts of lightning, which ran along the rods and died at the two balls placed at the tips and which seemed to be gathering the discharges.

"I hope everything's gone well…" Egil said wishfully.

"I'm sure it has," Annika said with a smile.

"Camu and Lasgol have already journeyed to the east before. Everything should've gone well," Egil said, hopeful.

The Portal finished forming in all its silver splendor.

Suddenly Camu and Ona appeared, coming out of the Portal and standing on the Pearl.

Egil, come, portal open now.

Egil drank the potion.

"Coming," he said, climbing up the ladder.

"Is everything all right, Camu?" Sigrid asked.

Everything perfect.

"Wonderful," the Mother Specialist said, relaxing her shoulders.

"The measuring dish?" Enduald asked Camu.

Be here.

"Egil, throw it down to me and I'll hand you another," Enduald said.

"Do I pick it up with my bare hands? " he asked uncertainly.

"Take my protective gloves," Enduald told him. He took them off and threw them at Egil, who caught them in the air and put them on. He picked up the dish from the floor. It now showed a series of concentric circles, which were shining yellow. He also noticed several symbols, some which were shining and others which were dull. He threw it at Enduald's feet, on the grass. Then he took off the gloves and also threw them down at him.

Egil stroked Ona, who did not seem scared, although they were before an open portal.

I calibrate portal, Camu messaged.

"Remember that we're going west. The nearer to the western coast, the better," Egil reminded him.

Yes, west, looking route.

Egil watched how Camu searched for the adequate rune, interacting with the portal.

Be ready. Rune west.

"Did you find it? Are you sure?"

I find. No sure.

"Not sure?" Egil looked at him blankly.

No sure. First journey west.

"That's true. I guess we'll have to take the risk."

Ready? Camu asked him.

"For discovery? Always," Egil smiled at him.

Come in portal.

"Very well, here we go."

"Good luck!" Sigrid wished them.

"May everything turn out well," Annika joined in as the others watched in silence.

Egil entered the Portal and at once lost consciousness.

Chapter 9

Egil, wake up.

A feeling of dizziness and unease had him struggling, but he managed to open his eyes and saw Camu and Ona beside him. They were in front of a White Pearl surrounded by gray, rocky formations, and the breeze that reached him suddenly moistened his face. He licked his lips and caught the taste of salt.

"Sea?" he asked, still confused.

West Sea, Camu messaged.

Ona chirped in the direction of the sea and jumped onto a big rock to indicate to Egil where it was.

"The potion didn't have much of an effect on me...." Egil got to his feet with his hands to his head. He felt it as if it was filled with cotton.

We notice.

"That's odd... it should have softened those negative effects."

You little body, much head.

Egil tried to laugh, but his headache would not let him.

"You mean that, although my body is small in comparison with an average Norghanian, my intelligence is bigger?"

Yes. Much head.

"It's better if you say 'much intelligence,' it sounds better and it will save you some bad interpretations."

Much intelligent.

Ona chirped once.

You strong, you stand well.

"Thanks, I wouldn't say that much. I'd rather avoid this experience if possible," Egil admitted, filling his lungs and exhaling three times in a row.

Now better?

"I think so." He took his water-skin out of his satchel and drank. "Much better now."

We happy you better.

Egil looked around. All he could see was the great White Pearl and groups of sizeable rocks that obstructed his sight. What he did notice was the smell of the sea, and when he concentrated, he was able to hear the sound of the breakers not far from where he was.

"I'm going to see if I can tell where I am," Egil climbed to the top of a large boulder, and from there he checked the landscape around him. To the east he saw a great plain covered in green. But to the south, the green blanket ended not very far from there and started turning brown, to then take on the color of sand further down. To the north there were vast green meadows, and beyond that a huge mountain range. To the west, the plain ended in a cliff crowned by large boulders that looked as if they had fallen from the sky at the dawn of time. On the horizon, he saw a rough, dark-blue sea.

"I can see the sea to the west, and to the south there seems to be dry land. Do you know where we are?" he asked and took out a map he was carrying to try and figure out more or less where he was.

South begin deserts.

"Deserts? Then we're close to Nocean territory."

We west.

"Yeah, that much is clear. I can see the Western Sea, and I hear it roaring. What I need to know now is where in the west we are," he said, checking his map.

Much south, no.

"And not very far north either, since we can see the beginning of the desert…"

Ona chirped once in agreement.

We center-west.

"I wonder whether we're inside Rogdonian territory…"

Not know.

Egil looked at the mountains in the north.

"No, that must be the mountain range south of Rogdon. We're on the other side, more to the south. Yes, I believe we're in the middle of Tremia and all the way west."

I tell, Camu messaged as if it were obvious.

"Yeah, but you didn't tell me with much accuracy or confidence. Precision in measurements is essential."

I much precision.

"Of course, it couldn't be otherwise," Egil smiled, knowing full well what Camu was like.

What do?

Egil looked in every direction and then consulted his map again.

"I have to go northwest, from what I was able to find out about the great weapon. To a village called Derfin, which must be at the foot of the mountains and above the Western Sea. I have to find the information I'm missing to know where it's hidden."

Village far?

"No, I don't think it's very far. We've come out a lot closer than I had guessed. This Portal is at an advantageous point and it's also pretty well hidden, being surrounded by all these large rocky formations."

I much good with Portal.

Ona chirped twice.

Yes be, Camu messaged back.

"I have to admit that you've brought us very close. This Pearl of the Midwest will come in very handy. It leaves us between the Kingdom of Rogdon and the dominions of the Nocean Empire. Gondabar will be very pleased to know about this location."

I tell others.

"Yes, do."

Need help?

Egil appreciated Camu's and Ona's company. They were of great help and loving companions. But he really did not need them for the rest of his mission. He was in neutral territory, and the weapon had to be buried somewhere. He did not need help; he could manage on his own. Besides, he would rather Camu and Ona were with Lasgol or whoever really needed their help.

"I don't really think I'll need you. At least not until I'm done, then I will. I will send Angus," he said and lifted a cage with a gray mottled owl inside it.

You send Angus when finish or if have problems. We come, pick up or help.

"Very well, I'll do that. I only hope I'll need you just to come and pick me up."

You much intelligent. All be good.

Ona joined in with one chirp.

"Thank you both. Me and my big head will go on from here," he replied, joking.

Camu tilted his head and blinked hard. He had not understood the joke.

Head normal. Much intelligent.

Egil smiled.

"You really are intelligent, my dear Creature of the Ice," he told him as he hugged him goodbye. Then he turned to Ona and hugged her too.

Wish luck.

"Thanks, I'm going to need it. Finding treasures isn't precisely one of my specialties."

You do, Camu messaged with great conviction, which Egil appreciated from the bottom of his heart. Only Camu could be so convinced he and his friends could do everything always. It was an admirable quality, although one day he would be greatly disappointed. This thought made Egil sad. He did not want Camu's good, brave heart to suffer the injustices of life. But that was precisely a part of growing up, and an important one. Your own successes and overcoming difficulties helped in personal development, but the failures and falls were even more crucial. You had to get back up and keep going, even if the disappointment was huge and the suffering great; only thus you grew up strong and complete.

"So long, friends," Egil waved at them. He adjusted his bow and satchel on his back, picked up the cage with Angus, and started on his way.

As he walked away, he had a funny feeling that made him look back. He could not see the Pearl since it was hidden among the great rocks, but he saw the Portal opening. There was no one in the area, but Egil wondered whether anyone might see it. Would the first men have seen it, when the last dragons used the Portals for the last time? Most likely not. From what they knew, there was only reference of one last dragon that had used the Portals. This is what Tor Nasser had told them in the desert. Humans and dragons had never lived at the same time. The dragons had disappeared before the arrival of humans.

Egil watched the beautiful silver Portal and wondered what effect it might have on humans to see the Portal now. It was something that had never happened, something as strange as it was wonderful and beautiful, at least from his point of view. The leaders and monarchs would not see them like that though. For them it would be a weapon to use against other kingdoms and tribes. The fact that an army could appear at once and all of a sudden was something powerful which many kingdoms would want to exploit. If the existence of the Portals was known, there would be wars simply for their control. Egil could not stop thinking about the implications.

He stood there watching until the Portal vanished. With a little luck, no one would have seen it. So far, only the Panthers and the leaders of the Rangers knew about the Portals, and he had the certainty that not only was that the most sensible decision, but also the most prudent one. Luckily, only Camu could use it, which would prevent greater evils in case their existence was ever found out. But this endangered Camu, since all the leaders would want him to serve their kingdoms. This would again create serious trouble for Camu and the Panthers. As well as the Rangers, who would try to protect them.

He sighed. Even if they did not know about Camu, sooner or later some erudite or mage or both would manage to open the Portal. Egil knew it was only a matter of time. When a mystery presented itself, humans had an innate disposition to try and find out the answer and get to the bottom of it. They might not be able to discover the secrets of the Portal, since the Portals used Drakonian Magic, but in any case, they would try without pause. No mystery could remain unsolved on the face of Tremia if there was something to gain from solving it. Magi and erudites and scholars would try to discover it by all means available. It was human nature. They would not let the matter be.

He went on walking with all these thoughts in his head about Portals and their future. The situation was half under control, except for the fact that a dragon might appear out of one of the Portals and wreak havoc. If Dergha-Sho-Blaska could use the Portals, it was more than likely the lesser dragons could do so too, since they were dragons, lesser or not. This thought made him uneasy. Their problems were multiplying, and they were not going to go away on their own. If the Panthers did not do something, they would grow and the consequences would be even worse of a catastrophic proportion.

He was so lost in his own thoughts that he did not realize he had arrived at a country road with a mule-drawn cart coming toward him for a distance. He went toward the person driving it, who looked like a middle-aged farmer, to greet him.

"Good morning!" Egil said, raising his left hand and using the unified language of the west.

"Good morning!" the man replied. He pulled on the reins to stop the cart and looked at him in surprise, most likely because of Egil's accent and looks.

"Would you be so kind as to tell me where I am, please?"

"You are in the Peninsula of Logon, southwest Rogdon. Everything that surrounds it is water except to the east."

Egil looked behind him and then ahead. This explained why it smelled so strongly of the sea on that plain. He was on a peninsula.

"Am I far from the village of Derfin?"

"A good half league following the road," the man told him, turning to indicate the direction he had come from.

"Thank you very much. I'll be on my way then."

"Visiting anyone?"

"No, only the village."

The man made a funny face.

"Few people come this way. This peninsula is a little forgotten by everyone."

"We are in Rogdon, aren't we?"

"That's right. But the least known and visited part. The kingdom is behind those mountains. On this side, and more so on this peninsula, they have forgotten about us."

"Sometimes being forgotten is a blessing," Egil said, smiling.

The man scratched his head.

"True, here we are safe from politics, the throne, and the madness of wars between kingdoms."

"And what about the Noceans? Aren't they a problem?" Egil asked, pointing south.

"On the contrary. They come to buy fish and seafood," he indicated the load he carried which, from the smell, was undoubtedly fish. "We sell it to them at twice the price we do to the locals," he laughed.

"Good business then."

"Indeed. Desert people aren't good fishers, at least around here."

Egil smiled.

"May your sales be good!"

"Thanks," the man smiled and went on his way.

Egil followed the road.

He arrived at the fishing village a little earlier than he had expected, lost once again in his own thoughts about Portals and the danger they meant for humanity. He had reached the conclusion that it was almost as dangerous that humans would want to take over them as it would be if dragons used them. In both scenarios there would be inevitable bloodshed.

The village was very picturesque with all the fishing folk houses painted blue and a silvery white. The kingdom of Rogdon was known for her Lancers and the colors blue and silver they wore. Well, the Lancers and all other soldiers, since these were the colors of the realm. He thought it fascinating to find all those small fishing folk houses made of wood looking out on a long wharf and the Western Sea. They seemed to be all dressed up waiting for the fishing boats to return.

In the street and on the wharf, he saw fishing folk working on the nets and fixing boats. There were as many women as there were men, and they were all quite old. The young folk had to be at sea fishing, or so Egil thought. He would have to ask. He walked along the houses toward the wharf. He was delighted by the little houses all with well-painted walls in silver-white and doors, windows, roofs, and balconies painted blue. They were very well kept and were a visual delight. Now that he was in the middle of the wharf and houses, Egil had a greater feeling that these were looking to the sea waiting for the return of the fisher folk.

"Good morning!" he said cheerfully and with a big smile they could all see as they worked on the wharf.

The people, both men and women, who were sitting on the wood boards of the floor and on crates stopped working to stare at him. No one rose. They only watched him as if he were an anomaly that had just arrived in their world.

"You're not Rogdonian," one of them said to him. He was one of the oldest men, probably in his seventies.

"Or Nocean," a woman who looked as old as him said, smiling.

"My accent and the paleness of my skin betray me," Egil replied with a shrug.

"You're not a warrior either, you talk too nice," another fisherman making complicated knots said.

"No, I'm not a warrior, and I'm not looking for trouble. I'm Norghanian, from the lands with mountains always covered in snow."

"Aren't Norghanians big and strong, with platinum-blond hair and beards, and brutes without much up here?" another woman in her sixties asked, pointing at her head.

"Those are the Norriel," a man replied.

"The Norriel aren't blond or so big," another woman corrected him, "and they use long swords. The Norghanians use axes, right?"

"I see our reputation precedes us," Egil smiled. "Norghanians are like you say, and the distinction with the Norriel who also live in the north is correct, but they live to the northwest."

"So, what happened to you?" the sixty-year-old woman wanted to know.

"Let's say I'm the exception that confirms the rule."

"And what does that mean?"

"That every rule has an exception, and in the case of the Norghanians, I'm it. The exception, I mean. The rule is accurate."

"I don't understand what he's saying," said another man.

"Because of the accent or the point I'm trying to make?"

"Because of the accent and how funny you speak," the man in his seventies said.

"My apologies, I'm not used to speaking to such honorable and hard-working folk of the sea."

"He's a good flatterer," one of the women said, laughing.

"Why are you carrying an owl in a cage?" another woman asked.

"Well… it's a long story…"

"Leave it, it's his own business. It might be his pet and they're inseparable," the woman in her sixties said.

"Something like that, sure…" Egil tried to wave it aside.

"Well, that's your business. Are you lost?" the older man said.

"No, very much the opposite. I've come expressly to this village."

"Here? What for?"

"Not to buy fish and seafood."

"No, I've come to find out some information… about a weapon of power…"

"Another fool who's come looking for the golden spear," a woman who looked older than all the others said.

"I'm not the first, right?"

"Nor will you be the last," she replied.

"Then you can help me."

"Not us," the older man replied. "You'll have to go and see Gordon the Sailor, although he's not much of a sailor anymore."

"Where can I find him?"

"Before you go, you should know that all those who've been to see Gordon, after speaking to him, left to never be seen again."

"You mean seen here in the village?"

"They have never been seen…"

"Perhaps they didn't come back this way and that's why you never saw them."

Once again, they all shook their heads.

"Nobles of Rogdon have passed through here, even kings' relatives. They were never seen again. They never went back to their possessions or titles."

"That doesn't sound very promising."

"That's why we're warning you."

"Thanks," Egil was left thinking. He had expected the search for the golden spear to have certain risks, but this was more than he had calculated at first. He had not expected to have to face a situation like the one they were telling him about. And the worst thing was that he believed these good people, which complicated things.

"You can go back the way you came and forget that crazy idea," a woman said.

"I'd really like to, but I can't …"

"In that case, Gordon the Sailor's house is the last one on the wharf."

"Don't say we didn't warn you," another fisherman said.

"Thank you all," Egil said, bowing his head, and went on toward the house they had indicated. Already, dark clouds were appearing in his head, just like the ones he could see forming in the sky.

Chapter 10

Egil arrived at the house and banged softly on the door with his fist. Although the sound echoed, no-one came to the door. Egil waited for a moment and then banged harder. This time the door creaked, but no-one came to open it. He was beginning to think there was no-one in or that the fishermen had pulled his leg. It was more likely the former, but he could never be sure.

Suddenly, one of the two front windows opened and the head of a man in his late eighties peeped out. He studied Egil from head to toe.

"I'm not buying owls, thank you," he said and closed the window again.

"No, I'm not selling the owl," Egil tried to explain.

There was no answer.

Egil snorted and knocked on the door again. He waited, since he did not expect the old fisherman to open the door quickly.

The window opened again.

"I said I'm not interested in the owl."

"I didn't come to sell the owl."

"Then why do you come to bother me?" the fisherman demanded angrily.

"I've come for the Golden Spear."

The look on the man's face changed to one of interest.

"You come looking for the spear that kills dragons?"

"That's right. I want to find it and recover it."

"Many before you have come looking for it and haven't found it."

"I'm different," Egil said, smiling.

"I seriously doubt it."

"I swear my reasons are different."

"Sure. Now you'll tell me that greed doesn't move you, that you don't want the fame and the glory of having such a powerful weapon."

Egil considered how much to tell the old man so Gordon would help him, because it did not look as if he was going to. In that case, it would be no good to lie to him. Most likely he would have heard all kind of lies and tricky answers. He decided to tell him the truth.

"I need the weapon to kill a dragon."

The old man's eyes widened in surprise.

"You're not being serious."

"I'm dead serious."

The fisherman closed the window again and Egil was left waiting, a little puzzled. Had the man taken it as a sign of disrespect? He hoped not.

Suddenly, the door opened.

You'd better not be pulling my leg. At my age, I don't take kindly to that kind of thing. I might be forced to gut you like a fish."

"I'm telling the truth. A dragon has come back to life, and I need the spear to kill it."

"If that's true, you'll need quite a lot more than a spear. It doesn't seem to me that you and your owl will be much of a threat to a dragon, even with the Golden Spear."

"Without it, we don't stand a chance."

"That's for sure. Come into my humble dwelling, foreigner, and we'll talk."

Egil came into a house as old and in as much disarray as its owner. Everything inside had to be at least a hundred years old, from the few rustic pieces of furniture, sailor style, to decorations as odd as they were dated. Nets were hanging on the walls, as well as harpoons, hooks, and other fishing tools. There were also pieces of wood with the names of what Egil guessed must be old vessels.

The ancient mariner invited him to sit down.

Egil took a reclining chair and the old man sat in another one beside him. Before them was a welcoming low fire. The house smelled of dust and time. The smell of the fire was the only thing that lightened the heavy atmosphere of the tiny house, which only had one more room at the back. Egil preferred not to see what was in it or in what state. He had enough with the living room and kitchen.

"I was told that Gordon the Sailor could help me..." Egil started, to prompt the old man to talk.

"Gordon the Sailor already has a feeble mind and one foot in the deep sea."

"But he could help..."

"I was piqued by your story. Many have come with false pretenses, not only in my time, but in my father's time and his father's before him, and even before that. All looking for the famed Golden Spear of Rogdon. I don't like liars. You're not lying, are you?"

"No, I'm not lying."

"What's your name, and where do you come from? Your accent sounds northern."

"I am from the north," Egil said, nodding. "My name's Egil, and I'm from the Kingdom of Norghana."

"You are far away from your land. As a rule, it's Rogdonian noblemen or adventurers who come looking for the famed spear. Some Noceans too, and the pirates of the Central Sea have looked for it. Even the Norriel, only to prevent Rogdon from having it. But no one had come from Norghana before, not in my time or in my father's time."

"We've had the misfortune of coming across a dragon," Egil shrugged.

"We?" Gordon raised a white, scant eyebrow.

"My partners and I. We're seeking for a way to kill him before he finishes off our kingdom or any other kingdom he might attack first."

"That does you credit. Few would do that."

"But it has to be done. We are men and women of honor."

"What if I told you that all who have gone in search of the spear have never come back? You'd still want to go? Would you still see it as something that has to be done?" Gordon's gaze showed malice and interest; he wanted to know what Egil was going to do.

"I had already guessed there would be danger. Also, that it wouldn't be easy, but I have to do it. There are many lives at stake."

"Do you really believe you'll find the spear and survive where men much stronger and noble than you have failed? Some from the royal lineage of Rogdon."

"I don't believe that lineage has anything to do with this, and if I'm less strong, I make up for it with a sharp mind," Egil replied, tapping his head with his finger and smiling.

Gordon started to laugh and Egil noticed that his wrinkles deepened and his skin looked languid. He was also missing several teeth. The man looked over a hundred years old.

"Let's see, what do you know about the Golden Spear?"

Egil sighed.

Not much, unfortunately. I know what is told in the Kingdom of the West of the alleged existence of a spear which an ancient king of Rogdon possessed, Gontel Dungers. This weapon was magic, capable of killing dragons. The famous mounted Lancers were created to serve King Gontel once he had the weapon in his possession. It's said they're unbeatable."

Gordon smiled and chuckled deep in his throat.

"Go on, don't stop now."

"Unfortunately, the weapon disappeared a few hundred years after the death of the monarch without a trace. It's said that his son Bernard hid it, jealous of his father's fame. Apparently, father and son didn't get along well."

"Jealousy and envy often undermine even the most royal of families."

"Is that what happened?"

"No one knows for sure, but I can tell you that Bernard came through here."

"He did?"

The ancient mariner smiled and nodded.

"He did."

"Then the stories are true."

"Not entirely, but they come close. Isn't that always the case?"

Egil had to admit it was usually so.

"That's what is said. There's no legend or myth that hasn't some truth in its origin."

"That's right. Bernard hid the spear and decreed that the Lancers should disperse and never wear the silver and blue of the realm again. His intention was to bury the large shadow of his father so it would never fall on him again, preventing him from growing. But by then he was just a small, wilted tree. He would never manage to grow and flourish."

"What happened to him?"

"He used all of his means to be better than his father. He created an army and searched for magic Objects of Power with the help of his magi who would lead him to glory, much more than his father ever achieved."

"Did he succeed?"

Gordon smiled bitterly.

"No, he did not. He died a few years after his father. Some say that the envy that ate at him, killed him as if his body had generated a poison that finished him. Others, that the immense rage he felt for not getting the people to love him like they did his father, corroded him until it dug a hole in his stomach that killed him. Whichever way it was, he died without achieving anything of merit. The Lancers were once again the elite corps of the Rogdonian Army after his death. That was like the cherry on top of his grave."

"And what about the spear?"

"Ah, the powerful Golden Spear of Rogdon. The one everyone is looking for and no one can find. I can tell you that my family helped Bernard hide it."

"Where?" Egil asked, unable to contain his eagerness to know.

"He hid it in the Triangle of Rogondel."

"I don't know that place, where is it?"

"Not very far from here," Gordon said, indicating west.

"In the sea?" Egil was surprised.

The ancient mariner nodded.

"The Triangle of Rogondel are three islands two leagues away from here. They're uninhabited. The late king hid the spear in one of them."

"Do we know in which one?"

"I'm afraid not, and that's where the mystery and the trouble begin."

"Because whoever goes to those islands never comes back," Egil guessed.

"I see you have a sharp mind."

"The Triangle of Rogondel is known as the Triangle of Pain," the ancient mariner said, stressing the last word intentionally.

"This pain isn't allegorical, is it?"

"I don't know what allegorical means, but the pain is very real. According to our folklore, a sea ghost lives in those islands and inflicts pain to the death to whoever it finds on them. The legend says it's the spirit of a sailor who went mad at sea and was wrecked on the Triangle and now lives there. They are his home, and he doesn't allow anyone to set foot there. Fishermen and sailors never go near those islands, but the shrill screams of those who have set foot there have been heard… on more than one occasion."

"I see… if I go to the islands, the mad sea spirit will find me and torture me to death, as it's done with others before me."

"As true as the sea being full of secrets and the souls of those drowned in it," Gordon smiled at him. "My advice is that you go back to Norghana and live a long life. The depths of the sea are filled with the skeletons of heroes who went in search of treasures to fight mythological beings."

"That's true. Luckily, I'm no hero," Egil said, smiling back.

"You certainly don't look like one, but I'm beginning to think you do have spirit. Unfortunately, fate makes no distinction. You'll die the same if you go."

Egil was thoughtful. He could ask for help from his friends, but they would be in similar situations as well. Besides, there was no proof that what the old man was saying was the truth and not another legend of the area. Tremia was full of myths, every region had them by the dozen.

"I'm afraid I do have to go looking for the spear."

"I'm sorry to hear that. I like you, I thought you'd be smarter than the others."

"Someone will find the Golden Spear, why not me?"

"Who says the spear can be found, and by you?"

Egil considered this.

"You're right."

"But even so, you'll go."

"I have to. My people need that spear. I must stop the dragon from destroying us."

"Is this dragon of yours real or a legend?"

"As real as I am."

The ancient mariner looked at Egil with narrowed eyes as if he wanted to see into his soul.

"I believe you, as unlikely as it seems. I see your need to go seeking the Golden Spear. It makes me sad to think that you're going to die, but I'll help you."

"Thank you for everything."

Chapter 11

Egil was sailing in the small one-mast boat Gordon had got for him. The old fisherman had also indicated the course. The Western Sea was a bit rough, and dark clouds in the sky bode ill. He had already left behind the small fishing boats of the village and was heading out to sea. Not being a great seaman and seeing the sea getting rougher, Egil was not at all easy. If what Gordon had told him was correct, it would not be long before he saw the Triangle of Rogondel, or that was his hope at least, because if the storm broke, he was going to have trouble in that small fishing boat.

He made sure the sail was well tied and that he was still on course: west and a little south. While he rode the waves, he found himself wondering about the sailor ghost that caused pain and death on the three islands. He did not believe such a ghost existed, or at least, he didn't believe in ghosts. He did believe in magic that lasted for centuries, but not in the ghost of some deceased person. On the other hand, the world of ghosts and spirits was one which he had not gone deep into. He had read about it, but most of the time he had dismissed it as a combination of imagination and fear, even terror, of the person telling the story or event. Fear could make one see things where there was nothing. On the other hand, in Tremia all kinds of strange things happened, so he could not dismiss the fact that there were ghosts somewhere on the continent.

He suddenly saw a shadow before him that startled him. He could not see it properly because there was a slight mist covering the area. He narrowed his eyes and tried to see what it was. At first, he could not make it out, but as he got closer, he managed to appreciate it fully. It was one of the islands of the Triangle, the smallest, which rose before his tiny boat. From what Gordon had told him, this island was called Regunde, and it was the closest one to the coast.

"Here I come," he told himself cheerfully.

He reached Regunde and, seeing that the sea was getting rougher by the moment, he searched for a beach where he might leave his boat and reach dry land. He had to go around the island along the eastern side, since all he could see were lethal-looking rocks and cliffs. He finally found a beach on the northern side and headed to it with relief. For a moment he had thought he would have to approach the rocks to reach land. That was always risky and the cause of a thousand wreckages.

He managed to reach the beach just as it started to rain hard. The rain in the west was a lot warmer than that of the north, so it barely bothered him. Except for the fact that because of the breeze coming from the sea, salty seawater was getting into his eyes and that was not pleasant. He jumped into the water and dragged the boat to the sand. The waves, which were much bigger now, helped him, and with three pushes as the waves broke, he managed to ground the boat.

He checked the sea and calculated that the tide would still rise a little higher. He did not want to lose the boat since he would need it to get back, so he pulled with all his might to drag it further up the beach. At that moment he really missed having his favorite bodyguard with him. The giant would have moved the boat with the strength of an ox. Egil had to struggle, pulling hard to achieve what Gerd would have done without breaking into a sweat. But he did it. He did not have much of a body, but he did have a lot of determination, and sometimes the latter made up for the former.

He sat down and watched the sea while he recovered from the effort. The rain was falling on his body. He felt it on his face and it was refreshing. The bodily punishment of the effort made soon went away, which surprised him. He was strong and fit. Then he realized why: he had been training with the Royal Rangers and he was in top physical condition. He got up and fetched the cage with Angus from the boat. The owl was wet and upset.

"I'd better take you further in," he told the bird, to which Angus replied by clicking his beak in protest.

Egil reached some rocks beyond the beach and found a small forest a little further into the island. The landscape was rocky, with some grass-covered clearings and a few groups of trees scattered as far as he could see. He headed to the nearest group of trees and went in among them, seeking shelter from the rain which was falling stronger by the moment. He walked to the thickest part and sat down under a tree with Angus at his side.

"We'll be fine here," he said to the owl, which bobbed its head and hooted.

The storm let down on the island, and Egil decided to wait until it passed before he went exploring the place. He was alert in case he picked up anything strange. The story of the ghost made him uneasy. He did not believe in ghosts, but every legend was based on something real. There was something here, whatever it was, and it made anyone it caught scream. That was not reassuring at all. He had his bow and arrows ready for whatever might happen.

The storm passed, and with it, day went and night began to fall. Egil decided to take a look before the light was completely gone. He came out from the trees carrying Angus with him, who began to liven up as night fell. He was looking everywhere with his big eyes.

"If you see a ghost, let me know," Egil said to Angus, although he did not have much hope that the owl had understood.

They reached a more elevated area where they could see a large part of the island. He was able to glimpse the other two islands in the distance, at sea. The one more to the west and a little north was the Island of Donger, twice the size of the one Egil was on. The one to the south and which was the biggest of the three was the Island of Ronwel. According to Gordon, they were deserted, which Egil could ascertain, since there was no one to be seen. There was nothing to be heard either. Not in the island he was on or in the other two.

Shortly after checking the three islands, night fell. Egil had to focus on the island he was on, since the other two vanished in the night as if the darkness and the sea had swallowed them. He looked up at the sky and could not see the moon or the stars. The clouds covered the sky, thick and threatening with the arrival of new storms.

"We'd better take a quick look around to see what we find. Don't ask me what we're looking for, because the only thing I can say is some trace that will lead us to the Golden Spear of Rogdon."

Angus looked at Egil with his large eyes and blinked hard.

"No, I don't know where it might be either, this golden spear," Egil said to Angus, who clicked his beak cheerfully. Egil knew the reason. "You like the night, me not so much."

Suddenly, Egil saw something in the distance, a white flash moving like a distant wake. He narrowed his eyes and watched it. The strange phenomenon was on the Island of Ronwel, to the south. It appeared to glide over the island and, in so doing, it lit up the terrain as it passed with a ghostly light.

Angus hooted.

"Yeah, I see it."

The ghostly wake was moving all over the island, flying aimlessly, making abrupt turns to change direction and fly over another area. It appeared to be flying over the whole island in an erratic course, without a fixed direction. It started zigzagging from the north to the south of the island.

Egil and Angus watched the anomaly.

"That doesn't look good."

Angus clicked his beak defiantly and showed his claws, banging on his cage.

"You're brave, my little friend, but I don't think it's in our interest to face that thing, whatever it might be. It looks bad. I don't think it's a ghost, but it's some kind of creature or being, that's for sure. That erratic flight isn't so erratic. It seems to be sweeping the whole island searching for something, or perhaps someone. In any case, it had better not find us."

The image was so fascinating that Egil kept looking at how it inspected the whole island, which was pretty sizeable.

Suddenly, the ghostly wake left the island and crossed the sea, arriving at the second island, the one more to the west and a little north: the Island of Donger. It began to sweep the whole surface of the island as it had already done in Ronwel. As it glided over the terrain, Egil was able to see the shapes the wake illuminated. There was not much on the island beyond rocks, some grass, and a few scattered forests. Very similar to the island he was on.

"I'm afraid the ghost is going to come to this island as soon as it finishes checking the other one. It's not going to like finding us here."

Angus clicked his beak again and banged the cage with it, showing off fiercely.

"You have a fighter's spirit, but it's best that we hide. I have a bad feeling about that ghostly wake," he told Angus, as he started looking for somewhere to hide. The thing was that, in the middle of the night, without light because of the clouds that covered the sky, it was not going to be easy to find a hiding place. Besides, this island was small, with little vegetation and not a single mountain.

In any case, they had to find shelter, so that's what they did. After a while of not finding anything, and to make things more complicated, the ghost began crossing over the sea toward the Island of Regunde, where they were.

"It's coming! Time's running out. You'll have to help me, Angus." Egil took the owl out of the cage and, holding him with both hands and looking into his eyes, he said: "Shelter!"

Angus hooted.

"Shelter," Egil repeated and launched Angus into the air. Angus was a Rangers' owl. He had been trained as a messenger and he was capable of doing other things, such as finding shelter for a Ranger. The key word "shelter" should serve to instruct Angus to find a place where Egil might hide.

While Angus searched all over the island, Egil kept his eyes on the wake, which was already reaching the north part of the island, the direction he had come from. Luckily, they were now south. He wondered whether that thing would realize there was a boat on the beach, which would indicate the presence of some person. Perhaps it was not sentient and only hunted what it saw. Not having any information about the ghost made Egil uneasy. You could not make decisions without good information.

The whitish wake began its strange movements with abrupt changes in direction. Egil nocked an arrow, although he was not confident he could wound the creature, since it did not appear to have a body, at least one to stick an arrow in. Instinctively, he began to withdraw, since the ghostly wake was moving toward his position and would soon reach him.

Now that it was closer, he was able to see it better, and he did not like what he saw at all. It really looked like some sort of spirit or ghost. He could glimpse a round shape that might be a head and a wake that must be the body, although it appeared entirely incorporeal and stayed in the air, parallel to the ground, about ten feet high. He watched it make several zigzags, and Egil realized it did not resemble anything human or any monster known to him. It was not reptilian, of this he was sure, which gave him some relief, since whatever that thing was, it had nothing to do with the Drakonians.

Suddenly, Angus appeared behind him and flapped his wings, brushing his head.

"Shelter?" Egil asked him, and Angus replied by flying around his head again. "Okay, I'll follow you."

Angus flew low before Egil, who ran as fast as he could after the owl. He had to go carefully or he would trip in the dark. The land was flat but filled with rocks of different sizes which seemed to have rained from the skies on the flat terrain. It was also slippery from the rain.

The ghostly figure glided behind his back, and Egil wondered whether it had seen him. It did not seem that way. It continued east while Egil ran after Angus to the south of the island. He leapt over several rocks and almost tripped over another, but he managed to recover and continue running. The ghost began to sweep the whole eastern area of the island in a zigzagging motion. It would soon reach the south where Egil was running. Angus was flying in front of him, staying low and flying slowly so Egil could follow him.

Suddenly, Angus rose. Egil reached the spot where Angus had soared and stopped, puzzled. Why had he risen here and vanished into the night? He went to take one more step and the sea breeze slapped his face and pushed him back, spraying him. He recovered and tried to see in the darkness of the night. What he glimpsed left him frozen. He was right on the edge of one of the cliffs of the island, half a step from falling off. Below, the sea was breaking strong against the high walls of stone.

Angus appeared behind him and started flying in small circles before Egil, over the void.

"What are you trying to tell me?" Egil looked over the cliff and saw that there was a huge drop.

Angus circled around in front of him again.

"I'm not going to jump into the void. There are rocks below."

He looked behind him and saw the ghost approaching. He did not have many options. If he did not hide fast, the ghost was going to reach him.

Angus kept marking the spot with his circling flight.

The ghost was inexorably coming closer. Egil saw the whitish wake and the sphere that looked like a head moving toward him with erratic movements.

He had no other choice—it was either jumping or being caught by that spectral being, and then the screams of pain would be his own.

He did not think twice and looked down below. He was about to jump. He moved his right foot toward the void when he saw a ledge a couple of feet away on the face of the cliff. His survival instinct kicked in and his foot returned to its place while his back arched backward as if an invisible force had pulled him back. That was what

Angus was indicating to him, not to jump into the sea.

The specter was even nearer.

He looked again toward the bottom of the cliff with the sea breaking strongly below. He had no other choice but to jump down onto the ledge. He took one last look back toward the ghost, which was already almost upon him. He turned around to jump, facing the cliff wall, but he closed his eyes. He dropped down to the ledge, trying to keep his balance and his descent parallel to the rocky wall. A feeling of falling into the void clenched his throat. He hoped he had calculated the fall well, because otherwise he was going to be killed.

Chapter 12

Nilsa and Camu were waiting for Tor Nassor, the Chief of the Desher Tumaini, the secret people who lived inside the Mountains of Blood. They had arrived a short while before through the Pearl, and they wanted to greet the Chief. A dozen warriors of the tribe who watched the Pearl had welcomed them. The Panthers had not encountered any trouble with them since Camu was a Greater Hor, a God for the desert tribe, and the Panthers had the Chief's permission to use the mountains' Pearl whenever they needed to.

Tor Nassor arrived, leaning on a staff, and came over to them. As was usual for him, he was not wearing a scarf on his head. Nilsa noticed his long, curly white hair, his brown skin weathered by the desert sun, and his wrinkle-covered face. No doubt he looked every one of his seventy years, and his eyes, like all the Desher Tumaini's, were a puzzling ruby red. In the middle of his forehead was a hand-drawn white circle, just like the first time they had seen him, and Nilsa wondered whether it might be a reference to the White Pearl.

"Welcome, Hor, welcome, Nilsa," he greeted them courteously with a big smile.

"Thank you so much for welcoming us," said Nilsa.

"It could be no other way. We must not offend a God and a friend of the tribe who have helped us so much in the past."

"It wasn't that much," Nilsa waved it aside, remembering the adventure they had experienced there, especially the giant worm that had almost swallowed Viggo.

Chief good person. Much nice, Camu messaged to Nilsa, who smiled.

"To what do I owe the honor of this visit? Last time Lasgol needed to use the Pearl to return to Norghana."

"In this case, it's the opposite. We've used the Pearl to shorten our journey because I have to go to the city of Albahrwalm in the southeast, by the sea."

"That surprises me. It's a city way out to the southeast of the deserts, far to the south. You'll have to cross the river Esher, then head to the Oasis of Wahazarqa, avoid the Live Dunes, skirt the Black Mountains of Aljibalalsaw, avoid the holy city of Almadinat and if everything goes well, then you'll reach the city of Albahrwalm. It's a long, dangerous journey through the southeastern desert, and you'll be dealing with extreme heat."

Nilsa took out the map Egil had given her and made sure she had everything the Chief had mentioned well marked on it. She was able to identify all the places, which eased her mind. The journey was going to be long and tough, she had already known that. She thought she had not been very lucky, since of all the missions handed to the Panthers, this one seemed the most complicated in her opinion. Crossing deserts was always insufferable, no matter how you looked at it, and the places the Chief had mentioned each seemed to have their own dangers. On the other hand, she was not going to be less daring than Lasgol, who had just traveled through half of Tremia, including the deserts. If it was her lot to walk through dunes, endure scorching heat and thirst, and go through a thousand dangers to obtain the golden weapon, she would do it. She was as brave and daring as any of the Panthers, and she was going to prove it.

"That's right, I have to get there. I have an important mission to carry out."

"May I ask what your mission is? Perhaps my people will be able to help you."

"Oh, thank you very much, Tor Nassor. Any help is welcome. I have to find 'Antior's Beam.' It's a javelin that can pierce through any armor, including dragon scales, those of a Lesser Hor. One direct throw of the javelin at the heart of the Lesser Hor would kill it."

Tor Nassor remained thoughtful.

"Our culture speaks of those who fought against the Hor, but I'm afraid they perished. No weapon is mentioned that could affect them."

Drakonians tough skin, Camu messaged to Nilsa.

"What they say is true, that no human weapon can pierce the scales of the Hor, but I'm looking for one that can."

"The Greater Hor agrees?" Tor Nassor asked.

Camu nodded several times, moving his head up and down.

"Camu agrees. The weapon isn't to hurt him but other Lesser Hor that pose great danger."

"I understand. If you have the approval of the Greater Hor, I will not only not stop you, but help you."

"I'll welcome any help you can offer with open arms," Nilsa

relied, smiling.

"Let's see. For this long journey you will need adequate clothing, camels, water, compounds for sickness, and, most of all, a traveling companion."

Nilsa threw her head back in surprise.

"A traveling companion?"

"Yes, a desert dweller, someone to help you survive the journey, because it is a long and difficult one."

"I have no doubt it'll be complicated," Nilsa was biting her nails unconsciously, thinking of all the difficulties she would have to overcome.

The leader of the Desher Tumaini turned to speak to one of his warriors, and a moment later the warrior left.

"May we offer you something to eat and drink?"

I want Eshe Baset.

"I'm fine but the Hor would like to try Eshe Baset, the incredible plant that grows inside the mountain."

"Absolutely, we'll bring it right away. It's an honor to have a God visiting us who wants to enjoy our Eshe Baset."

I much loved here. I be God.

Nilsa turned to whisper to Camu, "As Lasgol would tell you, don't let it get to your head."

No get head, but I be God here.

The warrior who had left came back with another young man. He must have been Nilsa's same age, maybe a year older. She found him very handsome, with that desert air and those incredible ruby eyes that shone when the sun touched them. His skin was tanned by the sun, but the tone was not very dark. Light-brown, curly hair bleached by the sun contrasted with his ruby eyes and skin and gave him a most shocking look. Nilsa forgot to breathe while she looked at him. She had never seen such an exotic and handsome youth before. He was slightly taller than her and wiry. In the desert no one was muscular or strong, but thin and tough.

"This is my son, Aibin Alfajir," Tor Nassor introduced him.

"Pleased to meet you," Nilsa said and bowed her head lightly as she blushed and tried to hide it.

"The pleasure is all mine," the young man replied in Norghanian, which left Nilsa with her mouth open.

"You speak... my language...?"

"I do. My father has been teaching me the languages he knows. Preparing me for the day when I might have to lead the tribe."

"Aibin Alfajir is my youngest son. His older brother, Abon Aleasor, has already left on his training journey. I believe I told you about this custom of our people."

"Yes, you did. The future chiefs travel abroad in order to become good leaders, versed in the ways of the outer world, not only these mountains and deserts."

"That's right," Tor Nassor nodded. "All the leaders of my people have been doing this for a long time. It's dangerous, as you can imagine. Not all those chosen to go return. Many die. In my case, I managed to come back, and I hope my sons will also make it. The world outside of these mountains is ruthless and cruel. I hope my older son comes back alive. I think this opportunity might very well be the beginning of my younger son's journey."

"Oh…" Nilsa was left not knowing what to say.

Tor Nassor explained in his language what Nilsa's mission entailed and the path to follow.

"It will be an honor and a pleasure to begin my journey of learning," Aibin Alfajir said, bowing respectfully before his father.

"I believe you are ready to fly away, young eagle. Don't let the desert burn you or humans hunt you. Fly free, travel throughout Tremia, and learn as much as you can. Go as far as the snow-covered mountains of Norghana, and when you get there offer my respects to the Snow Panthers."

"I will do that, Father," the young man said, bowing respectfully.

"He's coming with me then?" Nilsa said to Tor Nassor.

"My son will accompany you and so begin his journey of learning so that one day he may be a great leader for his people."

"It will be an honor," the young man said.

Nilsa had not been expecting this, but she was sure it was good news.

You not alone, you help, good, Camu messaged to her, seeming to read her thoughts.

"I'm going to leave this owl here," Nilsa said, showing Damien, a pretty, fearsome male owl, to Tor Nassor.

"We will look after it."

"Thanks. I'll use him to call Camu so he comes to pick me up once I've completed my mission."

"We wish you the best luck of the desert," Tor Nassor said.

"I didn't know the desert was lucky. I actually thought it was the opposite, that it was very unlucky."

"Not for those who survive it," Tor Nassor winked at her.

At nightfall, Nilsa was ready to begin her mission.

"Tell them everything's going well. I'll come back with Antior's Beam. That javelin will be mine, even if I have to travel the whole desert to find it," she told Camu.

I tell. I sure you get.

"Thank you, Camu, I appreciate the support."

I sure, sure, you come out with victory.

"You're a sweetheart, thank you very much." Nilsa hugged Camu's neck affectionately.

They said goodbye to everyone and set out. Traveling by night in the desert was a blessing compared to doing it by day. The temperature was pleasant and the moon shone bright in the sky, so they were able to see where they were going. The dunes could be dangerous if one did not tackle them correctly, something Nilsa quickly learned.

In the midst of the deserts and at night, Nilsa found herself missing her comrades, but she knew that this mission was hers to accomplish alone, that all the Panthers' missions at this moment were individual and they all had to complete them on their own. She knew her friends would complete their tasks, so she could do nothing less.

Nilsa was nervous about the giant worm, especially traveling at night. She had the feeling it was going to appear under her feet at any moment and swallow her.

"I notice that you seem very tense," said Aibin Alfajir.

"It's because of the giant sand worm."

"Don't worry, lately it's been a lot less active."

"That doesn't make me feel any better."

The young man smiled, and Nilsa saw his ivory teeth in the middle of the night shining in the moonlight, which made him even more dashing.

"We must do something about your name," Nilsa told him.

"Do something? What? Why?"

"Because it's too long and difficult to pronounce."

"Huh, I'd never thought of that. It might be for a foreigner."

"I'm telling you it is. 'Aibin Alfajir' is a tongue twister for me."

Her companion started to laugh and the camel started. He had to sooth it.

"Okay, how about shortening it to just Aibin?" he suggested.

"I like Aibin. perfect," Nilsa agreed.

"Aibin it is then."

"It suits you," she smiled.

"Because it's my name," he replied, laughing.

"Of course!" Nilsa said, joining in the laughter.

The first obstacle they encountered was crossing the great river Eshe. They arrived in the middle of the night and stopped to rest. It was a wide river, especially for one in the desert. Nilsa was surprised to find vegetation at the river bank. It cheered her soul to see some green in this world of sand. She slid off her camel, which refused to kneel so she could do so more comfortably.

"You're a very rude camel," she scolded. The camel completely ignored her.

"They have quite the personality," Aibin said, getting off after making his own camel kneel.

"I can see that. Yours obeys you though."

"You have to know how to command them," he said, smiling.

"Yeah…" Nilsa went to the river bank and put her hands in the water, splashing her face and neck.

"Beware of the crocodiles," Aibin warned her.

"You're kidding, right?"

"Absolutely not. There are crocodiles in this river, and they like to catch unaware humans who drink the water."

Nilsa jumped back.

"I just love this desert of yours…"

"You'll get used to it. Put the scarf on your head and cover your skin. The sun is beginning to burn you, and your skin is too delicate for this place."

"Are you saying that because of my freckles?"

"I say it because you're whiter than milk, and you'll roast here."

"I have a protective balm."

"Even so, I recommend covering yourself completely."

"Am I so ugly?" Nilsa asked with a coquettish smile.

Aibin was surprised by the question. His look changed to a more serious one.

"I didn't intend for you to think that. Of course, you're not ugly. On the contrary, you're beautiful."

"I am?" Nilsa was surprised by his answer.

"My eyes have never seen anyone with a beauty as radiant as yours."

"That's not that difficult, living in the desert inside the Mountains of Blood."

"I haven't seen much of the world, that's true, but I can still appreciate beauty," he said, slightly hurt.

"Aibin."

"Yes?"

"I'm just kidding, don't take everything so seriously."

"Oh, I didn't know you were joking."

"I think you and I are going to have to learn about each other in order to avoid misunderstandings."

"I think that's a good idea."

"So do I," Nilsa said, smiling. "Look, I see people upriver. Are they part of your tribe?"

Aibin shaded his eyes with his hand and looked.

"Yes, they're our people. They're fishing and gathering water plants that grow on the river banks. Remember, it was there where the Jafari Kaphiri patrols captured my people. Fish is a delicacy we don't have in the mountains, and we come down to the river to catch it."

"That's right, I remember. Should we keep going, or do we stop to say hello?"

"No, let's keep going. Everyone is busy with their tasks. We'll go a little farther south, then we can rest."

"Lead the way."

"They set off. Nilsa found it difficult to make her camel, which she had named 'Pighead' obey her, and it made her feel clumsy beside Aibin, who mounted and dismounted at will. Not to mention that he barely swayed with the camel's ambling, whereas she ended up with a sore bottom and half dizzy from so much rocking.

They followed a southern course, and Nilsa began to feel the weight of the desert sun. The heat was suffocating, and since she was wearing her Ranger's scarf up to her nose under her headscarf, she had trouble breathing. But it was either that or burn alive, and the latter was even more painful and difficult to deal with.

"Are you doing okay?" Aibin asked her.

Nilsa snorted.

"As well as a Norghanian with skin like snow can do while crossing a desert as large as this one. There's nothing but dunes and sand everywhere."

"That's the thing with deserts," Aibin said, chuckling.

"It's not my first time in a desert, and it's most likely not my last time in one either, considering our life as Rangers… but I'd like to get used to it."

"That takes time. Imagine if you took me to the frozen mountains of your homeland. I'd probably freeze alive on the third day of traveling."

"Or you'd slip and fall off a cliff."

"Yes, that too," he nodded, laughing.

They continued traveling, skirting several dunes which the camels had trouble going up. At midafternoon, seeing that Nilsa was having a hard time, Aibin stopped and prepared camp. In the blink of an eye, he put up a tent in the desert style so Nilsa would be protected from the scorching sun. It was also comfortable inside, which Nilsa was very grateful for. They sat facing each other with their legs crossed, and Nilsa was able to take off both her head scarf and Ranger scarf. She felt infinitely better. They ate and drank from their supplies to re-hydrate and for their bodies to recover their energy. Aibin did not really need it, but Nilsa did.

"We'd better rest," Aibin suggested. "At night, we'll resume the path."

"Path? We're crossing a sea of sand, there's no path!"

"You don't see it, but there is a path, I swear. It's here," Aibin said, pointing his finger to his own temple.

"Ah, well, if that's the case, maybe you'll teach me to see it too."

"It seems to me like you want to learn a lot in a very short time," he said, smiling.

"That's the way I am, impatient and nervous."

"Those aren't good qualities in the desert."

"They might not be, but they add to my charm," she replied, smiling from ear to ear.

"Undoubtedly," Aibin returned her smile.

"What's the next stage of the journey like?"

Aibin made a gesture with his hand that meant 'not that good'.

"First, we have to reach the oasis of Wahazarqa."

"That doesn't sound too bad," Nilsa said cheerfully.

"Yes, but then we'll have to cross a harsh area of the desert, with quicksand."

"Quicksand in the desert? Is that a thing?"

"I'm afraid so."

"Well, that's neat."

"Go ahead and rest, everything will be all right."

Nilsa lay down and tried to sleep. Having Aibin sitting beside her made her feel calm, but having to cross a desert with quicksand gave her terrible nightmares.

Chapter 13

Nilsa had the time of her life when they reached the oasis of Wahazarqa. The journey there by camel had been a small torture, although Aibin's company made everything better, even the scorching ride and the desert's sea of sand. The oasis looked like a true gift to Nilsa. It featured a large area of vegetation and a big pond of blue water.

"We'll rest here for a while," Aibin said.

"Wonderful!" Nilsa replied. She slid off Pighead and ran to dive, head first, into the pond.

Aibin watched her without getting off his camel. He was shaking his head.

"You shouldn't jump headlong into situations. It's dangerous," he warned her kindly.

"Stop lecturing me and get in the water. It's gorgeous!"

"Us, desert dwellers don't just dive like that into water."

"Well, you don't know what you're missing then!" Nilsa shouted, swimming on her back and enjoying every stroke.

Aibin dismounted and calmly walked over to the water. He bent over and used both hands to drink slowly. Then he went back to the camels and led them to drink. While Nilsa was swimming and laughing happily, enjoying her swim and the starry night above their heads, Aibin refilled the water-skins. Every now and then he glanced at Nilsa to see what she was doing and make sure she was all right.

Nilsa enjoyed the oasis as if it was the last thing in life she would ever enjoy. She was well aware that endless days filled with suffering in the desert awaited her, and she was not going to waste this wonder. Not only was her swim amazing, but the whole landscape was idyllic. The palm trees, the vegetation, the lake and dunes around it which were lit up by the perfectly clear, star-filled sky: they were all breathtaking.

"Come on, join me, the water is delightful!"

"Someone has to keep watch. The fact that it's night in the desert doesn't mean we are alone. Some other dweller might appear, or even bandits."

Nilsa stopped swimming.

"Bandits? Here?"

"There are, yes. They assault the caravans that come to the oasis for water and refreshment."

"Caravans pass through here?"

"Yes, they travel to the great walled city of Madinatalmusa. It's a little further east."

"Are we going to that city?"

Aibin shook his head. "We'll continue south."

"Oh, okay."

Nilsa could not resist doing a few more strokes and even swimming under the water. She could not see anything since it was night, but the feeling was so refreshing that she could not resist. Once she came out of the water, she lay down on the sand beside Aibin, who was sitting, sharpening a long, curved sword.

"What's the story behind the sword? I didn't know your people used swords."

"They don't. Only chiefs and their descendants learn to use these weapons. It's an ancient tradition."

"Why do they learn to use a sword?"

"This is a scimitar, and we learn to use it because it's the weapon used in duels between chiefs and nobles of the desert peoples."

"Oh... and are you good with it?"

The young man with ruby eyes smiled.

"Are you always so spontaneous? You ask the first thing that comes to your mind without stopping to think it might be offensive."

"Have I offended you? If I have, I'm very sorry, it wasn't my intention at all. It's just that my curiosity gets the better of me, you know… I have trouble controlling myself."

"Yes, I'm beginning to realize that, and no, you didn't offend me because I know your heart doesn't harbor bad intentions. But I have to warn you that you can't be that direct and intrusive in the desert. Privacy is highly valued among the Nocean peoples, and anyone asking questions about the personal life of others is frowned upon. Especially about the nobles or tribe chiefs."

Nilsa nodded, wrinkling her nose.

"Thank you for the warning. I'll keep that in mind. I know I'm a busybody and too curious for my own good, I won't lie to you, but I'll try to control myself. I don't want to get into trouble."

"I'll teach you the ways of the desert and the manner in which you should deal with people to avoid any problems."

"Good, a little diplomacy and good manners in the desert will be good for me, especially when we have to interact with others in order to find out where they're keeping Antior's Beam."

"That's what I think too," he nodded.

"Could you tell me—if you don't mind, of course—if you fight with sword and shield? Or only sword?"

"I don't mind your question. I fight with the scimitar and curved knife," he replied and reached back for a long knife similar to what Rangers used, only curved.

"Why are your weapons curved? I find it… strange…"

Aibin's eyes opened wide, and they flashed a bright ruby red.

"That's an odd question, although since you come from distant lands, I understand that our weapons and the way we use them might surprise you. The swords and knives are curved because of the way we fight. We value the cut, not the stroke. These weapons," he said, showing them to her," have an advantage when it comes to cutting in a slanted thrust," he accompanied his explanation with a demonstration in the air.

"I see…"

"Your straight swords and knives are better used for stabs and strokes."

"Aren't you at a disadvantage then?"

"Not if the cut is accurate," Aibin said with a wink.

Nilsa laughed.

"It'd better be!"

"It will be, don't worry."

Nilsa watched him. Seeing him in the light of the stars and moon, holding his scimitar and curved knife with those irresistible ruby eyes made something stir in her stomach. She blushed and had to look away so he would not notice.

"We should keep going, take advantage of the night," Aibin said.

"Fine. Just give me a moment to enjoy this dreamlike place, then you can take me to your nightmare of a desert."

Aibin laughed.

"Very well, enjoy the moment."

Nilsa had not been mistaken in thinking that the following day would be torture. Even protected from the terrible, merciless sun inside the tent, it was pure misery. It was almost impossible to breathe it was so hot. She had also found some burn blisters on areas of her body that had not been properly covered by her clothes.

She was holding up as best she could, but the extreme temperatures did not let her sleep. So later at night, when they had to move on through the desert, she fell asleep on Pighead and had been on the point of falling off on several occasions. The last time Aibin had grabbed her when she was already on her way down. One thing was clear to her—she was not made for the desert.

They were going south when Pighead decided to head west.

"Don't go near those dunes on our right," Aibin warned her in an urgent tone. He did not shout, but his voice sounded as if there was some danger.

Nilsa studied them, but to her they were only dunes. Then, suddenly, something happened that left her stunned.

"The dunes are running!"

"They aren't running. It might look that way, but they aren't."

"What do you mean they're not running? I'm looking at them moving like the waves of the sea! Am I losing my mind from the heat? Am I seeing hallucinations from the effect of the sun beating down on my head?"

"Take it easy, you're not going crazy, I promise. And it isn't a sea we're looking at, although some tribes do call it that. The Sea of Sand."

"Then what is it? Those dunes *are* moving from one side to another."

"And we have to avoid them, or they'll kill us. That's what some peoples of the desert call quicksand. It's a singular phenomenon that occurs in some desert areas."

"What do you mean by quicksand?" Nilsa was watching the sand dunes move like waves in a single direction. Then they changed and went in another.

"The wind from the sea pushes them. And these dunes aren't your typical ones, they have a different consistency which makes them move all at once, the dune is a small mountain of sand. The thing is, when the dune encounters an obstacle, it breaks and covers it. Dunes have killed many careless travelers who have ventured near them. The dunes move and cover everything in its path with the sand they displace."

"I can see that if you get in their way, they'll cover you completely."

"Yes, the sands move and cover you. They swallow you, so to speak. It's very dangerous."

"Tremia is filled with dangers we aren't even aware of." Nilsa had never seen anything like this before, and she was shocked. She would have walked into them without realizing it and never returned to tell the story.

"And isn't there any sign to indicate the danger they pose?"

Aibin smiled.

"Most desert dwellers know this area and avoid it. We're moving parallel to it."

"Well, I think there should be signs with skulls painted on them."

"An interesting idea," Aibin nodded. Nilsa's comments seemed to amuse him.

They continued making their way south, and Nilsa could not stop looking back to see the dunes moving like waves. It was extraordinary. Pighead, realizing she was looking back, seized the chance to veer, and Aibin had to come over quickly and grab the reins so the camel would stay on course.

"You have to go south, not west. You really are a stubborn camel," Nilsa said to it, and Pighead replied with a noise between a neigh and a grunt, which puzzled her.

A few days later, they reached a mountain range. The mountains were black. They looked as if they had been burnt by the sun to that shade.

"These are the Aljibalalsaw, also known as the Black Mountains."

"Scorched, rather."

"Yes, both. We must be wary as we pass through the mountains."

"Danger?"

"Yes, there's a tribe that lives in these mountains, the Aljisaw, and they're not friendly at all."

"Then we'd better take a detour to the west and then keep going south."

"Yes, but in that direction is the holy city of the Almadas."

"Let me guess. We shouldn't go near that city either."

Aibin nodded.

"That city is called Almadinat and is considered holy by the area's locals. We can't go near it. They kill any foreigner they find in the city or wandering near it. It is ruled by religious fanatics. Only those who belong to the Almadas religion can enter it."

"Not even you?"

"I'm not of their religion. They consider me a foreigner, a non-believer, and they'd kill me if they found me in the vicinity."

"Wow, they sound so friendly. Your father didn't inform us of this little problem. I guess he wanted us to find out for ourselves."

"That's right. I need to learn how to solve my own problems."

"A little help is usually a good thing."

"That's not how my people see things. I must travel this path alone."

"Not completely. You have me."

"That's true, and I am grateful to my father for letting me come with you in this, the beginning of my learning journey."

"Tell me, why is there a problem with this city?"

"Well, most of the large cities of the Nocean Empire aren't ruled by any religion, but there are a couple that are, and they're extremely fanatic. This is one of them and is considered very dangerous, even for other Noceans of the area. Emperor Malotas has had to send his armies more than once to pacify this area."

"Because of this city?"

"Yes, it doesn't get along well with the city of Madinatalmusa to the north, or with the city of Albahrwalm to the southeast, where we're going. Conflicts are constant. The city of Kabiramadina, which is the last great city in the south, is the only one with half its subjects belonging to the Almadas religion and supporting the holy city, although not openly so as not to infuriate the Emperor."

"All the desert cities are under the rule of the Nocean Emperor, aren't they?"

"That's right, but there are many cities and the territory is immense. The Nocean Empire is made up of numerous ethnicities and religions, and their interests don't always agree with those of the Emperor. There are often uprisings and revolts. The Emperor doesn't tolerate even the smallest sign of rebellion, and he crushes them with an iron fist."

"Does that happen often?"

"Yes, very. That's why it's common to see the emperor's army marching toward some city. Most of the times it's to quell the fire of some insurrection or revolt. Other times it's to show off Malotas' power so that no one will dare defy him."

"Interesting. And here I thought Norghana was busy."

"The desert never rests. That's a true saying we all know."

"Yeah, I'm beginning to realize that."

"Let's keep moving. We have to go between the Black Mountains and the holy city without the inhabitants of either seeing us."

"I love it when the plans are so simple," Nilsa joked.

Aibin glanced at her blankly and she realized he had not understood the joke. She waved him on.

Dawn arrived, and they had to stop to rest. Now the sun was an even greater enemy, since it burned them and made them visible from a distance. Neither of these things was good for them. The waiting in the tent was long and hot. Nilsa was sweating like she never had. The farther south they went, the hotter it became, and it was unbearable for her. Not only was it a nuisance, but it was also dangerous. No matter how hydrated she tried to be, the suffocation was such that she could not breathe. On a couple of occasions, she had to leave the tent, seeking air. The sun's rays attacked her as if a Fire Mage were throwing a flaming ball straight at her face and body.

With the arrival of nightfall, they continued on their way. Nilsa was feeling more and more tired from how little she was resting, and her head felt full of cotton. Pighead kept doing what he wanted, which did not help her feel any better. Luckily, Aibin was always alert to her needs. He was a gentleman in the desert, and his company and help were fantastic. If she had had to make the journey all alone, she would have been in big trouble.

They crested a tall dune with the Black Mountains on their right which seemed to stand as sentinels, ever watchful. They were so dark that at night they looked like a funereal, enchanted place. Nilsa did not even want to look at them, because they gave her the willies.

All of a sudden, they heard a light whistle.

Nilsa's head felt so heavy she did not even realize what it was until the arrow brushed her head.

"We're under attack!" Aibin warned her as he reached for his scimitar and curved knife.

With the shock, Nilsa's senses became alert at once. She bent over Pighead's neck as a second arrow brushed her back.

"They're shooting from the mountains!"

"Let's get away!" Aibin cried.

At that moment, Pighead decided to kneel down.

"Not now! Keep going! Run!" Nilsa cried, kicking him so he would move. The stubborn camel had decided Nilsa had to dismount and did not budge.

"They're coming to attack us, I see six Aljisaw!"

Nilsa reacted, leapt off her camel, and snaked up the dune to the top. She could not see the attackers, but she took out her bow and nocked an arrow.

Seeing Nilsa, Aibin jumped off his camel and crouched beside her.

"I don't see them."

"They're wearing all black. As soon as they come out of the shadow of the dune, you'll be able to see them."

Nilsa nodded and waited with her bow ready.

Another arrow headed to Aibin's torso, and he threw himself to the side in time.

All of a sudden, Nilsa saw two figures running, dressed entirely in black with short bows in their hands. She did not think twice. She released at the first one as he was nocking an arrow in his own bow. She caught him in the chest and he fell to one side. She nocked another arrow, and in a fluid movement she aimed and released almost at the same time. The arrow hit the attacker also in the middle of his torso when he was aiming at Nilsa. He could not release. They were not wearing armor, only tunics, black baggy pants, and a black scarf covering their head and face.

While she was nocking another arrow, she heard the sound of metal against metal to her left. She turned, aiming, and saw Aibin fighting two opponents. He cut one in the neck and the other one in the chest. Nilsa was about to release, but there was no need. Aibin had them taken care of, so she aimed at the mountains. Right then another attacker appeared at a run, a large scimitar raised with both hands above his head. He was shouting at the top of his voice. With almost no time to react, Nilsa released and the arrow hit the attacker in the mouth.

Nilsa threw herself to one side and the attacker stumbled past her from his own impulse and fell dead behind her. She jumped to her feet and drew her knife and axe to face the last attacker. There was no need. Aibin had already intercepted him, and after taking away his bow, he cut the attacker's throat with his curved knife in one clean slash.

The two looked to see whether there were any more attackers. They did not spot more danger.

"We have to get out of here, and fast. More will come," Aibin told her.

"This stubborn camel doesn't want…" she started to say when she saw that Pighead had gotten up and was standing beside the other camel. "I swear this camel is going to pay."

Aibin waved her along urgently, and they both grabbed their camels' reins. Without mounting, they headed southeast.

They mounted when they were already some distance away from their possible pursuers and then fled as fast as the camels and the desert night allowed them.

"I see you fight better than you let on," Nilsa told Aibin.

"My tribe's warriors prepare for these type of situations. I, as the Chief's son, must be even better than the others. It's my duty and obligation, since the future leader of the tribe must not only be wise and experienced, but also a better warrior in order to defend the tribe."

"Putting it like that, it makes total sense. Although, what a responsibility…"

"The same burden every leader must bear on his or her shoulders."

"If you knew the leaders we have in Norghana…"

"Aren't they honorable and wise?"

Nilsa burst out laughing.

"I'll tell you on the way. You're going to love our leaders."

Chapter 14

After camping as far as they could from the Black Mountains and the holy city, Nilsa and Aibin were preparing to begin another night's journey. Nilsa had lost count of the days they had been traveling, but for her body and spirit it was as if they had been traveling for a whole season without a day's rest.

"Not much longer now, cheer up," Aibin tried to lift her spirits as he smiled gently.

"You've been telling me that ever since we left your mountains."

"Because it's true," he replied with a laugh, and his laughter cheered Nilsa.

They packed up the tent, drank water, and went on. The city of Albahrwalm was very close now. Aibin showed it to her on the map, as well as where they currently were, and this made Nilsa feel better since she realized it was not that far. Then she remembered that distances on a map were deceiving and discouragement settled in once again.

As they were skirting some tall dunes they did not want to climb, they encountered an unpleasant surprise. In the middle of what looked like the beginning of a stone path, half covered by desert sand, a group of figures clad in white were waiting. They were standing in the middle of the path, armed with scimitars and short bows in the desert style. They had seen Nilsa and Aibin, so if they fled the figures would chase after them.

"Beware, they're fanatics of the Almadas religion."

"Okay, understood," said Nilsa, and at once she had her bow in one hand and an arrow in the other.

They went on, ignoring the group of eight warriors dressed in white from head to toe. Nilsa thought it strange they were wearing white baggy pants, tunics, and scarves in the desert when white attracted sunlight. Then she remembered what Aibin had told her about their belief that they were holy and proper and therefore had to wear white. As soon as they were closer, Nilsa could see that they each also had a white triangle in the center of their forehead.

Nilsa saw several white tents on one side of the path and camels tethered to a pole. This was a border post, which meant they were not going to be allowed to pass freely. She was not mistaken; they were stopped and ordered with signs and shouts to come closer. There were three of them armed with bows so Nilsa and Aibin could not run off. Besides, they had to consider that Pighead would do whatever he wanted with no regard for their safety.

Aibin motioned her to comply.

They reached the border post. The Almadas began to launch questions at them, waving their hands. Nilsa did not understand a word. Luckily, Aibin did, and he was answering calmly, in a demure tone, as was usual for him. Unfortunately, the men in white seemed agitated for whatever reason. Nilsa had the impression that the conversation was not going to end well, even if they had not done anything wrong. Unobtrusively, she nocked an arrow.

The man leading the group began to bark orders at Aibin, who raised his hands serenely in a peaceful gesture. Unfortunately, the group seemed to be looking for trouble. The leader walked up to Aibin and in one abrupt movement brandished his scimitar. Aibin did not flinch and with total ease delivered a kick to the man's face, which knocked him senseless. Next, Aibin drew his own scimitar and charged against the group on his camel.

Nilsa was astonished. She had never seen anything like that. The camel charged like a Rogdonian battle horse. Three of the fanatics were thrown backward from the impact, and Aibin killed two others with accurate scimitar slashes. One of the archers aimed at Aibin and was about to release when Nilsa shot him dead in the forehead, right where the triangle was drawn.

Aibin jumped off his camel and lunged at the second archer, knocking him down. They wrestled on the ground. Nilsa aimed at the other archer who was aiming at her and released an instant before he did. Nilsa's arrow hit his heart, and the impact pushed the archer's bow up, causing his arrow to fly over Nilsa's head.

Aibin stood up after finishing off the archer on the ground and turned to face two more of the white-clad fanatics, who came at him with their scimitars.

Nilsa did not dismount since they were all busy with Aibin, who was in the middle of the group, delivering slashes and blocking attacks with his knife and scimitar. This put her in an advantageous position, and she released against the fanatics as they tried to attack

Aibin. They took one step toward him and Nilsa knocked them down with an arrow to the heart or forehead. For some odd reason, Pighead decided not to move an inch in the midst of all the screaming and noise from the fighting.

A moment later, the eight figures in white lay dead on the ground, either with an arrow in their body or an accurate slash from the sword or knife. A grim silence took over the scene. They had died without any need, simply for their fanaticism.

"You couldn't persuade them we didn't want any trouble?"

"Unfortunately, they could not have cared less. They wanted to kill us for treading on their holy land."

"Holy land? Isn't their holy city further north?"

"They seem to be expanding their domains. Now it stretches out to here, or so they told me."

"It's awful that their fanaticism leads them to throw away their lives like that."

"That's not the awful thing, what's terrible is what they do to those who aren't as skilled as we are with weapons."

Nilsa nodded.

"You're right, they got what they deserved."

"The deserts are dangerous. We have to tread carefully."

"Yeah, I can see that."

"Luckily, everything turned out well. You're not hurt, are you?"

"No, you?"

"A superficial cut on my arm and another in the thigh, nothing serious."

"Let me see," she said, concerned. "An infection might be a lot more deadly than a slash."

"We should get away first. More might come."

"All right."

They rode away as fast as they could.

"By the way, you have to teach me how to charge with a camel like that. It was awesome!"

"I will, although I'm not sure whether your camel will obey you."

"Even so, teach me. It looked like a most effective tactic."

Nilsa tended Aibin's wounds with her Ranger's healing

knowledge. She was carrying everything she needed to heal: suture needle, thread, ointment against infections, and revitalizing tonic. Although in Aibin's case it was not necessary, because he was a son of the desert and his toughness and endurance were remarkable. Aibin also had some medicinal plants, which he chewed and then applied on his wound. From what he said, they worked against infections and also strengthened him. Something like what she had given him but a special desert remedy.

They were soon on their way. After such unpleasant encounters, Nilsa kept her eyes wide open and an arrow nocked in her bow. She had the impression that after skirting the next dune they were going to be attacked again by caravan robbers, or something similar. Aibin had explained that the fanatics frequented the stone paths they were following, which linked two large cities.

Luckily there were no more incidents, and they finally arrived at the city of Albahrwalm. Nilsa could not believe it—she was looking at the city by the sea from afar and snorting.

"Beautiful, isn't it?" she heard Aibin say.

"I don't know about the city, but the blue sea certainly is."

Aibin smiled. "You'll like the city. It's not very big, and its people are devoted to fishing and trade. They're friendly."

"Like the white-clad fanatics or the ones dressed in black from the Black Mountains?"

"No, order reigns in Albahrwalm, and there are no fanatics or ill-intentioned tribes."

"I'll believe it when I see it," Nilsa joked, although not entirely.

They arrived at the city gates, and Nilsa saw it was surrounded by a small, simple wall which was mostly unguarded. It did not look like the inhabitants suffered many attacks, which eased her fears a little. The city itself was a typical desert town, with small adobe and desert stone houses. There were a great number of houses, as well as many trading stalls and shops everywhere.

They left their camels in some kind of stables at the entrance of the city. It seemed strange to Nilsa that there were more camels and dromedaries than horses. Although the few horses she saw were beautiful specimens, with long, bright, black coats. They all looked purebred. She felt envious for not being able to ride one of them and instead having to deal with one stubborn camel.

"Well, Pighead. We're leaving you here for now, be a good boy," Nilsa said as the animal tossed its head up and down and grunted in the weird manner of camels.

"I believe he's saying 'no way,'" Aibin interpreted.

"That's what I was thinking. But, although the feeling isn't mutual, I do love you," said Nilsa.

Pighead snorted.

They headed to the first houses inside the city and noticed that everyone was staring at them in surprise.

"The first thing we should do is get more adequate clothes for the city, that way we'll draw less attention," Aibin said.

"I will, but you?"

"Me too. Remember that my race never leaves the mountains. We're a secret people. Better that they don't see me with these clothes and appearance."

"With your ruby eyes and my white freckled skin, I doubt we'll be able to avoid attention."

"We can try," he smiled. "Besides, we're dressed like desert dwellers from the north, and here in the south they dress differently. We'd better dress like them."

"Fine. Then let's go and buy some clothes," she smiled eagerly.

"They don't need to be expensive..." Aibin replied, accurately interpreting Nilsa's joy.

"I don't need anything expensive, just flattering," she laughed.

"Whatever plain clothes that cover our features and belong here will do."

"It doesn't make sense to buy clothes if they're plain and tasteless. If we're going to buy clothes, let's buy something nice."

"Really, with some scarves and plain tunics..."

But Nilsa would not hear anything else on the matter.

They went to a stall with clothes outside a market. It was modest in regards to its contents and pricing. Aibin chose the most adequate clothing. The people of this city wore lots of blue, so that was what he chose, darker for him and lighter for Nilsa.

"I like that you choose and buy clothes for me," she giggled. "Although they're not as pretty and luxurious as I'd like."

"I know they're not too elegant or expensive, but they'll do."

"I see, and I know we don't need them to be."

Aibin looked at her, puzzled.

"Weren't you saying…"

"You were right, but I didn't want to tell you," she made a face.

"Well, thank you for agreeing with me."

"Don't get used to it," she smiled.

"Do you find these clothes adequate?"

"Yes, I can tell you have good taste," she said, eyeing the tunic and scarf he had chosen for her.

In order to change behind the stall, which was in the middle of a square, the trader offered them the privacy of a big sheet. Nilsa blushed when Aibin held the sheet so close to her, but he behaved like a gentleman and did not look once. They changed fast and people suddenly seemed to stare at them less now that they wore shades of blue like everyone else. Nilsa covered her hair and face with a scarf so her features were hidden. Aibin also wore a scarf on his head and walked looking down so his eyes could not be seen.

They went through the entire market area without stopping to look at the sheer amount of clothes, jewels, and other merchandise exhibited for the customers. There were many stalls in the street, whereas there were fewer shops. Nilsa saw that all the trade was done at the foot of the stalls. There was quite a bustle, since the vendors called out their prices and the qualities of their goods at the top of their voices. Nilsa found the atmosphere of large numbers of people surrounding the stalls very lively, especially after spending so much time in the silence and solitude of the great desert. They went along several streets until they arrived at the door of an ancient building.

"I think this is the place," said Aibin.

Nilsa looked at it. It was a stone building that looked ancient. It had something carved on the stone on the right side of the door.

"What does it say?"

"Almarahan, studies and books," Aibin translated.

"This is the place," Nilsa nodded, opening her notebook and reading Egil's instructions again. In them he indicated that she should ask about the weapon here. Almarahan was a scholar and book collector, and he had recent information about the location of Antior's Beam.

They knocked on the door and had to wait a little. After a while, an old gentleman opened the door, and after looking at them up and down, he seemed to find the visit interesting and invited them in. They entered the ancient building and the old man led them to an inner open courtyard. They passed a couple of rooms, which Nilsa noticed were full of books. As they walked down the corridor, they noticed there was a lot of dust in the house and very old tomes. Aibin sneezed twice as they walked along.

Almarahan invited them to sit on some cushions on one side of the patio, in the shade. There were several piles of old books on the side too. They sat down and Nilsa noticed that, in spite of his old age, the man moved gracefully.

"Excuse the mess, I'm always trying to finish organizing my books, but I never seem to manage entirely."

Aibin translated. The man was so old that he spoke as if he could not remember the words and had to delve in the bottom of his mind for them.

"Thank you very much for seeing us," Nilsa said gratefully.

"The pleasure is mine. I do not usually get many visitors, least of all from foreigners," he said, smiling at them. "You have intrigued me."

A boy of about twelve appeared from one of the rooms, loaded with a dozen books.

"Asraf, bring something for our guests to drink, please."

"Yes, Grandfather, right away." The boy left the books near another pile and disappeared again in another room.

"Thank you again," Aibin said.

"To what do I owe this unusual visit?"

"We're looking for an ancient weapon, very famous," Nilsa said.

"The desert has many such weapons. Which one is it?"

"Antior's Beam. We were told we would find recent information here regarding that weapon," Nilsa explained.

The old gentleman smiled and nodded.

"Antior's famous Beam killed the dragon by piercing its scales and reaching its heart, thus avenging his brothers' death."

"Is that what the legend says?" Nilsa asked, interested. She already knew what the old man had shared, but she hoped she could gather more details.

"That is what it says, what isn't really known is whether it was really a dragon. That's the part of the legend that was never confirmed. Some say it was true, others that it was an invention.

Those of us who study the legend have to think it is both."

"Then there is a possibility he did kill a dragon with that weapon," Nilsa said cheerfully.

"Except for the fact that a dragon is a mythological creature of fantasy. Its existence has never been proven."

"Many desert peoples believe in them. So, there must be some truth in it," Aibin said.

"There are those who believe such. Unfortunately, no trace of any dragon has ever been found that might confirm this. Perhaps one day remains will be found that will confirm it."

"Let's hope so," Nilsa said, smiling. "The dragon killed Antior's brothers, then?"

"That is correct. The story tells that Antior's two younger brothers went to some mountains that shone with the gleam of gold in the middle of the desert. They entered a cave searching for a possible treasure of gold and precious gems. But they had the bad luck of encountering a dragon resting in the mountain's depths. The dragon gobbled them up for intruding. Antior had been away on a journey, and when he returned home and saw that his brothers were missing, he went looking for them. They had left him a note indicating the location of the mountain and the possible treasure. He went to the cave looking for his brothers and found the dragon there. He knew then that his brothers were dead. Enraged, he tried to kill the beast with his spear while it was sleeping, but he didn't manage to pierce the dragon's scales. He had to flee. The dragon seriously wounded him, but he managed to get away alive.

According to the legend, once he recovered, Antior went in search of a powerful Sorcerer of the Magic of Curses and asked him to create a cursed spear capable of killing a dragon. Unfortunately, Antior's wounds had left his left arm useless, so the Sorcerer made a light javelin of gold that he could throw at the dragon. To use a spear, you need both arms but the javelin only needs one. The Sorcerer told him to come back after one year and to practice throwing javelins in the meantime. He would have the cursed weapon ready at that time.

Antior spent the whole year practicing, throwing javelins with his right arm every day until he became a master. He went to see the Sorcerer, and when he arrived the weapon was ready, with the exception of one last curse spell. Antior asked him to finish cursing the weapon, and then the Sorcerer asked him whether revenge was so worth it. Antior replied that he lived for nothing else. This being the case, the Sorcerer cast the last great curse spell on the weapon, but he did so using Antior's life. Once the weapon killed the dragon it would kill Antior as well, since his life was the payment for the death debt which the curse required."

"And he accepted?" Aibin asked, unable to believe it.

Almarahan nodded repeatedly.

"He accepted. He went to the dragon's cave and killed it while it was sleeping with a perfect throw to the heart. The dragon died. The weapon required the curse's payment and took Antior's life too. Both the dragon and Antior died at the hands of the weapon."

"Wow, we didn't know that detail of the story. Only a few pieces," Nilsa said.

"It's a story with a moral," Aibin said.

"That's correct. Whoever wants revenge so desperately will die for it," the old gentleman said. "It's not a good path."

"I see," Nilsa nodded. "I wonder whether the story is true, because of that included moral."

"We will never know," the gentleman smiled. "It is an ancient story, a legend of the deserts. What part is true is what your hearts want to believe."

Nilsa realized that if the weapon had been cursed by a Sorcerer to give it the power it needed to kill the dragon, whoever used it would also risk death if that part of the legend was true, which she did not like at all. Perhaps that part was not true. The only important thing was that the part of the legend about killing the dragon was true. If she had to sacrifice herself to kill Dergha-Sho-Blaska, she was convinced she could do so.

Asraf came with the water, a tisane, and some dates.

Nilsa and Aibin thanked them for their hospitality. They drank the water and then enjoyed the tisane and dates.

"How come you have recent information about the weapon? Has anyone found it?" Nilsa asked, resuming the conversation.

"It has been found, yes. They brought it to me to make sure it was the real one. I am an expert on legends and history of this part of the desert."

"They brought you the weapon? Was it the real one?" Nilsa wanted to know, since she had not expected the old man to have held it in his hands.

Almarahan nodded slowly.

"In my opinion, it is the real weapon. Or at least it is the weapon which gave rise to the legend. It is made of a material that looks like gold but is not. It is much lighter. It barely has any weight to it. It glows with a golden gleam and is obviously a weapon of power."

"Does it have magic?" asked Aibin.

"It does. A powerful, ancient magic. The two sorcerers of the city examined it thoroughly once I had finished."

"Didn't they want to keep it? Magi have a tendency to take over any powerful object for their own personal gain," Nilsa said, raising an eyebrow.

"True, but in this case something odd happened. They could not use the magic and decided it was not useful to them. Really quite curious. I would say they got scared, something that seldom happens with sorcerers. On the other hand, considering the history of the weapon, I'm not surprised they did not want to suffer any misfortune due to manipulating its power."

"Yeah, that's true..." Nilsa was thoughtful. Was it fear of the curse or the power of the beam? In any case, this fear gave authenticity to the weapon. "Who found it?"

"The man who found the weapon and brought it to me was a treasure hunter. He found it in the central mountains of the desert, the Jibalalfajr, the Mountains of Dawn."

"The long mountain range north of Madinatalmusa?" Aibin asked.

"Yes, there. He never specified where in them."

"They are long and filled with countless caves."

"I see you know them."

Aibin nodded but said nothing more. He did not want to give explanations about his place of origin.

"What's his name? Where can we find him?"

"His name is Albahel Aldhar."

"Is he in the city?" Nilsa asked, unable to hold back her eagerness.

"I'm afraid not. He left a few days ago. Albahel is now in the great port city of Zenut."

Nilsa and Aibin looked at each other and exchanged an expression of surprise and shock. The city was near the Mountains of Blood. They had made the entire journey in vain.

"How did he leave? Did he take Antior's Beam with him?" Nilsa wanted to know.

"He went by boat, and yes, he did take the beam. Albahel is an expert in relics, apart from being a treasure hunter. Emperor Malotas called for him."

"The Emperor? Because of Antior's Beam?"

Almarahan shook his head.

"No, not because of that. Albahel has been summoned by the emperor because of what is happening in Salansamur."

Nilsa and Aibin exchanged glances again. This was most significant. They acted as if they knew nothing about it.

"What is happening in Salansamur?"

"Serious and mysterious things, I'm afraid. They say the city is cursed. Their inhabitants have gone missing, all of them. Not only that, everyone who enters the city vanishes without a trace, even soldiers. Several regiments have gone there and never been heard of again. All kinds of rumors are spreading among the peoples of the desert. There are some who say there are monsters in the city. Enormous monsters, beasts. Emperor Malotas has summoned a large army, of sorcerers and experts to find out what is going on in that city and clean it out once and for all. The rumors harm the Emperor's image. They make him appear weak for not being able to defend or rescue one of his cities from whatever it is that has happened there."

"Oh, I see…"

"Is the Emperor's army going to go there?" Aibin asked.

"A part of his army, yes. They are getting ready in Zenut and will march on Salansamur soon. This is the news we have here, at least."

"And are you sure Albahel has the Beam with him? Won't he have left it here, somewhere safe?" asked Nilsa.

"I'm confident. He never parts with the weapon. He thinks he's going to get a lot of gold for it. He will try selling it to the other sorcerers the Emperor is sending, or to some rich general. The high-ranking soldiers are nobles, from very good families. They have a lot of gold, and to possess such a wonderful, legendary gold weapon will be irresistible for them."

"They're so vain?" Aibin was surprised.

The old gentleman laughed.

"You have no idea. The vanity of some nobles and soldiers is greater than the desert their bones will rest in one day."

"It seems to me that we have no choice but to go to Zenut after Albahel Aldhar," said Nilsa.

"I wish you luck in your search," the old gentleman said.

"I'm afraid we're going to need it. Thank you so much for everything," Nilsa said gratefully.

They said goodbye, and Nilsa and Aibin left Almarahan's house.

"What should we do now?" Nilsa asked Aibin.

"Now we'll go down to the harbor and find passage to Zenut. If the Emperor is gathering part of his army there, there'll be many ships heading there."

"Good. Zenut, here we come," Nilsa said cheerfully.

Chapter 15

Gerd arrived at the entrance to the Camp and, as usual, found it shut. The barrier, which was made up of trees and brush, covered with snow, and looked like an icy wall, rose before him, imperturbable. Gerd knew there were several Rangers posted on duty, hiding in the heights.

He presented himself.

"Ranger Specialist Gerd Vang, requesting permission to enter the Camp," he said, loud and firm.

He waited a moment to be granted entry. He knew the various Rangers posted at the barrier were aiming at him, so he took out his Specialist medallion and rested it on his chest.

A 'crack' followed by the sound of branches and trunks dragging on the ground announced the opening of the barrier. A section of forest and brush opened like magic. Gerd had always found the opening of this gate mysterious and even a little dark, although he had overcome this feeling by now. He knew there were Rangers pulling on ropes and pulleys to open it.

Gerd entered the Camp and could not help feeling joy at the sight of this place which was engraved in his heart. As he went in and re-encountered the familiar environment, the memories of the years of training spent here assaulted him unwillingly. He had lived through so many things in this place. Some very hard moments, like the physical training and the teasing because of his fears, and other moments which had been priceless alongside his friends the Snow Panthers, overcoming the various tests and managing to graduate at last as Rangers.

Setting foot in the Camp once again gave him a deep, strange feeling. He did not think there was another place, with the exception of his parents' farm, that made such an impact in him. Seeing the stables with the beautiful horses, the kennels, the pens with the different animals, the cages with owls and hawks, his heart filled with joy. The truth was that he would not mind staying at the Camp for some time, looking after the animals, training them and teaching the new Rangers how to manage them. Yes, he loved this place. It had trained him and in large part turned them into who he was today, and he could not forget that.

He left his horse in the stable and chatted with the stable boys. He also went over to check the hounds and spent a while with them. He loved them. Then he headed to the center of the Camp. He crossed paths with a couple of first- and second-year contenders who stared at him with great interest. He also encountered Rangers of the Camp and greeted them as he did the sentinel at their high posts. As he walked by them all he remembered the good times he had spent here. For some reason, the bad ones had almost faded from his memory.

He reached the well in the center of the Camp and stopped to look at it as all the contenders ran by hurriedly on their way to their next lesson. They all looked at him with admiration and greeted him respectfully. He liked this. He had earned his stripes. Seeing them run off, he did not envy them, now that he was already a Specialist. After having been through the traumatic mental training, the last thing he wanted was more training.

He continued on to the Library and stared at the building, which was just as he remembered it. The time he had spent in there studying, or with Egil had not been as enjoyable as the time spent with the animals. In fact, he did not feel much like going inside. He knew it would be full of contenders from the different years studying the tomes of knowledge about the four Schools. Just thinking about it gave him a slight headache.

He decided it would be best to go to the House of Command and present himself. By now, the Masters would know he was in the Camp. News flew quickly as if the owls had delivered it from one end to the other. He crossed the bridge that accessed the island where the House of Command stood. The place where the Camp leaders met looked as regal and commanding as usual. The place where Dolbarar lived.

He found two Rangers on guard duty at the door. He introduced himself and asked to see Dolbarar.

"Please wait here, Royal Eagle," the more senior of the two told him. He was about forty years old and had recognized who Gerd was. "I'll see whether he can receive you."

Gerd nodded. "I'll wait."

The veteran Ranger went into the House of Command.

The other one, who seemed to be in his thirties, was looking at

Gerd with great interest.

"It's an honor to have you among us," he said respectfully, bowing his head.

Gerd eyed him with some surprise.

"Thank you… I'm only doing my duty, just like you."

The guard's eyes opened wide, then he shook his hand in disbelief.

"But you're a Royal Ranger, a member of the famous Royal Eagles. You've come so far compared to me and most of the Rangers. You're an example to follow."

The comment, and the respect it was said with, made Gerd think twice. Yes, he had come far since his first training days at the Camp with his team of the Snow Panthers. The path had been full of obstacles since day one, but he had managed to overcome them all, with pride and his friends' help.

Gerd smiled at the guard.

"Thanks, you keep striving and you'll be able to get to where I am."

"I appreciate your words, but I highly doubt I can reach that high. I'm happy with being a good Ranger."

"I used to say the same thing," Gerd replied with a wink.

The door opened and the veteran Ranger came out again.

"Our leader will see you now," he said.

Gerd saluted both guards with a nod and went into the House of Command. As soon as he set foot inside and looked up, he saw two friendly faces he greatly respected. Esben and Dolbarar were waiting for him beside a low fire.

"Dear Gerd, seeing you here at the Camp again brings joy to my soul," Dolbarar greeted him with his usual warm, kind smile.

Gerd bowed his head and replied to the Camp's leader.

"And it makes me happy to be here again, a place I have such good memories of." He remembered that they used to have to fall on one knee before their leaders, but now that they were Ranger Specialists, and Royal Rangers on top of that, they were exempt from that formality.

"Gerd, it's so good to see you again. You look even stronger than the last time I saw you," Esben greeted him as he moved to give him a bear hug.

"The joy is all mine, Master Ranger," Gerd replied, returning the hug, unable to hold back the joy he felt for being there and the warm welcome he was getting.

"Are you all right? Fully recovered?" Dolbarar asked him.

"Quite recovered. I wouldn't say fully, but I manage without too much trouble," Gerd said, tapping his hip with his open hand.

"A strong lad like you can cope with anything. Besides, us Wildlife Rangers are tough and strong, like mountain bears," Esben sentenced.

"I have a strong head, that's for sure. As stubborn as a mule," Gerd replied, smiling.

Esben and Dolbarar laughed at the joke.

The door to the House opened and two Master Rangers walked in.

"Well, this is a surprise, we weren't expecting to see you here," Ivana said.

Gerd looked at her. She was still as beautiful and cold as always. It seemed her iciness kept her in a perfect state of preservation.

"It was sort of unexpected…"

"Unexpected? Or without adequate planning?" Haakon said sharp as a dart, coming in after Ivana.

The Master Ranger of Expertise seemed to Gerd to be gloomier than usual and also more deadly. He did not know whether this was good or bad for the Rangers.

"We made a new plan," said Gerd.

"It shows a sharp mind to change the plan and follow a different course when the present one isn't the most favorable," Dolbarar said.

"It's also usually a sign of despair," Haakon noted, sitting on one of the armchairs in the room.

"Let's make ourselves comfortable," Dolbarar said, sitting by the fire. Ivana and Esben sat at the large oak table.

"Did you warn Sylvia?" Esben asked.

Ivana nodded.

"She'll be here presently. She's finishing a lesson with the third-years."

"Wonderful. This way we'll all hear the news firsthand," the leader of the Camp said with a smile.

"I'm afraid I don't have good news, it's actually rather troubling news…" Gerd warned them in advance.

"Yes, we know. Gondabar has been keeping us informed

regularly about what's going on," Dolbarar said, wrinkling his nose.

"Any news of the war?" Ivana asked coldly.

"Nothing new. Alliances are being worked out and also betrayals among the principal kingdoms of Tremia, or that's what Egil says."

"And he's not far off," Haakon nodded. "That Egil has a sharp mind, and he knows the treacherous hearts of those who plot in the shadows."

"Kingdoms will fall or triumph according to the alliances formed and the betrayals suffered," Dolbarar commented, nodding heavily.

The door swung open and one of the guards held it for Sylvia to walk in.

"Greetings. I was told we have an important, unexpected visitor."

"Important, not really…" Gerd said, going slightly red in the face.

"The visit of one of the Snow Panthers is always important," Dolbarar told him.

"More than important, troublesome, because they're always bringing us problems," Haakon commented.

"Which the kingdom must solve," Esben said pointedly.

Haakon made a face, meaning he did not entirely agree.

"Well, now that we're all here, tell us, Gerd, if you'd be so kind, what your plans are," Dolbarar said.

Gerd nodded. Calmly, he explained the meeting with Gondabar and Raner, what had happened with the Druid Queen, and how the Panthers had taken advantage of the occasion to leave in search of the weapons that would let them kill the Immortal Dragon. He told them who had gone in search of which weapon. He did so as best as he could, although he did not have Egil's ease for transmitting such things.

"It's a good plan, given the circumstances," Dolbarar commented thoughtfully. "We need to have some means to fight this Immortal Dragon."

"The problem is the time they have, which isn't much," said Esben.

"Indeed. Either the war will start, or our Queen will return and request their services," Dolbarar mused out loud.

"Those knives you mentioned interest me," said Haakon.

"Viggo's gone searching for them. He's also very interested in them."

"No doubt. I'll need to have a chat with Viggo about those knives if he finds them."

"If he does, I highly doubt he'll want to part with them," Gerd said, shaking his head lightly.

Haakon said no more, but he folded his arms and narrowed his eyes in an unfriendly gaze.

"Where will you be heading, Gerd?" Esben asked him.

"I have to go to the Frozen Territories, to the north of our kingdom."

"How come?" Dolbarar asked Gerd, interested and a little surprised.

"Here's the legend," Gerd said. "You see, according to the legend, Gim's Double Death is a two-headed war axe that can cut clean through the neck of a dragon. Gim lived in the Frozen Territories, and we believe he was Norghanian. The legend tells of a dragon of the ice that kidnapped his wife, Ursula. Without a second thought, Gim went to her rescue, found the dragon's lair, and fought the creature. The dragon won. It left Gim for dead and took Ursula deep into its lair. Some shepherds found Gim half dead and rescued him. Once he had recovered from his terrible wounds, he sought the best armorer in the north to make him an axe to kill the dragon. He found a dwarven armorer, Ripdis Ulken, who had been rejected by his own people for his short height. It was said he was capable of creating enchanted weapons. He created the Double Death for Gim, swearing it was a weapon capable of cutting through the neck of a dragon. Gim went back to the beast's lair, fought with the beast, and chopped off its head. He rescued his wife, Ursula, and they returned home to live a long and happy life."

"A lovely legend, I like it," said Sylvia.

"It doesn't sound very convincing," Haakon commented. "I for one don't believe it. In fact, I don't even believe the weapon exists."

"Do we know what happened to the axe?" Esben asked in an interested tone.

Gerd shrugged.

"It vanished from the north, and no one ever saw it again."

"There are several details of the story that I find quite interesting," Dolbarar commented.

"Any information will be useful," Gerd said, looking at the Camp leader with hopeful eyes.

"Ripdis Ulken, the famous dwarven armorer, existed, he's not fictional. I know the name," Dolbarar said. "There are Norghanian nobles who have exquisite weapons Ripdis made. If I remember correctly, he used to live in the north, beyond the Eternal Mountains and the Unreachable Range."

"That's good news!" Gerd cheered up. "I have to find any trace of him, even if he's already dead. His family might be able to help me. I'd guess they'd have information about the most famous weapons Ripdis forged."

"Yes, but there's something that doesn't fit in that legend. Supposedly, dragons and men lived at different times," Dolbarar went on. "If this is the case, Gim couldn't have fought against a dragon."

Gerd's hope and cheer vanished.

"Yeah, that's true.... But..."

"But?" Dolbarar asked, encouraging him to keep going.

Gerd scratched his temple.

"We believe that some dragons remained in Tremia when the rest of the species vanished. There are murals in the desert, in the Mountains of Blood, where the Desher Tumaini Tribe lives, which seem to indicate so."

"We believe? Who's we?" Ivana asked.

"We... the Snow Panthers," Gerd replied.

"That doesn't prove it," Haakon said. "It's one thing to believe something and a very different one to be able to prove it. Some primitive paintings of old aren't exactly concrete evidence."

"True, but we believe some dragons remained when the humans arrived in Tremia."

"It might be that some humans did interact with the last dragons of Tremia," Esben commented.

"That would explain why there are so many legends and so much mythology about them," said Sylvia.

"True, that would explain it, and it's possible, up to a point," Ivana commented. "Yet, it might be that all the mythology came from murals and thousands-of-years-old paintings and that humans and dragons in fact never really met."

"In order to convince me, you'll need more than a theory," Haakon said.

Gerd was going to tell them that there was also the theory that the magic of dragons had been passed on to some humans at that time. That, nowadays, there existed some humans with dragon magic running through their veins, and that those humans were the descendants of dragons and humans. But Gerd was not as good at explaining certain things as his friend Egil, so he left those tangled explanations for Galdason and Enduald.

"There's another incongruity in the legend," Haakon commented with the air of someone really thinking it over.

"Which is?" Esben wanted to know.

"I don't believe that any human being is capable of creating a weapon that could kill a dragon. It makes no sense, if you think about it carefully. The magic of humans can't defeat that of dragons, therefore, if we accept this premise, no matter how good the craftsman is who creates the weapon, if the magic imbued in it is human, it will never defeat the dragon."

"Hence, Ripdis couldn't have created that weapon," Ivana concluded.

"From what I could discuss with Gondabar and Sigrid," Dolbarar went on, "you're quite right on that point."

"It's correct? I had guessed as much," Haakon said smugly.

"Then who forged the weapons?" Ivana asked, frowning as she folded her arms.

"Based on Enduald's and Galdason's studies, Sigrid believes those weapons were created thousands of years ago, before the arrival of humans in Tremia, with the sole purpose of finishing off the dragons."

"Very interesting," Sylvia commented. "The question then is who created them, isn't it?" she asked, looking at the others who, after a moment, nodded.

"Enduald and Galdason lean toward the idea that the weapons were created by some gods, a very powerful race who came to Tremia before the humans, gods who defeated and expelled the dragons from this world," Dolbarar said. "They are more and more convinced of this theory."

"Do we know anything about these gods or their powerful race?" Sylvia asked.

Dolbarar shook his head.

"We don't have any information. I'm sure there have to be traces somewhere in Tremia if they really existed, but nothing has been discovered in Norghana so far."

"If those weapons existed, they would have left a trace," Ivana argued.

"They do exist. At least one of them does," Gerd intervened. "The Golden Bow Lasgol is carrying with him."

"True," Ivana nodded. "I'd like to take a look at it. I'll tell Lasgol to bring it here for examination as soon as he can."

"Ivar has already examined it at the Shelter with Enduald's and Galdason's help, you can talk to him," Dolbarar told her.

"I'll write to him. Even so, I'd like to feel the weapon in my hands," Ivana mimicked the action of nocking and releasing with her hands and arms.

"If what we've been discussing is true, then the legend of the axe makes no sense. It's wrong," Haakon said, "as I'd already predicted."

"Perhaps they embellished the story to make it greater than it actually was. This is very common in folklore, you know, in Norghana or any other kingdom," Sylvia said.

"That's more than likely," said Esben. "Every legend is part truth, part exaggeration and fantasy."

"In any case, Gim and Ripdis are a clue I believe worth investigating and seeing where it leads," Dolbarar told Gerd.

"I'll do that," Gerd said, nodding. He was not feeling very confident he would be able to find the weapon. If the legend was a fake, and that seemed likely from what they had been discussing, then the chances of its existence were vanishing into thin air.

"In that case, you'll have to go to the Frozen Territories, beyond the Unreachable Range," Esben told him.

"Are there any Norghanian villages beyond the mountains?" Gerd asked. "Or have they all been destroyed or abandoned after the wars with the Peoples of the Frozen Continent?"

"In the western area of the Frozen Territories, without venturing too much north, there are still the last Norghanian villages on that side of the great mountains," Dolbarar explained.

"The east coast, and the north in particular, are once again under the rule of the Wild Ones of the Ice. Best not to go near. The Wild Ones of the Ice have retaken those areas after the war," Esben added.

"I can't fathom why a few Norghanian fools still want to live so far north," Haakon commented, shaking his head.

"Because that's where their villages reside, where they've always been," Esben told him.

"It's safer to live on this side of the mountains," added Ivana. "Living on the other side is always looking for trouble. They won't have the King's help if anything happens."

"They won't?" Gerd was shocked. He did not think it was a good idea to abandon these people to their fate.

"It's been a while since Thoran tried to assault the Frozen Territories. He's been very busy with Zangria, the royal wedding, and now Erenal," Haakon said.

"Besides, every time Thoran's armies reached the eastern coast of the Frozen Territories, the Wild Ones withdrew north and regrouped. There they received reinforcements from the Frozen Continent, reinforcements of Tundra Dwellers and Arcanes of the Ice. It would seem that they now have a new leader and the strategies are less straightforward and more subtle. But effective indeed," Dolbarar commented.

"The Arcanes and their magic have managed to force Thoran's armies to retreat through confusion and have even bewitched them into fighting themselves. There was little direct confrontation. It's as if the Wild Ones are smarter now," Ivana explained.

"A very intelligent tactic which, no doubt, is due to their new leaders," Sylvia said, nodding.

"Yes, so we believe," Dolbarar agreed. "They are very different tactics from those the Wild Ones of the North used to employ."

"I'll take that into consideration," Gerd nodded and then was thoughtful. He hoped the new leader of the Wild Ones would be a friend of the Panthers. If it turned out he was not, he would be in trouble again. It had been a long time since they had heard of Asrael. He wondered whether he had managed to achieve the power of the Frozen Continent and rule over their peoples. He hoped this was the case, for his own sake.

"When do you leave?" Esben asked Gerd.

"At dawn. I'll leave the Camp through the secret passage and head northwest. I'll cross the Eternal Mountains through the Pass of the White Dragon's Gorge, then I'll head to the Unreachable Range."

"Very well, I'll come with you until you cross the Eternal Mountains. I feel like stretching my legs, and I want to visit the wildlife of the area. I've been neglecting it with so many new contenders. Well, if Dolbarar agrees, of course."

The leader of the Camp nodded.

"I agree," he said, granting his permission.

"I appreciate it, Master Ranger, Leader of the Camp," Gerd said, feeling very honored.

"We wish you good luck," Sylvia said. "Come by the Master House of Nature and I'll prepare some potions for the way, restoratives and something against the frost. The weather is getting worse, and you might freeze without a moment's notice."

"Thank you, I'm sure they'll be very useful."

"Good luck!" the others wished him.

Gerd felt honored. Crossing the mountains in winter was not a good idea. If they were already deadly, in winter they were much more so. He would have to tread carefully.

Chapter 16

Gerd and Esben left the Camp through the secret northern passage. The guards watching it let them through when they recognized the Master Ranger of Wildlife.

"Thanks for the company," Gerd said as they headed north.

"The pleasure is all mine, I was looking forward to making a short winter escapade," he replied, pointing at the sky, which looked as if it could unload at any moment.

"The temperature isn't too low, but the sky indicates a storm."

"Nothing better than a good winter storm above one's head to travel at the pace of a snow fox."

Gerd realized that indeed the pace they were making was that of a quick march, seeking to get away from the storm, and they were walking on the snow and frost at a fast rhythm. It was a pleasure to see how fit the Master Ranger was, since he was not exactly a young man.

They left the storm behind them when they crossed the endless pass in the Eternal Mountains, the Pass of the White Dragon's Gorge. Gerd walked, gazing up and ahead with his mouth slightly open, impressed by the greatness of the place.

"This Pass is one of my favorites," Esben told Gerd.

"It's breathtaking. It's as if the Ice Gods had given a massive axe blow to the mountain range to open a way for the poor humans."

Esben smiled.

"That's exactly what happened."

"Seriously?" Gerd asked in awe.

"I don't know, but I like to think so."

"It's not the first time I'm crossing it, but the feeling is always the same. It's awesome."

"The Norghanian Mountains and their passes are renowned, both for their beauty and the danger they hold."

"Both things are true."

They crossed the enormous gorge, and when they reached the other side, they found a wild, snow-covered landscape. It was as if they were leaving civilization behind and entering hostile territory.

They went on toward the northwest, talking animatedly, glad to see the storm was left behind and that the sky ahead of them was not so dark.

Esben would stop whenever he glimpsed animal tracks to examine them. If he found them interesting, he tried to see whether there was some specimen nearby.

"Interesting. On the way back, I'll stop to study this more closely," he would tell Gerd as he gave him some interesting explanation. But he did not waste time, and soon they were back on their way, chatting as they went along.

"What wildlife interests you?"

"All of it," Esben smiled at him, which made Gerd nod in agreement, "but up here, the great white and gray bears."

"I prefer dogs and wolves. I've studied them extensively with Elder Gisli."

"Gisli is a real compendium of wildlife knowledge. A scholar in everything that has to do with animals."

"The Master Ranger is one as well," Gerd replied, indicating Esben.

"Gisli is far more knowledgeable than I am," Esben said, smiling. "Wouldn't you like to have a familiar? After all, you're a Beast Master, and those Specialists usually have wild animals as familiars."

"To tell you the truth, I'd love to," Gerd admitted, scratching his head. "But I've never found the time. We're always in some tangle or another."

"If you want, I can see if I can find you a bloodhound, or a wolf pup."

"Thank you, Master, that would be wonderful."

"Leave it to me. You'll have one upon your return from this mission."

"It's a whole new responsibility..."

"It is, but one you'll never regret having."

Gerd nodded, "Yeah, I believe you."

"Then that's settled. Let's continue."

So entertaining was Esben's company, that Gerd found the journey from the Camp to the Unreachable Range very short. He could have sworn that the colossal mountain range was a lot farther. But he found them right before him in all their enormity of rock, ice, and snow. If the Eternal Mountains and their passes left one frozen in awe, the Unreachable Range seemed exactly that—unreachable due to their lofty heights.

"Your mouth's hanging open," Esben told Gerd as he patted his shoulder.

"It's because they're… colossal."

"Yes, they are. There are no mountains more impressive in the north, in my opinion."

"I agree. How are we going to cross them, being so far west?" asked Gerd as he studied the huge mountains close to one another, their high peaks covered by icy snow.

"Don't worry," Esben said, winking.

"It's hard not to, seeing how big and frozen they are."

"That's why I'm here. I know a shortcut that will save you time."

"A large one? Because you can't see any from here."

"Nope, it's a small, narrow one. It goes up between those two ranges," Esben said, pointing with his finger.

"Oh… I'll have to climb."

"Yup, there's no other way."

Gerd snorted. "I'm ready."

"Very well. I'll come with you to the foot of the mountain and show you the way up. It's risky, but you'll save a lot of time."

"I'll take the risk. I don't want to waste a lot of time going on long detours, and in this area, I can see that would take me forever."

"That's the spirit," Esben said with a big smile.

Gerd listened carefully to Esben's indications. He told him where to climb the first hills of the mountain and where, further up, to turn and face another climb. He finally told Gerd where he would find the narrow passage between the two summits.

"Thank you very much, Master Ranger."

"You needn't be so formal with me. You know I'm fond of you."

"Thanks…." The master's words touched Gerd's heart.

"Now, up you go, the mountain awaits you. See how it's challenging you."

Gerd looked at the impressive range and the two peaks through which he would have to cross high up and sighed.

"It is challenging. To me, and to all humans."

"I'll see you at the Camp when you come back with the axe."

"I hope so."

"I'm sure you'll make it. Good luck, and beware of the Wild Ones and the wildlife of the Frozen Territories which might make things complicated."

"I will be wary," Gerd nodded as he adjusted his rucksack, quiver, and bow, and prepared to climb. He breathed in the cold air of the mountain and started climbing carefully. The side of the mountain was partly rock and part snow. He went up first along the rock, which was safer. He found himself to be strong and well-coordinated, so he went ahead confidently. He knew there would be some trouble during the climb, but for now everything was going well.

Soon, he found there were no more rock areas not covered with snow, so he was even more careful. He looked down and saw Esben watching him climb. He waved at him one last time before the man vanished behind one of the mountain faces.

The climb became more difficult, and he had to tread more carefully. The snow and ice covering the whole mountain were not making things easy for him. At one point in the climb, his hip gave out and he lost his balance, but he managed to grab onto a protruding rock and recover. He was scared, but he had expected something like that to happen. He did not let fear overcome him and went on climbing.

After climbing almost all day, he reached the point where Esben had told him he would find the pass that was impossible to see from below. Gerd hoped it would be there. The Master Ranger did not fail him. He found the pass between the two peaks he saw above his head.

He snorted—the worst was over, he only had to cross the pass. Sideways, since it was very narrow, more than he had imagined. He set to it, and although it was stressful at times when he felt like he would get stuck between the two walls of rock, he managed to go through the mountains.

"At last," he exhaled.

Without wasting a moment, he started making his way down. It was going to be even more complicated because of the risk of slipping and falling into the void, but he did not lose heart and continued down. He had a couple of scares, first a big slip that nearly toppled him over the cliff. Second because of losing his balance, which nearly cost him his life. In both cases he had grabbed onto a rock with all his might to not fall to his death, and this had saved him.

He finished the descent and sat on the snow-covered ground to rest. It had been a harrowing experience. What discouraged him a little was finding that, in order to reach the Norghanian villages in that area, he would still have to climb one last mountain. Not as big as the one he had just left behind, but a considerably steep climb in any case.

"The life of a Ranger is like that. You overcome an obstacle and another appears," he told himself and smiled. He rested for a while, then he ate and drank from the supplies he carried in his rucksack before he resumed his journey.

Gerd stopped when he set foot at the summit he had been trying to reach all day. He inhaled and filled his lungs with the winter air, which at such great heights hurt as it went in, both his nose and lungs. But he enjoyed the winter cold of the mountains. It reminded him that he was alive, very alive, and that if he was not careful, he would not be alive for long. The Norghanian Mountains were as beautiful as they were ruthless. You fell in love with their snowy beauty and stoic magnificence, even as they killed you with their slopes, winter storms, and white abysses. Thinking about it, Gerd smiled. He had been spending so much time with Egil lately that he even thought in terms Egil used. Luckily, it was only in a couple of isolated occasions.

He looked upon the beautiful landscape of snow and rock he could appreciate from above. For a moment he thought he was at the top of the world, on the highest place in Norghana. That was not the case, and he knew it, but the view being so spectacular, he allowed himself to believe it for a moment. He turned around and saw the great mountains of the Unreachable Range, from his present position he could see them in all their splendor. The mountain ranges that separated the so-called civilized Norghana from the Frozen Territories were breathtaking and beautiful. For a moment, he delighted in the majestic beauty of the mountains behind him.

The climbs he had made had not been as hard as he had expected them to be. In another time, he would have found it a lot more taxing. He was pleased to find he was so fit in spite of his disability and that he was able to do quite well in this icy, mountainous terrain.

When his legs were sinking in snow to his knees, it was harder to lose his balance, although it was more difficult to walk. The descent would be a little harder. Keeping his balance on steep slopes covered with ice and snow had already proven hard. This concerned him somewhat. He would have to tread carefully, or else he would fall to a certain death from that height.

The sky was overcast and the storm seemed to be coming from the Northern Sea, to the west. So far, he had not really felt the harshness of the winter weather, which was worsening by the moment. The journey to the Camp had been quiet, and although it had snowed a lot, it had not been really cold, at least not a troubling cold. Gerd loved the snow and seeing the world draped in white. It was an idyllic sight which always filled his heart with joy. He had loved snow since he was a little boy.

He remembered with longing how, when he was a kid, he would get up early in autumn to see the first snowfalls and all the fields covered in white. Besides, at his farm, the arrival of the snow meant the fields could not be worked, which was always a reason to rejoice. His family did not feel the same way. Winter at the farm was always hard and they had to scrimp. Once he grew up he understood, but his love for the snow-covered fields, forest, and paths had never left him.

He looked at the mountains and a valley in the distance, to the northwest. It looked relatively protected, surrounded by high mountains. Within the valley he glimpsed two Norghanian villages. That was his destination, at least initially. He doubted he would be able to get to them before the storm caught up with him. A winter storm here would not be pleasant. Of this he was certain.

He began the descent, treading cautiously. The wind was beginning to blow strongly and the storm was rushing toward him, an added difficulty to the descent. Nothing like crossing mountains to get the heart beating faster. Gerd smiled and kept going down without taking his eyes off where he put his foot down.

He arrived at the bottom of the mountain and snorted. He had managed to come down without falling, and this was reason enough to rejoice, since it had not been an easy descent. He started walking toward the valley with renovated spirits. He would find the axe that could cut through the neck of a dragon, and with it he would confront the Immortal Dragon and his thralls.

He bent over when he saw some prints on the snow. They were

wolf tracks: a pack of about a dozen wolves with a large, heavy leader, judging by the tracks and how deep they sank in the snow. They were heading north, in the same direction he was. That was not good. He decided to let them get ahead, since the thick of the storm was still far away. He sat under a fir tree covered in snow to eat from his supplies and rest his legs.

He resumed his journey when he saw that the storm and night were almost upon him. He wrapped himself in his Ranger's winter clothes and quickened his pace in the direction of the valley. It surprised him that the storm was advancing so fast; at the summit he had calculated it would not catch up with him for at least half a day. He had been wrong in his calculations. The storm was moving a lot faster than usual, even so far north, where storms were famous for being not only terrible, but swift.

The north and its dangers. Whoever did not like it was better off not entering those wild and fierce territories. The icy wind began to whip him from behind and force him to move fast, gales stronger than he was comfortable with. If he already had trouble due to his disability, the strong western winds pushing him did not help at all. He wrapped his cloak around him tightly, adjusted his hood, and kept going as fast as he could.

He felt bad for not correctly calculating the speed of the storm coming from the sea at the west. He was an experienced Ranger, a Specialist—storms, no matter how unpredictable and unstable in these lands, should not surprise him. He would have to tell Egil. There had to be some study or tome that would help him better predict the behavior of those ice storms.

The icy, whipping wind punished his arms and legs. His back was protected by his rucksack, the bow and quiver forming a barrier now that they were half covered with frost and ice. His limbs were more exposed. A stronger gust of wind nearly toppled him. He recovered and picked up speed. He had to find shelter. The storm kept coming, and it was doing so too fast.

He saw the first of the two villages at the entrance of the valley and snorted. He wiped the frost off his face to see better, although the wind was now whipping him from all directions and it soon got in his eyes. He hurried. The cold of the winter storm was cutting and the wind was powerful. The first village was close, and that encouraged him to move as fast as he could. But it was hard to make way because of the strength of the storm breaking around him. Freezing rain, strong winds, ice and a terrible cold were punishing him.

He protected his face, covering his mouth and nose with his Ranger's scarf. Only his eyes were uncovered. The temperature was going down remarkably fast, and his eyebrows began to freeze. It was normal when a winter storm caught you in the mountains. It was also a clear warning that he was going to freeze to death if he did not find shelter soon. He thought that was what the Ice Magi liked to do to their enemies. Most likely they had developed their skills by watching the Norghanian storms.

He walked on with determination. This was not his first battle against a winter storm, and so far he had always come out victorious. A couple of times only by a hair's breadth, but he had always survived. He looked behind and saw a sky darker than an abyss coming upon him, sending terribly icy winds to turn him into an ice statue. It was not a good scenario at all, and fear started to grow in his stomach. He squashed it down with all his willpower. A Ranger was not afraid of storms, no matter how deadly they might be in the mountains. That was why he needed to find shelter. And the nearest shelter was the village. He had to reach it and get under cover.

He continued advancing with all his strength, fighting against the wind and the temperature that was dropping dramatically. Thunder began to sound, loud and close. Tremendous blasts of lightning and a great whirlwind were after him, as if an icy god wanted to kill him for having set foot on his sacred mountains without permission.

He arrived in the village at a run. It was not very big—he counted two dozen houses of rock and wood with a steep roof, Norghanian style. It was deserted, all the inhabitants sheltering in their homes. It was logical. They had seen the storm coming, and even the watch tower at the entrance was empty. Not even the guards had remained to weather out the storm. He did not blame them. If they stayed they could easily die, and no enemy in their right mind would attack in the middle of a storm.

He saw smoke coming out of the chimneys of the houses, which the hurricane winds blew away as soon as it came out. That meant the villagers were inside. The houses were solid and would weather the storm. Perhaps some roofs and windows might suffer some damage, but the Norghanian houses were built well, designed precisely to withstand winter storms.

He approached the nearest house and began to bang on the door with his fist.

"Open up! Norghanian friend seeking refuge!" he called at the top of his lungs to be heard above the din of the storm. Lightning was falling down around him, and the thunder sounded as if it would rend the sky in two. The wind was so strong Gerd had to grab the door frame to not be blown away.

"The storm is already upon me! Open up!"

But the door remained shut. Gerd thought about knocking it down with his shoulder, but the wind was so strong that it did not let him. If he let go, he would blow away. He was holding on for dear life, and he realized his arms and legs were freezing. The temperature was too low, and the wind was piercing through his clothes like ice daggers.

"Royal Ranger! Open up!" he cried at the top of his lungs above the thunder of the storm.

A blast of lightning fell on the watch tower and the strong wind carried away part of the structure. Things were getting worse, as impossible as it seemed. Part of a nearby house was blown away too.

Gerd thought he would not make it. He sought some place to hide from the wind. He considered going behind the house for protection, but the temperature was already too low. He was going to freeze on his feet.

The door of the house opened.

Chapter 17

"Royal Ranger?" a deep, masculine voice asked.

"Yes, I'm a Royal Ranger!"

"Come in!" the man said and put out a hand.

Gerd grasped the hand and the man pulled him inside. Gerd came into the house, tripped, and fell on the floor.

The door shut behind him and someone barred it.

Half frozen, unable to move, Gerd rolled to one side on the floor to see what he had stumbled into. He saw a man and a young boy staring at him with interest. The man had a war axe in one hand and the young boy had another.

Gerd wanted to raise his hand to indicate he meant no harm, but his right arm was frozen stiff and he could not move it.

"I mean you no harm. I'm a Norghanian Ranger."

The older man, who must have been in his early forties and looked surly, studied Gerd with suspicious blue eyes. He was tall and strong, with blond hair and beard, and he did not seem to trust Gerd's words, at least not entirely. The younger one was looking at Gerd with interest but also fear.

"I swear I'm a Ranger, and I mean you no harm. I only need shelter from the storm."

"If you're a Ranger, show me your medallion," the older man said.

"Yes... of course..." Gerd tried to open his winter cloak, but his arms would not respond.

"Trouble...?" the man pointed the axe at him, "or are you faking?"

"I'm a little frozen, my arms and legs. You can search for the medallions yourself. Go ahead, do it," Gerd turned over and remained lying on the floor.

"Don't do anything stupid, or we'll cut you to pieces."

"Take it easy, I'm not going to do anything. I couldn't even if I wanted to."

The man came over to Gerd and with his left hand rummaged around Gerd's neck while he kept his right hand raised, holding the axe. The young one was gripping his axe up too.

The man found Gerd's Wildlife Specialist medallion, which was the one he was now wearing. He showed it to the young boy.

"He's a Ranger, a Specialist."

"And Royal Ranger," Gerd added proudly, from the floor.

"This isn't a night to be wandering in the mountains, least of all in the Frozen Territories," the man said.

"Yeah… the storm came faster than I'd expected," Gerd replied, having trouble keeping his teeth from chattering. He was more frozen than he had realized outside.

"We'd better get you near the fire."

"Oh, that'd be good, yes."

"Son, help me drag him. This Ranger's larger than usual. He must weigh a ton."

"Yes, Father," the young man replied and, leaving the axe on a bench, he grabbed Gerd by his ankles. His father left his axe on a table and grabbed Gerd by his armpits.

"I appreciate it," Gerd said as they both dragged him before the hearth, where a fire was burning with a most appealing warmth.

"We'll leave you here for a while so you can get warm. Elof, bring a thick blanket to wrap around him."

"Yes, Father, right away." The young man went to one of the back rooms.

"My name's Gerd," he introduced himself and tried to offer his hand in greeting, but his arm barely moved.

"You'd better not force your arms and legs, being frozen, you might hurt yourself. My name's Frans."

"Pleased to meet you. Thank you for opening your home to me," Gerd said gratefully.

"You're welcome. We Norghanians help one another in the north, more so in the middle of a storm."

"Here's the blanket," the young man said, putting it around Gerd's shoulders.

"Nice, thank you."

"This is my son, Elof."

"Pleased to meet you."

"You thought you'd outrun the storm, didn't you?" Elof asked with the grin of someone who knew the answer.

"I thought so, yeah. It came faster than I'd expected," Gerd had to admit. "And I have some experience with storms."

"It's natural. Storms come from the sea in this area, from the west, and they're very fast and break with rage," Frans explained. "Only the northern storms are more dangerous. You were lucky. Many don't live to tell the tale. In your case, your experience most likely saved you."

"Yeah, it's been a real battle against the elements to get this far."

"That's the reason this village is so near the entrance to the valley, so that we have time to reach shelter before the storms break."

"You should put up a sign explaining this about a league away," Gerd said, grinning.

"That's not a bad idea, although we don't usually have many visitors, so we never saw the need."

"Or you could build a couple of cabins before arriving at the valley," Gerd suggested.

"We'll mention it to Fulker, the village chief," Frans said, nodding.

"I'm beginning to feel my arms again, that's good," Gerd told them.

"We'll make a northern broth for you. It'll help you get warm. Or would you rather have firewater? We have that too."

"I'd rather have the broth, my stomach likes being warm."

"Very well," Frans smiled and went to make it.

Gerd managed to move his arms and started rubbing his legs.

Elof sat down in a chair in front of him and watched him. He was a tall, thin youth, about sixteen, with blond hair and blue eyes. His face was Norghanian, but softer. He looked like a good lad. The average Norghanian had the face of a brute, but this boy did not.

"Are you two alone?" Gerd asked, pointing toward the kitchen where Frans was making the broth.

The lad lowered his gaze.

"My mother died last year."

"Oh, I'm sorry for your loss," said Gerd.

"Things happen… a white bear killed her in the spring while she was gathering berries in the forest to the north."

"Wow, that's bad luck…"

"Yeah, it was," the lad shrugged. "Life in the mountains isn't easy. If the cold doesn't kill you, the Wild Ones, Mother Nature, or wildlife will."

Gerd nodded, repeatedly and slowly. He felt bad for the poor boy.

Frans came back and finished making the broth on the fire. Then he filled a big wooden bowl for Gerd.

"It will do you good."

"The taste is strong," Gerd commented as he downed it with a large wooden spoon.

"It has white elder root, which is a good restorative."

"This broth has meatballs," said Gerd, eating one, happy at finding some in his bowl.

"Only way for you to recover quickly," Frans said, smiling.

"It feels so good, both the broth and the warmth of the fire."

"We're glad to be able to help a Ranger."

"I'm really grateful," Gerd said, finishing the broth.

"Are you on a mission for the King? Things have been pretty quiet in this area for quite a while," said Frans.

"It's a Ranger mission, not one for the King."

"Oh, funny. Then it's not because of the Wild Ones?"

Gerd shook his head.

"It doesn't have anything to do with them. I've come searching for a weapon."

"A weapon?" Elof said, looking surprised. "And you've come all the way here for that?"

"You see…" Gerd looked directly at him. "It's not just any weapon. It's an enchanted weapon."

"You've come for Gim's Axe?" Frans asked.

"Yes, I've come for just that. You know it?"

"Everyone in this area knows the legend of Gim," Elof replied. "It's one of the most popular legends this side of the mountains."

"Then you can help me find it," Gerd said hopefully.

Father and son looked at each other.

Gerd realized by their gazes that something was not good.

"What's the matter?"

"That the weapon was lost in the territory of the Wild Ones of the Ice."

"That's not good…"

"No, it isn't."

"Eat in peace. We'll help you with what we can," Frans told Gerd.

The following morning, the storm had unloaded hard enough and continued its course to the northeast. Gerd broke his fast with Frans and his son Elof and prepared to begin his search for Gim's axe.

They left the house and found it had snowed quite heavily. Several villagers were shoveling the snow from their doorsteps and workshops. It was a common scene in the north, and the sight of the villagers working with old wooden shovels gave Gerd a pleasant feeling.

"We'll go and see Fulker, the village chief. He'll want to know what you're doing here," Frans told Gerd as he made way through the snow that came up to his knees. Elof stayed behind, shoveling the entrance of their house. He said goodbye to Gerd with a smile and set to work with an old wooden shovel.

"Will he be able to help me with the axe?" Gerd asked as they walked.

"I believe he'll be able to do something," Frans nodded.

As they walked down the snow-covered street, the villagers began to notice Gerd's presence and watched him with interest. Frans greeted them all by name, which served to relax the tension that built when they realized the presence of the giant foreigner.

"You're causing quite the sensation," Frans told Gerd with a smile.

"I usually do, yeah."

"It's because you're so big. That draws their attention."

They arrived at the village's House of Command. It was unmistakable, since the building was the biggest in the village and was built Norghanian style, like a long ship with a high, steeped roof.

Frans knocked on the door. Since it was a very small village, there was no guard at the chief's house.

Fulker opened the door.

"Good morning, Frans. That was quite the storm yesterday, huh?" he greeted them.

"One that won't return," Frans replied.

The chief stared at Gerd from head to toe.

"We have a visitor in our small village?"

"This is Gerd, a Royal Ranger. He arrived yesterday in the middle of the storm. He spent the night with us."

"Well, and a Royal Ranger no less. It's an honor. Come in and we'll talk," the chief invited them.

The three went into the House of Command and, following Fulker's indications, they sat at a big, long table.

"If I remember correctly, Rangers don't drink, or I would offer you a strong liquor."

"No, we don't drink, thanks," Gerd replied.

"Frans?"

"Too early for me, Chief."

"Very well, I'll have one myself," he said and poured himself a dark brown liquor from a glass container. He drank, savoring the liquor. "You don't know what you're missing," he told them.

"The Ranger needs to talk to you," Frans told the chief.

"What does the King want now? He hasn't thought of us for a long time."

"I'm not here on a mission for the King," Gerd said.

"You're not? And not passing through either. There are only the last Norghanians villages here, and then the tundra and the villages of the Wild Ones of the Ice."

"I've come searching for Gim's Axe," Gerd said straightforwardly.

Fulker's eyes opened wide.

"Well, I wasn't expecting that. No doubt this news requires another drink." The chief poured himself a second glass and drank.

"Frans told me you could help me."

"Why does a Ranger want to find Gim's Axe? Shouldn't you be on some Ranger mission?"

"This is a Ranger's mission," Gerd confirmed firmly.

The chief threw his head back.

"Since when do Rangers seek weapons from fables and odes? Isn't there enough to do in Norghana?"

"We've just started recently," Gerd said jokingly. Then he became serious. "We need to find that axe, it's important."

"That axe is from a folklore tale of the Frozen Territories. It's never been found. I don't think it even exists."

"Why don't you think it exists?"

"Because many have looked for it and no one has ever found it."

"I see I'm not the first one who's come asking about it."

Fulker shook his head.

"Adventurers, treasure hunters, and the like have come by in the past. Rangers or King's men, none. You're the first."

"A long time ago?"

"In my grandfather's time, perhaps before that too, so yeah, long time," the Chief shrugged.

"Weren't any of them lucky?"

"I have to tell you that, unfortunately, none found it. Sorry."

"That doesn't mean it doesn't exist."

"I think that's exactly what it means," the village chief said.

Gerd wrinkled his nose. He did not like the chief's attitude. He could believe whatever he liked, but that did not make it the truth.

"Where did those adventurers and treasure hunters go?"

The chief scratched his chin.

"They searched the whole area, up and down, didn't leave a rock unturned. They searched in caves, lakes, ruins, and places that might have some kind of meaning and might be hiding the weapon. As I've told you, none of them found anything."

This was not the reply Gerd wanted to hear, but he did not lose courage.

"Did they go back home after their failure, or did they try to find the weapon someplace else?"

"There are three villages in this valley. They did not find anything here or in the villages around, so most of them went searching in the Village of Lorders."

"Why that village?"

"That's the village where Ripdis Ulken lived, the craftsman who supposedly created the axe," Frans told him.

"Exactly," Fulker joined in.

"Then I might find some important information there."

The Chief and Frans exchanged an unconvinced look.

"Those who go to Lorders looking for Ripdis Ulken's descendants end up going further north. To the territory of the Wild Ones of the Ice. They don't come back from there…" Fulker said.

"I see…." This wasn't good news. The last thing Gerd wanted was to stand up to a group of Wild Ones of the Ice.

"I don't know why you're looking for that legendary weapon, but I would advise you to quit. There are more important things than dying," Fulker said.

"He's right. An experienced Ranger like you could do a lot for us here. Don't waste your life going after a mythological weapon that doesn't exist," Frans said.

Gerd was thoughtful. He knew that both men were right, that it was a bad idea to follow the weapon's trail. He also knew he could be of help in this region forsaken by the King. But something inside him told him he had to keep going and find the weapon, that it was important to defeat the Immortal Dragon and his hosts.

"I understand your reasoning and good wishes, but I must stick to my mission. I've been ordered to find that weapon, and that's what I'm going to do."

Frans snorted, and Fulker sighed.

"As you see fit. Don't say we didn't warn you," the Chief said.

"How do I reach the Village of Lorders?"

"It's north from here, two valleys north to be precise," Frans told him.

"Then I'd better be on my way."

"I wish you luck, Ranger," Fulker added. "Don't let the Wild Ones end your adventure."

"I'll try."

"I wish you the best of luck," Frans told him. "Remember, you must run from the storm the moment you see it."

"I'll remember, especially if it comes from the west."

"That's right," Frans said, nodding.

Gerd took his leave of both men and started on his way. He crossed the small village at a lively pace. The villagers watched him, filled with curiosity. Frans and Fulker would later tell them who he was and the reason for his visit. Gerd could guess their reactions. Those men and women had enough work with surviving in that frozen landscape. They'd find Gerd's search absurd and reckless. Something only a fool would attempt out here, so far north and in the middle of winter besides.

Chapter 18

The soles of his feet landed on solid ground. Egil struggled to maintain his balance and not fall backwards and managed to remain on the ledge with his back to the abyss. He threw himself forward, intending to hug the rocky wall of the cliff and thus avoid falling.

But he was not expecting what happened next. He fell through the wall. Where there ought to have been rock, he met emptiness. A feeling of great fear overwhelmed him and rose up his throat. He tried to recover his balance and enter the darkness of the void he had stumbled into.

He stood, still trying to get his eyes used to the reigning gloom. While he waited, he bent over to touch the ground he was standing on. It was rock. He reached out to his sides and up but could not touch anything. He jumped upward and his fingers brushed rock. He took a step to the right and touched rock too. He stepped back and then to his left and touched rock again.

"I'm in a cave," he muttered under his breath.

He took a couple of steps forward, carefully, making sure he was on firm ground. Since he could not see anything and could not light a fire in there, he decided to stop and wait. He left his bow and rucksack on the ground and then sat down, facing outward, to the sea. He could barely make it out because of the blackness that surrounded him, but the sound of the waves and the cool of the saltwater reached him perfectly, brought by the breeze.

He wondered whether the ghostly creature would come here. He certainly hoped not. He did not think it had seen him, but he was not sure because it had come so close. If it had seen him, it must have thought he had fallen into the water. That was his hope at least. Now that he was thinking more calmly, the creature or ghostly being had to have seen him, even if it was night. It had been very near. Yes, it must have discovered him, unless its sight was impaired for some reason.

All of a sudden, something came into the cave at great speed. Egil threw his head and body backward from the shock just as Angus landed on the ground beside his feet.

"You scared me, Angus!" Egil cried, trying to keep his voice down so it would not echo.

The owl flapped his wings hard and then clicked his beak. Egil looked at him with his beautiful gray feathers and those owl eyes so characteristic and unique of his species and was infinitely glad to see him.

"Good shelter. Thank you."

Angus seemed to understand him, because he hooted happily.

"Shhhhhh, silence. That being might hear us," Egil told Angus, putting his finger to his lips and then pointing upwards.

Angus stared at him with his large eyes and blinked.

"We'll stay here until the danger's gone," Egil told his companion, not sure he would understand. He did not belong to Wildlife and did not know the way to make an owl stay with its Ranger. What he would not give to have Gerd or Lasgol with him right then! They knew and were able to communicate with an owl. He did not want to start exploring the place at night with a ghost lurking in the vicinity. He thought it would be more intelligent to wait until it went away without finding them out than risk being heard or seen, should he make a fire. He preferred not to take risks—a wary man reached a hundred, as the Norghanian saying went.

They waited for daytime to arrive. Egil was unable to sleep. He was constantly glancing toward the entrance, fearful that at any moment the sea ghost might come in through the opening to cause a pain so unbearable his screams would be heard in the sea leagues away. There were a couple of moments when his eyes drooped and, realizing he had dozed off, woke up startled to find Angus staring at him with his large eyes.

"You keep watch and give warning if the ghost appears," he told him every time he opened his eyes again.

Angus said nothing but turned his head toward the entrance, though Egil guessed it was more because he kept glancing that way uneasily than because the owl had understood the order.

With the first rays of sun sneaking into the cave, Egil was able to see where he was. It was indeed a narrow cave that continued on into the cliff. As he was already there, he decided it would be a good idea to check how far it went. He got to his feet and fetched his equipment.

"I'm going inside, follow me," he told Angus, who looked at him blankly.

He went forward, keeping to one side so that the sun's rays could go in as far as possible and this way see what was ahead of him. He arrived at a bigger cave, but he did not like what he found at the far end. There were over a dozen skeletons piled haphazardly in a sort of funerary mound.

He went over to see them. Those wretches had been dead many years. The first ones he identified, by their armor and clothes in blue and silver, to be Rogdonian. There were several noblemen among them, judging by their high-quality swords and some jewels that remained on the corpses.

A gleam of light on metal revealed a spear trapped between the skeletons. His eyes lit up. It might be the Golden Spear of Rogdon he was looking for, although this one was covered in dust and did not look golden. He pulled on it to study it. It was hard to dislodge from among the bodies that held it trapped. When he finally had it free in his hands, he saw that it was a Rogdonian Lancer's spear, but not the one he was looking for. Disappointment showed on his face.

Angus hooted as if asking whether that was the spear.

"No, my nocturnal friend, this isn't the spear. We'll have to keep looking."

He kept rummaging among the corpses. He did it unceremoniously. Those poor souls would not mind anyway, and he had no time to lose. His Ranger's training took away any qualms he might have had. Another group of skeletons he checked belonged without a doubt to a Nocean expedition. The scimitars and the turbans made that clear. As he studied the corpses, he came to another group that seemed to be from the far east, but in this case Egil could not be sure.

"They seem to have come from different corners of Tremia in search of Rogdon's Golden Spear."

Angus clicked his beak.

"Yeah, and they all found the same ending. A terrible one."

As he examined the corpses, Egil realized they had not died where they were lying, since they were all piled on top of one another. There was no trail he could follow, whatever there had been back in the day had vanished a long time ago. Something else he noticed was that all the groups carried torches. They had come prepared to search in caves and dark places. This could indeed be an indication. If they had all brought torches, it might have been because they knew the treasure was hidden in some gloomy place. It also might have been that they were just far-sighted. He also carried one in his rucksack just in case.

"What is certain is that something discovered them and killed them mercilessly. Yeah, that's what I think happened here. It killed them, most likely at the entrance, and then brought them here and piled them at the bottom of the cave unceremoniously. I'm starting to think it kills for fun and not to feed, since the island is deserted, which is even worse."

Angus hooted as if he agreed with Egil's guess.

"So, we have to avoid being found out, or else we'll end up like them," Egil told him, pointing his finger at the skeletons as if the poor owl could understand him.

Egil spent a good while studying the corpses and the cave itself. Unfortunately, he did not find anything that might help him in is search of the Golden Spear of Rogdon. He had the feeling those poor wretches had run into a dead end and the ghost had discovered them and killed them.

"We'd better get out of here. I don't want us to end up in the mound with them."

Angus said nothing and flew out.

Egil followed him, and when he reached the small ledge, he stopped. The breeze of the sea and the sound of the breakers reached him clearly. He looked up and realized they were no more than six feet to the edge. If he managed to climb a little way up the rock wall, he would be on the cliff top. The only problem was that if he fell, he would die. The height of the cliff was tremendous, and right below his feet he could glimpse enormous rocks where the waves broke.

The other thing was knowing whether the ghost was still hunting or not at the top. There was only one way to find out, so he began to climb the wall, seeking safe support spots and hoping they did not give way when he held on or set his foot on them. He had never been good at climbing, but this was easy if he kept his cool and secured every move. That is what he did and managed to reach the top. He stood up quickly. He still had to check whether the ghost was around or not.

He looked around with his eyes wide open, like one seeking death to avoid it, even knowing that, in the end, it is impossible to do so. But perhaps on this occasion he would.

He could not see the ghost, which eased his mind.

"You don't see it either, do you, Angus?"

The owl was flying not far away and made several passes. He did not seem to find the ghost, since he did not circle to indicate he had found something.

Egil felt better and let out the air in a long breath.

"Very well, let's resume the search," he told Angus, even if he was too far to hear. He hoped the owl would not go off on his own. If he did, he would have trouble going back. Anyway, that was the least of Egil's problems now, but he liked Angus's company, he made him feel less lonely, and although talking to an owl might be taken as a fool's act, Angus was a Rangers' owl, and Egil knew he understood a lot more than his wild counterparts.

He devoted half the day to find some clue on the island. He started with optimism and at a fast pace, but by afternoon he was quite certain the spear was not on this island, or if it was, it had been buried deep somewhere without leaving any mark that would enable him to find it.

He had to give up. It was not there. He had to go to the second island, the one more to the west and a little north, the Island of Donger. It was twice as big as the one Egil was on. He headed to the beach and waited for the tide to be right to launch his boat out to sea. To his joy, Angus appeared and landed on the boat in front of him.

"Welcome, partner. We're going to the second of the islands of the Triangle. It's going to be fun," he told the owl to release the tension he felt.

Angus hooted like a war chant, which Egil really appreciated.

They put out and were able to arrive at the Island of Donger without any problem. The weather had improved and the winds were mild. He found a similar beach to the one he had used on the previous island and landed. The effort of grounding the boat safely was greater though, and this did not make him too happy.

But he recovered fast, ate and drank from his supplies, and checked the land from the beach. It surprised him to see that, although this island was a lot bigger, it was similar to the first one in terrain and vegetation. After a first inspection, he wasted no time and began searching the island. Angus flew over the vegetation a little further ahead, acting as a scout.

Egil searched eagerly all afternoon without wasting time, since he had a lot of land to cover. Unfortunately, no matter how well he searched, he could not find anything. Not a signal, or mark, or significant skeleton, or place—nothing. But he was not downhearted. He had already expected it would not be easy. He was also aware of the fact that it was said that the Golden Spear of Rogdon was hidden there, but there was no guarantee this was so. It might very well not be the case.

Night began to fall, and although he did not want to stop his search, Egil knew he would have to find shelter.

"Shelter, Angus," he ordered.

The owl flew off and looked for a place for Egil to take cover. While Angus was flying, Egil saw with chagrin that the ghost had appeared on the Island of Ronwel. He realized it was already night. Egil guessed that because the creature only made its appearance at night, the locals thought it was a ghost. He believed it more likely to be a night predator they did not know about. He refused to believe it was a ghost.

Angus came back and brushed Egil's head twice to indicate he had found a refuge. Egil knew he had to follow him. He ran after the owl, which started circling beside a steep hill. Without stopping to check, since time was running out and he wanted to hide before the being arrived, Egil climbed the hill to the top, where he could make out the ghost already crossing the sea toward the island where he was.

"It's coming..."

He looked up and saw Angus circling above his head.

"Here?" he asked. He only saw the hill and rocks all around it. A small forest started a little further ahead. Since Angus did not change his flight and there was no shelter in sight, Egil began to go down the slope. Suddenly, under his feet, the slope vanished. Egil stopped abruptly and almost lost his balance, which he managed to keep by flapping his arms like a bird. He looked down and saw the entrance to a cave right under his feet.

"Now I see it. Thank you, Angus," he said, and sliding down one side, he stood before the entrance to the cave. It was dark and did not appear to be very big. He looked at the north side of the island and saw the ghost initiating its abrupt zigzags and turns. It was time to hide.

"Coming inside," he told Angus.

He went in and found it was a small cave with moss-covered walls. He waited a moment for his eyes to get used to the gloom before going further in. The cave looked deserted and empty. He moved away from the entrance so the ghost could not see him in case it passed in front of it. When he reached the end of the cave, he saw there was a passage he had not noticed upon coming in. Between the darkness and the angle the passage was in, it was hidden.

A noise behind him startled him, and he turned fast.

It was Angus, who had just flown into the cave. He hooted in triumph.

"Good job, Angus. Shelter, very good," Egil congratulated him.

Angus walked around the cave and then returned to where Egil was and stared at him.

"We're going to follow that passage. I want to know where it leads."

Angus clicked his beak. He did not like the idea. The cave was a good enough shelter according to him.

"It's a perfect shelter, but I have to investigate in case the spear is hidden here. It might be; you never know when you're looking for hidden treasure."

He entered the passage and followed it, groping along since he could not see a thing. He arrived at another bigger cave with an opening at the top to the east. A little moonlight came in through the opening, and what it lit up was another scene hard to swallow. He saw a new mound of corpses piled haphazardly on top of one another, without respect or consideration. This one was bigger.

"Not good…" he muttered and went over to check them.

Angus came in and stood behind him.

The corpses were mostly Rogdonian and, by the state they were in, more recent than those he had found on the other island. There was also a group of four that looked from the Kingdom of Erenal judging by the short, wide swords and what was left of their armor and clothes, which was not much.

Suddenly, Angus clicked his beak.

It seemed to Egil like a warning. He did not speak and carefully moved away from the light.

A moment later, the ghost passed across the opening of the cave through which light came in. Egil saw the white translucent wake and the ghostly light it emitted and shrunk back. But the ghost did not seem to have seen him, because it passed by.

Egil waited a moment, then he snorted. He went to say something to Angus, but the owl was staring at the opening with his big eyes fixed on it. This made Egil stay quiet.

The ghost passed over the opening at the top a second time.

Egil's heart missed a beat. He had thought it had left and he was safe. Big mistake. He stood as if petrified by a spell. He did not move for a long time. He had the feeling that the moment he moved, the ghost would appear and come through the opening to attack him.

He waited in total silence, Angus beside him. Neither moved nor made a sound. Somehow the owl picked up the danger that lurked around them, as if his raptor bird's instinct warned him that another predator, bigger and more dangerous, was near.

The ghost did not pass by again, and Egil managed to relax at last.

"I'm going to check the skeletons and remains in this place and see if I find anything."

Angus took a few hops to one side.

Egil checked everything he found without much luck. It was a frustrating search, since he could barely see and was relying on touch more than anything else. What worried him was that because of the lack of visibility he might miss some important detail. He thought about lighting his torch, but since the ghost might be close and the light would come out the upper opening, he dismissed the thought. He took his time and searched and searched like a mole that had found a treasure made up of weapons and armor. He found four spears, all common and Rogdonian.

In the end, he had to give up and lie down to sleep in front of the mound of remains. Angus stayed with him, which made him feel better. It was not exactly the pleasantest place to spend the night, although he was beginning to get used to it, since he had already spent two nights in a row sleeping in the Islands of the Triangle of Pain. The good thing was that so far, he had not suffered that pain.

With the first hours of day, they set off again. They did not see the ghost, nor any trace of Rogdon's Golden Spear. After searching the whole island, Egil had to admit the spear was not there.

"We still have the third island, Angus."

The owl hooted.

"Yes, we'll succeed there. Or we'll die at the hands of the ghost, since it seems to live there."

Angus clicked his beak and showed his claws.

"You'll defend me, I know, partner," Egil told him, and they headed to the beach for the boat.

Chapter 19

Egil and Angus had been searching through the third island of the Triangle of Pain for over half the day at a fast pace. The good news was that the ghost had not appeared. This did not surprise Egil, since it was daytime, and every time he had seen this ghostly being or spectral creature, whatever it was, it had only appeared at night. The bad news, on the other hand, was that he could not find any trace of the Golden Spear of Rogdon, no matter how much they searched and searched all over the island.

"It has to be here. It's the most logical answer," he told Angus, who was perched on a rock near Egil, as he checked what looked like a ruined house.

Angus hooted.

Egil smiled at him.

"Thank goodness you're here to cheer me up. I've always thought owls were fascinating and clever animals. You are both and a lot more."

Angus did not seem to understand the compliments, because he simply blinked hard.

At about mid-afternoon they found remains of some stone buildings. This interested Egil, since it indicated there had been human presence on the island, even though it was uninhabited now. He started to study the remains while Angus perched on a nearby tree.

"Someone lived here," he told Angus while he searched, turning over stones and moving remains.

For a good while he went on checking the remains, always at a hard pace, since time was precious and the day diminished, but he left nothing unturned. What troubled him most was making a mistake due to being too hasty. On the other hand, night was coming fast. They would have to find shelter to avoid the ghost.

He stopped for a moment to catch his breath. He looked at Angus, who was watching him from a branch with his usual serenity.

"I was certain this place would shed some light on our search. But it doesn't seem so. Anyway, I'm going to take one last look in case I missed something." He did not lose heart and kept searching among the ruins. Unfortunately, as he had anticipated, he did not find anything significant.

"We keep looking," he told Angus with a wave of his hand.

He went on searching throughout the rest of the island which, being a lot bigger than the other two, forced him to go fast, which is not good when you are looking for something. Luckily, the vegetation did not pose much of a problem and the terrain did not either, since it was pretty flat, with only a couple of peaks that were not too high. They wore out his legs a little when he climbed them, but Egil managed to do it without stopping and without any physical problems. He went up and came down and walked over the plain, searching among rocks, trees, and vegetation that was not too tall. But he did not find what he was looking for.

Tired and a little disappointed, he sat down to think on a relatively large rock. He had searched all over the island and, just like in the other two, which were similar in landscape, he was not having any success. The islands were not only uninhabited, but also the few remains left in them indicated it had been a long time since anyone had lived there. Most likely it was because of the ghost, although it might also be that the islands had been abandoned long before. In any case, there was no sign that indicated the place where the spear had been hidden.

He took out his notebook and went over it all in case he might get a new idea. This was something he did often, and many times it worked well. It helped him generate new ideas when the problem seemed to have no solution. But in this situation, the data he had only led him to where he was. There was no information that might tell him the possible place where the weapon had been hidden.

He sighed. After thinking, he realized there was only one more searching technique left which he had developed with Angus by accident, the "shelter technique" he had called it, and it had given unsuspected and positive results, so he decided to use it.

"Shelter?" he asked Angus.

The owl hooted and flew off.

Egil knew this was a desperate measure, but in the other two islands it had worked, so he hoped it would here too. It was not a very rational search method, but if something worked, rational or not, he had to try, especially when the situation was desperate.

He waited for Angus to come back with optimism in his heart, and as he had expected, Angus did not fail him. He appeared, gliding, and passed twice above his head. Egil picked up his bow and satchel and ran after the owl, who led him to the most northern part of the island. Egil did not like this at all, since that was the area where the ghost first appeared every night and the day was coming to an end.

"What's here?" Egil asked Angus when he saw him circling around the northern point of the island. "I see nothing but a clearing, and I guess it ends in a cliff. You're not preparing another fall into the abyss, are you?"

Angus continued flying in circles, always over the same spot.

Egil was surprised, but he went over to check. There was only grass and a few rocks scattered around the spot.

"Here?" Egil looked up at the sky. As he did so and stepped forward, the earth under his right foot gave in. He looked down and saw that the grass that covered the ground was actually covering a large hole. He tried to pull back so he did not fall in, but it was too late.

He fell into the hole, which swallowed him completely.

The blow was hard.

He fell on something hard, which he soon realized was another mound of warriors' skeletons. He had the good fortune that, although the blow was hard, he did not fall on any weapon or sharp, pointed object, and there were many. He managed to grab something solid and did not roll down the mound of remains, which would have been not only painful but very dangerous. Out of the corner of his eye he made out swords, spears, and knives in different positions.

"Phewwww!" he whistled without moving from the top of the pile.

Angus came down and perched on the helmet of a Rogdonian noble.

"You could've warned me…" Egil complained.

Angus blinked hard.

"I almost killed myself. Shelter is one thing. It's a very different thing to end up stuck on a bunch of rusty weapons."

A click of Angus' beak said clearly that the owl did not think the same. It seemed to say, "shelter is shelter."

Carefully, Egil sat up. He saw that what he had grasped was nothing but the femur of a soldier stuck between the bones of two other skeletons. From where he was, he could see that the number of skeletons here was at least three times that of the other two he had found. He thought it was horrible and at the same time hopeful, since the large number of dead bodies indicated this might be the place.

He got to his feet as best he could and saw that the hole he had fallen through was about six feet above his head. He figured it would be easy to get out of there. He carried a rope in his satchel, and with the number of weapons in there, he would have no trouble making a hook or using a spear for the end of the rope. He started down the pile and realized it might be difficult. When he stepped on the skeletons they sank or the bones broke, so he could lose his footing or get caught in something and fall on his head.

He proceeded down carefully. As he had to go slowly, he also examined what was under his feet and around him. In this new mound of corpses, he found many Rogdonians, Noceans, and Erenalians. It seemed they were the three most interested in finding the spear. He was also puzzled to find several groups of adventurers whose origin he was unable to determine. While he went down, he gathered information as slowly and carefully as he could. He had the feeling that, at any moment, that mountain of bones and steel was going to crumble under his feet.

Once he reached the ground, he moved back just in case. The last thing he wanted was to be buried under a mountain of dead bodies. It would not be a glorious end. What a hero he would make. Just thinking about it brought a smile to his face, although the place did not exactly bring joy to the heart.

He realized he was in a cavern and that the hole he had fallen through was at the top and lit up a clear area of blackish rock. He decided to check the cave and its wretched inhabitants before going on. One thing he found out was that, besides the number of skeletons being greater, the quality of their weapons and armor was as well. All these were nobles and adventurers who were well financed if they came seeking the Golden Spear of Rogdon.

One thing that left him worried was that among the corpses he found at least four magi or warlocks. He guessed by their robes and because they had staves with runes that looked arcane with gems at their tips. If the ghost had been capable of killing magi, things became even more complicated, since it meant this being was extremely powerful. It was one thing for a sword or spear to be unable to pierce an incorporeal silhouette, and a very different one that it could endure magic attacks. It could also have been that it had surprised the magi, but seeing that they had been with soldiers of different groups, he guessed they had come with different expeditions. He did not think it was likely the ghost would have surprised them all.

He snorted hard. No, they had not been taken by surprise, since he himself had seen the creature in the distance every night. Expert soldiers and magi with them had surely seen it too. It was more than likely they had faced the ghost and it had killed them. If magic had not been able to defeat it, Egil wondered what could. He did not want to confront the spectral being—the piles of corpses he had found were clear indications that it was better not to approach that creature. He would rather find the spear and get out of there before it caught up with him. On the other hand, if he did not finish off the ghost, whoever came to the islands would meet the same fate.

"Or maybe not…"

One thing came to his mind. All the corpses he had found were of nobles, soldiers, and magi. He had not found any fishermen or people who were unarmed. The dead had come without a doubt seeking Rogdon's Golden Spear, and that's why they were piled up. But, where were the normal people who had also arrived at the Triangle of Pain, because these islands were close to the Rogdonian coast. Did it scare them and cause them to flee? Did it kill them too but not add them to the pile of bodies? If this was the case, where did it take the remains then?

These matters were turning over and over in his mind. Since he did not have the answers, he decided to take advantage of the remaining daylight to explore the cavern properly. He found it only had one other entrance, through a tunnel to the south. He went over to check and saw a passage that could easily either be an entrance or a way out, meaning that it must lead to another cave or outside. He would have to follow it and see where it went.

"I'm going to check this passage," he told Angus.

The owl hooted and went after him, hopping.

The passage turned out to be shorter than Egil had expected. It did not go outside but into another cave which he went into, down a long ramp of rough stone. The cavern was large, and in the middle there was a pond of dark water. Light came in through two openings at the top, and although he could not see the whole cavern, it did allow some visibility. Egil went to the pond and examined it. The water seemed to come from one of the walls, along which it fell down as if the rock were weeping.

He walked around the pond, checking the cave. Suddenly, he saw something that caught his attention. He saw a flash at the end, beyond the pond. He thought it might be a gold coin. He bent over to see it better. He passed his glove along it to clean it and something odd happened. The metal object cut the glove as if it were silk and cut his finger too. Egil felt the sting of pain and withdrew his hand. He took off his glove and saw he had a pretty deep cut in his finger, which was now bleeding.

"All I did was brush against it…" he muttered to himself, baffled.

Angus heard him and hooted.

He had to put his rucksack and bow on the ground to look after his cut. He took out the water-skin to clean the wound. A metal object in here had to be rusty, and it would surely get infected. He took out an ointment to prevent infections and made a quick cure. While he was doing this, he watched the object, which had not moved when he touched it. It was fixed in the ground. It was not a coin, but it might be an indicator or clue he could follow.

He used his knife to dig out the object, since he could already see it was not what he had thought. The earth around the object was moist from being so close to the pond, so it was easier than he had expected to dig around it a little. The problem he met when he had taken out some earth around the object was that it was long, round, and went down farther into the ground. It was buried in the dirt floor of the cavern.

"It looks like I'll have to dig it all out to see what it is," he told Angus, who was staring at him, moving his head from side to side.

Egil started digging with his knife and axe. It took him a long while to reveal the upper part of the object. It was buried diagonally. It was metal and round. Being covered in earth, he could not tell exactly what it was, so Egil took water from the pond and wiped the object carefully, except at the tip to avoid getting another cut. Once he had it clean and looked at it from a distance, Egil stared at it with his mouth open.

"It can't be…"

The round object gleamed with golden flashes caused by the light falling on the metal surface. He was looking at the tip of a spear, a golden one.

"It's the Golden Spear of Rogdon!" Egil cried, unable to believe his eyes.

Angus was startled by his cry and clicked his beak.

Egil was staring at the upper end of the weapon in astonishment. It was beautiful, the color of gold, and it had some runes or strange symbols all along the weapon. He had no doubt it was a weapon with power.

"I found it! It exists!" he cried joyfully.

He set out to dig up the weapon eagerly. The excitement gave him renewed strength and vitality. But shortly after that he encountered obstacles. The spear was longer than he had expected, and not only that, the earth it was stuck in was hard and there were stones and pieces of rock mixed in it.

"This is getting complicated. You wouldn't have a spade by any chance?" he asked Angus.

The owl hooted.

"I thought so. I'll have to improvise."

He went back to the other cave, to the pile of skeletons, and searched among the weapons for something to dig with. He found several spears to break the hard surface and some helmets to bail out the earth. He went back to where Rogdon's Golden Spear was and continued working hard. Now that he had better tools, he was making progress, even if he went slowly and the effort was great.

He continued until only the back end of the spear was still buried. He started to pull on it as hard as he could, but it would not budge. He hung from it using his weight so it would dislodge at the base it was buried in, but that did not work either. He had to dig again and remove earth and rock. He had been so concentrated on his work and with such spirit that he did not notice that day had passed and night had already fallen. He could barely see a thing, but the golden weapon seemed to emit a faint light which was enough to keep working.

He almost had it. The Golden Spear of Rogdon was almost in his hands.

And at that moment, the water of the black pond started to glow.

Angus clicked his beak and took off.

Puzzled, Egil turned around.

Floating in the pond of black water, the ghost appeared. It was as if it had been there the whole time, submerged, and now had come up to the surface of the pond.

With the shock, he gave a start and jumped to the other side of the golden spear. In the middle of the pond, as if it were the corpse of a drowned person, the ghost was floating. It began to ascend, hovering above the pond.

Egil swallowed. He was doomed.

Chapter 20

Egil watched with disbelief and fear as the ghost rose above the dark pond from which it had appeared. The fact that it came out from the bottom of the pond with the intangible head and ghostly white body fit perfectly with the legend that said it was a drowned sailor, just as Gordon had told him.

He felt lost. If it was indeed a ghost, his bow and arrows or his knife and axe were useless against it, since it was already dead and incorporeal. He tried to keep calm, something almost impossible to do in such a situation, and think of a solution to the huge problem right in front of him. From what Egil had read about ghosts, and he did not believe in them, they could only be killed in a certain way. You had to use sacred or light magic or weapons. He looked at his bow beside his rucksack and quiver on the ground. Unfortunately, he had no sacred or light weapon, or magic. He understood the concept—it was rational, founded even—even though he did not share it. The ghost was an evil being of darkness, therefore only something that was good, sacred, or light focused could kill it.

But now that he saw it so close, and once he had controlled the panic that rose through his throat from his stomach, he had the feeling this was no ghost. From what he was witnessing, under the glow and ghostly light it emitted, it looked rather like some kind of being or creature. The head, though rounded, was not that of a human. It was too domed; in fact, it looked like the head of a large white mushroom. The body, to call it that, was not human either. He could see hundreds of traces of thick, long threads that made up a bright whitish wake. They gave the impression of tentacles stuck to one another. They looked most curious. If it were not for the fact that he knew he was in a life-death situation, he would have found the creature fascinating and the encounter absolutely fantastic.

He narrowed his eyes and gazed at the whole creature. It reminded him of something, of another creature. He continued studying it, since it was not moving. It appeared to be slowly waking up but not fully awake yet. Suddenly, he realized what the being reminded him of: a large jellyfish. This thought puzzled him. Could this be some kind of giant jellyfish? It had come out of the water, so it might be that. Yet, this being flew, or at least levitated, which burst his theory. On the other hand, jellyfish had venom, and the sting of some species was very painful. If this creature was some kind of giant jellyfish, its sting could be extremely painful for a human and, after time, the amount of venom it could inject into a person would surely kill him or her and they would die in insufferable pain. This did fit in with the screams the fishermen had heard.

At the thought that this creature might sting him, Egil shivered. For the moment it was just hovering and had not seen him, which was odd. But, as soon as it did, it would surely come at him to inject him with its venom. If he remembered correctly, jellyfish stung with hundreds of tiny stings. This giant jellyfish must have thousands of them. This explained the screams of pain of the poor people it attacked. Just thinking about it gave him gooseflesh.

The giant jellyfish seemed to be waking up from a deep lethargy. It was going to activate any moment now, Egil could sense it. He would have to defend himself. Slowly, he bent down to pick his quiver. He put it on his back without rising. Then he picked his bow and carefully nocked an arrow and prepared to release. The distance was too close, so he tried not to make the slightest noise. He took a couple of steps back, leaving the Golden Spear between the jellyfish and himself. He aimed at the body, at the bunch of tentacles. The bright whitish light the creature was emitting in the middle of the darkness of the cavern made it look indeed like a ghost hovering in the air.

Egil looked at the Golden Spear of Rogdon he had been working on to dig out. It had been buried parallel to the ground but at a slight upward angle. The tip was sticking out of the ground and the end was a little deeper. He had taken all the earth out around the weapon and there was only the end part of it that he had not had time to free. The golden weapon was between the jellyfish and the hole in the ground Egil had excavated, which was no more than three hand-spans deep. It was fully visible.

The creature finished waking up. Suddenly, it shook the tentacles that made up its body. Egil was able to see that they were indeed luminescent tentacles which glowed white when they moved, giving the creature that ghostly aura. The oval head turned and faced Egil. He saw no eyes or nose; it seemed to have none.

Then it turned, spinning completely in the air. The tentacles faced Egil and the head faced the other way. The body of tentacles was swaying, seeming to want to embrace him. The creature began to move toward Egil without the least sound, like a spectral assassin capable of levitating.

"I don't want to fight..." said Egil, who was already prepared to jump.

The creature did not reply and continued approaching slowly without changing either the pace or the height that separated it from the ground.

"I only want Rogdon's Golden Spear. I'll take it and leave. There's no need to fight," Egil said as he took two more steps back. His back touched the rocky wall. There was nowhere left to go.

The giant levitating jellyfish continued its advance.

Egil released at the body.

Something entirely unexpected happened. With a swift movement, the tentacles glowed white and moved. They hit the arrow and deflected it, preventing it from hitting any organ. Egil was struck dumb. The creature's reflexes were amazing. He nocked another arrow and released again. The giant jellyfish deflected the arrow with its white, translucent tentacles.

Now he understood why all those soldiers had not been able to kill it. The creature's reflexes and its multiple tentacles had stopped swords, spears, and arrows from reaching and killing it.

Seeing it was coming at him and he would not have time to release again, Egil decided to try and dodge it.

He moved to the right.

So did the creature.

Egil stood behind the Spear in the center, and the creature tried to pass over the golden weapon as a shortcut to get to him. As it did so, the spear flashed gold and something affected the creature, because it was thrown back while it gave off a white flash which ran from the head to the tip of its tentacles.

Egil realized the Golden Spear of Rogdon had reacted to the creature's presence, which surprised him, since he had been pulling on the spear with all his might, touching it, and nothing had happened. He thought for a moment. It had to have something to do with magic. The creature must have some kind of magic the Spear had detected and rejected. He found all this fascinating. The only problem was that he was about to die in the midst of insufferable pain with thousands of stings buried in his body, injecting him with venom.

He moved again to stand with the Spear between him and the creature and nocked another arrow. This time he used an Elemental Arrow, since the regular one had been useless.

The creature came straight at him, and now it did so at great speed, maintaining its height. Egil released and the Earth Arrow headed to the tentacles. These reacted and hit the arrow to deflect it. In so doing, the arrow burst and there was an explosion of earth and smoke. The creature did not like this at all, and it withdrew at once with an evasive movement as if it were swimming in the ocean, only it was levitating in midair.

"Well, that's something..." Egil muttered.

The creature lowered several of its tentacles into the water, and these began to glow as it appeared to drink the water. But it was not drinking, it was healing itself, using the water to that end. Once again, he found it fascinating and thought of something as he saw the tentacles in contact with the surface of the water. He nocked another Elemental Arrow and, without waiting for the creature to react, he aimed and released. This time he shot at the water, right at the edge but just under the surface. The Air Arrow entered the water and burst upon contact with the rocky bottom. There was an electric discharge that ran throughout the surface of the pond and reached the creature's tentacles. The discharge ran up them and reached the head of the jellyfish.

Egil watched as the creature withdrew quickly as if it had received a tremendous lash. The discharge had hurt it, he had no doubt about that. Seeing he had achieved a small advantage, he nocked another Air Arrow and released. The creature had already withdrawn from the pond, which proved its intelligence, and, spreading its tentacles, it allowed the arrow to pass through its body and hit the far-end wall. The detonation and the discharge did not reach the creature, which attacked again.

Seeing it was coming to get him, Egil shielded himself behind the Spear once again. The giant spectral jellyfish came straight at him, infuriated by the discharge it had received. It changed course when it reached the Spear and tried going around it on the left, so Egil moved to the other side of the Spear, keeping it between him and the jellyfish. The creature continued going around the Spear without passing over it. Egil was trying to make the jellyfish pass or brush over the Spear in the hopes that the Golden weapon would act. He managed after a few movements left and right. The Spear gave off a golden flash. The jellyfish gave off a whitish one. Both magics collided and the jellyfish was thrown backward. The Spear's magic was more powerful than that of the jellyfish, which Egil had been hoping for and expecting. After all, the Spear was a legendary weapon, capable of killing a dragon, a more powerful creature than this jellyfish. On the other hand, the jellyfish had killed all kind of nobles, magi, soldiers, and adventurers. Egil was no rival for this being.

The creature withdrew to one side of the cave, out of the water and far from the Spear. It made a move as if it were approaching the water, and Egil nocked an Air Arrow. The creature wanted to heal its wounds in the water, but it saw Egil's movement and changed course. It made a couple of swift abrupt movements and began to go up and down. Egil realized he was in serious trouble; the jellyfish was calculating how to go around the Spear with swift movements and changes in height. It would come at him now.

The jellyfish went straight for the Spear, but at the last moment it rose and made to pass over it, close to the ceiling. Egil released his Air Arrow and the jellyfish spread its tentacles to let it through. It flew above the upper part of the Spear, which did not react. It was coming at him, and he was going to die.

Suddenly, something hit the jellyfish hard, making it come down. It was Angus. He had ploughed into the creature, claws first.

"Angus, no!" Egil cried, watching the owl fall to the ground and start shaking in pain with its beak open. The sting of the tentacles had reached him.

The jellyfish hit the upper part of the Spear and tried to rise. The Spear emitted a powerful flash and the jellyfish was thrown against the ceiling of the cavern. It crashed hard and fell at Egil's feet.

The creature seemed unconscious from the blow and the effect of the Spear's magic. Egil grabbed a Fire Arrow from his quiver, dropped the bow, and grasped the arrow with both hands. He buried it in the creature's head with all his strength. There was a detonation and a flame. Egil was expecting it and moved his face away as fast as he could. He singed his arms and hands, but his Ranger's gloves and leather vambrances held pretty well. He took a second arrow and buried it in the creature's head as it tried to rise in the air with part of its head in flames. The second arrow made the jellyfish catch on fire more, and it fled to the water to put the flames out and heal itself.

The second burst of fire did penetrate the singed protections Egil was wearing, and he got burned. He held back a cry of pain, clenching his jaw firmly. He composed himself and picked his bow, looking for another Air Arrow in his quiver and finding he only had one left. He nocked it. The jellyfish was still half-submerged, head first. If it went completely underwater, it would put out the fire and escape.

He released and hit the tip of its tentacles as it was going completely under. There was the discharge, which passed from the tentacles to the water and electrocuted the jellyfish.

The creature was left floating dead on the water.

"Phew..." Egil snorted, relieved and sore. He turned at once to the brave Angus. He dropped the bow and tended to him. His heart had stopped from the effect of the jellyfish's venom. Egil started giving him a cardiac massage, pressing rhythmically with two fingers, trying to restart the brave owl's heart.

"Come on, Angus, come back to me," Egil was saying as he continued to give him the cardiac massage. He felt awful for what had happened to the bird.

"Don't die on me now, we defeated it, and we have Rogdon's Golden Spear," Egil was telling Angus as he kept massaging his heart.

Suddenly, Angus opened his eyes wide and started emitting a shrill sound. It was a cry of pain.

"I know it hurts a lot. Hold on, Angus, don't give up."

The owl started flapping his wings on the ground and shrieking with screams that broke Egil's heart.

For a long while Egil witnessed his partner's agony. He had no antidote for jellyfish venom, and he could do nothing except focus on pulling out the stings left in Angus's body. They were pretty big and he could see them easily. He managed to get them all out and Angus fell unconscious, exhausted. Egil also applied an acid similar to vinegar on Angus's plumage, which he carried to fight insect bites. This should help with the venom. He waited a moment to make sure the owl's heart did not stop again, but he seemed to be stable.

While he waited for Angus to come to, he looked at the Golden

Spear of Rogdon. It was beautiful, made entirely of gold, with engraved symbols and runes which glowed with golden flashes. It ended in a sharp tip that looked lethal, so he would need to not touch it under any circumstance or he might lose a finger. He had already tasted how sharp it was in spite of the passage of time, and also witnessed how powerful its magic was.

Determinedly, he set down to work and finished freeing it entirely.

He picked it in his hand and noticed that, although it was as tall as Gerd, it weighed no more than a knife. How could such a weapon be so light? He moved it from one side to another with his right hand and delivered several cutting and penetrating thrusts. His arm did not feel the weight or any resistance with the air. This weapon had been designed to be able to fight with it for days without getting tired.

He was amazed.

Not only that, he felt powerful, invincible.

Chapter 21

Aibin was right. When they got to the harbor of Albahrwalm, they were met with a flurry of activity and several ships headed to Zenut. He did not have much trouble finding passage for him and Nilsa on one of the cargo ships. He avoided the military vessels or those who carried troops: the officers would ask too many questions, and it was best to maintain their anonymity. He chose a ship that carried food, water, and other supplies for the army. Nilsa had some gold Egil had given her, so they did not run into any problems.

The journey by sea had an interesting start, since shortly after leaving the harbor Nilsa could see the large silhouette of Cinders Island in the distance. She then realized how far south they were. Seeing the island brought back the memory of the adventure the Panthers had lived there, when the search for the Dragon Orb had taken them to this place by using a Pearl to open a Portal. She remembered the dangerous natives who inhabited the jungle island and the great volcano, which had housed the fossilized body the dragon claimed for his own. It had been an intense adventure and terribly dangerous.

Nilsa mused about her life and adventures. Little by little, she was traveling throughout much of Tremia. She had never imagined she would travel so extensively. As a rule, the Rangers served in Norghana, and most of them had never set foot outside Norghana their whole lives. She and the Panthers had traveled through much of the continent, which she loved and found fascinating. She had seen distant, exotic lands and met interesting people—people like Aibin, who fascinated her.

She looked at her partner in her current adventure, who sat beside her and was looking overboard at the sea.

"Have you ever been at sea?"

"No, never. It's awesome."

"And the sea? Had you ever seen it before?"

"Not like this. I've seen it from the desert. It's overwhelming, so immense once you're in it. I feel a little lost."

"Yeah, the immensity of the sea can do that. But you're with me, don't worry," Nilsa said to make him feel easier.

"All this water around us..."

"Don't drink it, it's salty," Nilsa chuckled.

Aibin smiled.

"I knew that."

"Do you know how to make it drinkable?"

"Well... no... how?"

"I'll show you. It's a seamen's trick for when they run out of water on the ship."

"There's so much left for me to see, experience, and learn." Aibin's gaze was lost in the horizon.

"Take it easy. You have all the time in the world."

"Not really. One day I'll have to return to my land and rule, if my older brother doesn't want to follow my father's footsteps."

"Doesn't he?"

"He's not sure. He wants to learn, see the world. Lead the tribe? Not so much. I hope he sees reason after his learning journey and takes the post."

"Me too. Well, if that's what you want. Or do you want to be your father's successor and lead the tribe?"

"I only want my father to be proud of me. If I have to take over the responsibility, I will. If that's not necessary because my brother takes it, I'll also be happy."

"I'm impressed you feel that way. You have a noble heart."

"I've been brought up that way. It's my parents' merit, not mine."

"They did a good job."

"Thank you. I'll try not to disappoint them."

"And you won't."

"I'll have to struggle every day to achieve that. Difficult situations, tough decisions... I'll have to make them as they come and hope I don't make mistakes."

"Erring makes us human. Admitting it and doing the right thing is what matters in the end."

Aibin looked Nilsa in the eye.

"You're right. I'll make mistakes, I'll just have to learn from them and try to fix them."

"But don't forget to live," Nilsa said, chuckling.

Aibin laughed. "Forgive me, I got too serious. I just don't want to fail in my duties toward my father and people."

"I completely understand you. Don't be too hard on yourself. Enjoy the sea," Nilsa said with a wave of her hand that encompassed the beautiful view in front of them.

"I'll enjoy the sea and your company," Aibin added, and he looked into her eyes with his intense ruby ones.

Nilsa felt her skin crawl and butterflies fluttering in her stomach. Neither said anything for a long time. They enjoyed the sea and each other's company. The sailors came and went, but Nilsa and Aibin did not even notice, lost as they were in the moment.

The days they spent on the sea flew by since the wind was pushing them, and the climate was not as intense as it had been in the desert. Nilsa enjoyed being on deck with Aibin and the good weather. The desert had been left behind, along with the insufferable heat, and at sea she felt fantastic. She still had to cover herself from the sun, since at some stages of the journey it was too scorching. The sailors and the ship's captain paid no attention to them; they had other concerns. From what Aibin had heard, the ship had left port a few days late and the officers waiting for the supplies in Zenut were likely unhappy.

One day at noon, a day with a strong, warm breeze, Nilsa discovered they were finally arriving at the port city.

"There it is. Zenut," she pointed the city out to Aibin.

"Indeed. That's the walled city of Zenut, an important port city of the Nocean Empire."

"Have you been there?"

"No, but it's one of the cities I have to visit in my learning journey through the desert lands. I've always wanted to visit it."

"Well, look at that, today your wish comes true," she said, smiling.

Nilsa was sorry that the journey by sea was coming to an end. She had enjoyed it a lot—the peace and quiet, the good weather, and the best company. Unfortunately, duty called, and she had to respond and find the gold javelin.

The entrance to the harbor was complicated because of the large number of military ships and cargo vessels anchored there. The soldiers of the Nocean Empire preferred to travel by sea rather than crossing the desert in order to go from one city to another whenever possible. For Nilsa, it made all the sense in the world. Crossing deserts was crazy, even for its dwellers. So, they had to wait until they found a mooring in one of the cargo docks. The shouts of captains and bosses, and the arguments about who had precedence over who, continued all afternoon. Finally, when the sun was already going down, they arrived at the pier and were able to set their feet on solid land. Really, only a few came on shore, like them, coming to Zenut to do different things, because the crew could not set foot on land. They had to stay to unload everything they had brought in the hold. Nilsa felt bad for them; they would have to work well into the night.

When they set foot on the pier, they met officers and soldiers waiting. Nilsa and Aibin looked down and headed unobtrusively toward the larger north docks, hoping to enter the city from there. The soldiers were there for the precious cargo that had arrived late, not for them. There were many people everywhere, not only soldiers, and everyone seemed to be in a hurry for some reason or another. The cries and the urgency were ever present, which favored them since no one was paying attention to who landed but to what they had to do. Later, on the bigger docks, they saw large numbers of Nocean soldiers being organized into groups by their officers. They were grouping them and leading them off the pier in lines of two. No one noticed Nilsa and Aibin, and they were not stopped when they entered the lower part of the city.

The city of Zenut was a wonder, much bigger than the city of Albahrwalm and dedicated to sea trade and fishing. It was also a martial city, with several huge buildings in the center in the Nocean military style. The wall protecting the city was also imposing, about forty-five-feet tall and thick. By the way it was strengthened facing the sea and the number of sentinels on the battlements looking toward the ocean, this city had been attacked from the sea on more than one occasion.

But what really captured Nilsa's attention as she walked through the city was how different the Nocean architecture and the buildings were compared to the Norghanian style. Here everything ended in cupolas, many of which were golden, and the walls were made of desert stone and sand-colored, not the grayish blue of the quarried rock of Norghana. The windows and doors were also domed in contrast to the straight, square shapes of the Norghanian buildings.

Carts with supplies, groups of soldiers, and officers on horseback were hastening along the wide avenues, heading toward the north gate to leave the city. The question was where might Albahel Aldhar be. They had to find him, and in such a large city in the midst of so much hustle and bustle due to the presence of the Emperor's armies, it was going to be complicated

"We'd better ask discretely," Nilsa said to Aibin.

"Yes, you wait for me here."

"Where are you going?"

"To the market. It's the best source of information in any city. At least, that's what my father says."

"Yes, that's most likely true."

"I'll be back quickly," he said and went to ask in a bustling market.

While Nilsa waited, she watched the soldiers marching toward the gate. The Nocean soldiers were very different from the Norghanians. Nilsa was fascinated by their dark skin, black eyes, and long, dark, curly hair. They were not tall and strong like the Norghanians; they looked much thinner, agile, and fast. They wore long blue tunics over black baggy pants. They were protected by long chainmail armor that covered their thighs. On their chest and back they wore a cuirass, and this was engraved in the center with the image of the sun, the Nocean emblem. They wore the typical Nocean helmet, rounded and crowned by a sharp tip, a handspan high. They carried scimitars and each had a long, curved knife at their waist. They were marching at a martial step, spear in one hand and small round shield in the other.

When she saw them pass, group after group, Nilsa had the feeling that these soldiers were seasoned, dangerous, and knew how to fight and did it well. They would be tough to defeat in battle. The officers that led them rode white and black horses with coats that shone with a special glow. They were desert horses, slim and beautiful, of a race Nilsa had never seen in the north. Another thing she found curious was that the Nocean army used camels and dromedaries, and not only for cargo. She saw several mounted regiments passing which rode camels and dromedaries instead of horses. Nilsa wondered what they would be like in battle. It was one thing to ride a war horse, a strong creature capable of charging and knocking down a soldier or another mount. It was an entirely different matter to ride these desert animals which, although they could charge, as Aibin had proven, did not seem like the best animals to use as cavalry. On the other hand, if the battle took place in the desert, horses were not the best choice either. Nilsa was watching a Nocean mounted regiment, wondering about all this, when Aibin came back.

"Did you have any luck? It took you a long time."

"It was difficult, but I found the information."

"Good?"

Aibin made a face.

"Albahel Aldhar has already left the city."

"Oh dear…"

"He's headed for Salansamur, to the outskirts of the city where the Nocean army is gathered."

"Do you think the information is trustworthy?"

"Yes, I think so. A merchant Albahel Aldhar deals with gave it to me. He told me Albahel spoke to him about Antior's Beam and that he's looking for buyers."

"Then the information was good. He won't have sold it already, right?"

Aibin shook his head.

"He's asking for too much gold. So far, he hasn't had any buyers. He hasn't found anyone who'll pay the amount he's asking for."

"I don't know whether that's good or bad…" Nilsa was thoughtful.

"We'll have to go to Salansamur."

"Exactly," Nilsa said, troubled.

"Is that bad?"

"You have no idea. Very bad."

Aibin looked at her blankly, and Nilsa realized she would have to tell him something about what was really happening in the city, which would lead her to reveal the existence of the Immortal Dragon. He deserved to know the truth, especially if he was going to help her get the Beam and travel with her to that cursed city. Needless to say, it was going to be an interesting conversation.

"What should we do?"

"Look for supplies and camels and head to Salansamur."

"Alright."

"On the way, I'll tell you what's going on there and why it's so important we find Antior's Beam."

Aibin said nothing and just nodded. Nilsa saw concern in his ruby eyes, and that same feeling overwhelmed her heart too.

Chapter 22

The journey through the desert to the outskirts of Salansamur was quiet. They moved behind the large caravans of the Nocean Army, keeping their distance and without walking on the stone path that linked both cities. They veered toward the oasis of Tanwalha first, but they found it taken up by the army so they went on, moving carefully so they did not draw the soldiers' attention. Nilsa had used the time during their journey to tell Aibin what was really happening in the cursed city and why it was so important they find the gold javelin. To Nilsa's surprise, Aibin did not doubt a word of what she told him for a moment. He believed everything, something she really appreciated.

He did not ask much about the matter, and Nilsa did not say more than she thought was necessary. If Aibin wanted more information, she would give it to him when he asked. Anyway, she trusted him fully, and based on what the handsome desert dweller with ruby eyes was proving, he also trusted her. This was important to Nilsa for several reasons, the most important of which was that they were heading into terrible danger.

They reached the top of some dunes, and what they saw in the distance left them speechless. In the plains of sand before the cursed city of Salansamur, thousands of soldiers belonging to the Nocean Army were getting ready for a potential battle. They were some two thousand paces from the city, which remained deserted and silent, as if it had been robbed of its soul.

A little further back, they could see several hundred tents where the army had been preparing. They could see large numbers of servants who worked with the supplies carts and quartermaster who had arrived at the camp. But there were no officers left in the camp itself; they were all ready for the upcoming battle and maneuvering before the camp, their eyes set on the cursed city.

"Awesome. How many soldiers do you think there are?" Aibin asked Nilsa.

"I'm counting, give me a moment... about fifteen thousand soldiers, five thousand mounted and ten thousand infantry."

"You have a good eye for these things. I couldn't count them."

"Let's say it's part of my trade. I have to be able to pass relevant information to my superiors. The number and type of enemy troops are part of that information."

"I see. Maybe you can teach me how to do that."

"Better if you don't find yourself mixed up in that kind of task."

"Fair enough, but if you teach me, I can teach my people."

"No problem, I'll teach you."

"Thank you. One day it'll come in handy."

"I can see the flag of the Nocean Empire, the sun emblem in bright gold on a black background, right?" Nilsa said, not missing a detail. The desert plain was covered with men in black, blue, and gold, proudly carrying banners that showed a radiant gold sun.

"That's right. Whenever you see that emblem, it's the armies of Emperor Malotas."

"How many soldiers make up the Nocean Empire? I mean in total, do you have any idea?"

"My father says the armies of Emperor Malotas are immense. He calculates he can count on over fifty thousand soldiers, seasoned children of the desert."

"Wow, that's what I call a real army," Nilsa shook her hand to emphasize the fact.

"Yes, hence the Emperor has only sent a third of his forces here today to face the threat."

"It seems like he doesn't believe the threat is serious enough to worry about it," Nilsa guessed.

"Well, he obviously is worried because he sent fifteen thousand soldiers, and that tells me he's concerned."

"True, which makes me think something else…"

"Which is?"

"Why Emperor Malotas is sending such a large army. You told me he heard rumors about the cursed city."

"Rumors harmful for the Emperor. Since he hasn't stopped the problem in one of his cities, it makes him appear weak."

"Yeah, but I wonder whether those rumors have spread a lot or little."

"They've spread throughout the desert, that much I can tell you. We all knew, and we're a tribe that lives hidden in some out-of-the-way mountains. In every city of the empire, there was talk of what was going on in Salansamur."

Nilsa nodded thoughtfully.

"Doesn't it sound weird that word has spread about a problem in one specific city?"

Aibin thought about it.

"Now that you mention it, there has been trouble in other cities, revolts, and in general we didn't hear about it until much later. Some I'm sure we haven't even heard of."

"That's what I mean. The Emperor is covering his problems to minimize the impact on his rule. Why is he not hiding what's happening in Salansamur?"

"I don't have an answer to that question."

"I think I do. Someone has been spreading the rumors from city to city."

"Who?"

"I think I know who's spread the rumors, forcing the Emperor to act. Someone very intelligent who uses information well."

Aibin was staring at Nilsa expectantly.

"Do you know this person?"

"Very well. He's a good friend of mine. Very intelligent. A master of plans and skilled in the art of information."

"Well, he's done a great job. He's managed to make the Emperor send this great army here."

"Who leads it?" Nilsa asked, changing the subject.

"I asked around in the city. General Muleine is in command. From what I've been told, he's skilled on the battlefield. He has proven experience, and is who the Emperor sends to pacify areas where the worst revolts are. He's ruthless and bloodthirsty: that's why Emperor Malotas appreciates and trusts him."

"Some people appreciate the bad in people instead of the good."

"Men like that are needed to lead armies like the Nocean."

"Well… there are very few honorable soldiers then."

"Sometimes one of the four regents who rule the empire accompanies the army. I don't think that's the case here, I can't see a large retinue surrounding a nobleman with the banner of a regent."

"Regents? Doesn't Emperor Malotas rule the empire?"

"Yes, but the empire is too big, and Malotas has it divided into four large areas ruled by the regents. The regents and their armies, and each one has his own. They only mobilize for big battles from what I understand," Aibin said. "Anyway, I don't know much about these matters. The best known is Mulko, Regent of the North, who has a great sorcerer and master of spies, Zecly, feared by everyone in the empire."

"Sorcerer and master of spies?"

"Yes, Sorcerer of Blood Magic. Powerful and evil magic. Besides, he has a network of spies who travel throughout Tremia and keep him informed. Rumors say they can kill anyone just by uttering their name."

"It can't be that bad..." said Nilsa.

"Maybe not, but that's their reputation."

"I think we don't pay enough attention to the Nocean Empire in Norghana, and we should," said Nilsa.

"Let's dismount and hide the camels. They'll surely have sentinels and patrols. If we're found out, they'll want to know why we're spying."

"They wouldn't believe us if we said it was only out of curiosity, would they?"

"I'm afraid not."

Nilsa and Aibin lay down on the sand, behind a large dune, where they would not be seen from the lower plain. They got close enough to have good visibility but were careful to remain hidden by the sand dune.

The Nocean Army was maneuvering. The cavalry placed itself at the front, forming five lines with the infantry behind in ten lines of a thousand soldiers. At the rear there were three groups on horseback that looked like nobles, generals, and officers. General Muleine began to give new orders from the rearguard, and several officers rode off at a gallop to transmit them to the regiments.

"Do you think Albahel Aldhar might be in those rearguard groups?" Nilsa asked Aibin.

"I guess so."

"Wouldn't he stay in the camp?"

"I doubt it. I only see servants over there working without pause and some sentinels."

"But he's not a soldier like the rest who are on the front lines," Nilsa argued.

"He's also not a noble or general like the group in the center of the rearguard. I'd say he must be in the third group, the one to our left. They look like nobles, but they're not. Yes, he should be in that group," Aibin guessed.

"Yeah, I think so too, let's not lose sight of them," Nilsa said, and then, "Who are the people wearing long red robes and standing with the nobles and generals?" she asked.

"Those are the Sorcerers of the Blood Magic. The ones wearing green-brown robes are those of the Magic of Curses," Aibin explained.

"Wow, we'd better not lose sight of them either. I count two of Blood and two of Curses."

"Yes, I do too."

"They look grim, although I can't see them properly from here."

"Neither can I, and I've never seen one before, but I can identify them by their clothes and the staves they carry. No nobleman or general carries a staff with a gem at the tip, only sorcerers or magi. Or at least that's what I've learned in my tribe."

"I'm sure you're right."

The Nocean troops finished forming a line, and General Muleine gave the order for the officers to advance on the city. Horns were sounded and desert drums were played as the army started moving with disciplined step.

"I have a bad feeling about this," Nilsa told Aibin.

"Because of what your friend Lasgol found in there?"

"Exactly because of that," Nilsa nodded.

And suddenly, Nilsa's fears came true. Flooding out of the city streets like a plague of terrible nightmare creatures sent by a vengeful god, thousands of giant snakes, scorpions, and crocodiles launched themselves at the Nocean Army. Nilsa watched with her mouth open, unable to comprehend what she was witnessing. An immense horde of terrifying creatures was pouring out of the city to attack the Nocean Army. Aibin was watching with his ruby eyes wide open.

"The Gods… are sending a plague of giant creatures… to punish us," Aibin muttered.

"It's not the Gods, it's Dergha-Sho-Blaska sending them. He's been creating them inside those mountains by the city."

Aibin watched the scene that looked like something out of a horrific nightmare.

The royal scorpions were chilling and they advanced at the front, their colossal size like that of a loading cart pulled by two Percheron horses. The huge pincers could cut a person in two as if they were butter. The head with those horrendous jaws foretold a painful death. Their bodies were long and covered by a black shell supported by eight legs, four on each side, also shell-covered. The most fearful part of the creature, though, was the long tail that ended in a huge venomous stinger they carried above their bodies. Chief scorpions led them, larger still and red.

The royal cobras, that came after the scorpions, were also a horrible size, over nine feet tall. They moved slower and rose on their bodies, as wide as a Norghanian and over six feet tall, bearing their fangs. They slid their forked tongues in and out of their mouths quickly. Their scales were olive colored with yellow stomach patches and black heads. Several red cobras, larger still, were leading them.

Moving even more slowly and at the rear came the giant crocodiles. Horrendously sized, three times as big as a large river crocodile, they came, showing the lines of teeth in their lethal, long muzzles.

The Nocean soldiers saw the army of nightmare creatures coming toward them from the city and seemed at a loss for what to do, as if they were witnessing some kind of witchcraft that simply could not be true.

In a moment, the advance of the Nocean Army came to a complete stop. The soldiers and officers watched the flood of giant reptiles pouring out of the city, paralyzed by disbelief and fear. The great reptiles were terrifying. Nilsa noticed though that they were not fast at all. In fact, it was hard for them to move fast on the sand. Their size helped some, but Nilsa had the feeling they were neither fast nor agile. At least it was a small advantage for the humans, although she wondered whether it would be any good.

While the Nocean Army stood in shock, more and more giant reptiles were pouring out of the city. The thousand and five hundred paces that separated them were filled with the creatures coming to contend with the army of desert soldiers. If they kept coming like that, soon they would be as numerous as the Nocean Army itself, which was not good at all for the Noceans.

"They're paralyzed by terror, something I find completely logical," Nilsa commented, not missing a detail of how things unfolded.

"They might be for a moment, but they'll recover. That's what they've been trained for," Aibin assured her hopefully.

"You think so? They're up against terrifying monsters. They haven't trained for that."

"The children of the desert are seasoned warriors."

"They might be. But will they fight against nightmare creatures?"

"They'll fight, because the desert children are well acquainted with suffering and horror. They'll overcome their fears and fight."

Nilsa did not want to disagree, especially since they were his fellow countrymen of the desert and Aibin did not wish to see them die. Neither did she, although she had the feeling they were all going to die there today.

General Muleine finally reacted and started shouting orders to everyone around him, officers, sorcerers, and nobles. The officers seemed to react at last and transmitted the orders to their soldiers to attack. They gave the order to charge against the beasts at the same time the nobles and officers at the rear shouted orders at the top of their voices.

The soldiers obeyed the orders and launched the attack. Nilsa and Aibin watched the beginning of the great battle, and they both feared a result of the most bloody and horrendous kind.

The clash between the Nocean cavalry and the giant scorpions came with brutal violence. The riders on horses, camels, and dromedaries, armed with spears and scimitars, attacked the giant scorpions lunging at them. The first line of riders attacked headlong with all they had against the nightmare beasts. Spears and scimitars hit the shells of the beasts, and something unexpected happened. The tips of the spears did not penetrate the shells and the blades of the scimitars did not cut their pincers or legs. They could not penetrate the flesh of those reptilian monsters.

On the other hand, the scorpions attacked with pincers and stingers, amputating the arms and legs of the riders or piercing holes in the torsos and faces of the Nocean cavalry. They began to fall off their mounts, dead by the dozens. Those who were able to avoid the pincers and stingers defended themselves with their small shields, realizing they could not wound the scorpions that continued advancing. They moved to attack the giant royal cobras instead.

They were in for an equally unpleasant surprise. The spears and scimitars could not pierce through the scales of the colossal cobras. The soldiers attacked the snakes with all their might, but there was no way of hurting those monsters unless they struck the inside of their mouths or the eyes, which seemed to be the creatures' only weaknesses. The snakes spat venom at the cavalry and bit them with their tremendous jaws, tearing their limbs apart.

If the situation was not complicated enough for the cavalry, their mounts were frightened and reared in front of the giant snakes, throwing off their riders. The cobras took advantage of the panic and attacked them on the ground, killing them moments later.

The cavalry officers were ordering to continue the advance, penetrating the lines of enemy monsters, seeking some beast they could kill. They reached the giant crocodiles, and their luck did not change. They could not pierce the tough hide of the crocodiles with their weapons, and their mounts reared and bucked and threw off their riders when the enormous beasts attacked their legs.

The cavalry was practically annihilated without causing any damage to the monsters which kept coming, now at the infantry.

Chapter 23

The infantry officers called a halt, and the lines stopped. The next order was for the archers to move forward. They ran through the lines of soldiers to the front and formed three rows. They were dressed in black and carried short curved bows in the style of the desert.

The scorpions were already close, less than two hundred paces away. The archers aimed, the order came to release, and thousands of arrows flew and fell on the scorpions. As with the cavalry's attack, the archers' bore no results. The arrows hit the shells that covered the scorpions' bodies but did not pierce through.

The officers ordered another volley, and the Nocean archers released. The arrows flew over the hundred paces that separated them from the beasts and fell on the monsters. Apart from a few that hit the flesh in the grooves of the shell, most bounced off without causing any harm. Seeing that this did not work, they gave the order to the archers to withdraw, and just as they had reached the first rows they retreated to the rear at a run, passing through the infantry lines. Meanwhile, the scorpions covered the last paces that separated them from the infantry lines.

General Muleine gave the order for the infantry to stand their ground. The lancers took over the first lines and prepared their shields and spears to repel the attack. The monstrous scorpions reached them and crashed against them like a wave. Nilsa thought the beasts would make the soldiers fly through the air, but the huge scorpions did not have enough inertia since they walked so slowly. The first line of lancers slowed them even more using their spears, although they had to step back. The first three lines compacted, forming a single one while the scorpions tried to make their way forward by tearing the soldiers apart with their pincers and stabbing them with their deadly stingers.

At an order from the officers, the rear lines of infantry divided in two and attacked the scorpions' flanks. They surrounded them, making a large U, and attacked their legs, the monsters' weakest spot. The officers' order sounded loud and clear, passing from officers to soldiers, and soon they were all shouting the same thing, thousands of voices shouting the same order.

"What are they shouting?" Nilsa asked Aibin.

"Only attack the mouth, eyes, and joints."

"Oh.... The monsters' weak spots."

"Yes, since they're so big, most are attacking the leg joints."

"That's a good idea," Nilsa said, somewhat cheered.

The order started bearing fruit. The first giant scorpions fell with their legs maimed. They collapsed like huge structures whose foundations had been destroyed.

General Muleine shouted another order, which immediately spread.

"And what's he saying now?"

"Don't finish them off."

"Don't finish them off?"

"That's the order."

Nilsa was puzzled. She watched what was happening.

Once a great scorpion went down, the soldiers did not bother to finish off the creature, and Nilsa realized why: they were no longer dangerous. They could not move. They were trying to reach the Nocean soldiers with their pincers and stingers, but the soldiers moved away quickly and nimbly. They left the scorpions where they fell and went for the next enemy.

"Wow, this general is clever. They're beginning to succeed."

"Yes, they're doing well. They're fighting with bravery and resilience, as they should be," Aibin said with a certain pride in his voice.

This tactic worked well against the scorpions. Each one was surrounded by six infantry soldiers, and while some defended themselves from the scorpion's attack and tried to avoid being torn to pieces, the others attacked its legs from every direction. The Nocean soldiers were fighting with courage and daring.

When they reached the royal cobras, the scene changed entirely. These creatures were a lot more agile, and they dodged the soldiers' attacks with ease. On their part, the soldiers could not pierce the scales that covered the snakes' bodies, and the cobras attacked and killed with skill. They first showered the soldiers with venom which they spurted from their fangs, then they attacked, stabbing them with those huge, deadly fangs.

If the battle had begun to lean in favor of the soldiers, this quickly changed when they confronted the giant royal cobras. Even with several soldiers surrounding them, they could not manage to kill the beasts. They had to get to their eyes or the inside of their mouth, which was almost impossible.

"Now the order is to attack the mouth," Aibin said to Nilsa.

"It won't be easy."

"They have to wait for the cobras' attack."

"It's all or nothing. If they wait until the last moment and miss the mouth, they'll die."

Nilsa was right. The battle continued and the Nocean soldiers slowly killed the cobras, but for every one that fell, the cobras killed over a dozen soldiers. The battle leaned toward the monsters. No matter how hard they tried to kill the cobras, they lost too many lives. The Nocean soldiers were losing.

And to make things even more impossible, the giant crocodiles had now entered the fray. Their mouths were full of teeth, ready to destroy the Nocean soldiers. They caught the soldiers in their muzzles and tore them apart. It was a horrendous spectacle. The soldiers attacked the legs, mouth, and eyes like they had with the scorpions, but the crocodiles' hides were tougher than an armor breastplate, and the soldiers only managed to maim them. The problem was that, like the cobras, the cost in human lives was terrible.

The officers were not calling for a retreat, but for Nilsa it was clear that the battle was lost. The monsters were annihilating the Nocean forces.

"Why aren't they retreating?" she asked Aibin.

"Retreating from the battlefield is considered a great dishonor."

"If they don't, there won't be a single soldier left alive."

Aibin nodded, and in his face, she could see the sadness he felt for what he was witnessing.

The Noceans were fighting and dying, staining the desert sands red. At that moment, the call for retreat sounded. The surviving soldiers ran to the Nocean camp. In the rear, three thousand archers were getting ready with fire arrows to cover the retreat.

The reptilian monsters chased the soldiers as they retreated. They were not going to leave any soldiers alive if they could catch them.

Run!" Nilsa cried, unable to contain herself.

Aibin put his hand on her mouth and stopped her from rising.

"You must stay quiet. If they discover us, we'll die."

Nilsa nodded, and Aibin took his hand off her mouth.

As the soldiers withdrew, the archers started releasing at the monsters with flaming arrows, hoping the fire would hurt them. The arrows plunged into the ground or bounced off the bodies of the enormous reptiles. Areas formed where the fire reached the bodies of the fallen soldiers and they caught fire. It was a terrible scene, witnessing the bodies of the brave Nocean soldiers in flames. The monsters did not like it either. The fire frightened them, and they started to retreat or go around the flaming areas. The soldiers kept fighting, even after their deaths.

Suddenly, the four sorcerers came forward to stand in front of the archers and started casting a spell. The two of Blood Magic in their red robes had threatening amulets decorating their waists and were holding their staves of power over their heads. The two of Curses Magic, also with disturbing amulets hanging from their waists, were waving their staves before them in circles, as if they were invoking or creating something.

"The sorcerers are going to attack," Aibin warned Nilsa.

"I wonder if their magic will have any effect on those creatures."

"Why wouldn't it?" Aibin asked blankly.

"Magic doesn't affect dragons. They're protected against it."

"These creatures aren't Lesser Hor."

"No, but they've been created by them."

"I doubt they'll have the power their creators have."

"We'll find out soon," Nilsa said and squinted to better see in the sun.

The sorcerers of the Magic of Blood attacked the royal cobras while the sorcerers of the Magic of Curses attacked the giant crocodiles, all while the fire arrows continued falling upon them and more dead soldiers' bodies caught on fire.

The first thing Nilsa noticed was that around the snakes, on the desert floor, a red circle appeared. She was not even sure it was real—it looked like part of a large spell. The circle filled with a crisscross of lines in every direction as they continued conjuring. She found it very strange. The cobras did not seem to notice what was going on under their bodies.

The second thing she saw was a greenish mist that began forming over the crocodiles. The green color of the mist was alarming, like bile. Nilsa had the feeling that it was the shade of illness, of suffering. It expanded over all the crocodiles, filling the area where they were advancing to avoid the fire. The mist became thicker and more ominous as the spell continued.

The sorcerers were concentrated and continued casting their spell. They did not even appear to be present in the world. They kept enlarging the targeted area with the two great spells. The red circle continued to grow and the area covered by the mist was spreading. The sorcerers were trying to reach the maximum number of enemies. Behind them the archers were still releasing, more to slow the attackers from coming forward than anything else. Behind the archers, General Muleine and his nobles maintained their position. The rest of the surviving infantry was fleeing and regrouping at the camp.

All of a sudden, from inside the red circle the Blood Sorcerers had created, a beam of red light rose toward the sky. All the royal cobras affected by the beam of red light began to hiss in pain and suffering. Something strange and terrible happened—blood began to pour from their bodies. From their mouths, eyes, and between their scales, blood began to flow as if attracted by the beam of red light. The royal cobras started losing large amounts of blood while they suffered in agony.

The crocodiles under the mist of sickness also started to suffer. Green bile started to pour from their mouths as if they were poisoned. Their skin was quickly covered in sores and rashes which oozed a putrefied, green liquid. They were deathly ill, and in a few moments the suffering increased. The giant creatures lay in their backs amid spasms and died with green liquid dripping from their mouths.

The royal cobras were losing a lot of blood and were suffering. The spell was killing them by making their blood come out from every nook and cranny of their bodies. Their bodies soon ran out of blood and they began to die in groups.

"It's… horrible…" Nilsa muttered.

"Magic of Blood that seeks the blood of the enemy. Magic of Curses that seeks to curse and sicken the enemy. Both forms of powerful magic, magic of the desert."

"Magic of the desert?"

"It's been practiced for a long time in the desert. Only by great sorcerers. And those four are great, they've proven that."

"You can say that again."

The cobras and crocodiles were dying by the thousands, writhing in pain from the magic of the four sorcerers.

Suddenly, the lead crocodile and the lead cobra, both larger than the rest with red skin, turned and stopped the rest from advancing so they would not enter the area afflicted with the powerful enemy magic. They did not succeed right away, and by the time they managed to stop their followers, thousands of reptiles had already died. But many still remained, and these withdrew to the city.

The two Sorcerers finished casting their powerful spells, and all four seemed to be left exhausted. Several acolytes came from among the troops and helped their masters to retire. They took them to some horses, helped them to mount, and got them out of there at a full gallop.

"Those sorcerers used up all their magic. They used it all up on those two spells," Nilsa said.

"In that case, the battle seems to be without a winner."

At that instant, the sand started to whirl at several points between the archers. Enormous circles formed, and the sand in them seemed to move in spirals. Suddenly, four giant rhinoceros beetles appeared from the ground. They were colossal, larger than elephants, each with a huge horn on the front of their heads. They looked completely armored with their dark shells. They attacked, squashing the archers or hitting them with their huge horn. The situation soon turned tragic for the Noceans.

General Muleine ordered a retreat with loud shouts and wild arm waving.

The four beetles charged against the nobles, the General, and the other groups at the rear as they tried to escape. Unlike the reptiles, the colossal beetles moved with great speed thanks to their size, and they massacred the groups trying to escape from them.

Nilsa could not bear to watch.

The General, a few of the nobles, and their retinue managed to escape at a gallop, but most perished. The giant beetles had destroyed them. The battle was over. The beasts had won, and the human survivors were running for their lives.

For a long while once the fighting between the humans and

beasts was over, the desert returned to a state of peace, silence, loneliness. The surviving monsters returned to the city slowly, quietly, entering the city and vanishing inside it. No doubt they were returning back to the depths of the accursed Mountains of the Past.

What little was left of the Nocean Army fled to the city of Zenut, which no doubt would prepare for war. The explanations General Muleine would have to give to Emperor Malotas were certainly going to be complicated. He ran the risk of not being believed, and he might lose his head. On the other hand, he had the testimony of the survivors on his side. In any case, Zenut would shut its gates and strengthen its walls. The General would ask for reinforcements to defend the city.

But it did not seem like the monsters of Salansamur were going to follow the defeated Nocean Army to Zenut in order to attack it. What was left of the horde, which had also lost thousands of members, was sheltering inside the city and mountains. Nilsa did not know why or for what purpose, which intrigued her greatly.

"It seems everyone has left the battlefield," Aibin said to Nilsa.

"Yes, only the bodies of the fallen in battle are left."

"There are many thousands of them from both sides."

Nilsa looked at the plain filled with dead bodies and did not know what to say. Over ten thousand Noceans had died, and almost as many monsters. The sandy plain now looked like a giant graveyard for monsters and humans.

"What a horror…"

"My father says that all wars are."

"Your father is a wise man. Well, at least we've learned something from all this death," Nilsa commented.

"And what's that?"

"Dergha-Sho-Blaska's servants can resist steel but not magic. They can be killed with magic."

"Yes, indeed. That has been proven."

"Come, follow me," Nilsa told Aibin as she motioned him to come with her.

"Do you want to go to the battlefield? Among the dead?"

"Of course," Nilsa replied as she started down the dune they had been hiding behind.

They came to the place where the rearguard of the Nocean Army had perished. Everything was calm, the strange calm which death brought. There was no sign of any enemy, so they rested somewhat easy, although since they could appear from under the sand, it was not too reassuring.

Nilsa started to rummage among the Nocean dead.

"What are you doing?" Aibin asked her.

"I'm looking for Albahel Aldhar."

"Oh… it's a bit grim to be rummaging among the dead, but okay."

They searched for the adventurer among the dead. They would turn the bodies over and find tremendous wounds, which Nilsa knew would give her nightmares for a long time, but she would endure them. What was important was the weapon, and she had to find it. Since they did not know what Albahel looked like, they were going by the clothes. After a long while of searching, Aibin found something.

"Here, Nilsa."

She ran over to him to see what he had found.

Aibin showed her a body. It was not a soldier or an officer, and based on his clothes he was not a nobleman either. His clothes were good, but not that much.

"It might be," Nilsa said as she started searching his body. He had a quiver with arrows on his back, and on the ground beside him was a bow. Nilsa searched on his back. Beside the quiver, he was carrying a weapon wrapped in a leather casing. Nilsa took it. It was long. She unwrapped it and found a gold javelin with strange engravings. It weighed almost nothing and was as light as a feather.

"This is it! Antior's Beam!" Nilsa cried, bouncing up and down.

"We're in luck," Aibin smiled at her.

"You bring me luck!" Nilsa said to him and hugged him hard and kissed him, carried away with joy.

Aibin was left not knowing what to say or do, a look of surprise on his face. His surprise lasted only a moment. He hugged her and kissed her back.

"Well, this settles another matter," Nilsa said, smiling.

"Yes, it does," Aibin replied, a little embarrassed.

"We'd better get out of here. I don't want to be surprised. Something smells rotten in all of this," Nilsa commented, gazing at the battlefield and the many fallen.

"You mean what happened here?"

"Yeah… no lesser dragons took part in the battle. I find this very strange, but I can't explain why. With their power, they could've dealt with the Sorcerers of Blood and Curses."

"Maybe the Lesser Hor aren't here."

"That's what I'm thinking. Lasgol said Dergha-Sho-Blaska had left. And now his lesser dragons seem to have departed as well. Where have they gone? And more importantly, why? They're planning something important, and I have the feeling we still haven't found out what it is."

"More important than creating an army of monstrous reptiles and other creatures to conquer Tremia?"

"Yeah... I don't know… my intuition tells me we're missing something…"

"Well, for now you have the javelin and the army of monstrous creatures had to withdraw. I think we've achieved a lot."

Nilsa looked at Aibin and could not help smiling.

"When you're right, you're right. Let's get out of here."

"Let's go."

Chapter 24

Gerd continued traveling north, even more concerned than he would like to be. What he was learning about the axe and this region was not very favorable, and it was indeed quite disturbing. Perhaps the fact that adventurers and treasure hunters had not come back might have some explanation that did not imply that they had died at the hands of the Wild Ones of the ice or the winter storms, but he doubted it.

He went down a snow-covered hill and saw several huge oaks covered in ice and frost. The people before him had most likely died at the hands of the Wild Ones, no matter how much he did not want this to be the case. It was not good news, but this was not going to make him give up on his goal of finding the weapon with the power to kill dragons. Besides, the Wild Ones did not scare him. He had encountered them already, and he was no longer afraid of anything he knew. His fears no longer dominated him like they used to. Not even the unknown caused him enough fear and anxiety to make him lose control. He had learned to control his fears and was doing pretty well.

He had already fought the Wild Ones before. They were powerful and fearsome, good warriors, but so was he. He hoped he would not have to fight them, but if he was forced to, he would. The destiny of Norghana, the lives of his friends and that of thousands of other people, were at stake. He could not fail them. He had to find the axe and help kill the Immortal Dragon, his lesser dragons, and his reptilian monsters. If in order to achieve this he had to fight some Wild Ones of the Ice, he would.

The snow and gusts of icy wind of the area accompanied him on his journey but he did not really mind. Snow did not bother him, and the icy wind made him remember how precious life was every time it whipped him with its freezing lashes. His winter gear was holding up well. Since he was dressed entirely in white, with the exception of his bow, he blended in well with the landscape around him. He was not worried since there should not be any Wild Ones in the area, not yet at least. He had not seen more bear or wolf tracks, another danger to consider. In all likelihood, they had hidden from the storm of the previous night.

He reached the summit of a high mountain and stopped to look at the landscape. He could see behind him, in the distance, the valley he had come from. Before him he saw two valleys that went on parallel toward the north. From the directions he had been given, he had to go east, inland. In the other valley was the village of Gurenbern, which he might have to visit, but that was not the initial destination. He also glimpsed wildlife, which filled him with joy. Several large reindeer with big racks were looking for food to the east. A snowy eagle was flying over the area, looking for some small quarry to hunt. Gerd hoped the mountain hares hopping to the east through the snow-covered bushes would notice before it was too late for them. He also glimpsed a white fox sniffing the snow, looking for the trail of some smaller animal. Seeing all the wild nature of these beautiful frozen territories made him want to stay and study them. He would love to be able to spend some time here and discover the wildlife which was as interesting as it was diverse. He would surely discover some species that had not been catalogued. From what Esben and Gisli had told him, there were animals in the north that were unknown and hence had not been studied yet. He wondered what kind of animals they might be, perhaps predators hiding from humans. He would have to come back when he had some more time.

He continued toward the valley that protected the Village of Lorders. He went down the mountain. It was hard because of the amount of snow that had accumulated and his own problems with his hip and balance. Once down, he headed to the valley at a firm, brisk pace. He had to stop at nightfall to rest. It would take him at least another day to get to Lorders, if he did not encounter storms or any other difficulties.

He sought some trees to protect himself and improvised a small shelter to spend the night. He had come prepared and had brought a Ranger's tent. He had known it would come in handy. As he was putting it up, he wondered whether he would have survived the storm in that tent. Most likely not, and he was glad he had decided to go to the village for help instead of setting up the tent and trying to survive the night in it. As a Ranger, he had to trust his instincts always. Knowledge and instincts—only those could save him.

The night did not seem long, even being on his own. He did not feel the least fear, which made him very proud. Previously, it would not have been so. In fact, he felt a great calm and peace here, in the Frozen Territories, sleeping outdoors in the middle of a snow-covered forest. It was as if his destiny were becoming real. He had doubted whether being a Ranger was what he wanted, what he was destined for. He doubted that no more. He was convinced that being a Ranger was his fate. Being a Ranger and helping his friends and the kingdom.

At dawn, he resumed his journey. It did not take him long to travel the remaining distance. He arrived at the entrance of the village. Two men armed with short bows came out to meet him from behind two oaks. Gerd had already spotted them and assumed they were the village watchmen, so he did not worry too much.

"Who's there?" the one aiming at him from his left asked him.

"Gerd, Royal Ranger," he replied calmly.

"A Ranger?" the other archer asked.

"And Royal? What are you doing here?" the first one asked, surprised.

"I'm here on a Ranger's mission. If you don't mind, stop aiming at me."

Both watchmen looked at each other and a moment later lowered their bows.

"Sorry, we mistook you for a Wild One," the tallest one said.

"Me?" Gerd said blankly.

"Because of your size," the other one replied. "Every now and then some Wild One appears at the village."

"Seeking blood?"

"They did before, not anymore. We think they come down to spy, and we flush them out. They usually withdraw without confrontation."

"Well, that's a relief," said Gerd.

"Yeah, it's a much better time now, but even so, it's not prudent to go much further north. This territory is already entirely theirs," the tall watchman said in warning.

"Yeah, I know."

"Every once in a while we also have Ranger visitors. On scouting missions. Are you here for that?" the other one asked.

"No, my mission is different. I'm looking for the family of Ripdis Ulken. I was told I would find them here in the Village of Lorders."

The two watchmen exchanged looks.

"Ripdis' grandson has his house to the east of the village. There's no mistaking it, it's the biggest in the village," the short watchman said.

"He's the wealthiest member of the village, because of his grandfather, the craftsman."

"I see. I'll check him out."

"If you need anything, go the House of Command. There you'll find Chief Ulgentonen. He'll help you with anything you might need."

"Thank you both," Gerd said and went on to the house they had indicated. As he was crossing the village, the curiosity of the villagers was stronger than their reservations, and they came out in the street to see who the newcomer was.

It was not hard at all to find the house, since it was not only the biggest but it was the best looking one. It was the house of a Norghanian nobleman, robust, good-sized and long-lasting. That's what gold was good for—it could provide houses and comfort, even so far north.

He knocked on the door.

"I'm a Ranger. I'm looking for the great grandson of Ripdis Ulken," Gerd said in an authoritarian voice, as if he had come to take him into custody.

"One moment," a voice replied, and the door opened very slowly. An elderly man appeared in the threshold.

"Good morning," Gerd greeted him.

"May it be good," the old man replied. "Do you wish to see my master?"

"I think so," Gerd guessed that this old man was a servant.

"Please, come in. I'll announce you."

Gerd stood waiting beside a spectacular armory that covered one of the walls of the hall from side to side. It was a mixture between a glass cabinet and an armory where many handcrafted weapons were exhibited. He took a look and noticed they were weapons of great value and quality. He could not help but look at them like a child presented with a chest full of toys. Most were swords and axes of different styles and sizes. All of them were inlaid with gold, which caught his attention.

"They are magnificent, aren't they?" a voice behind him said, and Gerd turned around. The speaker was a man in his mid sixties with long white hair which he wore loose, with the exception of two braids that fell along his cheeks.

"They are indeed. Exquisite weapons," Gerd replied.

"My great grandfather was an artist of steel and gold. A forger with no rival and with a special ability to create weapons as beautiful as they are deadly, which many have wanted to replicate but no one has ever equaled."

"I'm not a connoisseur, but I can appreciate that they are very good creations."

"A Ranger recognizes his bow and his knife," the man replied, smiling.

"Which are simple weapons without any filigree, not like these I see in this cabinet," he said, pointing at the weapons housed there.

"Very true," the man nodded with a smile. "I'm Henerik Ulken, master of this house," he said with a slight bow of his head.

"Thank you for seeing me. I'm Gerd Vang, Royal Ranger."

"We don't get many visitors around here, not for a very long time. Conflicts with our neighbors of the Frozen Continent and the harsh climate make it difficult to visit our cozy village. The Rangers are the few people who visit intermittently, to see how things are going around these northern valleys. Are you on a surveillance mission of the area?"

Gerd shook his head.

"I'm on a rather more complicated mission."

"To my house? I'm surprised. There's only my great grandfather Ripdis' collection of weapons that are of any interest here," he said, indicating the armories that covered the four walls of the hall.

"That's exactly why I'm here."

"Well, I do find that strange. The Rangers have never shown any interest in my great grandfather's weapons. They consider them too elaborate."

"There's always a first for everything. I've come for Gim's Double Death."

Henerik's eyes opened wide.

"That weapon vanished during the time of my great grandfather. I don't have it in my collection."

"If it vanished, that means it existed…"

"Yes, of course it existed. The axe at least."

"Do you have any proof that the axe really existed?"

"I do. Wait here for a moment," Henerik told him as he left the hall.

Gerd waited, looking at the swords and knives. They were really beautiful. He could appreciate Ripdis' personal style. The dwarf engraved the weapons with drawings that resembled the waves of the western sea in gold on the silver blades.

Henerik came back a moment later with a tome in his hands. He was leafing through it and stopped at a certain page.

"Look, this is the drawing of the weapon. It's my great grandfather's handwriting. He also noted down the measurements of the great axe, as you can see here."

Gerd looked at the drawing, which was very detailed.

"Yeah, this must be the axe…"

"You don't seem happy to see proof that it existed," Henerik said, raising an eyebrow.

"Oh, it's not that. I am happy there's evidence that the weapon existed. The thing is that the weapon has a reputation of having power, of being enchanted…"

Henerik shook his head.

"My great grandfather's weapons were true works of art, created by a craftsman with prodigious knowledge and hands, but they were not enchanted. There's no magic in them."

"In none of them?"

"Not that I know of. All his weapons have some drawing, sketch or notes, and I've never seen anything that indicated the use of magic in any of them. Besides, my great grandfather did not have the Gift. He would not have been able to use magic even if he wanted to. Around here we've had the occasional witch with the Gift, but only for healing."

Gerd wrinkled his nose. That did not fit. If the weapon existed and it had been created by Ripdis, as everything seemed to indicate, then it was not a weapon with power, and that meant it could not kill a dragon. What he was finding out did not fit with the hopes they had for the weapon being similar to Aodh's Bow. For an instant Gerd felt a little disappointed and unsure of what to do. Everything pointed to the fact that the famous craftsman had created the great axe Gim had killed the dragon with, but if Ripdis had created the weapon it would not be able to kill any dragon, so the legend was false.

"I guess you've heard the legend of Gim and the axe?"

"Of course. Who doesn't know it in the north? It's part of our folklore. It's also part of the reputation that made my great grandfather into a legend among the weapon forgers."

"Do you believe in the legend?"

"Well… legends are just that, legends…"

"Then you don't believe in it."

"I didn't say that." Henerik began to pace before the armories, looking at his precious collection. "My great grandfather created the axe for Gim. Whether Gim killed a dragon with it or not is another thing entirely."

"Then you don't think so."

"I can't lean to either side with real facts. Because of romanticism, I tend to think he did kill the dragon and, like me, so do most of those who live in the north."

"But there's no evidence of that…"

"We're talking about a dragon. There's no evidence of their existence as far as I know, not here or in any other place."

Gerd nodded. His investigations were not going the way he wanted. How he wished Egil were there with him. He would surely think of some brilliant idea to get out of this tangle. Unfortunately, he did not have the luxury of counting on his friend right then, so he would have to think of something himself. He would have to solve this mission 'Gerd style.' And there was only one way of knowing whether the legend was false: checking the weapon. The key to the whole thing was in the great axe. It seemed evident that it existed. There was only one way to prove it could kill dragons, and that was by obtaining the weapon and examining it. The best thing to do in this situation was to act like a bloodhound and find the quarry. That was what he would do.

"Any idea where the weapon disappeared?" Gerd asked.

Henerik looked out the window and gazed at the frozen landscape.

"What was found out is that the weapon disappeared in a territory under the control of the Wild Ones of the Ice north of here. Some have tried to find the famous axe but never came back to tell."

"The Wild Ones?"

"Probably, or a storm, or the wolves, white bears, who knows. The thing is, no-one has ever found the axe."

"But you believe it exists."

“It did exist. What’s become of that weapon, I have no idea,” Henerik shrugged.

“Its last location?”

“Are you sure you want to go searching for it? I don’t think you’ll ever return if you do.”

“I have to, it’s important.”

“I hope it is, because you’re risking your life.”

“It is.”

“Very well. I’ll tell you on the map where the weapon is believed to have disappeared. I have no certainty it was there, but that’s all I can tell you.”

“That’s enough, thank you.”

Henerik nodded and went to a table in the next room to get a map from one of the drawers. Then he marked the place with an X.

Gerd went over to see.

“It’s here, in the Pink Caves.”

Gerd threw his head back. “I’ve never heard that name before.”

“It’s a very special place. You’ll see when you get there. Only one warning: the Wild Ones are accustomed to visiting it. It’s sacred for them. They say there’s a semi-giant who lives there. I don’t know whether this is true, but we humans don’t go near it just in case.”

“And it’s there that the weapon vanished?”

Henerik nodded.

“From what I’ve been able to find out, Gim left the weapon in the cave where he killed the dragon. That’s supposed to be the cave.”

Gerd nodded. “I see. If that’s the place and the weapon is still there, I’ll find it.”

“That will make you famous. That weapon has a reputation.”

“I don’t want fame or glory. I only want to protect my people.”

Henerik nodded. “That does you credit. I wish you the best of luck. You’re going to need it.”

“Thank you very much.”

Gerd left the house after consulting a few more aspects with Henerik. He left the village, greeting the neighbors he passed, and headed north, to the Pink Caves. A feeling of unease was churning his stomach, and no matter how he tried to make it disappear, he could not. It was time to enter territory controlled by the Wild Ones of the Ice.

Chapter 25

Once he left behind the last valley, Gerd knew he was entering the territory of the Wild Ones of the Ice. With every step he took to the north, he went deeper into Wild territory and the more danger his life was in. He was well aware, so he took extreme precautions. The weather was no ally either, as he had expected, since it was winter, and this was an area known for the terrible winter storms that killed with just the freezing breath of the winds.

He watched the sky while he recovered his breath. He was able to identify two storms coming toward him, one from the north and the other from the west. Since he had already had a bad experience with a storm from the west, he decided it would be wiser to avoid this one first. He inhaled the cold wintry air and headed northeast, going around the storm to put distance between it and himself. He would deal with the second storm later.

He managed to outrun the western storm and left it behind him. He snorted in relief. He had had to pick up his pace in order to avoid it. Unfortunately, the other storm was fast approaching and from the direction he was supposed to move in. He wondered what to do. It was not a good idea to retreat south, since the storm was coming that way and would break upon him. After thinking about it, he decided to run toward the storm and reach the caves before the storm found him. It was terribly risky, but trying to avoid the storm would force him to take a long detour to the east which he would rather not do.

He started running north. The danger and the presence of the storm closing in made him run at top speed, faster than he thought he could run. He tripped a couple of times because of his hip, but he managed to recover without falling. Suddenly he glimpsed several pink flashes coming from the skirt of some mountains ahead of him. The icy wind of the storm whipped his face, even protected by the Ranger's scarf, and he had to shut his eyes so, for an instant, he lost the reference of the flashes. The storm blackened the whole sky, creating a gloom that only the lightning bolts and the thunder seemed capable of rendering. They heralded cold and death. The pink flashes appeared again, and he ran with all his might.

He came to about three hundred paces from the central mountain and found an entrance to a great cave. Although he could barely stand with the wind and the cold, he stopped in his tracks. He looked at the great opening and was amazed by the flashes of light coming from it when it was hit by the lightning flashes of the storm on the mountain. They were all pink, a bright, pale pink. He had to rub his eyes because he had the feeling he was not seeing properly, that what he was seeing was some kind of weird optical effect. It made no sense that he saw pink luminescence coming from the mouth of a cave. If he told anyone, they would not believe him.

He had to go in and find out whether the axe was inside. He nocked an arrow and, careful not to make any sound, he approached the entrance to the cave. He had the feeling that the beauty of the flashes and the singularity of the place would likely hold some deadly danger. More than one, in all certainty.

He sighed. A little danger was not going to make him retreat. A little danger would not sway him, neither would a lot. He was going to complete the mission. If the axe was inside, he would find it and he would take it, and if anyone or anything tried to stop him, they would regret it. He went into the cave, aiming his bow in every direction in case danger appeared. All he was able to detect were the pink flashes coming from the walls of the cave. It was as if the entire interior was covered in pink-toned crystals.

Every bolt of lightning the storm produced outside broke the gloom, and the cave responded with multiple pink flashes coming from its walls. He went further in to shelter from the storm and noticed that the flashes were due to some kind of pink-colored crystals embedded in the rock walls. It made it look like a cave filled with pink diamonds, if such a thing existed at all, which he did not believe. His jaw dropped, and he had to touch them with his hand to make sure his eyes were not tricking him. It was some kind of pink crystal formation, and there were hundreds of them embedded in the floor, walls, and upper part of the cave.

Meanwhile, outside the thunder was terrible and the temperature was dropping to deadly levels. Gerd was going further into the cave, not only for shelter but also to explore. He headed to the back, where he could glimpse more light. It was rather strange to see light, especially if the place was uninhabited. Soon, he had an unpleasant encounter.

Two Wild Ones of the Ice were guarding what looked like the entrance to another cave.

Gerd stopped and studied them. He was always impressed by the sight of a Wild One of the Ice. They were taller and bigger than him, more muscular, but what most impressed him was their skin, an intense sky blue, and their eyes, such a pale gray that they looked almost white. Their eyes did not seem to have irises. Their whitish hair and beards seemed to be frozen like ice. They wore white bear skins, as was typical of their people.

The two Wild Ones stared at him in surprise and walked toward him, wielding huge two-headed war axes.

Gerd aimed his bow at them, first at one and then at the other. He knew they were brutal and would not yield to formality.

"Stop, if you don't want to die!" he warned them, although he doubted they understood Norghanian.

The two Wild Ones stopped when they saw Gerd's attitude with the bow. They might not understand his words, but the language of weapons was universal. Bow against axe, at a distance, led to a result known by any warrior, regardless of race or ethnicity.

The Wild One on the left started talking to him, but Gerd did not understand a word. From his gestures with his axe and the way he pointed at Gerd's bow, he did not look very happy.

From what he had been told at the villages, the Wild Ones had not been aggressive for quite a while. Gerd attributed it to Asrael's leadership, although the Panthers did not know for sure whether the Arcane led the Peoples of the Frozen Continent or not. It was only a guess and a hope. He thought about using Asrael's name—it might have some effect. Most likely it would not, but he lost nothing for trying.

"I friend of Asrael," he said, lowering his bow a little.

The two Wild Ones said something in their language, but Gerd was unable to understand anything.

"Asrael, friend, me," he tried to make them understand.

Unfortunately, communication was not going well. Both Wild Ones shouted more and more and seemed ready to attack him.

"Asrael!" Gerd shouted.

The two Wild Ones stopped shouting, waving their arms and looking at each other. Then they looked at Gerd again. Perhaps he had managed to make himself understood, although he did not know how Asrael was pronounced in their language. He hoped they would understand, although he doubted it.

The Wild Ones pointed at him with one finger while they held their enormous axes in the other hand. They shouted unintelligible words at him.

"Asrael!" Gerd repeated in his attempt to mention a name they might respect.

His stratagem did not work.

The Wild One on the left lifted his axe above his head with both hands and attacked.

Gerd had no choice but to defend himself. He released, and the arrow caught the Wild One in his right shoulder. He did not flinch and continued his charge with a war cry. Gerd stepped back while nocking another arrow. He released before the distance was too short to use the bow. He hit the man again in the same shoulder. This time, the Wild One stopped and lowered his axe, screaming in pain and rage. A moment later, he raised his axe again to attack. Gerd remembered that in order to stop a Wild One, you had to hit him several times.

He retreated to the entrance of the cave and felt the icy breath of the storm outside on his back. He released a third time and hit his opponent in the same shoulder again. The Wild One nearly lost his axe as his right shoulder failed him and threw him off-balance with the weight of the axe. He lowered his axe and glared at Gerd, who was alert to the movements of the other Wild One. He was watching the fight as if it were a duel, without intervening.

The wounded Wild One took a step toward Gerd, dragging his axe with his left arm and hand. Gerd left his bow on the ground and reached for his Ranger's axe and knife. He waited for the Wild One's attack. The Wild One put all the strength of his huge, muscular body in his left hand and tried to split his adversary in two with a colossal axe blow. Gerd slid to the right, the wounded side of the Wild One, and avoided the blow which hit the rocky floor, sending shards of rock and pink crystals through the air.

Gerd measured the blow and delivered a tremendous kick to the support knee of the Wild One. There was a 'crack' and the Wild One stumbled. With a round blow with the blunt side of the axe to the Wild One's chin, Gerd brought him down. He left the Wild One unconscious on the floor. Gerd watched him for a moment in case he got up again, although he had hit him with all his might and was hoping he would not. He did not get back up. He was knocked out.

"My, you're tough," he said, snorting.

The other Wild One roared and prepared to attack.

"Very well, it's your turn now," he told the other Wild One, and motioned for him to approach while he stepped back to his bow.

The Wild One charged.

Gerd bent down and picked up his bow, leaving his axe and knife in front of him. He nocked an arrow, aimed, and released with a sigh. The arrow went straight at the Wild One's chest. It hit and detonated, although it was barely heard over the booming thunder outside. But the Earth Arrow left the Wild One half blinded and a little stunned. He stopped and rubbed his eyes with his arm.

A second arrow hit him when he was beginning to attack again. This one was an Air Arrow, and the burst that followed was eclipsed by the terrible lightning from the storm outside. The Wild One was left stunned, and Gerd finished him off with a second Air Arrow. This time the burst made the Wild One drop to the floor, unconscious.

He stared at the entrance to the back cave in case any other Wild One came out to see what was going on. Luckily, the blast of the storm outside had completely muffled the sounds of fighting, and no other watchman appeared. While the storm raged, he tied up the two Wild Ones with ropes he carried in his rucksack. He used strong knots in case they woke up, which he hoped would not be soon.

Once he finished dealing with the two Wild Ones, he gathered his weapons and went further into the second cave with his bow raised and an Earth Arrow nocked. He walked in carefully and saw that the inner cave was larger and also filled with the strange crystals that gave off those pink flashes. There were no watchmen, but there were a couple of torches lighting it up which indicated that the Wild Ones used it. He walked around the cave and saw that it had five exits. This puzzled him, and he did not know which one to follow or whether the one he chose would lead him to another encounter with Wild Ones.

"Let's begin with the one farthest to the left," he muttered to himself, not very convinced.

He ventured into the next cave, which turned out to be a passage to another larger cave with an exterior opening, where the storm was breaking as if it were trying to punish all the mountains for some sin committed against the Ice Gods. There was no other way to go but out, so he doubled back.

He took the next exit and found that it went up to another cave that also opened out. He was beginning to understand why he had seen so many pink flashes coming from different locations in the distance as he approached the mountain. It was the caves. He found another cave that opened outside.

The other two exits led to two large caves. In a huge one there were about two dozen Wild Ones who seemed to live there, since they had fires, tables, chairs, and armories, as well as an area with something that looked like beds. He saw them roasting several reindeer and boar they had hunted. The guards were thinking more about the roast than keeping watch, so they had not seen him. The problem was that he could not go through there, and neither did he see a golden axe anywhere. All the axes he saw were the usual ones the Wild Ones used.

The other exit led to a smaller cave where there were three Wild Ones on watch. Gerd thought about attacking them and making his way through, but the risk was too high. Not only were the Wild Ones strong, talented warriors, but the rest might hear the sounds of fighting and discover him, which he definitely wanted to avoid.

He watched, hidden, and did not like the idea of attacking or trying to escape. He would not be able to. But he had an idea that might work. He went back to one of the caves that led outside which he had already explored. He put his head out to check the profile of the mountain. At once, his face started to freeze from the terribly low temperature. He endured the cold and saw more pink flashes further up toward the north, just as the sky seemed to crack as a bolt of lightning fell, splitting in two.

The pink reflections indicated there was another cave further up. He tried to see whether he could reach it and found a way up the rocky wall he thought he could tackle. The cold embrace of the storm was hitting him, and the ice that covered the rock was not a good omen, but if he could reach that cave from the outside, he could get past the three guards. He had no other option, so he adjusted the scarf over his mouth and nose, fastened the bow and quiver on his back, and went out to the side of the mountain.

The first thing he felt was a tremendous cold lash at his body.

The storm winds were strong, and they froze him to his core. He calculated that he would not be able to bear the cold out here for more than a few moments, so he started climbing the wall immediately without wasting an instant. He put his feet on the lower ledges of the rock with great care and grabbed the upper ones with his hands, well aware that he was risking his life. A gust of wind whipped him so hard that it almost pulled his fingers from the wall, even though he was holding on for dear life. But he did not let go. He held on, hugging the rock.

He recovered and slowly continued climbing as the storm broke over the mountain. The cold began to be too much. His face was freezing, as well as his limbs. He kept climbing. He knew that if he did not get to the cave, he was dead. He would freeze and fall off the mountain. Every step he took along that wall was horribly painful. He clenched his jaw and went on. It was a matter of reaching the cave or dying. He had to reach it.

A moment later, he was at the entrance to the upper cave.

"Done..." he muttered proudly.

He fell inside, half frozen alive, and dragged himself in with the last bit of strength left in his arms. His legs simply did not respond. He was so tired and frozen that for a long while he just lay there, unable to do anything. At least he had managed to drag himself deep enough inside for the storm not to reach him. He stayed there for a while, staring at the dozens of pink crystals on the wall in front of him.

He snorted hard. He was still alive, and that was what mattered. By a hair's breadth, but alive.

He waited until he had recovered from the cold. His legs took longer to recover feeling and then more to be able to move. For a moment, Gerd became really worried. To have his eyebrows and forehead frozen was one thing, but his legs? That was entirely different. Without legs, he was dead. With great relief, he noticed feeling returning to his legs, and he rubbed them vigorously to help the circulation.

It took him a long time just to be able to walk again. His balance was dodgy at best, and being barely able to feel his frozen legs did not help things. He managed to take a few unstable, unbalanced steps around the cave. He was in no condition to fight anyone, least of all a Wild One of the Ice in his lair. He saw an exit at the back and decided to go that way. He moved slowly and stomped his feet to finish waking up his legs, which still did not fully respond. He found a tunnel with no light and went along it. If there was no light, most likely it was because there was no one inside.

He reached the end of the tunnel and threw himself on the floor to watch. He saw an enormous cave lit up by a hundred torches. On its walls were thousands of pink crystals that flashed when they were hit by the reflection of the torch fire. The vastness of the cave and its great height impressed him—a whole army of Wild Ones of the Ice could easily fit in there. The tunnel from where he was watching had to be about fifteen feet high, and it was half hidden between two folds of rock in one of the walls.

In the center of the cave he saw a Wild One of greater size than usual. He was taller and wider than a regular Wild One. He looked like a chief, based on his size and also by the marks on his skin. His strength and appearance made him most intimidating. Gerd sensed that fighting this Wild One would entail a painful death.

Together with the chief, there were about twenty Wild Ones forming a circle, all armed with their two-headed axes at their backs and holding what looked like large wooden shields, as large and wide as themselves. This puzzled Gerd; the Wild Ones usually did not carry shields of that kind. He noticed the shields were very rustic. They looked more like the top of a table than a shield.

If he was puzzled by the shields, what he witnessed next confused him even more. They were singing some kind of chant that sounded like a ritualistic prayer and in a tone that leaned toward brutal. The more they sang, the louder they became, banging the rock floor with the bottom of their shields as if they were calling something or someone to their circle. Gerd had a bad feeling about the circle and the chanting. Something was cooking here, and it was going to end in a blood bath.

All of a sudden, eight Wild Ones came into the cave through an entrance at the far end. They were carrying long iron poles that ended in leather nooses, and they were pushing and pulling an animal they had trapped by the neck with them. They were leading it to the circle of Wild Ones, which took Gerd aback, and he had to rub his eyes to make sure he was seeing the animal correctly. It was a wolf with long white fur, only it could not be a wolf because it was twice as big as a northern wolf, both in height and complexion. Beside the colossal wolf trotted its pup, which looked tiny in comparison. It could not be more than a month old.

The Wild Ones were having serious trouble managing the great wolf and were applying all their strength and the weight of their bodies to control it. The animal was pulling in every direction, trying to free itself while growling with bloodcurdling, aggressive sounds. The little pup was whimpering, not understanding what was going on. Gerd had the feeling the great wolf was a female and the little one following her was her pup.

The Wild Ones led the great wolf to the circle where the rest of them were intoning their chanting. Those closest to the wolf parted so she could be led to the center. Once they had her there, the chanting increased, becoming a roar of discordant voices. The ones who had parted closed the circle again, placing their large shields as a barrier.

The great wolf did not like this at all and fought harder to free herself. The Wild Ones who were controlling her pushed her with their long iron poles, which oppressed and strangled the beautiful animal.

"Cowards..." muttered Gerd under his breath, wishing he could go down and free the beautiful animal.

Suddenly, one of the Wild Ones holding the wolf slipped and fell face-first on the ground from the strength the wolf was pulling with. Before the others could help him, the huge animal pounced on him and killed him with a tremendous bite on the nape. The Wild Ones of the circle cheered at the strength and deadliness of the beast that had just killed one of their own in a moment of distraction.

Another Wild One from the circle took his dead comrade's place, picking up his pole and joining the rest in the task of keeping the wolf in the middle of the circle. The wolf kept jumping, pulling and struggling to get free, but she had six nooses around her neck, and the strength and weight of the Wild Ones was too much for her. She was strangling herself the more strength she exerted.

Gerd could not understand what was going on here and what this terrible bloody ritual was, but what he did know was that he did not like it.

Not at all.

Chapter 26

The Wild Ones' chief remained a couple of steps back, watching. He began to shout words at the top of his lungs that could be heard over the ritual chanting of his circle of Wild Ones.

The eight holding the great wolf suddenly released the iron poles they were holding her with and took shelter at top speed behind their comrades with the large shields. The giant wolf, finding herself free even though she still had the poles hanging from her neck, began to attack the shields that formed the circle surrounding her. She pounced and hit the shields, and the Wild Ones withstood the blows without allowing even a crack to open up between them that she might escape through.

The wolf jumped and attacked with growls while the chief of the Wild Ones gave them orders. Gerd assumed the orders were to maintain the circle so the wolf could not escape. The power of her attacks made the Wild Ones step back, but immediately those on their sides covered them, pushing the wolf with their shields to make her retreat. It was obvious this was not the first time they had performed this ritual. They were well trained and all knew what to do.

After several attempts to escape, the wolf, who was burdened with the poles hanging from her neck, turned to her pup. She protected him, growling, enraged at those surrounding them, showing them her teeth which were tremendous for a wolf, larger than a tiger's. The sight of her maw caused fear and respect, especially if it was accompanied by a growl that promised a painful death.

Suddenly, from another cave entrance three Wild Ones appeared, armed with two-headed axes, with their torsos, thighs, and arms painted red. They went to their leader who was waiting for them. When they were before him, they knelt. The chief said some words while the chanting continued. He pointed at them from left to right and then, raising his arms, shouted something at the top of his lungs.

The first Wild One he had pointed to, stood up and headed to the circle. One of the shields moved, and the Wild One marked in red entered the circle of shields. Gerd guessed he was going to face the great wolf. He could not believe his eyes. Were these Wild Ones mad? Why were they doing this? What was the need? It was crazy!

The Wild One gave a shout and, raising the great axe, initiated his attack on the giant wolf. The pup whimpered and his mother growled. Then the wolf pounced and caught the Wild One in mid-run, falling upon him. She knocked down the Wild One with her momentum and the weight of her body. Gerd's jaw dropped. The leap had been powerful, more so considering the poles dragging her down. The warrior tried to hit the wolf with his axe, but she went for his throat and tore it with two bites. The Wild One was dead in a moment.

The chanting developed into shouts and cries of surprise. The wolf stepped back, with blood on her muzzle, to where her pup was. Two Wild Ones entered the circle swiftly and carefully to retrieve the body of their dead comrade. The wolf was going to jump at them, but she held back and continued protecting her pup.

The chief shouted something to the second painted warrior, and he entered the circle while the rest cheered and shouted. Gerd was shocked at such an inhuman spectacle. The Wild One attacked the wolf, but he was not as aggressive as his comrade. He advanced and feinted but then stopped. He waited for the wolf to attack first so he could catch her in mid-leap and get her with his axe. The wolf came forward, biting the air, but did not leap. She was moving slowly and carefully, her body ready to leap but without doing so.

The Wild One, seeing that she was not leaping at him, calculated and, stepping forward, delivered a strong axe blow parallel to the floor at mid-height, seeking to get the wolf's head as she bared her fangs and growled. It looked like the blow was going to hit and kill the animal, but she stepped back with amazing agility and the axe cut only air. The Wild One took another step forward and delivered the same blow but in reverse. The wolf retreated again, letting the edge of the axe pass in front of her muzzle. In a swift move, she leapt while the warrior recovered his position after cutting air. The wolf fell on him with great force and knocked him down. They fought, the Wild One took out a knife, and stabbed her with his right hand. The wolf bit him with her terrible fangs. The fight did not last long. The wolf killed the Wild One on the floor with tremendous bites.

The shouts and cries of his comrades were heard again, filling the cave and echoing on the walls. The chief did not seem very happy and was shouting at the last Wild One marked in red.

They waited for the wolf to step back. She was wounded. She had several cuts she was licking. Once it was safe, they retrieved the dead warrior's body.

Gerd wanted to go down and stop this atrocity, but he knew that if he did. he would be killed and would not achieve anything. There were too many Wild Ones down there. He had to hold back, no matter what happened.

The third Wild One entered the circle and started toward the giant wolf. He was wary and did not attack first. He started going around the wolf, who was eying him without leaving her pup's side while she threatened the warrior, showing her teeth and growling. The wolf pup whimpered in fear. He knew something bad was going on and that he was in danger of dying.

The Wild One stood behind the wolf, forcing her to turn, dragging all the poles from her neck, and at that moment he attacked with a vertical blow. The wolf reacted and leapt onto the Wild One, but the edge of the axe hit her from behind. Even so, she attacked fiercely and bit him savagely in the thigh and arm, which made the warrior back up until he bumped into his comrades' shields.

The wolf withdrew with her pup. She was lame and bleeding from her right hind leg. The Wild One recovered and attacked the wolf. He delivered another vertical axe blow. Both wolf and pup leapt to one side. But the attack was accurate and cut the wolf in her chest. Even wounded, she leapt forward, ignoring the pain of the wound, and knocked the Wild One down. They fought on the floor, the wolf trying to finish him and the warrior defending himself with a long knife.

The chanting and shouts had ended. Everyone was watching the fight without missing a detail. All that could be heard were the growls of the wolf and the shouts of rage of the Wild One. After a moment, the warrior became still under the weight of the huge wolf. He was dead. The wolf stepped back and sought her pup. She was bleeding from multiple wounds that looked pretty bad, but she was not giving up. She was still showing her teeth at those surrounding her, defiant.

The chief began to wave his arms furiously. He was shouting and pointing at the three dead bodies that lay outside the circle. He pounded his chest with his fist and said something to one of the Wild Ones, who ran out of the cave. The Wild One returned after a moment with a weapon for his leader. A weapon which, the moment

Gerd saw it in the light of the torches, he had no doubt it was Gim's Double Death.

The weapon shone with golden flashes, and it was beautiful and impressive. The Wild One handed it to his leader, who took it with one hand as if it did not weigh anything at all, although it was a huge two-headed axe. He raised it above his head and let out a terrible war cry. He walked to the circle, which opened to let him through.

Gerd knew what was going to happen next. The chief was going to finish off the giant wolf. Gerd grabbed his bow and nocked an arrow. He looked at the wolf. Her wounds were fatal—she was not going to live, even if he intervened. He would not accomplish anything if he took the shot, and all those Wild Ones would come after him. He would not make it out alive. Not with the storm still raging outside. When he looked at the wolf pup, defenseless, he had to lower his bow.

"I'm sorry... you don't deserve such an end..." he muttered, heartbroken.

The chief began to deliver blows left and right with great speed and power as he walked toward the giant wolf, who was waiting beside her pup. The chief kept delivering blows to prevent the wolf from leaping at him. Mother and pup withdrew until their backs touched the shields. Finding herself cornered, she attacked them to try to escape the axe, but the Wild Ones withstood the animal's charges. The chief reached the wolf, and she had no choice but to attack him. She leapt forward with courage and aggressiveness. The axe caught her, and the blow nearly split her in two. She died instantly.

The chief gave a long shout of triumph, which was echoed by the rest of the Wild Ones.

Gerd sighed, saddened. At least death had come swiftly with that last blow from Gim's axe. He did not understand the purpose of it all. They had killed a beautiful, magnificent animal of an unknown wolf species, a noble, courageous animal who was just protecting her pup. How could people be so cruel and heartless? Gerd could not understand it. He could not fathom the fact that there were rituals in which animals were hurt for pleasure. It was demented, no matter how rooted it might be in their culture.

The worst part was that the celebration of the chief's victory went on for a long while amid cries and chants of joy. The Wild Ones sang around their leader. They hit the floor with the lower rim of their shields as if they were drums. The chief raised the axe over his head, holding it with two hands.

Gerd had to get the weapon, but he could not do it with the chief and all those Wild Ones present. He had to endure their celebrations, which left him with a bitter aftertaste. He waited for night to fall, for the strange ritual to end and the Wild Ones to withdraw to rest. Hiding where he was, he did not seem to be in great danger. As long as they did not see him, and he was quite deep inside the tunnel, there should be no trouble.

The great cave slowly emptied until only the three dead Wild Ones and the wolf's body were left. They had left the pup with his dead mother, and he refused to leave her side. He was whimpering and trying to wake his mother up with his muzzle, pressing up against her chest and head. The scene broke Gerd's heart.

For some reason, they had not taken any of the dead bodies away. The Wild Ones' habits were most strange. The chief went to rest through one of the back exits. Gerd seized the chance now that no one was left in the cave and searched in his rucksack for some rope, thin but strong enough to bear his weight. He found a place to tie it, a ledge that looked like a horn, a bit further back. He tied the rope and pulled hard. The ledge held.

He dropped the rope down along the wall. He took in a deep breath and started down. It was holding. He reached the floor and crouched by the wall. Several torches had already gone out, and the cave was half dark. He moved forward, hugging the wall cast in greater darkness. He stopped for a moment to check on the pup, who was not leaving his mother's side. He had to keep going. The axe was the priority. He raised his bow with an arrow already nocked.

He reached the exit the chief had vanished through and found a tunnel. At the end of the tunnel were two Wild Ones on watch duty. The distance was about twenty-five paces. Without hesitating, he released and hit the first guard in the forehead. His head was thrown back from the impact. The other Wild One opened his eyes wide and reached for his huge axe. He took a step toward Gerd and an arrow hit him in the throat. He stopped and dropped his axe, putting his hands to his throat.

Gerd knew he had caught them by surprise but that they would recover quickly. They were Wild Ones of the Ice, as hard as icebergs.

He dropped his bow and ran toward them. While he ran, he reached for his knife and axe.

The first Wild One brandished his axe. Gerd could hardly believe it. He had an arrow stuck in his forehead and still did not fall. The truth was that Gerd's shot had not been as accurate as he would have liked. It was a little to the right. The Wild One delivered a horizontal blow with his axe when he saw Gerd coming at him at a run.

Gerd stopped in his tracks, and the axe brushed his chest and hit the rock wall hard. He leapt forward and, with all his strength, buried his axe in the middle of the Wild One's forehead beside the arrow. The Wild One threw his head back from the tremendous blow and took a step back. Then he tripped and fell on his back on the floor.

The other Wild One, with one hand to his throat to stop the hemorrhage, and a long knife in his other hand came for Gerd. The Wild One's knife came straight toward Gerd's heart, but he deflected it with a strong defensive block using his own knife. He followed the block with a tremendous kick to the Wild One's stomach, who doubled up without air. Gerd buried his knife in a downward movement in the man's nape with a dull blow. Half his knife came out the Wild One's throat. He pulled it out and the Wild One collapsed, dead.

Gerd hastened to recover his axe from the forehead of the other dead Wild One. At that moment a figure appeared in the tunnel, coming from the back cave. He asked a question in the Wild language, which Gerd did not understand. What he did know was that the figure was the chief, because he was carrying Gim's Double Death in his hands.

Before the great Wild One could realize what had happened there, Gerd launched his attack. The chief saw it and raised the axe at top speed, as if it weighed no more than a feather. He delivered a vertical blow with all his might, trying to destroy the enemy coming at him. Gerd saw the attack and calculated quickly, stopping in his tracks and letting the axe hit the rocky floor before him. Then he raised his right arm and with all his strength threw his short axe at the chief. Seeing the axe coming at his chest, the chief deflected it with the great axe, raising the weapon defensively. The force of the axe made it bounce upward, and it hit him in the face. He was left half stunned.

Gerd seized his chance and jumped forward while the chief tried to hit him with the golden axe. The side blow the stunned chief delivered came toward Gerd's body who, seeing the move, leapt forward with his knife in front of him. The golden axe hit Gerd in his ribs at the same time he buried his knife in the chief's neck.

Gerd doubled up from the tremendous blow he had sustained and lost his knife. He looked down at his side, thinking he had been killed, but saw that the blow had been with the metal handle of the axe, not with the double head. It had broken a couple of ribs, but he had not been cut. He looked at the chief and saw him stepping backward with Gerd's knife stuck in his neck. He had dropped the golden axe. Gerd calmly picked it up from the floor and noticed that it was indeed as light as a feather. Now he understood how it was possible for the chief to wield it with such ease and speed. He advanced toward the leader of the Wild Ones as the chief withdrew to his cave. The leader did not make it. Gerd delivered such a terrible axe blow with both hands that it nearly split the Wild One in two.

The pain in his ribs made him double over, but he did not let go of the golden axe. It took him a moment to recover, and once he did, he looked at the dead chief on the floor.

"That's for the wolf," he said with contained rage. "Whoever mistreats an animal for pleasure deserves an exemplary punishment. Enjoy yours."

He breathed in deeply and exhaled. Then he inspected the weapon. He had to make sure it was Gim's Double Death, although its lightness and the golden reflections indicated it was. When he examined it, he realized it had engravings along the handle, but they were not Ripdis's. His were shaped like waves, but these were incomprehensible symbols that did not even look manmade. The discovery baffled him.

If Ripdis had given the axe to Gim, and so it seemed based on everything Gerd had found out so far, and the Wild Ones had the axe, as was the case, then why did the axe not have the characteristic wave shapes Ripdis marked his creations with?

He thought about it for a moment, as Egil would, seeking a connection. The solution to the enigma was, as a rule, the most direct and logical answer. In this case in particular, the most logical and simple answer was this: Ripdis had not forged the weapon Gerd now held. This being the case, if the legend had a basis in reality, Ripdis must have given Gim a weapon with power to help him, but it was not a weapon he had created. Gerd would have to run these conclusions by Egil, but he was sure this was the case. Ripdis had found or obtained the weapon and given it to Gim, passing it off as his own creation when in reality it was not. That would explain why it was a magical weapon and the rest of what had happened.

Gerd turned, picked up his weapons, and left.

As he left the place, he held his ribs. They hurt, and he was sure a couple were broken. He was going to have trouble escaping the cave. Luckily, he did not see any other Wild Ones. No one came to find out what was going on.

He reached the main cave where the fallen bodies from the terrible ritual ceremony still remained. He glimpsed the rope he had to climb up and headed to it at a quick pace. A whimper reached him from the pup, who was still beside his mother. Gerd stopped and looked at him. The poor wolf pup was mourning the death of his mother. He had already realized she was dead and would not wake up to look after him.

"Poor little thing…" Gerd said under his breath.

The wolf pup looked at him with moist eyes.

Gerd could not resist and went over to him. He bent down and offered him his hand. The wolf pup growled and showed him his teeth threateningly.

"I can see you have a fighting spirit, but I'm not your enemy," Gerd said, although considering the fact that he was carrying Gim's axe in one hand, he did not exactly make a calming figure.

The little animal, scared and sad because of his mother's death, was trying to defend himself by showing aggressiveness. Gerd stroked his head with his right hand while not letting go of the axe with the other. The wolf pup looked into Gerd's eyes, as if he were trying to guess his intentions.

"Take it easy. I'm not going to hurt you. I was hoping they wouldn't kill you. You were lucky."

The pup growled again.

Gerd thought about getting up and leaving the pup there. He had to get out. He had already obtained the axe, which was the most important thing. But, something inside him stopped him from leaving. He could not leave this poor animal to his fate there. Not after witnessing what those Wild Ones had done to the pup's mother.

"Look, I can't leave you here... you're coming with me," Gerd said, and he picked him up with his free hand, holding him to his chest. The wolf pup resisted at first with growls and bites, but as soon as he realized Gerd meant him no harm, he quieted down and kept silent.

Gerd stood up with the golden axe in one hand and, holding the wolf pup against his chest with the other, walked over to the rope.

"This is going to be complicated," he told the wolf pup, who stared at him with wide eyes. He adjusted the great axe on his back, crossing it with his quiver and bow so that it was held in place and would not fall off. As he did so, he realized how big the weapon was, even larger than he had calculated. Since it did not weigh anything at all, it seemed to not take up space, but it did. Once he had it secured fast, he concentrated on the next problem: the pup. He put him inside his shirt.

"Stay still until I reach the tunnel," Gerd told him, although he knew the pup would not understand him.

To his surprise, the pup did not shift and stayed very still against his chest. He was surprised the pup was not more aggressive. Then he thought of all the pup had been through and reasoned that he must be exhausted.

Gerd did not have time to waste, so he jumped to reach the rope. He propped his feet against the rock and started climbing. He pulled himself up with the strength of his arms and 'walked' up the rock wall. His legs moved as the strength of his arms propelled his body upward.

He reached the tunnel, and with one last effort he got inside. He stayed there for a moment, lying on his back and snorting. Climbing vertical walls aided by a rope had never been a strong point of his, and he was thankful for how strong the Ranger's rope had proven. Suddenly, the wolf pup's head popped up among his clothes and stared at him. It was a strange situation, since Gerd was lying on the floor and the little animal's nose was touching his chin.

"I'll have to give you a name..." he told the pup while he wondered what would suit him. He found one after a moment. "I'll call you Argi. Yeah, I think the name suits you."

The wolf pup stared at Gerd and licked his chin.

"Now I won't need Esben to look for a familiar for me. You'll be my familiar, little big guy with sharp teeth."

Argi licked his chin again, and with that gesture their bond was sealed.

Chapter 27

Ingrid was watching the majestic walls that protected the city of Orecor in the distance from the middle of the wide road that led to it. She had been watching them for a while already, as she approached the gates. She had had to stop to make sure her eyes were not tricking her. The closer she got, the more impressive those walls appeared. And this could not be the case, because already in the distance they looked about ninety feet tall.

She was studying them with her hand shading her eyes from the sun which, although it was winter in this eastern part of the continent, shone more intensely. Because of some strange optical effect, the walls seemed taller still. She wrinkled her nose. Now they looked to her to be over a hundred and twenty feet tall, which only the largest fortified cities of Tremia were. This was not only impressive, but also very interesting, or, as Egil would put it, fascinating. She had already known that both the city and its walls were legendary; she had been hearing about them since she was a little girl, and it was a place she had always wanted to visit. But as her aunt used to say, "you have to see it to believe it, the rest is exaggeration."

She went on toward the city, whose reputation she was already beginning to see was no exaggeration but a patent truth. She loved everything that had to do with military aspects, and a walled city-state, renown for the ferocity of its troops and its impenetrable nature, fascinated her. She was delighted that her search for Neil's Dragon-killer had led her directly to this city. She would be able to fulfill one of her childhood's dreams, to visit the famous, unconquerable city-state of the east, since in all its history it had never been conquered by any foreign army.

As she walked, the cage where she was carrying Lisa, her white owl, was hanging from her rucksack. It swayed, and every now and then the beautiful bird complained with a click of her beak. Ingrid thought about taking her out of her cage, but they were already too close to the great city, and there might be hunters or soldiers who might hurt her. Ingrid had let her fly free all the way from the

Eastern Pearl, which was where Camu had brought them using the Portal from the Shelter's Pearl. Now she had the owl in the cage just in case. She did not want anything to happen to her.

"What a wall… and what impressive double gates," she told Lisa when she stopped to look at them.

The owl hooted, although she could not see much since she was behind Ingrid's back.

She approached the city and stood in line to gain access. The colossal double gate that accessed the city was open, and a cordon of over a hundred soldiers were guarding it. From what Ingrid knew, that was the only gate with access through the wall, so you could only enter or exit the city through there. The gates were forged from metal, and their thickness awed her. From what she could see as she stood in line to enter the city, the gates had a width of nine feet. They were so big and heavy that the pulley mechanism needed to open them had to be ten times as big and complex as those of a large city like Norghana. Each of the two parts of the gate had to weigh as much as a house, or more. They had four squares depicted on each, and within those squares she could admire the profiles of large lions roaring. Ingrid was in awe. Knocking down those gates would require such powerful siege weapons or magic that it was possible a method did not even exist yet.

Ingrid noticed the soldiers guarding the entrance and supervising who could enter the city and who could not. They wore simple classic armor. Their limbs were covered with vambrances, and greaves that looked bronze in color but which Ingrid guessed were steel. On their torsos and backs they wore a short sleeveless cuirass, with the head of a roaring lion depicted on the front and back. She was surprised to see that they wore some sort of short white skirt down to their knees, with long, thick, copper-colored plates as protection. They wore helmets that covered their heads with two long slits for their eyes at the front. Their feet were protected by sandals with metal tips.

She moved toward the long line waiting to enter the city. As she got closer, she noticed that all the soldiers, with the exception of the officers, carried a steel spear and a large round shield that covered almost their whole body. The large shield also had the roaring lion engraved on it. They were not as big and strong as a Norghanian, but they were lean, which meant they were accustomed to hard work. She glimpsed dark-brown eyes under the helmets. The soldiers' skin was slightly darker than the Norghanians or those of the kingdom of Irinel, but it was still quite light.

She got in line to enter the city. The soldiers were inspecting everyone who wanted to go in one by one, and there were many. Most of those in the line were traders, artisans and farmers who were coming to the city to earn a living through trade. The five cities of the east coast formed the Confederation of Free Cities of the East and were cities that lived off trade, particularly maritime, since they all had large commercial ports. The city of Orecor was also famous for its army and military regime. The city-state was ruled by a military system.

She noted that the soldiers seemed well prepared and concentrated on their duty. It was said that the city's soldiers were the best, unbeatable on the battlefield. Luckily for other kingdoms, they usually did not leave their great walled city and their main job was to defend it. No one had attacked them in a long time, although in the past, wars between the five cities had been as terrible as they had been long. Control for the maritime routes had caused innumerable wars involving the five cities, and alliances and betrayals had been as unexpected as they had been bloody. Luckily, the five city-states had signed an alliance a few years ago, and now the eastern sea and its coast were at peace. How long this alliance would last, no one dared to predict.

Along the middle of the road were several lines where the traders were waiting for their turn to enter the great city. Along two side lines on each side, a large number of carts were leaving the city, loaded with all kinds of materials. Ingrid watched how the traders gained access to the city after stating their intentions to the officers. Some had permits, while others paid a fee to be able to enter the city to trade.

She waited patiently for her turn to arrive. Gradually and calmly, the lines entered the city. Not everyone gained access though. The soldiers dismissed whoever they thought did not fulfill the prerequisites to enter. They did this without disturbing the peace in a formal, serious, threatening manner, but without any altercation. The soldiers were obviously well trained.

An officer stopped her and spoke to her in the language of the place. Ingrid did not understand him.

"Sorry," she replied in Norghanian, "I don't understand the

language."

The officer examined her from head to toe and then turned. He addressed a couple of older men with white hair wearing green robes with white borders. They approached and stood by the officer, who asked Ingrid something in his language again.

"I'm sorry, I don't understand. I come from the north," Ingrid pointed in that direction, although she was leagues away from home.

One of the elders addressed Ingrid.

"Are you from the kingdom of Norghana?"

Ingrid's eyebrows rose with surprise.

"I am. You speak my language?"

"I do. Yours and twenty-five others. I am an interpreter."

"That's great. My name's Ingrid. Pleased to meet you," she greeted him, delighted to be able to speak with someone who understood her. Egil had already told her that because of all the trading that took place in the five city-states, they had a number of interpreters who spoke most of the languages in Tremia. For the eastern cities, trade was essential, and they made things easy with interpreters and other services like money-loaners, dealers in coin, and similar professions—anything that facilitated making financial and commercial deals.

The officer said something to the old interpreter.

"State your nationality and reason for your visit to our city," he said.

"Ingrid Stenberg, Norghanian. I'm here to trade in weapons."

The interpreter translated to the officer.

"Weapons? Wholesale or retail?"

"Retail. I look for very precious weapons, relics."

The officer was thoughtful when the reply was translated.

"Weapons trade is always welcome in the city. That of special or singular weapons, even more. There's a tax you have to pay in order to come in and trade."

"A tax?"

"You must pay a sum in gold in order to enter the city. Here in the east, this is common practice. You can't access any of the five city-states without a commercial reason and you must always pay a tribute when you do, for the privilege of trading in our cities."

"Oh… I see…" Ingrid played dumb, but she already knew about this. Egil had explained it all to her and given her the gold she would need to enter the city. He had also told her to play dumb and poor, otherwise they would ask for an astronomic figure.

"You must pay for access to the city."

"The thing is that… I don't have much gold with me… I didn't know I'd have to pay at the gate."

The officer listened to the translation and barked something. He seemed upset.

"How do you intend to buy precious weapons if you don't have gold to access the city?"

"My master has a financing line with one of the commercial agents of the city," Ingrid explained, just as Egil had told her to.

The officer seemed happier with that reply.

"It will be ten gold coins to enter the city."

"Ten coins? That's a lot."

The officer was adamant.

"Fine," Ingrid said, drawing her money pouch and paying the ten coins. She thought it was sheer robbery of huge proportions. Ten gold coins was a lot. But Egil had already calculated that, and he had not been wrong. They had to pay dearly to enter the city and trade in weapons of great value.

The officer said something to a scribe beside him and wrote a permit which he later sealed with the emblem of the city.

"This is a permit to trade in weapons of great worth. Valid for one month," the interpreter told her.

Ingrid bowed.

"Thank you very much," she said and, taking the permit, she passed the control post and headed to the colossal gates, following the rest of the traders who had just passed by the entrance control. Along the two sections of the gated city, soldiers were in position with their spears and shields.

She went in and was amazed not only by the height but by the thickness of the walls. She counted fifteen paces wide as she crossed the threshold. Not only that, the wall was thicker at the bottom and then tapered gradually in tiers so that the battlements were much narrower than the base. Without a doubt, it was built to endure an attack with siege weapons.

She continued watching, and another thing that drew her attention was the rock used to build the wall and the houses she could see in the first streets of the city. These were not the ugly gray and blackish rocks of Norghana. They were a yellow-orange earth color that added life and beauty to the buildings. The buildings were also perfectly aligned with every stone in place. The outer wall was smooth like marble and did not have any handholds or seams. Climbing up that wall without the help of ropes or ladders was impossible. The great defensive wall that surrounded the city was beautiful, apart from being impressive. The shade of the stone it had been built with made it pleasant to the eye, and all the stone was perfectly preserved.

She entered the city, and as she walked along one of the main avenues several things caught her attention. First, all the houses were built with the same rock that had been used to build the wall. The houses were only two stories tall, square with flat roofs. They all had a small porch, located at the front or back, with two columns that went up to the roof. They looked like small temples to Ingrid. She also noticed that they formed perfectly rectangular blocks, limited by wide avenues. Someone had gone to great lengths to organize and lay out all the houses and streets.

The second thing that caught her attention was that there were soldiers everywhere. Not only upon the battlements with guards, but also inside. Wherever she looked, she saw soldiers with their round shields and spears. There were many posted along the avenues, standing so still they looked like warrior statues, only living and breathing, and beside the fountains in the gardens. Not only that, but every few paces she crossed paths with a city patrol on guard duty made up of a dozen soldiers who marched up and down the streets without pause. They seemed to be patrolling the city without missing a street. The surprising thing was that, as a rule, in large cities there was usually only one patrol for several neighborhoods. Here, every block had its own patrol, and then there were additional soldiers who patrolled the great avenues throughout the entire city. She thought it was impressive. It was the most well maintained, safest place in all of Tremia.

The third thing that drew her attention was the fact that, being a predominantly military city, the avenues were filled with carts and wagons with lots of goods to trade. Ingrid was beginning to realize that the city was not only a military power, but a commercial one. It made sense, since during her journey from the Pearl to the city she had barely seen any villages or farms, as were customary around large cities. Here it seemed that the city itself was a commercial center where gold and goods were exchanged for other products and gold. She found this interesting.

She decided to tour the city to familiarize herself with it. She had permission to stay and trade, so she likely would not run into any problems in spite of the large number of soldiers she could see. She felt like the city was at war and waiting to be attacked at any moment. But from what Egil had told her, the city-state was not at war with any other kingdom. Ever since they had signed the alliance to form the Confederation of Free Cities of the East, the wars had ended, and now they were a continental power precisely because of all their economic power, as well as their military might, judging by what she was seeing. The other four city-states were not as militarized as this one. They each had their own culture and peculiarities that made them unique. What made Orecor unique was its military regime and its huge army of quality soldiers.

She arrived at the central area of the city and found a huge square where about thirty large statues had been erected. She stopped to look at them. They were all the same size, about thirty feet tall and nine wide, and all featured military men and women. There was no doubt they were military, because they were all dressed in armor with a sword at their waist and a helmet under their arm. All of the poses were also similar, with a raised chin and a triumphant, sharp air to them, as if the men and women were looking at a recent conquest. She approached one of the female statues and saw her name and rank detailed on the stone, but Ingrid could not read the strange writing. It was not the same alphabet used by the Norghanians. She guessed the woman had been a great soldier. Seeing several women among the statues made her feel good. This city might be a place where she could prosper—well, not her in particular, but women like her.

A group of about thirty children around eight years old passed through the statues. They were running in formation with rucksacks strapped to their backs that appeared loaded. They were following a youth of about sixteen who wore full armor and set the pace for them with a military song. Ingrid found it amusing. They seemed to be training, but they were too young for that. She saw them cross the square of statues and continue to the east.

Ingrid shrugged and went on her way toward the sea. She wanted to see the big port she knew the city had on its eastern side. To her surprise, when she got to the foot of the eastern wall, she found there was no possible way to reach the port, which had to be on the other side of the wall. She noticed there were some stairs in the rock that wound up to the battlements. On them were soldiers on guard duty, but she also saw people going up and down in an orderly manner. They were not soldiers but civilians, the few who lived in the city, since so far more than half the people she had seen were soldiers or related to the military somehow.

"If they can go up, so can I," she told Lisa.

The owl hooted, which Ingrid took for a 'yes'. At least it was not a 'no'."

She walked to the huge steps. There were two soldiers on guard who ignored her entirely, so she started up. The stairway was six feet wide and hugged the wall diagonally. She went up determinedly until she got to a point where it changed direction and continued climbing diagonally but in the opposite direction, which baffled her. At the turn there were two more guards, but they did not stop her, so she continued going up. The stairs changed direction twice more before she could reach the battlements. The height was enormous, and the stairway system was simple but ingenious.

At last, she reached the battlements, and from the extreme height she looked down at the sea. Her jaw dropped. The view was spectacular. She put Lisa in her cage on the battlement so the owl could also see such beauty. The ocean spread before them, blue and immeasurable. She could see the line of the horizon in the distance where the blue sea met the gray winter sky.

"Isn't it awesome?"

This time Lisa said nothing. She was staring at the great ocean with her huge eyes wide open.

Below, at the foot of the wall, she saw a large bay of rocks without a beach, around which a colossal harbor had been built. She counted more than a hundred vessels docked or moored, mostly commercial and massive. Further at sea, she saw about twenty war triremes with large orange sails and the unmistakable roaring lion head in the center of each. This was part of the city's military fleet.

There were two wide paths that came up from the harbor. One went to the south wall and the other to the north. Carts and wagons came and went along the two paths. They both ended at the city gate Ingrid had entered through. She thought it would make more sense to build a gate in the eastern wall where she was standing, but she soon understood the logic of not doing so. If a more powerful fleet took the harbor and the bay, it would be able to access the city through the sea. This way, they had to go all the way around. The defenses made the city much safer.

"They're certainly clever, very clever," she told Lisa, who was still staring at the sea, spellbound.

For a while they stared at the awesome harbor, enjoying the sea and the view. Not only the view to the east but also of the city, which they could enjoy from up here. Ingrid identified the main military buildings, the residential quarters, and the large trading area, which occupied almost a quarter of the city with thousands of stalls, workshops, boutiques, and shops of all kinds.

The city impressed her indeed. Its martial order, its bet on trade, its soldiers, its harbor—she thought it all most impressive.

Happy to have seen the great harbor and the bay, she went back. It was time to start asking about the sword. There was only one problem: she did not speak the local language. Thinking about it, she remembered the elderly man in the green robe. He was an interpreter. She would have to find one for herself. She headed to the trading area. All business was conducted there, and there had to be interpreters, or so she hoped. Surely, where there were gold and other goods to exchange, there was also bound to be someone to help translate.

She left the wall and went to the main square with the big statues, heading for the trading area. She reached the commercial section and entered. Even here, with thousands of people trading, order and peace reigned that Ingrid had never seen in any big city. The fact that there were soldiers everywhere must be part of it.

She searched among the stalls and shops and came to an area with more soldiers. She saw it was a block of artisan workshops where jewels and precious metals were crafted. She also saw several high-ranked officers with white streaks in their hair buying jewels, and also several women in armor taking a look at the jewels. There were only a few people wearing robes who were buying, civilians, and they were not all from the city, judging by their clothes and the color of their skin, since there were quite a few Noceans among the customers. This surprised her, since the Noceans and the city-states were rivals when it came to maritime trade. Perhaps there was not as much rivalry as Norghana thought.

Suddenly, she saw a figure in a green robe going into one of the shops. She wasted no time and walked in after the figure. The shop was a jeweler's. The salesman greeted the two arrivals: a foreign trader and his interpreter. She stood close to them and listened. She did not understand a word, but the trader showed the foreigner a large sapphire, and after a long conversation between the three, the foreigner paid in gold and took the sapphire. At the door, he paid the interpreter and they parted ways.

Ingrid approached the man from behind and tapped his shoulder just as he was leaving the shop. The interpreter turned.

"I need help with the language. Do you speak Norghanian?"

The interpreter listened to her attentively.

"Norghanian?" he asked.

"Yes, Norghanian," Ingrid confirmed with a nod.

The interpreter signaled for her to follow him, and she complied. The man navigated through the crowd that filled the area's streets and squares and stopped before a house with a large sign over it. He turned to Ingrid and signaled to her to wait there, then he went into the house.

After a moment, another interpreter came to the door.

"You're looking for a translator who speaks Norghanian?"

Ingrid could barely contain her joy.

"Yes, please."

"Then I'm your man," he smiled. He was in his seventies and had brown eyes.

"My name is Ingrid, and I am Norghanian."

"I am Celopus, an interpreter," and he pointed at the sign above the house.

"What does it say?"

"House of Interpreters," he smiled.

Ingrid sighed and shrugged.

"That's good to know."

"How can I help you?"

"I need your services. I've come looking for an extremely valuable weapon."

"I see. Do you know which trader has it?"

"That's the problem. I don't."

"In that case, it may take a few days. As you can see, the city is a place with a lot of trade. There are weapons, artisans, and dealers by the hundreds."

"Yes, I noticed that already… it's going to be like looking for a needle in a haystack. Will you help me?"

"For a price, of course," the translator smiled.

Ingrid showed him a pouch of gold she carried at her waist that Egil had procured for her.

"Let's get started. I'm anxious to find that sword."

Chapter 28

Ingrid and Celopus, her interpreter, went by several large buildings with about twenty tall columns on their façades. Celopus wanted to consult a couple of acquaintances in the wealthy part of the city before heading to the commercial area where they would have to go shop by shop, making enquiries and hoping with their fingers crossed for some luck.

By their look, Ingrid had no doubt these were not palaces but military buildings. They heard voices, and Celopus invited her to go and take a look. The soldiers posted by the columns were stoically doing their duty. In fact, they looked like statues and said nothing to them.

Ingrid saw large squares behind the buildings filled with soldiers practicing with spear and shield in compact formations. They were divided into regiments, and each one had several officers in charge of giving orders and exercises to perform. They saw that one regiment, which was ten men wide and ten men long, all very close together, was fighting another regiment with the same proportions. This intrigued Ingrid, who wanted to stop and watch.

"Our infantry regiments with their spears and large round shields are well known and feared," Celopus told her.

"Why do they stand so close together? Don't they interfere with each other when fighting?"

"It would seem so, wouldn't it? But it's the other way around. That formation is called a phalanx, and it's extremely effective against less organized groups of enemies. You'll see."

Ingrid nodded and watched.

At some commands from the officers, both regiments began to advance at mid-pace to fight. The officers marked the rhythm. The first lines of both regiments met in the center of the square. The officers halted them and both regiments stood still, awaiting the next order. Ingrid noticed they were not the only spectators. There was quite an audience watching the soldiers practice. They were on the east side on some sort of stone steps. She felt a little out of place watching the soldiers, since she was a foreigner. On the other hand, if the practice was open to the public, she was entitled to watch just like the rest.

After a moment, the officers on both sides gave the orders. The regiment on the left attacked, stepping forward and hitting the one on the right with their spears against the defenders' shields. All the shields had the figure of a roaring lion, the same as their cuirasses. The spears hit powerfully, and they could hear the echo on the shields as the soldiers exhaled hard. At an order from the officers, the attack was reversed, and now the regiment on the left was attacked hard by the one on the right and withstood the clash firmly.

They repeated the exercise a dozen times. First one side attacked and the other defended itself, then they switched. She was surprised they did this without a single soldier losing their place or stumbling. What she understood the moment she saw it, was the strength of the phalanx formation. The tight line they formed with their huge, round shields ensured they covered one another perfectly and made a thick barrier of impenetrable shields. Only the feet and helmets could be seen. There was no way to break the line. Besides, the spears kept the enemy at bay and killed them if they attacked with a shorter weapon, like a sword or axe.

"I can see why this phalanx formation has proven so successful for your people."

"Impressive, isn't it? We're very proud of our army."

"Are they all professional soldiers? I mean, not only these practicing here now, but everyone I've seen in the city."

"They are. It's their career. Since the age of eight, they train to be soldiers. The best are chosen for this profession. Whoever is not chosen is considered a dishonor to their family."

"But perhaps not all of them want to be soldiers and fight. They might want to be fishermen, artists, farmers…"

"Not in this city. Here everyone, women and men, dream of being soldiers of the city, soldier-citizens as we call them. It's an honor to serve the city like this, to defend it from the enemy. Those who don't manage to become soldier-citizens are disavowed by society and their own families."

"That's surprising. I'd never seen such a strong, positive feeling toward belonging to the army."

"We risk our lives. This city only survives because of its army."

"It's the same in many kingdoms, but that doesn't mean everyone wants to be in the army."

"Then they must be weak kingdoms. Here, it's an honor and a privilege to be a soldier-citizen."

"Interesting…" Ingrid was thoughtful.

When the exercises finished, the audience applauded. It seemed strange to Ingrid. At a new order of the officers, both regiments practiced movements to the sides, front, and back. Ingrid was surprised to see how synchronized they all were; they moved as one in any direction, as if they were one thick mass and not a hundred different people.

At another order, the two regiments halted. The officers called out a special formation, and the soldiers on every side of the rectangle who formed each regiment stood looking outward with their spears ready. The inner lines stood, reinforcing each outer line. Ingrid saw the formation and knew what it was. It was an anti-cavalry formation. If the enemy army was mounted, it could not break the defense of the spears on the four sides of the rectangle.

"Very interesting, yes," she murmured, nodding, pleased with what she was seeing.

"I'm glad you find our small civilization so interesting."

"I wouldn't say small. I see a military power."

Celopus smiled, pleased.

"That's what we like to believe. Let's continue our search for your weapon. You'll be able to see more entertainment as we travel around the city."

Celopus' acquaintances were unable to tell them who specifically might have information about the weapon they were looking for, but they did tell them about a few traders who were most likely to know anything about the matter. This reduced the search greatly, although she was not sure they were going to find the weapon. The list was still long, it would take them several days.

Celopus got Ingrid a simple room at one of the innumerable inns and hostels in the commercial district. Ingrid would be able to rest and leave Lisa there, as well as her gear.

A couple of days later, at mid-afternoon, Ingrid and Celopus went into the shop of yet another weapons dealer. They had already visited over a dozen, so far without any luck.

"Let's hope we're lucky in this one," Celopus said with an encouraging smile as they walked into the luxurious shop.

"Yes, let's hope so," Ingrid nodded, not so optimistically.

The shop was large and, from how well decorated it was and the weapons she could see at the entrance, higher quality than others they had visited. A trader of advanced age came over quickly. He was wearing an elegant, long white robe, and on his right shoulder there was an engraving of a spear and shield. Celopus had explained to Ingrid that this identified him as a weapons dealer. In the commercial area, everything was very well organized and maintained. Shops of the same type were organized into quadrants within the great mercantile area to facilitate trading with the buyers. Every shop was identified over the door with its type, name, and the emblems this man wore, and this way no one was misled. Besides, it made things easier.

Ingrid was delighted with all this military order. She wished things were like this in Norghana, where disorder was rampant. Things worked differently there.

"This is Dopemus, weapons dealer, famous for the exquisite pieces he trades with," Celopus introduced him to Ingrid.

Ingrid made a slight courteous bow.

"A pleasure," she said, and Celopus translated.

"What kind of weapon does the young lady want?" the trader asked.

"A very special one, I'm afraid," Celopus translated.

"Then you've come to the right shop. My pieces are exquisite and very special," Dopemus said, waving his hand toward the shelves and cabinets where he exhibited worthy weapons.

Ingrid walked around, studying them.

"We're looking for a sword," she said, and Celopus translated.

"The sword is the weapon of a general, a leader," Dopemus said, pleased.

"Don't soldiers carry swords in this kingdom?" Ingrid asked, realizing she had not seen a single soldier carrying one.

"No, of course not. Soldiers and officers of low and mid rank use spears. The spear is the weapon of this city-state—the legends of our ancestors have been forged with them. The sword is a noble weapon, but the spear is what wins battles.

"Didn't you know that? When you see our army in action, you'll understand."

"I'd like to see it, indeed."

"They usually practice in the martial district. You can go and watch them. It's open to the public. All the citizens of the city must realize the sacrifice required to obtain the skill and strength of our soldiers, and all our army as a whole. They must respect them. Civilians have the good fortune of being protected by them in a city-state that has never fallen into enemy hands in all its existence," Celopus said proudly, the same pride Dopemus had expressed with absolute certainty. It seemed almost every person in the city felt that same level of pride.

"From what I've seen, there aren't many civilians, not like in other cities or kingdoms," Ingrid commented.

"Here there's a great military tradition. Most people want to be in the army, ever since early childhood. They don't want to be civilians. In fact, there are benefits to having enough civilians in the necessary areas of life in the city, such as healing, or obtaining food from the earth and the sea. In many cases, already trained soldiers are allowed to do civilian jobs for a few years, given that we never have enough civilians available," Celopus explained.

"In fact, my son and I," Dopemus said, pointing at the young man watching them from further in the shop, "were in the army before turning to the family business."

"That's not only a great military tradition, it's much more than that. This doesn't happen in any other place in Tremia, as far as I know."

"And that's why we're so proud of our military city and culture…" Celopus said almost apologetically to Ingrid.

"Come inside with me. I'll show you my most valuable swords," Dopemus said and led the way. They followed him to a hall with glass cabinets and armories that only had swords. He had all kinds, from Nocean scimitars of different types, with different curves of the blade; to short, wide, double-edged swords from the kingdom of Erenal; some other swords that were similar although not so wide, which generals and high-ranked soldiers in the city carried; or the long, rectangular spider swords; and even lengthy Norriel swords from the region to the north of the kingdom of Rogdon. Dopemus' son showed them to Ingrid, giving all kinds of explanations about their main use and origin. Celopus translated while she studied each sword they let her examine and test out.

"Do you like them?" Dopemus asked.

"I not only like them, I think they're amazing," Ingrid said as she made movements with a long double-edged sword and straight crossguard.

"Are any of them what you're looking for?"

Ingrid stopped tracing slashes with the sword and gave it back to Dopemus' son.

"I'm afraid not. The sword we're looking for is made of gold," Ingrid said.

Dopemus made a face.

"There are no gold swords, not for fighting. They're no good. Gold doesn't have the qualities required for fighting against steel."

"I know, forgive me, but the sword I'm looking for has been described as gold."

The trader was thoughtful for a moment.

"It could be a ceremonial sword, or a sword created for prestige or ostentation, but it can't be a battle sword."

"The sword I'm looking for is called Neils' Dragon-killer."

Dopemus was thoughtful again, which surprised Ingrid since, up till then, every trader they had asked had replied immediately with a negative. No one knew the weapon. No one had ever heard about it. And yet, Egil's studies and research pointed to this city, and that was why Ingrid was here. Egil was rarely wrong, but this was a complicated search and he might have made a mistake. She decided not to think like that and maintain her optimism. If she had to return home empty-handed, she would, although it would be very disappointing.

"Do you know of it? It's supposedly a gold sword capable of piercing the scales of a dragon," she insisted, in case she was lucky, since she saw something odd in the eyes of the trader.

"That weapon…" Dopemus turned. "Wait here a moment," he said and went out the back door of the house.

Ingrid questioned Celopus silently to see whether he knew what was going on. He replied with a shrug.

"He'll be back in a moment," Dopemus' son assured them.

They waited, and meanwhile Ingrid continued admiring the wonderful swords. They were not very elaborate or ornamented. They were real swords, for real combat. She had found the same thing in almost all the shops they had been to. The priority was swords for battle, not for nobles or rich merchants. In fact, she had been shown very few ornamental weapons, with jewels or gold plated, which had surprised her, since in other kingdoms what was considered a beautiful, special weapon was precisely the one that had been finely wrought and had all kinds of luxuries, such as jewels or gold engravings.

Dopemus came back with a tome in his hands and showed it to her.

"The name rang a bell, but I couldn't remember where I'd seen it. It's here, in this tome. It's a tome about our mythology, with legends and stories of our culture."

Ingrid could not understand anything written in it, so she waited to be given some kind of explanation.

"Neils Dragon-killer is a sword that's mentioned in the legend of General Neils Usmentus, the Defender," Dopemus explained.

"Who was he? What did he defend?" Ingrid asked.

"Well, there are several theories about that. On the one hand, there are those who say he was one of the founders of the city who took his own life in an outburst of madness. Others say he was one of the first generals of our army who went mad in battle. And some others say he was a madman who had visions and led his regiment to their deaths…"

"Which is the true story?" she wanted to know.

"Well… all of them and none," Dopemus said with a gesture of apology.

"Isn't there one that has more weight than the others?"

"I'm afraid not. In all the stories it's mentioned that he was a soldier, one of the first, when the wall hadn't even been built yet and the city was being shaped. And they all agree that he lost his mind."

"I see… hence the legend of the dragon."

"Exactly. The reason why they say he lost his mind is because he claimed that a dragon had returned and was coming to raze the city."

"They didn't believe him," Ingrid guessed.

"In our culture, well, in all the eastern coast of the continent, dragons are considered semi-gods who sought power and riches."

"And no one believed a semi-god would appear and rob them."

"That's what it appears, according to what we know. For some reason, Neils believed there was a dragon with hostile intentions, and he went to defend the city from it," Dopemus said as he read from the tome. "He took his regiment with him and they never came back."

"And the sword? Is the gold sword mentioned at all?"

"Yes, it is. According to the stories, Neils believed he had found a gold sword that could pierce the scales of a dragon. He was going to kill it with this sword. As we all know, a gold sword can't even pierce wood, let alone the defenses of a semi-god in the form of a dragon. That also contributed to the increasing belief that he had lost his mind."

"Does anyone know what happened to the sword?"

"From what it says here, they only found the armor and weapons of Neils' regiment. The bodies had vanished."

"Very curious."

"Well… we can't believe all this. It's only a tome of legends, compilations of what people say happened. It's more rumor and fantasy than reality."

"I understand. That's the sword I'm looking for though. What could've happened to it?"

"Perhaps it got lost, or it never existed," Dopemus said.

"I'd like to think it did exist," Ingrid insisted.

"Well, if it did exist and was found, it might have been kept as a mythological relic."

"Kept? Where?"

"At the Victory Museum. It's where we have relics of the victories of our heroes. They have weapons on exhibition there, those used in the great battles of the past."

"Then, it might well be there," Ingrid said, encouraged.

"That's saying a lot, since this sword might not have even existed. We're not even sure Neils existed."

"I believe he did exist and that he wasn't crazy. I'll go to that museum to look for the sword. Where is it?"

"By the Square of the Heroes. It's a circular building, you can't miss it," Dopemus told her.

"I'll take you to the museum," Celopus offered.

"Thank you both." Ingrid took her leave of Dopemus and his son and headed to the Victory Museum with Celopus. For some reason, she had the feeling the sword would be there, although the odds were minimal. Something told her that Neils had existed and so had his sword, and that she would find it with the weapons of the other heroes of the great city.

Chapter 29

The Victory Museum was undoubtedly that—a museum devoted to the great victories of the city-state. All its glorious past, and some of its present, was represented there in large areas within a circular building which, from what Ingrid had seen so far, was one of the few. Everything in this city was square or rectangular, except its soldiers' shields and this building.

Large representations hung on the walls, depicting great battles of the past. In most of them, the great city and its impregnable walls were the center of the exhibition. Cabinets, armoires, tables and showcases were set around the tapestries, murals and paintings with remains from the battles. Most of them were pieces of armor and weapons used by the soldiers and generals of the city, as well as those of its opponents. The date and place of the battles, as well as the names of the generals who took part in them, were shown in large boxes.

Only a few areas were devoted to battles that had taken place in open fields. It seemed that in the past they had preferred to fight within the safety of their walls or that they had been attacked by foreign forces many times. In fact, she noticed that many of the battles had been fought against the other four City-States of the East Coast of Tremia. The rivalry between them and the struggle for the supremacy and control of maritime trade had written a large part of the city's history.

Hence the many depictions of naval battles. Triremes and other war vessels from different time periods appeared on canvas and murals. Remains of maritime battles were exhibited and well preserved. There were sails and keels of ships on exhibition, as well as oars, rudders, and endless remains of triremes. Of course, there were also weapons and the armor used by the ships' soldiers.

Ingrid asked Celopus to translate the information about the places and dates of some of the most important battles, as well as the forces of both sides and the final result. If the city had resisted all the attacks and ultimately been victorious at sea, things would have been different, but from what Celopus was translating, the people of this great city had lost quite a few maritime battles, as well as won some. Things looked pretty equaled in the final toll. The five City-States of the East Coast, the Noceans of the South, and the Coporneans of the Central Sea had gone through an infinitude of battles. They had even fought against the Kingdom of Irinel in the northeast.

After spending a long time at the museum, it was clear to Ingrid that this city lived for, and by its army and military tradition. In fact, many of the museum's visitors were not foreigners like her or civilians of the city, but were soldiers and officers admiring their great city-state's past and present glory.

"How many people live in the city?" she asked Celopus.

"Over a hundred thousand, according to the last official reckoning."

"And out of all of them, how many are soldiers?"

"More than half, about sixty thousand."

"I see. And how many work to support the army in other professions?"

"Another ten thousand, more or less."

Ingrid nodded.

"So, seven out of every ten people are in the army one way or another. That's a high number. That's not the case in any other city or kingdom."

"We are a great city-state with a deeply rooted military tradition. That's why we've always survived all attempts at invasion or conquest. You also have to understand that part of the population goes from being a soldier to other professions when necessary."

"But still, the profession par excellence is that of a soldier."

"That's right. There's nothing more noble than defending your own country with spear and shield. We all wish for that when we're little children. We start training to be soldiers at the age of eight, at school."

"I see. So your schools are really military academies."

Celopus nodded.

"They are. First you learn to be a soldier and then, according to each child's characteristics, they are assigned a profession at the age of fifteen."

"So, they are all trained to be soldiers until the age of fifteen. Women and men equally?"

"That's right. Every citizen, woman or man, is prepared to defend the walls and fight in the triremes."

"How come you're one of the few people here who's not a soldier then?" Ingrid asked Celopus, looking around. They were surrounded by soldiers and officers.

Celopus smiled.

"In my case, they discovered that at fifteen I was already skilled with foreign languages, and language itself. The army supports and helps establish trade. Translators, interpreters, and scribes are necessary for trade."

"But you trained as a soldier until you were sixteen, right?"

"That's right. We all have to do so, although it's not simply as a soldier per se. We also have to learn to write and read, as well as receive instruction in geography and other subjects of interest."

"But mainly military."

"That's the essence of our people."

"Yes, I've gathered that already. You make for a very interesting civilization."

"I can tell we please you," the interpreter said, smiling.

"You certainly do. I like the military model you follow in your city, although it must have its disadvantages too. I doubt that art and culture are two shining areas here, to mention just two…"

Celopus could not help but smile and nod.

"Indeed. Our focus is on military and commercial might. Let's say the other areas suffer a little. It's the price we have to pay for living in this wonderful city. On the other hand, no one is forced to stay here. If anyone wants to leave the city, they're free to do so. But that's a step you must consider carefully and thoroughly before you take it, since being accepted again after you decide to leave is not guaranteed. A military tribunal decides on each case, and many are denied re-entrance for having abandoned their responsibilities."

"I expected that to be the case, being such a militarized society. I guess justice is also imparted by the soldiers."

"That's right. Specialized soldiers who serve as both judge and jury. In order to be a military judge, you must first have a decorated career and demonstrated your worth on the battlefield and in defense of the city."

"I think that's good. Who names them? The military judges, I mean."

"The representatives of the five Glorious Families."

Ingrid frowned.

"Glorious Families? Who are they?"

"There are five families that have ruled the city since its beginning, since it was founded. Those families are the rulers, and they govern the destiny of all the inhabitants of our society."

"Military families, I guess."

"Of course, the most decorated and distinguished."

"And how are decisions made between the five?"

"There's a Ruling Council in which a Captain General from each family represents them. The Captain Generals are the ones who make the decisions in the council and name all the ranks of the army, both of land and sea, from generals to under-officers, as well as the posts in the government of the city, which are usually of high rank."

Ingrid pondered for a moment.

"And what if the five don't reach an agreement?"

"That's why there are five. They each have a vote, and since there's an odd number, there is always a majority."

"Interesting system, indeed. And are there no rivalries?"

"Oh, many. The five families have a very strong rivalry between them. But that's viewed as a good thing, because it drives them to always excel and not dwell on past victories, which could happen."

"I see… and what if a non-glorious family wants to become glorious? What if the family achieves enough merit?"

Celopus's expression changed, shifting to one of worry.

"That's the greatest point of contention regarding our beloved hierarchical system. Until one of the five families disappears or decides to leave the council voluntarily, the other families can't enter it, no matter how well deserving they are."

"Well, there's no such thing as a perfect system. They all have some disadvantage or problem. Otherwise everything would be perfect, and perfection doesn't exist."

"Well put. Here we say that we seek perfection, but one must be satisfied with excellence."

"I like it. Both your society and your philosophy."

"I'm pleased that you do."

After looking through the museum and searching for the sword in every showcase without finding it, Celopus suggested asking one of the museum guides for help. They found one who looked about ninety years old. Ingrid thought he was the right one to ask, since they needed someone who knew ancient history well, especially the legend of Neils the Defender.

They approached the guide, who was wearing a red robe. He had so many creases in his face that he actually looked closer to a hundred years old.

"Good morning, Guide," Celopus greeted him.

"Good morning to you too," the guide replied, and seeing Celopus translate for Ingrid, he was interested.

"Foreign visitor?"

"That's right, from Norghana."

"Oh, the land of eternal snow in the North," he said in a hoarse, melancholic voice.

"Do you know it?" Ingrid was surprised.

"No, I've never been able to go, but I've read about the North of Tremia. The Norghanians and the Norriel have always interested me a lot."

"The Norriel are further west, but still to the north, yes," Ingrid explained.

The guide smiled and nodded, which made even more creases appear on his face.

"My name is Jotus, I'm the Senior Guide of the museum. Would you like a tour of the exhibits? It would be my pleasure. I greatly enjoy explaining our history to foreigners. As you can see, it's long and glorious," he said with a wave at all the exhibits around him.

"Thank you for the offer, but we've already taken a look at everything. What we want is information about an illustrious person of the past."

"Which of our heroes and their conquests do you want information on?" Jotus asked, interested.

"About Neils the Defender."

Jotus' face shifted to one of surprise.

"Not many people know the legend of Neils the Defender."

"We do, and we're searching for information about him."

"That's a real surprise for me, seeing as you're a foreigner. It's an ancient legend, from the time when the city was beginning to take shape. Those were tough times, dangerous and bloody."

"We know he wanted to defend the city from a dragon that was going to destroy it," Ingrid said.

"That's what the legend claims, yes."

"Do you believe that's the truth?"

"It's a legend. They all consist of a small kernel of truth and a great helping of fantasy and imagination."

"Yes, that's usually the case," Ingrid had to admit.

"I don't know whether you know that dragons are semi-gods in our mythology. It's possible that that's the fantastic part of the story."

"Then it's possible he defended the city from some danger."

"A great danger, because only the weapons and armor of his regiment were ever found," Jotus said, and with a wave he indicated them to follow him.

Ingrid and Celopus followed the guide to a corner housing a set of shelves with tomes. He picked one up and consulted it.

"Yes... we don't have them on show because, after all, it's nothing but a legend."

"But you have the remains?" Ingrid was surprised.

"Yes, we do. Come with me to the storeroom and I'll show them to you."

Ingrid was cheered up. She was close to her goal.

Jotus guided them to the storeroom below the great circular building. He had to open several doors with a bunch of keys he carried at his waist.

"It's the advantage of being the most senior member of the place," he said with a smile as he opened the door that went down to the basement.

They walked along a large section of the great basement used for storage which was lit by a few oil lamps. If everything was well organized and tidy in the floors above, here it was exactly the opposite. There were endless crates that stored all kinds of relics of the past, and they were neither organized nor catalogued by what Ingrid could see. They could also see objects of all kinds that were not even in crates or boxes, but that had been left on the floor or on top of the boxes themselves.

"There are so few of us, and there are so many historical objects to catalogue still..." Jotus apologized when he saw Ingrid's look.

After walking through half the storeroom, Jotus stood before a sizeable crate. He checked what was written with white paint on two of the sides.

"It's this one," he said.

"Should we open it?" Ingrid asked, unable to hold back her

eagerness to find the weapon.

"Go ahead. I'm a bit old for these things."

"Sounds good." Ingrid set to work. She took out her Ranger's knife and climbed onto the crate, which was taller than she was. She pried the top open with her knife, pulled hard to get it off, and found that there were indeed armor and weapons in the crate. She started to take them out carefully and set them on top of the other boxes and crates around her. First she took out a dozen spears which were in a poor state, rusty from the passing of time and smelling damp. The armor was a bit better, but she could also notice the effects of time in their metal. They were similar to the armor the soldiers now wore but more rudimentary, less carved, and they were pretty heavy, especially the cuirasses. The grieves and vambraces also looked heavy, and she realized they were quite thick.

She took out everything that was in the large crate. She even had to climb inside to reach the last pieces. She did not find any swords. Frustrated, she clambered out of the crate and jumped down to Jotus' and Celopus' side.

"There's no sword."

"Sword? Is that what you're looking for?" the old guide asked her.

"Neils' Dragon-killer, his sword. The one he is supposed to have killed the dragon with."

"Let me see," he told Ingrid, and he picked up a tome that was stuck to the side of the crate. He opened it and leafed through it for quite a while.

"Here it is," he said at last.

"What is?" Ingrid asked.

"The sword. It was taken. It appears it was a unique weapon which drew interest."

"Who took it?"

"The Gotirus," Jotus said.

"And who are they?"

"They're one of the five families on the Ruling Council."

Ingrid shut her eyes and sighed. Things were starting to get complicated.

Chapter 30

Lasgol arrived in the vicinity of Mirkos' Tower. He studied the building before getting closer, as he always did. It was an outstanding building, a jet-black, tall, slender tower with a large round patio in front of its door. It was not inviting, given its look. Besides, a powerful mage lived in it, so few people came close. It was quiet and there did not seem to be any danger. He decided to approach slowly.

While he approached, he was thinking about how much he missed the company of Ona and Camu, but he knew they would be busy helping the rest of his friends and he did not need their help for the time being, even though he missed them horribly. In fact, he hoped he did not need their help, because if he did it would mean he had gotten in dangerous trouble, and that was not his intention. The mission that had brought him here was finding a container for the Pearls of Power, and it should not, at least in principle, entail danger. That was his hope at least, but with magic and magi, one never knew what might happen.

He dismounted and knocked on the door. A moment later, a servant opened it.

"I need to see the great Mage Mirkos the Erudite," Lasgol said.

"My lord doesn't accept visitors," was the servant's reply.

"I've come from Norghana to see him. It's about something very important, otherwise I would never dare bother him."

The servant nodded.

"Wait here. I will see if my lord wants to see you."

Lasgol waited, a little nervous in case the Mage did not want to see him.

The door opened, and Lasgol saw an old man leaning on a red staff edged with gold and crowned with a large translucent pearl. His face was stern and his eyes intense. He had a long, bushy white beard; large, snow-white eyebrows; and long, straight hair that was almost entirely white. He wore a silver robe edged in black, with the emblem representing the jet-black tower they were at embroidered in the center of his chest. He was just like what someone would imagine a mage to be.

The Mage studied him from head to toe carefully.

"My assistant tells me you are Norghanian, is that so?"

Lasgol felt a bit uncomfortable with the scrutiny but decided to hide it. Besides, the Mage had addressed him in Norghanian, which made things a lot easier.

"Yes, I am Norghanian. A Ranger," he replied. "I am pleased to see that you know our language."

"Yours, and many others. It is what a life of study gives you."

Lasgol nodded.

"The languages of Tremia aren't my strong point," Lasgol had to admit.

"And what is your strong point?"

The question befuddled Lasgol. He had never thought about it. What was his strong point?

"Well… I don't know… I guess being a Ranger Specialist…"

Mirkos studied him again closely.

"There is more in you," he said with interest.

Lasgol knew he was referring to his magic. Since Mirkos was an eminence in magical subjects, he saw no reason to hide it, since he most likely already knew.

"I have the Gift, the Talent," he admitted.

Mirkos nodded, and the ghost of a smile appeared on his face.

"True. You have it. And from what I pick up from your aura, it is a powerful Gift and a very interesting one."

"Interesting?" Lasgol was puzzled.

"It is not like the Gift of most magi, the basic composition of your magic I mean…" Lasgol guessed what he meant. What surprised him was that the Mage could pick it up just like that, without any tool, or making a study or casting a spell. This was remarkable. On the other hand, Mirkos was considered an Erudite in the magic arts, and perhaps that was why.

"It seems that way, from what I've been told…"

"Do not feel uncomfortable. I say it purely out of academic interest." The Mage watched him out of narrowed eyes, which made Lasgol become even more nervous.

"You see, I've come from Norghana…" Lasgol changed the subject.

"True. A long journey," Mirkos nodded. "Why did you wish to

see me, Ranger?" he asked. "Relations between Norghana and Rogdon have never been very stable… or very good…. Right now they're cordial, but knowing the Norghanian monarchs and the Norghanian people in general, I expect they will become hostile at any moment."

"I see the Erudite doesn't hold a very good opinion of our people."

"Why should I? Have the Norghanians not been a brute people, quarrelsome looters of the cold lands of the north, abusers of tribes like the Masig, and the cause of multiple continental wars in the past, including one with my beloved kingdom of Rogdon?"

Lasgol did not know how to defend Norghana. Everything the Mage had said was true, no matter how much it bothered Lasgol to admit it.

"We aren't a beloved kingdom, that's true."

"Or one to trust in. Its monarchs have always sought power and gold at the expense of other kingdoms and peoples, which sooner or later has always ended in wars, causing death and suffering to half the continent."

"Perhaps times are changing, and with them the monarchs and their actions."

"Wishful thinking, young Ranger. Unfortunately, a fool with bad intentions reigns in Norghana."

"Maybe he will soon reign no more. Perhaps new times, happier and prosperous, are on the horizon for Norghana."

Mirkos opened his eyes wide.

"I never thought I would hear something like that out of the mouth of a Ranger, and I assure you it is not easy to surprise an old scholar like me, who has seen practically everything in this life."

"I'm not just any Ranger."

Mirkos looked at him again, analyzing him.

"I am beginning to realize that."

"I assure you I'm not here on any official mission, in spite of being a Ranger Specialist," Lasgol said.

"That is even more interesting. You are not here on behalf of your warmonger king?"

Lasgol shook his head.

"No, sir. I am here on a Rangers' mission."

"But not on King Thoran's… very interesting…." Mirkos raised one eyebrow and eyed Lasgol with obvious suspicion.

"I know it's difficult to understand, but this mission concerns the Rangers, not King Thoran."

"And is that why you carry a Bow of Power at your back?"

Lasgol glanced over his shoulder almost unconsciously at the bow.

"This is Aodh's Bow, and it is indeed a Bow of Power."

"I thought you would deny it, which would not have helped you in your intentions here. I can feel the magic of the bow, it is powerful…" Mirkos closed his eyes, "it is an ancient magic, one of the founding magics."

"Founding magics?"

"I see you are not well-versed in magic knowledge."

"No… I'm not…" Lasgol blushed, feeling out of place before the great erudite mage.

"There are three original founding magics, the basic ones all other magics derive from."

"Three? Aren't there only two?"

"Well, you do know something about the subject."

"Not much, I'm afraid."

"There is always time to learn. As long as one is alive, that is. That bow is powerful and has Golden Magic, also known in a more colloquial way as Magic of Gold, of the original."

"I didn't know… but if this bow has Magic of Gold, I guess that another of the types of original magic would be Magic of Silver."

Mirkos looked impressed.

"You learn fast. That is correct. The second base magic is what we call Argent Magic, or Magic of Silver. My magic, for instance, comes from the Golden Magic, as does that of the bow."

"I see. And the third?" Lasgol asked, filled with curiosity.

"That, you will have to study to find out," Mirkos said, smiling. "I am not going to show you the easy path. One must forge his or her own path through study."

Mirkos crossed his arms behind his back and smiled.

"You increasingly intrigue me, young Ranger, possessor of the Gift. Yet, I am a Royal Mage, faithful to Rogdon. My King would not appreciate the fact that I took an interest in Norghanian matters. As you can understand, King Solin of Rogdon would not like it if his erudite mage helped a rival kingdom whose monarch he does not see eye to eye with."

"I understand. King Solin did not come to the royal wedding…"

"And for good reason."

"Because he doesn't trust Thoran and his allies."

Again Mirkos's eyes widened, and he even threw his head back a little.

"I would never have thought I would meet a Ranger who spoke like that of his king. And it is even stranger that I do not see malice, hate, or grudge in your eyes. Very remarkable."

"I'm here for an important reason concerning Norghana, and for all of Tremia. My feelings toward the King are what they are, and I have expressed them so that the Erudite will know it is not His Majesty who sent me."

"Funny way of appearing to ask for my help."

"The time I have is scarce. I've chosen to be direct and transparent in my intentions and message, since I can see that my lord erudite is not inclined to helping Norghana."

Mirkos smiled.

"I am a Rogdonian Mage of the Four Elements, a Royal Mage before all else, including my role as a scholar. My duty to my King and my Kingdom requires me to be prudent in situations like this. What would you say to a Nocean Sorcerer who came to your door in Norghana asking for your help?"

The question befuddled Lasgol again.

"Well… a Nocean… Sorcerer… in Norghana… yeah, I can see the problem I pose for the Erudite."

"You do, indeed. They might execute me for treason."

"I understand… you can't help me."

Mirkos looked at him harshly. An instant later, his face relaxed.

"I didn't say that."

Lasgol looked up hopefully.

"Will you help me? And commit treason to your kingdom?"

"King Solin is a personal friend. He is not going to hang me for treason. He knows I would never betray Rogdon. I would die for my King and my Kingdom, but betray them? Never." The Erudite's tone was as firm as the earth.

"I swear that what I need from you won't compromise you."

"Very well, come into the tower and we will talk in my office. You have piqued my interest, and that does not happen often."

The Mage's studio was like Lasgol had imagined, filled with tomes about magic and magical objects he did not know the purpose or design of.

"Explain yourself, please," Mirkos asked, sitting in a comfortable armchair and inviting Lasgol to sit in another one with a wave of his hand.

"You see, we're in possession of some very valuable magical objects..."

"We?" Mirkos interrupted.

"Yes, my fellow Rangers and I. We call ourselves the Panthers."

"Very well, continue."

"There are enemy forces that want these objects of power, and they can detect their power from afar. We need a container that prevents their power from escaping and being detected."

"When you say enemy forces, you do not mean Rogdon, do you? Because if that is the case, I cannot help you."

"No, sir. It isn't Rogdon."

"That is even more interesting. What objects do you want to hide?"

"Some objects of great power which must not fall into the hands of evil."

"Objects of great power, huh? Now you have all my attention. You know that we magi cannot resist them.... Tell me about these Objects of Power."

Lasgol hesitated about continuing with his quest. If the mage became too interested and ended up wanting the objects for himself, he would have a very big problem before him. From what they knew, Mirkos the Erudite was one of the most powerful magi in Tremia.

"I'd like to tell you..."

"Yet, you're not going to."

"I'm sorry, it's just that..."

"You don't trust me, and yet you are asking me to trust and help you. As you can understand, this is not something I can accept blindly."

"I am being honest, completely," Lasgol said.

"That might be true, but I do not know you. You come to my door asking for me, and you ask me to help you when you refuse to tell me what truth there is behind your plea for help. I have many years on my shoulders, years loaded with wonderful experiences and knowledge, but also with treachery and lies. Life has taught me that, much to my chagrin, there are many people who are not noble and honest in this world. I cannot help you if you do not show me that you are trustworthy."

"The Objects of Power are pearls, and I believe they have Argent Magic."

Both of Mirkos' white eyebrows rose.

"That is very interesting, my young friend."

"It is? Why is that...?"

"Because there are very few Objects of Power known to have Argent Magic. Very few, and that makes them twice as valuable, because of their power and base magic."

"Oh ... I hadn't thought of that."

"I would love to be able to analyze these Objects of Power with Argent magic."

"Right now that's impossible... they're being sought after..."

Mirkos scratched his beard.

"I understand. It's dangerous."

"It is, sir, very dangerous."

"Well then, I suggest a deal, my new young Norghanian friend. I will give you what you ask me for on the condition that, in a near future, you will let me study those objects."

Lasgol thought about it. He did not have much choice. On the other hand, Mirkos seemed like an honorable Mage. Lasgol did not think he would steal the pearls.

"All right, you have a deal," Lasgol offered Mirkos his hand.

The Mage shook it and smiled.

"The world is full of little surprises. Wait here. I will bring you the container."

Lasgol waited. All those tomes of magic fascinated him. He wished he had all their accumulated knowledge.

Mirkos came back after a moment with a coffer. It was medium sized, more than large enough to keep the pearls.

"This coffer has a powerful masking spell. Its function is what you are looking for. Many magi have this kind of container. We hide objects in them, objects that arouse envy in other magi..."

"I understand, sir."

"Very well. Take it, and remember our deal."

"I won't forget, you have my word."

"Go, young Norghanian Ranger, possessor of power with two of the three basic magics."

Lasgol was once again speechless. Mirkos had read him like an open book. He took his leave courteously and left. He had the container, which was what mattered.

Chapter 31

Lasgol was returning from the Tower of Mirkos the Erudite and was feeling happy: he had obtained the container they needed. Now he had to join Camu to take the container to the Pearls and hide them inside. He hoped Camu had finished helping the others with the Portals.

Night caught up with him when he reached the great river Utla, and he decided it would be best to wait until dawn to look for a pier to cross it. He tethered his mount to an ash tree and looked for some timber to build a fire to spend the night. It was not snowing on this side of the river, but it was cold. He was in desert land, and nights on the Masig Steppes were cold.

He used his *Blue Fire* skill and made the timber burn. He rubbed his hands and sat down to enjoy the warmth the fire gave off. He felt strange, alone in the outdoors. The thing was, he was usually always in the company of his friends, Ona and Camu especially, and not having them with him when he was on a mission felt weird. He resigned himself. He had to learn to fend for himself too, since he was not always going to have the good fortune of being with his friends on every adventure.

He had Aodh's Bow beside him, and he stroked it. When he did, the bow seemed to respond with a golden flash.

"You're my new partner," he said, as if the bow were sentient.

"Not a good sign to be talking alone," a voice said in the gloom.

Lasgol looked up and saw a figure coming toward him. At once and subconsciously, Lasgol started calling on his combat list. The skills activated as Lasgol stood up with the bow in his hand.

"Who are you?" he demanded distrustfully.

"My name is Sigurd," the figure said, approaching the fire and revealing himself. It was a man, Norghanian, in his mid-thirties. From his white, long hair, snow-white clothing, and the white staff with a blue gem at the tip, Lasgol knew what he was.

"You're an Ice Mage."

"I am," the Mage nodded.

"I think I know you," Lasgol said, realizing he had seen the man with Maldreck.

"Yes, and I know you, Lasgol,"

"Funny meeting you here," Lasgol said, glancing around.

"Not really, I've been following you."

"Oh, I see. I thought it strange that an Ice Mage would be wandering these lands all alone."

Sigurd smiled.

"You're intelligent and, they say, a very good warrior."

Lasgol shrugged.

"I guess it depends on who you ask."

"I've also been told you have the Gift."

"Well, that's not something I go around telling just anybody."

"My lord, Maldreck, confided in me. As a warning. He says you're dangerous."

"Not to my friends."

The Mage smiled and nodded. "Then, let's try and be friends."

"I don't see why we couldn't be."

"First, you must give me what Mirkos has given you."

"Why should I?"

"Because my lord told me to follow you and find out what you're plotting. I've seen you visiting Mirkos, and I saw you come out with the coffer."

"How did you follow me? I made sure no one did."

The Ice Mage indicated Lasgol's horse.

"I put a tracking spell on the saddle. It's Water Magic, only an Elemental Mage could have picked it up."

Lasgol sighed.

"I see. Yes, I've been to see Mirkos. I only wanted to know whether he took on apprentices."

"You're lying, and you lie badly, Ranger. We're not going to be able to be friends this way."

"In that case, I'll ask you to leave and let me be."

"I can't leave before you give me that coffer and tell me what you wanted it for."

"I can't do either of those things."

"You can, and you will, one way or another."

"Now you're threatening me? We're surely not going to be friends this way."

"Last warning. Give me that coffer and tell me what you want it for, or you'll regret it. I have permission from our leader to attack you if you don't collaborate."

"I know you're a powerful Ice Mage, but I don't fear you, and I certainly don't have to give you or tell you anything, and I won't."

"As you wish, don't say I didn't warn you," The Ice Mage cast a spell and raised two protective spheres with great speed. The first one, transparent, was anti-magic. The second, solid frost and ice, was designed against physical attacks.

Lasgol took two steps back to put distance between him and the Mage and summoned his protection against physical attacks: *Woodland Protection.* There was a green flash that ran through him from head to toe and his whole body became covered in braided creepers, tree branches, hard earth, and pieces of rock and foliage, creating a tough layer of protection.

"That won't save you from my magic," Sigurd warned him.

"We'll see," Lasgol said as he nocked an arrow and aimed at the Mage.

"And those arrows of yours won't be able to pierce through my icy protection," he smiled condescendingly. "The fact that you think you can defeat me shows very little sense on your part. You disappoint me. I thought you'd use a trick of some kind. In direct combat at this distance, you don't have a chance. You know the saying: 'if the Mage reaches two hundred paces, the archer dies.'"

"I'm not just any archer, I have magic too."

"Which is good for nothing. You won't be able to do anything to me with my defenses raised."

"I wouldn't be so sure."

The Mage cast a spell rapidly and an ice stake flew off. Lasgol took the blow in his chest. The blow was hard, but he had released an instant before being hit. His *Woodland Protection* held, but a piece of it flew off in the air. Similarly, his arrow hit the protective sphere of solid ice and frost of the Mage and he only managed to chip a bit off.

Before the Mage could cast again, Lasgol released again, using his *Multiple Shot* skill. Three arrows flew against the Mage, which hit the sphere in three points, disturbing some frost but without really damaging the protection.

The Mage attacked again, and this time he did so with a steady beam of ice which came from his staff. Lasgol took the blow in his torso. The protection held but started to freeze over. He could feel the icy cold trying to penetrate his defenses and reach his body. If it did, he would be frozen on the spot and the fight would be over. He sent more energy to strengthen his *Woodland Protection* while Sigurd kept the beam on him and increased its power, sending more energy himself.

Lasgol realized that, although his protection was holding, since it was not deteriorating, still it could not protect him properly from the cold and the freezing effect of the spell. For that he needed anti-magic protection, which he did not have. He had not been able to develop it yet. He decided to use distraction tactics. He released using his *True Shot* skill and hit the crystal gem of the Mage's staff where the ice beam was coming from. Upon impact, the staff was thrown back and the beam went upward.

"That does nothing but avoid the inevitable!" Sigurd shouted at him, annoyed. The Mage quickly cast a new spell and sent a dozen ice stakes against Lasgol. Thanks to his *Cat-like Reflexes* and *Improved Agility* skills, Lasgol threw himself to one side and was able to avoid the stakes. One hit his side, but the *Woodland Protection* saved him.

The Mage conjured a huge ice stalactite that fell from the sky. Lasgol once again used his skills and reflexes to leap forward and rolled over his head, avoiding the attack. He finished off the move with a *Powerful Shot*, which did manage to make more frost skid off the Mage's defense.

"You'll never manage to break my defense," Sigurd told him, and he sent more energy to strengthen his defense of ice and frost. Lasgol noticed how all the impacts from his arrows vanished as the Mage repaired the sphere.

He stepped back and called upon his *Elemental Arrow* skill. He released against the Mage with an Earth Arrow, which impacted with a loud blast and made the Mage lose his concentration. He could not finish casting the spell against Lasgol.

"More little games? You can't defeat me with that."

Lasgol next tried an Elemental Arrow of Fire, which upon explosion did manage to damage the Mage's defense, although not enough.

Sigurd began to create a winter storm above Lasgol, who realized when he saw some dark clouds over his head and noticed the temperature beginning to drop. He did not think twice and moved swiftly to one side to get out of the storm's range. But he was not counting on the storm following him, and an instant later it was once again over his head. This was not good news for him.

"You can't run faster than the storm." Sigurd laughed and sent more energy to make it more powerful.

Lasgol wondered what he could do, and while he thought, he kept moving around the Mage and releasing Earth Arrows to stop the man from concentrating. And then he had an idea. The defenses of the mage were similar, albeit less powerful, to those of a lesser dragon, and he had already managed to defeat a dragon with the help of Aodh's Bow. Yes, that was the solution. He had to combine his power with that of the Bow and pierce the Mage's defenses. He only needed a moment to do so.

He had another idea. First, he called upon his *Multiple Shot* skill and tried to combine it with *Elemental Arrow* to send Earth Arrows against the Mage. There were two green flashes, almost simultaneous. Three Earth Arrows flew from his bow, all three exploding when they hit the spheres. The blast and the cloud of earth, dust, and other substances they produced left the Mage stunned and without vision.

"You're doing nothing but delaying the inevitable!"

He was not wrong; Lasgol was beginning to freeze under the storm and the winds that hit him so hard he could barely stand, but he had a respite, and he was going to seize the moment.

He called his *Powerful Shot*, then he sent energy to Aodh's Bow, which he could now interact with without needing to call on his *Arcane Communication* skill, since a bond had formed between his magic and that of the Bow when he was fighting against the dragons. He could send energy to the weapon, just like he did with his own skills. There were two flashes, one green and another golden—one was Lasgol's and the other one, the Bow's. The arrow flew and hit the Mage's two spheres. It pierced through them, making a hole, and came out at the back of the spheres, also piercing through them. Lasgol had not aimed to hit the body of the Mage, only to make a hole on the side of the spheres.

"What? How? It can't be!" Sigurd was nonplussed.

The cold was about to finish off Lasgol, but now he had a hole to reach the Mage. He called on his *Blind Shot* and *Elemental Arrow* skills.

As he threw himself to one side in a desperate attempt to get out from under the storm, there were two green flashes, one after the other. The arrow went in through the hole, and this time he did hit the Mage right in the middle of the forehead. This was where Lasgol had aimed, with an Elemental Air Arrow. There was a burst and a discharge hit the head of the Mage, who fell to the ground, unconscious.

Lasgol rolled on the ground, trying to escape the storm. A moment later, the Mage's spheres vanished, and then the winter storm, which evaporated into the sky. Lasgol was left lying on his back, covered in frost and half frozen.

He smiled.

"Being able to combine my skills and also use the power of the Bow is going to be quite interesting," he said to the sky and smiled from ear to ear.

Chapter 32

Ingrid and Celopus were walking through the Square of the Heroes, between the great statues. They had taken their leave of the good guide Jotus, who had thanked them for brightening up his day. It did not happen that often.

Ingrid was thoughtful. One of the five ruling families had the sword, and she was already assuming it was not going to be easy to get.

"They won't grant me an audience, will they?" she asked Celopus.

"I'm afraid not. The five ruling families see almost no one, least of all a visiting foreigner without noble blood who's searching for a legendary sword."

"I guessed as much."

"You must understand that they are important, busy families. They carry the weight of the whole city. They can't see everyone who asks for an audience."

"And least of all a plebeian without rank or connections."

Celopus looked at her and shrugged.

"That works the same way everywhere, I'm afraid."

"Yeah, that's also been true in my experience."

"Look on the bright side. Until now you didn't even know whether the sword existed. Now it appears that it does, that it is indeed real."

"That's true," Ingrid nodded. "Would you take me to the Gotirus' house?"

"I'll take you, but it's not a house, it's a whole district in the city."

Ingrid nodded. They were important indeed.

They arrived at the district where the Gotirus family lived. Ingrid noticed it was well protected. There were a large number of soldiers around the first houses of the district. They looked like regular soldiers, no different from those she had seen throughout the city, but something told her they all served the Gotirus family. She checked the block and saw that it was also being watched on both sides.

Celopus put his hand on her shoulder.

"Wait here for a moment. I'll try to get you an audience, although I doubt I'll succeed."

"Thank you, I really appreciate that."

Ingrid watched her translator leave. He headed to a large building made of rock with several portico columns. It looked like an official building of some kind. They let him through, and Ingrid stood outside and waited.

While she waited, she walked over to another of the main buildings, this one more military-looking, and noticed there was a group of people waiting in line. They were mostly soldiers. They were allowed in one by one, after some officers interviewed them briefly.

Celopus came back after a short while. By his look, Ingrid already knew he had not succeeded.

"I'm sorry. No one is received unless they have been called, not even the lesser members of the family."

"I was expecting that… thanks for trying…"

"You are welcome."

"Does the whole family live there?"

"Yes, the family and those closest to them. They have many people working for them."

"I see. They occupy a lot of buildings then."

"Well, they use the biggest and most elegant. Those in the middle with the gardens and fountains are used only by the family."

"How big is the family?"

"About fifty people. Those with rank, I mean. Sabis Gotirus is the Captain General. Generals Demisus and Noteasus are his brothers, and Yerminus and Saletirus are his sons. He has ten nephews with the rank of captain, and then there are the rest, up to the fifty I mentioned."

"A united military family," Ingrid smiled.

"That's what they say, yes."

"Tell me, what's that line over there for?"

"I don't know, let's go and see."

They went over, and Celopus chatted with one of the guards on watch duty.

"It's for the aptitude test," he told Ingrid, who looked at him blankly. "Oh, forgive me, I forgot you don't know our customs. You see, all the great houses, including those of the rulers, have an annual aptitude test to recruit talent to serve in the ranks of the Family

Guard."

"Talent? What kind of talent are they looking for?"

"Military talent. Fighters."

"Oh… interesting…"

"What are you thinking?" Celopus asked, raising an eyebrow.

"Can a foreigner try out?"

The interpreter scratched his head.

"Well, actually yes… there are no restrictions, as long as you're a skilled fighter."

"Then that's my way of getting in."

"Are you going to apply? They'll make you fight with other warriors, and let me remind you that they are very skilled here and don't fool around. People end up injured in these fights, sometimes even dead."

"Don't worry, if there's something I know about, that's fighting."

"Are you sure? It's a pretty radical approach."

"This isn't radical at all compared to other things I've done with my comrades. I'll be fine."

"As you wish… but do be very careful…"

"Don't worry, I will."

"Another thing… come to think of it… there's usually a winner out of all the fights. Captain General Sabis Gotirus grants a prize to the winner. It's the tradition among warriors."

"That could definitely come in handy."

"I still think it's very risky."

"Let me give you a hug to thank you for all the help you've given me."

"It's not necessary… it's my job as an interpreter, and you've already paid me very handsomely."

Ingrid hugged him anyway.

"You've done much more than just being an interpreter, and gold is no guarantee of good service."

Celopus smiled politely.

"I'll stay around, just in case…"

"You're a good man, Celopus."

Ingrid stood in line and waited for her turn. It was a long line. There were many who wanted to apply. When her turn finally came, the officer studied her from head to toe. Then he shook his head and told her to leave. She did not understand him, but his gestures made it very clear. Ingrid did not move and stared at him defiantly. The officer went on gesturing and raising his voice, demanding she leave.

Without flinching, Ingrid pointed at her own torso and then at the parchment where they were writing down the names of those who had applied. The officer would not give in and continued telling her to leave rudely. Calmly, Ingrid reached for the bow at her back. The soldiers stiffened. Slowly, so as not to create an altercation, she reached for an arrow from her quiver and showed it to the officer. Then she pointed at a fountain about three hundred paces away and twelve feet tall in the shape of a soldier. The water fell from an amphora under the arm. Ingrid touched the middle of her own forehead with the tip of the arrow and then pointed it at the statue.

The officer understood what she was going to do and motioned her to go ahead.

Ingrid nocked the arrow. All the soldiers in the area raised their large round shields nervously. Ingrid pulled the string to her cheek and aimed. An instant later, she released. The arrow flew straight at the head of the stone soldier and hit it right in the middle of the forehead.

The soldiers murmured in surprise. The officer looked at Ingrid and nodded. He let her in and said something to the soldier with the parchment. She guessed he would write foreigner with bow or something similar, since they had not even asked her name. What was important was the fact that they had let her in, and that filled her with pleasure.

She followed the others who had been standing in line with her, and some officers led them along a street between several military-looking buildings. There were guards posted at the corners and along the streets. There were more at the doors of nearly every building she saw. They clearly did take the safety of these families seriously. Thinking again, considering there were so many soldiers in the city, they had to put them to work doing something. Watch duty, guarding, and protection assignments were usually the most common, but something that surprised her was seeing nearly a hundred soldiers repairing the façade of a building that seemed to have been raised even before the great walls.

She also saw soldiers cleaning other buildings and streets, as well as doing gardening work. She had the impression that in this place, though soldiers were soldiers, they were used for almost everything, which was quite smart. There was no point in having thousands of idle soldiers when there was no war. It also did not seem like this civilization was very aggressive and launched conquests on other kingdoms, unlike the kingdoms of Central or South Tremia, and she liked this. They were a strong kingdom, militarized, that did not use their superior strength to lord over weaker kingdoms and nations. She remembered what Celopus had told her about the rivalry between the five City States of the East. Maybe so many years of useless war among them had made them see reason. Otherwise, she could not explain why they did not go out to conquer other regions.

The officers made them stand in line in a large square before a building so big and majestic that Ingrid had no doubt it had to be one of the main buildings of the Gotirus family. They stood in formation and waited for the last applicants to join them. They were left there all afternoon, and when evening came Ingrid thought they would close the lists and move them elsewhere. She was wrong.

The soldiers left them standing in formation all night. The officers and guards watching them rotated, but they were kept there. They were not even given water or food or allowed to move. Ingrid was beginning to suspect what was going to happen to them and smiled. It was not going to be good. She looked around and counted ten lines of ten. There were a hundred of them in all, a small regiment, although she had the feeling many of them were not going to survive the Gotirus family's selection process.

Dawn came and they were ordered to continue standing, without water or food. Ingrid wondered whether she was the only one who did not know what was going to follow. Perhaps the rest already knew how these selection processes worked in the city. It surprised her to see that almost half of the applicants were women. Rather than surprise her, it pleased her. Here, women were warriors and talented fighters. She found this interesting and advanced in comparison with other cultures like the Norghanian way of life. She also noticed that many of those who had come did not have weapons or armor. She was one of the few who carried weapons, and they were heavy.

By evening on the second day, Ingrid's legs were beginning to cramp, and she had to shake them. They were not allowed to move from their spot. Several had tried to move and stretch, but the officers had made them go back to the formation at once. They were expected to stay firm and in their place. Some were having a hard time, but they were holding up. No one wanted to fail. In the faces of the women and men around her she could see that they were stubborn. They would stay strong, although perhaps their minds would endure and their bodies would not. Ingrid no longer had any doubts that this was a test of endurance, and she estimated that they would still be forced to stay on their feet one more night. She was not wrong.

On the evening of the third day, with a dozen applicants about to collapse but who were holding themselves up through sheer pride, the officers gave the order to move. They were ordered to form a line and parade to the back of the great manor building. The first steps were the most painful and clumsy, but they soon recovered, their bodies soon remembered how to walk in a straight line, and they managed to reach the back part.

Ingrid saw another square between four magnificent buildings with gardens at the front and large flat porticoes with huge square columns. At the top of the square was a long table with a hundred tall glasses. The officers made them go by the table in a line, and everyone was able to drink the contents of one glass, and only one. The soldiers made sure the rule was enforced.

Ingrid drank slowly when she got to the table. Her mouth was parched, so first she moistened it before letting the liquid go down her throat, which had become a desert. She found it was water with lemon and honey. She wondered why they were being given a restorative drink when the soldiers had left them without drink for two-and-a-half days.

The reason was soon evident. They were divided in two equally sized groups and the soldiers placed one group at the eastern part of the round square and the other at the western side. The square was over five hundred paces in diameter.

People began exiting the four buildings boxing in the street, a couple dozen from each building. Ingrid watched them. They were dressed mostly like officers, although with gold-and-silver armor and expensive clothing. Ingrid guessed who they were: Captain General Sabis Gotirus, Generals Demisus, Noteasus, Yerminus, Saletirus, and the rest of the ruling Gotirus family. Ingrid identified the one who had to be Sabis by his figure and the respect he was shown by all those around him.

They had come out to watch the selection of the new members of their guard. For them it must be a show, one that started as soon as the family was placed to watch, every group looking from its privileged position under the arches of each building. The servants, who were also soldiers, brought out chairs and snacks so the nobles could enjoy the show.

The officers explained the rules, which they read off a scroll. Unfortunately, Ingrid did not understand a word, and there was no one to translate. She would have to learn the rules as events unfolded, which was dangerous and might cause her to do something she should not and be disqualified, or worse. But she had no choice. The officers were not going to make exceptions with her.

A group of soldiers brought several armories with different types of weapons. She could see there were different kinds of spears, axes, swords, knives, maces, bows, and crossbows. These caught Ingrid's eye—she had heard about them and knew they were used in the East, and she had always wanted to use one. But she had not seen the soldiers in the city carrying them. They also brought other armories with shields and armor of different kinds. Things were beginning to get interesting.

Suddenly, they called out two names. This she did manage to guess, one from each group at both ends of the square. The officers gave them instructions and they both headed to the armories. They chose weapons, armor, and shields. Ingrid found it curious that they both chose the weapons and armor typical of the city soldiers. They both picked a spear and a large, round, steel shield and cuirass to cover their back and torso, as well as grieves and vambraces for their arms and legs. On their hips they were protected by a skirt that went down to the knee made of steel plates.

At an order from an officer, who seemed to be acting as the referee, the two hopefuls stood in the middle of the square. The officer gave an order and they stood in position, flexing their legs, one a little before the other, and hiding behind their shields, presenting the long steel spear in their right hand and arm. They looked like two mirrored, identical figures. At another order from the officer, the fight began.

The fighter in Ingrid's group leapt forward without uncovering his defense, holding the great shield in front of him as he launched a sharp attack with his spear. His opponent stood firm. He planted his feet and protected himself behind his shield. The spear hit the shield but bounced off to one side. The defender did not yield a single step. The attacker lunged at the defender and both shields crashed. The sound of metal against metal rang out when they did, and both fighters were thrown back after the impact. At once, the defender countered with a swift movement with his spear directed to his opponent's feet, which he saw and lowered his shield to protect them, leaving his face and neck uncovered. With a movement Ingrid could not have even imagined, the defender spun on himself and hit the attacker with the rim of his shield. The attacker fell back and was knocked out. The officer declared the one still standing the winner and told him to go to the north of the square.

More pairs were called to fight, always one from each group. Ingrid noticed that almost all chose the spear and shield, which were the city's traditional weapons. She soon understood the reason why. It turned out to be a solid way of fighting. They had a formidable defense behind the great shield. With a long spear the rival could be kept at a distance of six feet, and they wielded it skillfully, not only in piercing attacks but also in cutting ones, since the tip was as sharp as a knife's. In one of the fights, one of the warriors from the opposite group left his opponent unconscious with a blow to the helmet with the butt of the spear. It sounded like he had been hit with a hammer.

She was beginning to understand why those shield and spear soldiers had such a good reputation and why the city had never fallen. The shield defense, combined with the advantage of distance the spear granted, was a lethal combination. What she was thinking was demonstrated when one of the fighters chose a doubled-headed axe in the most Norghanian style. As he attacked, delivering a two-handed stroke, he was already dead. The tip of the spear hit him in the cuirass, one step away from finishing his attack so that he was unbalanced to one side. He delivered another lateral blow that was deflected by the shield, and when he tried to attack again the tip of his opponent's spear caught him in the thigh in a swift attack. The officer stopped the fight, and Ingrid realized the winner was decided 'at first bloodshed,' the goal not being to kill, which eased her quite a bit.

The fights continued. They were mostly spear and shield against spear and shield, women and men, which made for quite balanced fights and was somewhat boring, except when there was a fighter who brought innovation with new attack moves with the spear and shield. And when there was one who used shield and sword, it became more interesting. But the result was always the same—whoever did not choose spear and shield was defeated. The superiority of those fighters made Ingrid wonder whether the Invincibles of the Ice could beat them with their swords and shields. Maybe not. The spear reached further than the sword, and the shields these fighters used were almost twice as big as the ones used by the Invincibles. Luckily, they would never need to find out what would happen if they did fight, or so she hoped.

When nearly all the applicants had taken their turn, it was hers. It was not difficult to understand they were calling her because, when she did not respond, the officer-referee came over to her and jabbed his finger at her rudely. With cold calm she went over to the armories, although she did not need anything from them. She was carrying two bows at her back. She had held up under their weight during the endurance test, so they should let her use them. They did not refuse. Ingrid chose her composite bow and walked back to the edge of the square, where the rest of her group was. Her opponent chose shield and spear, which was not a surprise.

She breathed in calmly and waited for the signal to begin. She soon realized that her fight had sparked expectation, because many members of the ruling family had come to watch. Ingrid guessed it was because she was a foreigner, and because they must not have many like her in the tests. In fact, she was the only foreigner that year, or so she believed.

The officer gave the order for the fight to begin.

Ingrid aimed at her opponent and he wasted no time, lunging into a run to try and shorten the distance between them as soon as possible. He wanted to run at her and attack at close combat, which did not favor Ingrid. Luckily, she was already expecting that strategy and she was ready. As the soldier ran to her, she aimed at his torso, which was protected by his cuirass. As he ran, he was not protecting himself with the shield. He simply carried it in his left hand and had his spear in his right.

Calmly, Ingrid waited until the distance was good enough to release with her bow and too short for the soldier to react. She waited, and when she was sure, she released. The soldier saw the arrow fly and tried to cover himself with his shield without slowing down. He was not fast or coordinated enough. Ingrid had already foreseen that his movement to cover himself with the shield would be from left to right, so at the last moment she had aimed toward the right, aiming at his arm. The arrow brushed the inside of his arm and drew blood. The soldier was charging at her so blindly that he did not even realize. He reached Ingrid and attacked her with his spear. Ingrid slid to one side, avoiding the blow, and pointed at his arm. The soldier looked and cursed in his own language. He withdrew, showing the scratch to the officer, who proclaimed Ingrid the winner. It surprised her that the soldier was so honorable and did not try any tricks.

The fights continued, and Ingrid soon realized they were actually qualifying fights. Once one half had fought the other half, several officers took away the defeated hopeful. The half who had won were once again divided in two, and the process was repeated. Ingrid fought a girl and was sad to defeat her, but she needed to be noticed, and this was the best way. She hit the girl's hand that held the spear: just a glancing blow, but it was enough. The warrior stopped the attack and, nodding to Ingrid, she withdrew.

The ruling Gotirus family seemed delighted with the fights. Its members, spread out in the different buildings, were applauding and cheering after every combat. It even looked like they were placing bets on who was going to win. They were not obvious about it, rather contained, but it was clear they were enjoying the fighting and the skill of the fighters.

The qualifying tests continued. The losers were taken away by the officers, and judging by their looks of defeat, it did not look like they were going to serve the ruling family. Ingrid had to fight several more opponents. Two of them did not use either shield or spear. One had a sword and a knife, and the other used two short swords. She had seen them fight and they were good. They had gotten rid of several phalanx-style soldiers and were agile and coordinated, but unfortunately for them they had never encountered a Ranger before, and without a shield they had nowhere to hide. They both tried to avoid Ingrid's shots, but she got them both with the third arrow. They did not even get close enough to her to be a problem.

The fights continued, and some turned out to be quite competitive. Ingrid watched and made up her mind on how she would fight against her rivals, their strong and weak points, before she realized that with her last victory, she was a finalist. There were only two contenders left, herself and a lean phalanx soldier with long, curly hair.

The Gotirus Ruling Family was paying close attention, especially Sabis, the Captain General whom Ingrid was sure had the sword. She had to win the last fight and ask for her prize. The only problem was that she had already seen her opponent fight, and he was skilled—agile, strong, wary, intelligent, and precise. He was going to be a problem.

The officers signaled for them to take their positions.

Ingrid relaxed her shoulders and stood ready. It was time to fight and win.

Chapter 33

The final combat between Ingrid and Sopelus, her rival, created great expectations. The whole Gotirus family was standing, and it was obvious they had stakes in the fight. Ingrid guessed they had bet against her. After all, Sopelus was fighting phalanx style, and she was a foreigner with a bow. She did not let this fact affect her. All she had to do was defeat him and claim her prize. All the rest was unimportant.

The officers announced the beginning of the fight. In the next instant, Ingrid already had an arrow nocked and was raising it to aim at her opponent. To her surprise, Sopelus did not rush into an attack to try and shorten the distance, which was what most infantry soldiers would do when facing an archer. It was the most logical approach. They had to reach the archer and kill him or her. Remaining at a distance against an archer meant death nine out of ten times.

Ingrid aimed at her opponent and he hid behind his shield, his spear at hip level parallel to the ground. He began to advance slowly, making sure his body was well covered by the large shield. In fact, he was doing a good job. Ingrid could only see the man's spear, large shield, and helmet showing over the rim. It was not going to be easy to hit him. She decided to try taking a shot to see her opponent's response. She shot at the helmet. The arrow flew from the bow and went straight to the target. For a moment Ingrid thought she was going to hit her target, but at the last instant Sopelus raised his shield. The arrow struck the top and bounced off.

Swiftly, she nocked another arrow, raised it, and aimed. The soldier was coming toward her slowly and remained well covered without leaving a clear target. The shield looked huge when the soldier hid behind it. Since she was not going to hit his head, she decided to shoot at his feet. He was wearing odd sandals with a steel tip which Ingrid had seen other soldiers wearing in the city. The protected tip had to be so that their toes would not be attacked in combat, since they were what little could be seen and so entailed a weakness.

She released, and the arrow flew swiftly at the soldier's ankle. Just like with the shot to the helmet, Sopelus protected his feet by lowering the shield. The arrow bounced off. While Ingrid nocked another arrow, the soldier took two large strides to shorten the distance between them. Ingrid released again twice in a row, at the helmet and feet of the soldier, trying to confuse him, but she did not. Sopelus defended himself skillfully and finished shortening the distance that separated him from Ingrid while she nocked another arrow.

All of a sudden, Ingrid saw the tip of the spear coming straight at her torso, and with an instinctive movement she stepped aside and the attack did not hit her. She realized that the reach of the spear was great and the way her rival wielded it very skillful.

She needed to be alert, or else she could lose. The soldier turned to Ingrid, always with his shield raised high and covering himself. Ingrid leapt back, and while she was in the air released the arrow she had ready. The shot was a diagonal, downward one, but the soldier still managed to defend himself well and deflected the shot with his shield. He attacked with his spear with two leaps forward while Ingrid was nocking another arrow. The spear nearly cut her shoulder, but she was able to throw herself on the ground and roll away to avoid the second sharp attack of the spear.

Sopelus turned again toward Ingrid and faced her. In doing this, Ingrid noticed something she could use to her advantage. When the soldier turned his shield and spear to the left, he was slightly slower. Both the shield and spear were metal and heavy. Turning toward the off side since he was right-handed, Sopelus was not as quick as he should be. Seeing her chance, Ingrid prepared her strategy. She released again, leaping backward, and almost landed out of the fighting area. The soldier covered himself with his shield and then launched two powerful forward attacks.

Ingrid had been expecting this attack and finished nocking her arrow when she threw herself on the ground to the left side of the soldier. She did not roll but let her body slide along the ground on her side without letting go of her bow, which she was aiming at the left foot visible under the shield. The soldier turned left to face Ingrid and, just as she was expecting, the turn was slightly slower than desirable. Sliding on her side, she released. The arrow hit the soldier in the left ankle just as he was lowering his shield to protect it. He cried out in pain. He had not had time to cover himself.

Ingrid stood. The soldier was staring at his ankle. There was no doubt he had been hit, since the arrow was sticking out of the side of his ankle. Ingrid knew it was not a serious wound. Sopelus would recover in a couple of weeks. The soldier conceded victory to Ingrid, pointing at the arrow in his ankle with his spear.

The applause and cheers of the Gotirus family underlined the fact that the fight was over. Ingrid snorted. She had won. It had not been easy, but she had done it. She slung her bow on her back. The officer proclaimed Ingrid the winner. Sopelus accepted his defeat and saluted Ingrid with a slight bow of his head, which she returned.

The officer came over to Ingrid and said something she could not understand. Then he motioned her to follow him. Ingrid nodded and followed behind him. He led her to the building where Captain General Sabis Gotirus and his family and guests had watched the fighting from.

Ingrid walked up the stairs to the great arcade with columns and stood silently before Sabis, who ordered the officer to stand at ease to one side. Sabis was a man of average height, neither too tall or too short. He had a lean build and his hair and beard were short. His eyes were brown and his skin was a light brown. Ingrid noticed that all those present looked the same, only the faces were each slightly different. The women sported pretty, long, curly, dark hair, and their eyes were also brown, ranging from light to medium dark. Ingrid found them beautiful in contrast with the Norghanians she was used to.

The Captain General addressed Ingrid, but she did not understand a word. Sabis changed languages and tried again, with the same result.

"Norghana," she said, indicating her face.

Sabis understood and nodded. He turned toward one of his assistants and gave him instructions. The assistant vanished inside the building. Sabis offered water to Ingrid, who was thirsty and dehydrated, so she accepted, delighted. She drank three full glasses of water almost in one go.

She noticed that everyone was watching her while she drank. Not only that, other members of the family were coming over from the other buildings and, after greeting those already there, also stared at her while they enjoyed some snacks or picked at food that looked tasty. She could see there were strawberries and pieces of watermelon mixed with melon. There were also olives and pickles. She was starving. She was about to reach for something, but she was feeling slightly uncomfortable in front of all those generals in their gold-and-silver armor, although it was their fault she had gone without food for three days.

One of the generals asked for her bow and she handed it to him. When she did, they noticed she was carrying a second tiny bow, Punisher, which interested them. She also handed over that one for them to look at. They were all watching her and commenting among themselves, saying things she was unable to understand.

She was the star of the day, although she hated drawing attention to herself. She thought of Viggo. He would love to be there, victorious. He would puff up so much that his shirt would burst. He would strut before all those generals as if he were a king and they, simple soldiers. Her little numbskull would certainly enjoy all that attention. Thinking about Viggo made her yearn to see him, kiss him, and hold him in her arms. As soon as they finished their respective missions, she was going to show him what a passionate Norghanian in love was like.

A man in a green robe appeared, walking behind the assistant, and Ingrid recognized him. It was Celopus, who smiled at her. Ingrid smiled back.

Sabis said something to Celopus.

"Yes, my lord, I speak Norghanian," Celopus replied in Norghanian and then in his own language. The Captain General seemed satisfied. He began to talk in Ingrid's direction, and Celopus translated.

"Congratulations on winning the event of the annual aptitude test. It is an honor few achieve."

"Thank you, sir," Ingrid said, bowing respectfully.

"I do not know why a foreigner like you wishes to enter the ranks of our family's guard..." he said, looking at those surrounding them and listening to the conversation with interested looks.

Ingrid had to meditate on her answer. She did not want to get into trouble.

"Well, sir... that's really not my intention..."

When they heard, the members of the family cried out and grunted. Voices were raised, as Ingrid had expected. The veteran soldiers looked upset and even offended. She would have to tread carefully, or she was going to find herself in deep trouble. She did not want to lie to one of the ruling families, right in front of them to their faces. It would be suicide if afterward the truth was found out, which is what usually happened. The truth, sooner or later, always came out, and it was prone to do so at the worst moment. If Ingrid knew one thing, it was that soldiers were not very understanding. And they never forgave betrayal.

"My brother, General Demisus, demands an explanation," Sabis said, waving his hand at one of the generals in a gold cuirass who looked very upset.

"Well… I'm here for something else, and the only way to gain an audience with the Gotirus family was this…"

Sabis threw his head back and looked at his relatives. Another of the generals in a gold cuirass began to talk rudely and wave his hands in a displeased way.

"My other brother, Noteasus, thinks this is not a dignified way to behave."

"My most sincere apologies, gentlemen. It was not my intention to offend anyone, very much to the contrary, since I come seeking the help of the Gotirus family," Ingrid replied, doubling down in a bow of apology.

This seemed to please Sabis and his two brothers, who lifted their chins at the sight of Ingrid bowing before them.

Another of the soldiers of the family, in a silver cuirass, gave his opinion.

"My oldest son, Yerminus, wants to know where you learned to use the bow that way. We do not have archers of your level in the city."

"I appreciate the compliment. I am a Norghanian Ranger Specialist."

The soldiers started talking to one another. Ingrid had the impression that some of them, the most experienced, had heard talk of the Norghanian Rangers, while the younger ones did not seem to have heard of them. From what Celopus translated, which was not everything, Ingrid realized she was not mistaken. It was curious. Everyone around her looked quite alike: their facial features, height, and complexion were very similar. It was clear they were one big family.

"My other son, Saletirus, asks what your specialty is. My brother,

Demisus, thinks it's related to Archery."

Ingrid was surprised the general would know that, but then she thought again. He was a general—part of his job was to know the enemy, their generals and officers of more renown, their military tactics, the specialties of their armies, and similar.

"General Demisus is right, I have Specialties in Archery."

"More than one?" Saletirus asked, surprised.

"Yes, sir, I am an Archer of the Wind, Infallible Marksman, and Man Hunter."

Once again, the soldiers started talking and arguing among themselves. It appeared that the fact that Ingrid had three Specialties had surprised them, and they were discussing it.

"How is that possible?" Sabis asked. "Specialists only have one specialty, according to our reports."

"You are well informed, but there are certain exceptions, and I am one of them. I have obtained two additional specialties through a special training program."

"That is most interesting," Sabis scratched his short, well-trimmed beard. "Elaborate, we're interested to learn more."

Ingrid found herself in a compromised situation. She did not wish to reveal anything to these soldiers. After all, sometime in the future they might be an enemy, even if they were not one now. They were not currently allies either, so it was not impossible that they might meet on the battlefield at some point, and the less knowledge they had about the Norghanian forces, the better. Besides, it was forbidden for the Rangers to reveal information about their corps, locations, tactics, or training. In fact, any information at all. She would have to answer vaguely, without revealing anything important.

"Some Rangers may achieve more than one Specialization if they keep training for it. A few, like in my case and that of some of my comrades, were chosen to continue our training in order to achieve new Specializations."

"Then you must be very skilled," Noteasus said.

"I have trained extensively, yes," Ingrid replied.

"Man Hunter—is that Specialization what the name indicates?" Demisus asked.

"It is. The main function of a Man Hunter is to track, find, and catch a fugitive."

"A fugitive or a rival, am I wrong?" Sabis said.

"You are correct."

"Through mountains and forests?" Saletirus asked.

"In Norghana it is most commonly through mountains and forests, with ice and snow as well."

Once again, conversation among the relatives broke out, and Ingrid had to wait for them to discuss concepts and comments among themselves. What was killing her was seeing all that fruit and other delicious food on the tables. Her stomach was growling, and she was tired. Celopus kept throwing her knowing glances, which helped a little.

"We understand that you are an advanced, expert Ranger. We have seen you fight, and what you can do with that bow of yours is exceptional," Sabis said. "We also believe you capable of following a trail until you catch your prey. What interests me to know is why you are here. It certainly is not to serve and protect us," he said, waving a hand toward his family.

"It would be an honor to serve such a distinguished family in a city as magnificent as this one," Ingrid said flatteringly, following Egil's advice. He had told her many times that a few well-placed compliments to noblemen delivered at the right moment would open many doors, doors an accurate shot to the heart could not. "Unfortunately, I am here for another reason, one of great importance to the Rangers."

"Go ahead, we're listening," Sabis said.

"I am here for Neils' sword, the Dragon-killer."

Sabis' eyes opened wide, and those of his brothers and sons did as well. Ingrid's motive was something they had not expected. As soon as the surprise subsided, they started arguing among themselves. They did not seem very happy about Ingrid being there for that weapon. Celopus was trying to translate, but the conversations were private and he had to stop.

The leader of the family ordered everyone to be silent, since the arguments were escalating. Then he turned to Ingrid.

"Why does a Norghanian need the legendary weapon of one of our heroes, the founders of this city?"

"I thought he wasn't a hero…"

"He is for some. For others, not so much. His legend has different interpretations," Sabis explained.

Ingrid had been afraid they were going to ask for her opinion. If she replied with the truth, they would think she was crazy and throw her out, or worse. It was better to give the answer she already had prepared.

"From what we know, that weapon is one of power. We wish to study that power and see whether it truly is capable of piercing the toughest metals and the most resilient hides. In recent times, great reptiles have appeared in Norghana with extremely hard scales and we've had to fight them. That's why we're interested in studying the sword's power. That's why I'm here and why I need the weapon."

"Great reptiles? How great? What kind?"

"Gigantic. Sea serpents, colossal desert crocodiles, and others. All very difficult to kill. We can't pierce their scales. The legend says that Neils' sword can do just that."

"Interesting. Rumor has reached us of great reptiles in the desert. We did not know they had traveled so far north."

"They have, and we fear there are more."

"Curious that something like that should happen. We live in very strange times. My Magi have studied that sword, and they say it has a very ancient, powerful magic."

"Then you have the weapon," Ingrid cheered up. This was a step forward.

"Yes, I do. It's in my ceremony hall, hanging above the fireplace."

Ingrid was surprised.

"Didn't you say it's powerful? Don't you use it?"

Sabis laughed, and the rest of the family joined in. The laughter made Ingrid feel bad, not understanding what they were laughing at.

"It is powerful, yes. Or so my Magi tell me, but no one can use that power, and without its power it is nothing but a ceremonial weapon."

"I don't understand... I thought...." That could not be. The sword was supposed to be capable of killing a dragon. Its power had to be usable, if not it would be worthless for them. Maybe it was not the famous Dragon-killer but instead some enchanted sword and they did not know how to use it? That would make more sense. Ingrid was nonplussed. It had to be possible to use it; if not, it had to be some other weapon.

"Yes, I also thought it was a sword that would grant me an incredible advantage in battle. I was going to become legendary. That was what my Magi promised me. We searched for it for a long time, and when at last we found it, we suffered a terrible disappointment. The sword does not pierce metal or tough hides. It is light and sharp, but its power does not activate. Not in my hand, not in that of any of my relatives, or of my Magi, no matter how hard they tried to make use of that power."

"It's only decorative," Demisus said, making a face.

"A gold sword with magical properties that's nothing but a common sword. One that's very light," Noteasus added.

"It's an advantage…"

"Not if it doesn't do anything else it claims to do. I cannot wield Neils' famous sword if it does not give me its power. What good is it to me? It won't make me a legend like it did for him."

"A legend who died with his whole regiment," Yerminus said.

"Some people believe the weapon is cursed," Saletirus added.

"Perhaps its curse is to make anyone who wields it believe that it gives them power," said Demisus.

"Here everyone has their own opinion, but no one wants to wield it," Sabis said. "Including me. I prefer my own sword. I like its weight, looks, and steel. And the fact that it's not bewitched or unlucky," he added.

Ingrid saw an opportunity. If no one wanted the famous sword, maybe she could take it.

"In that case, I'd be delighted to take it with me and have our Magi study it. They might find out more."

Sabis eyed her intensely. He was trying to calculate whether Ingrid was lying, whether it was a trick.

"It's a weapon that belongs in our city," Noteasus said.

"It's an ancient legend. We can't give the sword to a foreigner," said Yerminus.

Sabis thought about it for a moment, rubbing his beard.

"I'll offer you a deal."

"I'm listening, my lord."

"You've won the test, and you have a right to a prize. Since you want the sword, I'll give it to you."

The whole Gotirus family started to protest and raise their voices. Sabis instantly quieted them.

"Shut up, all of you! I'm the head of this family, and I decide!"

There was a silence.

"I'll give it to you on one condition. If your Magi manage to find the way to use its power, you will bring it back to me exactly one year from today."

"And if they don't find a way to use its power?"

"In that case, you will come here and serve in my guard, as you should do for applying to undergo the test."

Ingrid saw the trick. If the weapon was one of power, she would have to return it and Sabis would win a powerful weapon he did not have now. If they could not get it to work or it was not really Neils' Dragon-killer, she would have to serve Sabis. In both cases, he won.

"And if I don't take the deal?"

"I will give you a gift of gold and you will serve me for having applied to the test. I appreciate good fighters, and you are excellent, apart from having other qualities. You will be a welcome addition to my guards, bringing much value with all your specializations. A soldier like me knows how to appreciate both military and martial talent, and you have a lot of both."

Ingrid saw no way out. She had to take the deal. The game had ultimately not been in her favor. This man was smart and knew how to seize opportunities. She had risked too much and could not back up now. They would not let her go scot-free.

"Very well, I accept the deal."

"That's what I like to hear," Sabis smiled broadly, although some of his relatives were not smiling. They did not like the idea of this deal and what it implied.

"You'd better keep your word," Noteasus threatened her, jabbing his finger at Ingrid.

"I'm a person of honor. I'll honor the deal."

"She will. I know it," Sabis said. "Yerminus, bring the sword," he said to his son.

Murmurs spread once again throughout the place. While they were all commenting about what had happened, Celopus was looking at Ingrid with commiseration. Ingrid winked at him unobtrusively.

"Don't worry," she mouthed silently.

Yerminus soon came back with the weapon in his hands.

"Here is Neils Usmentus the Defender's sword." He gave it to his father, who showed it to Ingrid.

"It's a beautiful sword. It looks gold," she said admiringly.

"It looks like gold, but it's not," Sabis said, handing it to Ingrid.

Ingrid noted the engravings in a strange language that ran all along the edges of the sword. She knew it was an ancient and powerful weapon; at least she hoped so. It had all the signs of Neils' Dragon-killer. Unfortunately, she could not prove it until she was back at the Shelter. In any case, she was pleased. She had the sword, which was what mattered, and she would return with it.

"Thank you. It's been an honor to make the acquaintance of the Gotirus Family," Ingrid said as farewell.

"One year. Remember," Sabis said and dismissed her with a gesture.

Chapter 34

Viggo was not happy at all. His search had not been going as well as he would have liked. He was looking for Sansen's Knife, a weapon you could use to tear out the heart of a dragon to then eat it, and thus obtain its power. Unfortunately, his search had led him to many informants or traders, either dead or with their tongues cut out for lying, and he was left without his precious treasure. For now.

The idea of having a weapon in his hands which could kill a dragon was already enough incentive for Viggo, but that it could also grant him the dragon's power seemed unbelievable to him. His friends had not considered that detail, or they had dismissed it as untrue. Whichever was the case, it was a mistake. He had the clear feeling that his knife would grant him the power of a dragon, and with it he would become a semi-god. What more could a human ask for but to become a semi-god? Just thinking about it made him drool.

He was in a border city between the kingdoms of Irinel and Moontian called Dulbelin. It was a curious place. Besides housing inhabitants from these two kingdoms, there were also quite a few people who came from the five City States of the East. It seemed to be a city that traded in all kinds of objects, especially valuable ones. There was a steady flow of caravans in three directions: north to Irinel, south to Moontian, and east to the city states. Especially to the east, from what Viggo could tell after the three days he had spent checking out the city.

"Do you speak my language? I hope so, for your own good." Viggo was on top of the merchant he had surprised and knocked to the ground. He had one of his knives resting on the man's neck and the other one at his ribs.

"Yes… I speak Norghanian and five other languages…" the man muttered, afraid.

"You traders are very smart. You learn whatever you need to make money. Tell me and I won't ask twice—where is the golden knife?"

"Golden knife? What knife…?"

"Don't make me lose my patience. It's not one of the many

virtues I have. You know perfectly what knife I mean."

"Hon…. honestly…. I don't know where it is…"

"Let's see, first you tell me you have no idea what knife I'm talking about, and now you say you don't know where it is. That's an incongruity."

"Incon… what?" the merchant was trembling and did not understand, he was so terrified.

"I've paid a good sum of gold to learn what trader could have a gold knife with power, and I was given your name: Mortises. That's you, right? And think carefully before you lie, because you could easily lose your neck."

"Yes, yes, I'm Mortises. I have money… hidden in the shop…"

"I'm not here for your gold. I'm an Assassin, the best one in the eyes of many, not a simple thief. I want the knife."

"Yes… I had it… but I don't anymore… that was a very long time ago, over fifteen years...." The man—who was in his fifties, fat, with the look of someone who had lived a good life—was perspiring profusely, prostrate on the floor at the back of his elegant shop.

Viggo, sitting on top of him, was looking around the place. There were swords and knives, elaborate pieces worthy of prestigious nobles, and, of course, gold. Mortises was a well-known dealer of exquisite weapons. He knew highly skilled artisans and sold their products, for three times the price he had paid, at his ostentatious shop in the main square of the city.

"Then you know what knife I mean," Viggo used a threatening tone.

"Yes… I know the one you seek, Assassin, but I don't have it… honest, I don't."

"I've traveled through half of Irinel and half of the east of Tremia, and to tell you the truth, I'm fed up with going around chasing after the weapon. If you tell me that the knife is in the kingdom of Moontian, I'll be very upset, and that doesn't bode well for you."

"Nooo, it's not in Moontian!" Mortises cried in panic.

"Then where is it? And consider your reply carefully, because I'm feeling rather annoyed tonight. You know, the full moon and all that…"

"I'll tell you everything, Assassin, please don't kill me," the trader whimpered, which Viggo didn't particularly like. He didn't like people who panicked easily in critical situations.

"Tell me, and explain yourself clearly. I want to know how you came by it and who has it now."

"I bought the knife from an eastern trader, Marcus Fratis, over fifteen years ago. I was having some money issues and he owed me money. He offered it to me as a way of payment. I don't usually accept goods to settle bills, but I had already heard that Marcus was about to go broke, and he owed me an important sum. I needed to hold onto whatever I could. At that time, I didn't have much gold either, my business wasn't going as well as it is now. He offered me the knife, said it was a gold relic with power."

"Gold relic with power, we're on the right track."

Viggo stopped pressing his knife against the trader's neck so Mortises could speak easier, although he did not fully withdraw it. He also kept his other knife at the man's ribs. He had already had a couple of unpleasant experiences with traders who looked inoffensive and had nearly cut his throat and poisoned him. Now he took no risks—all those who made their living by buying and selling gold had no qualms with selling a dead body, even if they had killed the person themselves.

"The legend of Sansen… is known around here… there are many who try to sell his famous knife," the trader explained.

"Curious, I don't know that legend. Enlighten me," Viggo said, sitting on the man's torso and making himself comfortable.

"I'll explain everything, but don't kill me, I beg you…" the trader said with tears in his eyes.

"Firs tell me, and then I'll think about letting you live or not."

"The legend says that, hundreds of years ago, some people think even over a thousand, a terrible white dragon appeared in this region and razed fields and villages."

"Wait, a white dragon? I've never heard about white dragons."

"The legend says it was white, the color of snow."

"How many versions of the legend identify the dragon as white?"

"Ours does, and six in this area, at least if I remember correctly. Then to the south and east there are just as many, and in all of them the dragon is white."

"It doesn't fit, but go on."

The trader swallowed and continued.

"The legends say that the white dragon killed the nobles and their soldiers who confronted it. It set itself up as king of this region and made everyone else serve it."

"As servants?

"As slaves. Its wishes were law, and no one could say a word against the dragon or they were killed. The legends also say the white dragon froze those who dared to look upon it with its frozen breath. Those who stood up to the dragon were ripped apart with its claws and eaten."

"You don't say. Hah, I like this dragon, it doesn't fool around."

"It terrorized all the regions of these parts, regardless of kingdom, and the dragon's base was the Castle of Mirtell."

"I think I've seen it, it's the one half ruined at the top of the hill behind this city, isn't it?"

"The one and the same. For over a hundred years, the white dragon ruled over these lands without anyone capable of bringing down the beast."

"And then our friend Sansen appeared," Viggo interrupted him.

"The legends say Sansen grew up here and suffered under the slavery the dragon had imposed on the whole region. He was one of those in charge with bringing the creature cattle to feed on. He brought the dragon well-fed animals which it devoured in two bites."

"But something happened, didn't it? Something always happens in legends." Viggo smiled.

"Apparently, one day the animals brought to the dragon weren't up to the dragon's standards, and it became enraged and killed all of Sansen's men. He survived by a hair's breadth, but he was badly wounded. The dragon thought him dead. Among the dead were Sansen's father, who had taught him the business, and his uncle, who worked with his father."

"That must've upset Sansen quite a lot."

"The legend tells that, broken by the loss of his loved ones and friends, Sansen prayed to the Gods to give him a weapon to kill the dragon with."

"What Gods? There are so many."

"It doesn't… say… it depends on the region, it's some gods or others."

"I was afraid of that. So, we don't know what gods. With so little exactitude, we won't get very far," Viggo said.

"That's all I know, I swear."

"Go on with the story, you have me spellbound," Viggo smiled at the man as he showed him his knife.

"Well… according to… what is believed, the Gods answered Sansen's pleas and sent him a weapon which could not only kill the dragon, but could tear out its heart and take its power."

"Now we're getting to the part I'm interested in."

"Sansen took the golden knife the Gods had given him and hid in wait with the next load of cattle. When they served it to the dragon, the beast ate them all and lay down to sleep."

"The glutton. Of course, what bad behavior."

"Sansen, who knew where and when the dragon would be fed and that it would rest afterward, killed the dragon in its sleep."

"Smart boy."

"That's what the legends say."

"And did he get the dragon's power?"

"Yes, and he became king of the ancient kingdom of Gormos, which is now gone. He reigned over five hundred years."

"That's a lot of time, too long for a mortal."

"They say the power of the dragon prolonged his life."

"You don't say… hmm, that's interesting."

"Well…. they're only legends…"

"Even so, I'm interested. So, regarding the weapon this Marcus Fratis brought to you, did you examine it and determine that it could be Sansen's Knife?"

"Yes… I'm convinced it was."

"If you want me to get off your chest and not kill you, you'd better persuade me that it *was* the knife."

"Yes… it was a gold knife, only it wasn't gold. It was made of a material similar to gold but a lot lighter. It didn't weigh anything."

"What do you mean it didn't weigh anything?"

"It was very light, like brandishing a feather."

"Interesting, continue."

"And it had power."

"Was it enchanted?"

"Mage Eldritch confirmed it. Very ancient and powerful magic."

"Who's that mage? And why didn't he keep it if it was a weapon of power?"

"He's the city's Mage. He's a scholar who possesses the Gift. He's really more of a Healer than anything else. He uses his knowledge and magic to make healing potions and balms. He's not interested in the weapon and its power, or in anything that has to do with death or power that causes pain."

"What do you know, a good-natured, pacifist mage. I'd never heard talk about one like that until now."

"He's a good person… he helps people…"

"I'm sure the gods will reward him in the afterlife. Now, persuade me that the knife is authentic and that everything you've told me is the truth."

"It is! I haven't lied! It's the truth!" Mortises cried, tearing up again with fear.

"Okay, I'm convinced. Now I need to know who you sold it to and where to find that person. If you lie to me, you know I'll come back for you and you'll lose your jugular."

"I sold it to a Zangrian Noble! Count Zolatan!"

"Zangrian Noble?"

"Yes, he knew the legend of the knife, and he came in person to see me, along with about twenty Zangrian soldiers who were escorting him."

"Hmmmm… I don't like the turn this is taking."

"I had to sell it to him, he offered me a lot of gold! He wasn't going to take no for an answer! The Zangrians are terrible losers!" Mortises cried.

"I know the Zangrians. Small, ugly, quarrelsome—oh, and hairy."

"I had to sell it to him. It's been fifteen years since then and I've never heard anything about the knife."

"Then Zolatan has it."

"I sold it to him, that's all I know. It's been a long time."

"Yeah… it seems I'll have to have a talk with this Count Zolatan. Where do I find him?"

"In the County of Zoltanmagen, in the heart of Zangria. Now isn't a good time to go there… the war is about to begin."

"Thanks for thinking about my well-being. I'm flattered."

"Don't kill me, please!"

"I'll make a deal with you. You don't tell anyone what happened here tonight, and I won't kill you."

"Yes! I won't say anything"

"You won't say anything about what?"

"Nothing about nothing! This hasn't happened!"

Viggo smiled from ear to ear.

"That's what I like to hear." Viggo rose, and with three steps and a leap he left through the window he had forced open. He melted into the night and vanished in the back alley.

Chapter 35

The merchant Mortises was not wrong when he said it was a bad time to enter Zangria. The kingdom was on the warpath, and there were soldiers everywhere, which did not make Viggo's task easy at all. It had taken him over a week to get to the center of the country. He had needed to travel practically always at night and by secondary roads, crossing forests and rivers where there were no checkpoints by the Zangrian Army, which had them practically everywhere.

He was already in the County of Zoltanmagen, in the heart of Zangria, and he could glimpse a large castle on a clear hill in the moonlight. A little apart, by the river and at the foot of the mountain, he saw a walled city. According to the map of Zangria Viggo had procured himself, the city was Saprost. It was quite big, and it must be at the center of the county. A wide, clear road led to the city. The problem was that there were at least two checkpoints controlled by the Zangrian Army. He also saw a patrol of four soldiers on horseback patrolling the forests.

Suddenly, he heard a noise and looked behind him. It was Milton, the owl. He was in a cage next to the saddlebags of his horse. He could not understand why—of all the Rangers' owls, they just had to give him the most rebellious and the one he hated the most. And yes, he was sure the bird hated him too.

"Shhhhhh, you hopeless owl, don't make any noise."

Milton ignored the order and started hitting the cage with his claws.

"If you don't shut up and stay still, I swear I'll pluck off all your feathers and roast you like a chicken, you scrawny flying rodent!" Viggo said in an angry whisper.

Milton clicked his beak loudly.

Viggo snorted and continued riding until he found a forest, not too big but quite thick. He entered the trees and then jumped off his mount. He led the horse to a stream in the middle of the forest and put Milton on the ground by the horse.

"Now you can make all the noise you want," he told the owl.

Milton hooted loudly.

Viggo climbed a tree and lay down to rest on a high, thick branch.

The mounted patrol of four Zangrian soldiers soon passed nearby. Milton's noises seemed to draw the attention of one of them, who stopped his horse. He peered into the center of the forest where they were. Seeing he had stopped, the rest of the patrol also came to a halt a little further ahead. The first one dismounted and made a sign for his comrades to follow him.

The four Zangrian soldiers entered the forest. They were armed with spears and triangular shields. They wore the unmistakable Zangrian colors: flashy yellow and black, both on their clothes and shields. Since they were short people, they had chosen bright colors to appear bigger than they actually were, or that was what other kingdoms said about them.

They parted the bushes and thicket to reach the center, where Milton hooted when he saw the four Zangrians. Viggo's horse panicked and backed up as the soldiers moved toward them. They reached Milton who, always quarrelsome, was showing them his claws and clicking his beak menacingly. But the soldiers were not interested in the owl and the horse, they wanted to know where the rider was. It was not long before they found out.

Viggo jumped down from the branch he had been waiting on and hit two of the Zangrians on their backs with all the force of his fall. The two soldiers were thrown forward and ended up face-first on the ground. As soon as he landed, with tremendous speed, Viggo delivered a strong blow in the temple to the Zangrian soldier with the pommel of his knife as the man turned to attack him. Viggo stunned him, although he did not knock him out since the helmet muffled the blow. The other Zangrian had turned and lunged to attack with his spear, but Viggo flew forward and, with a strong right punch holding the hilt of his knife, broke the man's nose. The Zangrian stepped back, dropped the spear, and put his hands to his nose.

Viggo finished off the stunned soldier with two punches to the chin, holding his knives in his hands. Then he took a powerful leap and with his forward leg hit the one with the broken nose full in the forehead, who promptly fell backward and lost consciousness. The other two soldiers were getting up and trying to pick up the spears and shields they had dropped when falling on their faces. Viggo did not give them the chance. He leaped up to reach the first one and kicked him in the groin. When the man doubled up in pain, he knocked the soldier out with a right hook, never letting go of his knives. He turned for the other one, who already had his spear in his hand and tried to pierce Viggo, who moved to one side and then onto the soldier as he was trying to withdraw his spear to launch another piercing attack. Viggo cut both the man's hands at lightning speed, and the Zangrian was forced to drop the spear. As Viggo was landing again, he knocked out the soldier with two blows, one to each temple.

"What did you think of that, Milton? Spectacular, wasn't it?"

Milton hooted, and the way he did it sounded to Viggo as if he was not too impressed.

"You don't know what you're saying," he told Milton and gestured at him with his hand.

He checked the four soldiers on the ground. They were short, wide as oaks, but short. All except one, who was slightly taller than the others, although not by much, maybe just four fingers. He was the only one whose beard was not a mess.

"You'll do." Viggo took off the man's clothes and then took ropes out of his saddlebags and tied up the four soldiers. He also gagged them with rags from their own uniforms.

He put on the taller Zangrian's uniform and took his spear and shield. Then he began to walk half-crouched, because he was much taller than the Zangrians and wanted to pass off as one of them.

Milton hooted, and Viggo had the feeling the bird was laughing at him because of the way he was walking.

"I have to practice, and don't laugh, or I'll roast you on a slow fire."

After practicing a little, Viggo thought he looked pretty convincing. He took Milton's cage and hung it from his saddle, then mounted.

"Now we'll head to the castle. It's a silent mission, so no noise whatsoever."

Milton hooted loudly.

"I swear I'm going to roast you…."

It was the early hours of the morning when Viggo left the battlement of the north wall behind. He quickly headed to one of the towers and stood still, as if he were on duty, with the yellow-and-black shield covering his body and the spear in front. The helmet was too big for him, and he had almost lost it climbing the wall. Luckily, the Zangrians were not the best builders in Tremia—the castle wall was not too tall or well built. The stone used had not been polished or leveled, so Viggo had been able to climb the wall with his hands and feet without needing a rope. He had slung the shield and sword on his back and climbed without too much trouble. That did not pose a problem for an Assassin of his caliber—the best Assassin in the north, and soon of all Tremia.

He heard footsteps and counted them: four guards on the battlement doing their rounds. Attacking them was not the best option, as it would make too much noise. The short Zangrians were hard to knock out, as he had just experienced, and it would make a racket and alert the rest of the sentinels. From what he had seen while he waited for the change of guard before he climbed, there were more than twenty sentinels on the battlements in the north and east sections. This mission required stealth and intelligence. He could not go in fighting, or they would sound the alarm and he would have to flee without reaching his goal.

Leaning against the wall and bending slightly to appear less tall, he saw the four sentinels pass. They did not even notice him. They walked in a roundabout way, looking toward the outside. At night and in a place without much light, like the situation he was currently in, they would never notice he was not a Zangrian. With more light, things would get complicated. He waited for the right moment and quickly opened the door of the tower and went in, closing it behind him.

He waited and listened carefully, but he did not hear footsteps or noise. He began to walk down the spiral stone stairs of the tower. He reached the top floor under the battlements, put his head out, and saw two corridors, one to his right and one to his left. They were lit with torches, and between each corridor was a soldier on duty. Viggo knew that Count Zolatan would not be sleeping on such a high floor. Nobles, no matter what kingdom they were from, did not like to climb many stairs. They preferred lower floors, although they did not live on the lowest level because they had to be above soldiers and servants.

He continued down the tower stairs for three more floors, and at each one he poked his head out. He found two corridors each housing two sentinels, but on the third there were three guards in each corridor. This might be the area where the Count had his rooms. More guards were a sign that something important was here, in this case the castle noble's quarters. The problem now was getting rid of the sentinels without them sounding the alarm or making too much noise that other guards would hear and come over to investigate. The good thing about being an Assassin and having another Assassin in the Panthers' ranks, like Astrid, was having someone to exchange new techniques and tactics with, and sometimes they managed to develop really good tricks. There was one they had devised and which Viggo had not had the chance to try yet. But he was sure it would work. After all, he had found the best way to use the trick, using a throwing knife, his favorite.

He reached to his belt for three throwing knives. They were special, and Egil had helped him forge them. They were knives very much like his own throwing knife, only that half the knife was made of hollow glass. He held the first one in his right hand, ready to throw, and with his left hand he held the Zangrian shield and spear. With absolute composure, he started toward the nearest guard in the left-hand corridor. It took the guard a little while to notice Viggo coming, a little longer to realize there was something odd in this Zangrian solder, and still longer to react.

Too late for him, Viggo did not even have to throw the knife. He passed the guard nonchalantly. The guard filled his lungs with air, and when the man was about to speak, Viggo plunged his knife in the man's mouth with a sharp blow. The glass tip broke, and the Summer Slumber it contained flooded the guard's mouth, nose, and throat. Viggo continued walking toward the second guard as if nothing had happened. The wounded sentinel tried to speak but could not. The Summer Slumber knocked him right out and he slipped along the wall until he was sitting on the floor.

The second guard saw Viggo coming and that something had happened back there. He looked blankly at the guard, already in a deep sleep, while Viggo kept walking, unfazed. The sentinel was about to say something when Viggo whipped out his right arm and the second glass-tipped knife flew straight to the guard's Adam's apple and the tip broke. The guard could not speak from the blow, and the Summer Slumber knocked him out a moment later. Viggo reached the man just as he was falling and held him to gently deposit him on the floor.

The third guard noticed something was going on just as Viggo was facing him and starting toward him. The guard turned to Viggo and the glass-tipped knife flew like an arrow toward the forehead of the man, who tried to cover himself with the shield when he saw something flying at him. Viggo kept walking with absolute calm while the knife passed over the shield and plunged between the guard's eyes. The tip broke and the gas had the guard sleeping by the time Viggo reached him. He had to rush the last few paces to hold him before he fell to the floor, and he deposited him gently, making sure his shield and spear made no sound.

Viggo looked around. Everything was silent, and the three guards were sleeping on the floor. He took two steps back and breathed. He did not want to be knocked out by the effects of the gas. The Summer Slumber knife had worked perfectly, just as he had told Astrid it would. She had not liked the idea of using a throwing knife much. He would have to tell her, and this brought a smile to his face. He liked it when he had good ideas, especially when he was right about something.

He turned and went back. When he had passed the guard in the middle, he had noticed an interesting door. He stopped before the door to a room and checked it. It was undoubtedly the Count's—the door was oak, double and engraved. There was even one engraving Viggo guessed was the coat of arms of the Zolatan House.

He took out his lock picks and skillfully forced the lock open. It was one of the good ones, but not good enough to withstand Viggo's skill with his tools. He carefully cracked open the door and peeked inside with one eye. He saw a huge room with another chamber at the back. From the elegance of the furniture and the decoration, he thought he was in the right place—this might be it. He went in silently.

He went straight to the back chamber, since the first was an office with a large oak table that served as a desk. He left the spear and shield on the floor and went on. He took out his two Assassin's knives. He found two back chambers. The one on the left looked like a reading room. There were armchairs, a round table in the middle, and bookshelves. This Zangrian liked to read.

He made his way to the chamber on the right. He was expecting it to be the Count's bedchamber and that he would be sleeping in it. Viggo had been watching the castle for a few days and had seen the

Count come out with an escort a couple of times. Count Zolatan had just returned that evening, so he should be resting after the journey. Well, that was if Viggo had not mixed up his nobles and the one he had seen was indeed Count Zolatan, whom Viggo did not know. From the escort and the respect shown to him by the officers and soldiers when Viggo had seen him arrive at the castle, Viggo was taking for granted that it was indeed Zolatan. He hoped he was right, because if not he was going to be in deep trouble.

On the bed, asleep, was a man in his mid-forties. He was Zangrian without a doubt, judging by his stature and complexion. But unlike most Zangrians, who wore their hair and beard messy, this man had them well groomed. This told Viggo he was a noble, as well as the high-quality, bejeweled sword left on an armchair and the silver armor resting on a wooden mannequin. On the other side were an armory with spears, a large rectangular shield in gold-and-black steel, and a glass cabinet where he could glimpse an important collection of swords and daggers. By the look of them and the jewels decorating them, they were very expensive.

Viggo walked to the cabinet to see whether Sansen's Knife was there. If it was he could steal it easily and get out of there with the prize and a smile. He checked the weapons while the Count snored peacefully. He checked them one by one, but Sansen's Knife was not among them. He cursed under his breath—it would have been one of his most perfect missions if it had been there. Now he would have to do it the rough way, which he did not really dislike. Ingrid would scold him for the feeling, but since she was not there, he could relish in it. He smiled and approached the Count, who was sleeping like a log.

Swiftly, he put the knife on the Count's neck. The Count felt the cold metal and pressure on his Adam's apple and woke up. Viggo put his other knife over his mouth when the Count's eyes opened so he did not have time to scream. Viggo pressed down with both hands so he would stay quiet and still. The Count understood and did not try to struggle.

"Do you understand me?" Viggo asked.

The Count made a horrified face, and his eyes widened even more.

"I'm not here to kill you."

"You Norghanian," the Count said in Norghanian with a thick

accent.

"Yes, I am. But today you're lucky, because I'm not here on an Assassin's mission."

The Count looked at him blankly.

"No understand."

"No Assassin."

The Count understood then.

"No Assassin," he repeated.

"That's right. Count Zolatan?"

The Count considered his answer.

"Don't lie to me, it'll be worse. Not lie."

"I Count Zolatan."

"Great, for a moment there I was worried."

The Count did not understand a word, and the look on his face showed it.

"No understand."

"Don't worry. Sansen's Knife."

The Count's eyes widened again.

"No understand."

Viggo showed him his knife and then pointed at the cabinet and repeated the name of the weapon.

"Sansen's Knife."

"No understand."

"Knife," Viggo showed him his own. "Sansen's" he repeated.

The Count either did not understand or was an expert pretender. His face showed terror.

"Sansen," Viggo repeated.

And suddenly the Count seemed to understand.

"Sansen," the Count said in another accent.

"Yes, Sansen, I've been telling you for half the night already. Sansen, Sansen. Sansen," Viggo pronounced it, trying to imitate the Count's accent.

"Yes, Sansen," he repeated with another accent.

"I need to learn more languages, this is getting frustrating. Where is Sansen?"

"Where?"

"Yes, where?"

"Gift."

"Gift? To whom?"

"Gift, General Zorlten."

Viggo snorted loud.

"When?"

"Ten years. Favor."

"Let's see if I understand. You gave Sansen's Knife to General Zorlten so he would do you a favor. Is that it?"

"Political favor. Big."

"Yes, I imagine that if you gave away a legendary weapon with power to a soldier, I'm guessing someone powerful, it had to have been for a huge political favor."

"Zorlten, Sansen."

"Are you sure he has it?"

"Zorlten, Sansen," the Count repeated, and from his look and how he was sweating, it was clear he was telling the truth.

"Okay, it's clear that Zorlten has Sansen's Knife. I don't like it one little bit, but we have to accept it when things don't turn out as well as we hoped."

Count Zolatan was staring at Viggo with a look of incomprehension.

"No…"

"Take it easy," Viggo kept one knife on the Count's neck and removed the other one. With his free hand, he took out a container from his belt under the Zangrian uniform and armor. He poured the contents down the Count's mouth and nose without a word.

Zolatan shut his mouth and tried not to breathe, but he could not resist for long with a knife to his neck. A moment later, he was unconscious.

Viggo, who was holding his breath, covered the container and put it away again. He moved away from the Count, who was knocked out, and headed for the door. He picked up his shield and poked his head out. There was no sign of danger, so he went out into the corridor. He closed the door behind him and started moving away, only daring to breathe when he was halfway down the corridor.

"Well, let's see what this General Zorlten can tell us."

Chapter 36

The journey to reach the base of the Fighters of the New Sun in the south of Erenal had not been at all easy. Going into enemy territory as a spy when a great battle was brewing was at the least risky, if not suicidal. Astrid had needed to take extreme precautions, traveling only by night, through forests and hills that allowed her to hide at all times. She was not dressed as a Ranger and went around control posts belonging to the Erenalian army and stayed away from villages and towns. This last requirement saddened her quite a bit. Erenal was a beautiful kingdom, and the capital, Erenalia, was the prettiest Astrid had ever visited. She would have loved to enjoy its beauties again, the large avenues with statues, the elegant buildings, the Great Library of Bintantium, but it could not be. If she were caught, she would hang as a spy.

It was mid afternoon when Astrid finally arrived at the fortress where the Fighters of the New Sun had their base and residence, south of Erenalia. From what Egil had uncovered about them, King Dasleo used them as bodyguards, spies, and for special assassination missions, so Egil had had no trouble finding them. In a way, they were like the Rangers, only they were all women with the specialties of Archery and Expertise.

What concerned Astrid was whether she would be accepted or not. From what Egil had written down in his notebook, they accepted any candidate who was a woman and a good fighter, or had the potential to be one. Nationality did not matter, and neither did ethnicity, height, size, beauty, or strength. Those factors made no difference as long as you were a woman. The problem was that once you became a member of the Fighters and you took the oath, you could not leave the sisterhood. This was a slight inconvenience which Astrid was considering as she approached the walled fortress.

In any case, first things came first: she had to get accepted and avoid being hanged as a Norghanian spy, which was going to be more difficult than later escaping with the Gauntlet.

She sighed. That Norghana was at war with Erenal did not make her mission any easier. She checked the gate in the wall. There were six women in front of the gate. One of them was sitting at a table with an open tome in front of her, most likely the Inscription Log. The first thing that drew her attention was the women's clothing. They all wore reinforced leather armor and leather skirts with high boots, also leather. The armor was dyed a faded gold. Cloaks fell from their shoulders in the same aged gold color. They were armed with composite bow on their backs, with a sword and dagger at the waist. The sword and dagger were not in the Erenalian style but longer. They all wore their hair long, in different shades, and a headband, also in aged gold, with a green emerald gem in the middle. They were all in their mid-thirties.

One thing became clear to Astrid. They were not discreet, and anyone would notice the group from afar. She also noticed that those six women were muscular. They were wiry and had no trace of fat on their bodies. They were well-trained warriors. The good reputation they had in Erenal seemed to be well-deserved.

As she watched them she had an idea, one that might work. She remembered that Valeria had worked for Erenal before going to Irinel, for General Augustus if she remembered correctly, so they might also know about the Dark Rangers. She could not pass herself off as Valeria because someone might have met her, although the odds were low. But, she could pass herself off as Valeria's sister. She knew her story, her motives for treason, her entire past. She could tell that story as if it were her own. It bothered her to no end to have to use Valeria since she loathed the woman, but it might work. Yes, it might work very well indeed. She would introduce herself as Astrid, Valeria's sister and a fellow Dark Ranger. This gave her a reason to seek shelter here as a Norghanian.

She approached the warriors. She was wearing a common blue-hooded cloak, and under the cloak she wore breeches and shirt of the same color. She looked more like a trader than anything else, and she was not carrying her bow, Ranger's knife, or axe.

"Good morning," she greeted them with a nod of her head in the language of Erenal. She only knew a few sentences she had learned to get by.

One of the warriors returned the greeting and then delivered a couple of sentences Astrid did not understand.

"I don't speak Erenalian," she said as best she could.

The warriors looked at one another. The one sitting at the table asked her something else, but Astrid did not understand a word.

"I want to join the Warriors of the New Sun," she told them in the language of Erenal. She had been practicing that sentence for days.

The warriors understood, because they started talking among themselves.

The one sitting at the table with the tome showed it to her and asked her to write down her name.

Astrid nodded and wrote, 'Astrid, Norghana.'

When they saw 'Norghana', they all understood and grew tense. They reached for their weapons.

Astrid raised hers slowly. She was only carrying one throwing knife in her belt at her back, so when she raised her arms and her cloak opened, they saw she was not carrying weapons.

One of the warriors came over and pushed back Astrid's hood.

The six women stared at her as if gauging her possible worth. Then they spoke among themselves. One of them went into the fortress. Astrid remained as she was, hands in the air. The other warriors stared at her without saying a word. They waited for the warrior, who had gone inside and returned with another woman, who was slimmer and less than thirty.

"Hi, I'm Julia," she introduced herself in Norghanian with a strong Erenalian accent.

"Hi, I'm Astrid. Glad there's someone who speaks Norghanian," Astrid said, smiling and lowering her hands slowly.

"I'm local, from Erenal, but I spent half my childhood in Norghana. I still remember the language."

"You remember it well," Astrid told her.

"You want to join us? That's very strange. You are Norghanian, and we're at war…" Julia said, puzzled.

"Yes… and suspicious, I understand. My story is complicated…."

The warrior at the table said something.

"She wants to know whether you can fight?"

"Tell her I can, I'm a Ranger Specialist."

Julia's eyes opened wide. Then she translated.

The warriors began to talk and argue among themselves. Some started to reach for their swords.

"They want to kill me, don't they?"

"You're Norghanian and a Ranger, what would you think in their place?"

"Yeah... tell them I can explain why I'm here and that I haven't come to spy on you."

Julia translated Astrid's words and the argument stopped.

The one at the table, who was surely the officer in command, spoke.

"She wants to hear your story, and she says you'd better be convincing, or you won't go back to Norghana."

Astrid heaved a deep sigh. She hoped her idea worked, otherwise she would have to kill some of the warriors and escape if possible. There were two towers in the wall with archers in them—maybe fleeing was not a good idea.

Slowly, she told the story of her life with as much sincerity and drama as she was capable of, imagining herself as Valeria's sister and belonging to the Dark Rangers. She added that she had been banished like her sister and that she had been wandering Tremia ever since. She could not go back to Norghana or she would be hanged, so she had thought that here, among the sisterhood in Erenal, would be an ideal place for a Dark Ranger, especially since they were at war with Norghana. Once she finished, she studied the faces of the warriors to see whether they had believed her or not.

After a moment, the officer said something to Julia.

"We will check your story. If it's not true, you'll die."

"Understood, thank you," Astrid said, nodding.

The officer talked to Julia for a moment.

"Come with me. I'll give you food and a place to rest until the Test of Worth."

"What's that?"

"It's the test that decides whether you can join the sisterhood or not."

"Oh, I see."

"If you're a Ranger, you won't have any trouble passing it."

Julia took Astrid inside the fortress. The main building was a large military keep with four other buildings around it, two storehouses, and some stables. It looked like an army keep. There were women working everywhere, as well as a large number practicing the sword with instructors teaching them how to use it in training. They used fields with wooden mannequins for the sword and dirk, and targets for the bow. At first count, she saw almost four hundred women in all.

The workings of the sisterhood were fully martial, and she began to distinguish the officers, who each had a red ribbon on their left wrist. The instructors wore a blue one.

Julia took her to one of the adjacent buildings. It was long and had all the looks of being a bunkhouse. Astrid was right—that's what it was, with over a hundred beds, trunks at the foot of each one. There were about a dozen girls there, resting. They were not dressed like the warriors of the order.

"This is the newbies' bunkhouse."

"Oh, I see."

"Choose one that's free and put your things in the corresponding trunk."

"Okay."

"Dinner will soon be served at the cafeteria-dining room. It's the rectangular building, smaller than the rest. Since you haven't been accepted yet, you can't access any other building but this one. Later I'll bring you something to eat. Remember, you can't leave this bunkhouse. The guards will detain you or worse if you wander alone around the fortress."

"I understand. Who leads the sisterhood?"

"That's Belona. She's the leader of the Fighters of the New Sun. She's nearly sixty already, although no one would be able to tell. She's in excellent shape. She has two lead warriors with her. Victoria is in charge of Swordsmanship, and Diana of Archery. They're our teachers in how to wield those weapons, and they lead the rest of the warriors. Don't worry, you'll meet them when you pass the test."

"Thank you. By the way, how long have you been here?"

"About five years. My story is sad, like yours, only I came seeking revenge."

"Revenge from a warrior of the sisterhood?"

"Oh no. My father and brother were killed in Rogdon. I know who did it, a rival merchant. But the Rogdonian justice wouldn't listen to me. I didn't have proof, and he wasn't tried. There was nothing I could do: he has gold and armed soldiers to protect him. I knew of the legendary warriors of the New Sun—they have a great reputation in Erenal and King Dasleo finances them—so I came here to be trained and fulfill my revenge."

"And have you?"

"Not yet, that's still pending," she said, bowing her head and looking a little embarrassed. "But I will one day. I swore on the graves of my father and brother, and I intend to keep my oath," she said with anger.

Astrid nodded.

"Be careful with revenge, she's bad company."

"I know, but nothing's going to stop me. I'll do what I promised," she said and then left.

Astrid chose a bunk at the beginning of the bunkhouse. She put her rucksack in the trunk and lay down to rest. She was in. It had gone better than she had expected. So far the story she had invented was working and had opened the door for her. Now she had to get accepted. Then find out where they kept the Gauntlet and grab it. The fact that she was surrounded by about four hundred well-trained, alert warriors made it slightly difficult, but she decided not to let it worry her. Perhaps an opportunity would present itself; that, or she was going to have to work hard to get out of there alive with the object.

Julia came back with dinner for her as she had promised, and Astrid noticed that others had brought dinner to the ten girls there with her, which meant they were in her same situation. She ate the stew, which was very good.

"Meat with tomato and green pepper, it's really delicious."

"I'm glad you like it. We have very good cooks."

"I imagine," Astrid smiled as she continued eating the delicious stew.

"You're in luck," Julia told her.

"Am I? Why's that?"

"Belona has announced at dinner that tomorrow morning we'll have the test. These girls have been here over two weeks, waiting," she said, glancing at them.

Astrid looked at them too. They were of different races, which surprised her.

"They're bored of waiting."

"As a rule, we wait until there are a dozen candidates."

"That means that not all of them pass."

"No, only those who can be warriors. Many girls come to us with traumatic pasts, with stories so horrible you can't even begin to imagine. They believe we'll take them in and help them."

"Like in your case."

"Yes, but with even more dramatic stories. The problem is that if they're not good for fighting, and many aren't, they're not accepted, no matter what horrors have led them to knock on our door."

"I see, this isn't a charity."

"No, it isn't. Belona only accepts warriors. Otherwise, the sisterhood would grow weak and die out."

"That makes sense."

"It's a pity, but we can't help or take in all the women who deserve help."

Astrid nodded.

"This is a cruel world, and it doesn't know forgiveness or justice."

Julia nodded.

"Belona asked King Dasleo to create another sisterhood to help women and take in those our sisterhood rejects."

"And he refused."

"On the contrary, he thought it was a good idea. He created the Sisterhood of Aid. It's north of the capital. Those who don't manage to enter our sisterhood are sent there."

"Oh, wow. This king of yours doesn't seem like such a bad man."

"No, he isn't at all. Dasleo is a great King."

"I'm happy for you," Astrid smiled, thinking how unlucky they were with Thoran and the Druid Queen.

"Rest now. Tomorrow is an important day."

"Thank you, I will."

Julia left, and Astrid lay down in her bunk. She could feel the nervousness of the other ten girls from where she was. It was as if a light tremor ran through the bunks. She felt bad for them. They had not had her good fortune of becoming a Ranger, of being a Snow Panther. She thanked the Ice Gods for her good luck. Then she reconsidered. She did not believe in any god, of the ice or of any other place. The luck she had, she had earned herself with her own effort.

"Good luck to all," she whispered in the dark.

Chapter 37

Early in the morning, they came for the candidates, six warriors in their aged gold armor and cloaks, each sporting the headband with an emerald in the center and armed with a sword, dirk, and bow. In the morning light, they shone like golden warrior goddesses.

They made all the girls come out and form two lines, then they were taken to a wide, tiled long quadrangle in front of the large keep. The quadrangle was surrounded on all sides by warriors there to witness the Test. The girls were told to stand inside the quadrangle, at the far end, on the other side of the keep.

Astrid wondered what the Test of Worth would consist of. She observed the girls waiting with her. She did not know where they were from, but they obviously came from different origins. She saw two Noceans with skin the color of ebony; a Masig with red skin; one girl from the mountains of Moontian, unmistakable for her violet skin and pink eyes; and others she could not place.

They heard trumpets, and Astrid located two warriors standing before the entrance of the keep who were doing the calling. She soon realized they were announcing their leaders. Three women came out of the keep, followed by a dozen warriors. Astrid guessed who they were from what Julia had explained to her. The first one in the lead heading to the rectangle was Belona, the leader of the Fighters of the New Sun. She was over sixty, her wrinkled skin and white hair were proof of it, but her body looked like that of a much younger woman. She obviously took care of herself and exercised a lot, Astrid guessed. She was followed by her two lead warriors. Victoria carried a broadsword at her back, as well as a long sword and a short sword at her waist. She was tall and strong, with white skin, black, straight hair, and intense green eyes, and she must have been in her mid-thirties. Beside her was Diana, with her composite bow on her back and two daggers at her waist. She was blonde, and her hair fell down her shoulders. Her eyes were blue and she was beautiful, average height, and thin, with wiry arms. She must have been in her late thirties.

They arrived at the quadrangle and the warriors moved back to let them inside while the trumpets continued to announce the Test.

The three leaders and the dozen warriors who had to be their guard stood at the entrance of the quadrangle, on the opposite side of where the candidates were standing. Belona addressed all the warriors in the language of Erenal, so Astrid could not understand a word of what she said. She did understand though that this was a speech to raise morale, because the warriors broke out in cheers and shouts with raised arms and clenched fists. Belona went on with her haranguing, speaking right and left, gesticulating strongly and with a powerful, raspy voice. Astrid did not know what the warriors were shouting, but she suddenly felt like joining in the cheering. One thing was clear. Judging from the way Belona spoke to her warriors, the power of her gestures and words, and how they had received the message, she was a charismatic leader.

The leader finished her speech and the trumpets rang again. Astrid guessed the test was about to begin. She was right. Two officers stood in the center of the quadrangle. One of them was holding a scroll. With a powerful voice, she called out a name. It was not Astrid's. One of the Noceans of the candidates' group stepped forward, and the officer signaled for her to come to the center. The Nocean did so. She was about twenty and thin but wiry. She must have come from the deserts and was wearing a cream-colored robe.

The officer with the scroll called out a name that sounded Nocean to Astrid, and from among the group of warriors, one woman with ebony skin stepped forward. Her aged gold armor and gold-colored cloak made her a sight to be seen. She came over to the candidate and spoke to her. The candidate nodded and started talking in her own language to the leaders. As she did so, the Nocean warrior translated what the girl was saying. Astrid, who did not understand either Erenalian or Nocean, guessing it was some kind of introduction. But after a moment, and since the girl kept talking and at moments seemed to have difficulty continuing, Astrid realized it was more than that. This girl was recounting what had happened to her, the horrors she had been through that had led her to be there. She was doing this in front of everyone, and Astrid was surprised and a little shocked.

Once she finished, Belona addressed the girl in a kind tone, and the look on her face was sad. The leader of the Fighters of the New Sun felt bad for what had happened to that woman. She waved her hand in a clear sign to go ahead.

The other officer called someone, and from the warriors on the right side emerged a muscular warrior, who headed to the center of the quadrangle where the two officers and candidate were standing. When she reached them she greeted Belona first, bowing from the waist and then acknowledging all the rest with nods.

Astrid guessed this was the warrior the young Nocean would have to fight. The warrior was tall and strong, her blonde hair in a bun. Astrid could swear she was Norghanian. She soon realized this woman knew how to fight and had well-worked muscles. She must be as strong as a horse.

The officers explained the rules of the fight, and the candidate and fighter stood three paces from each other in the center of the quadrangle. Trumpets rang and the test began. Astrid noticed this was not a fight with weapons, since the warrior had handed hers to the officers and the candidate was unarmed.

The candidate advanced toward the warrior and at once attacked her eyes with her bare nails. The warrior saw her coming and delivered a tremendous right hook to the girl's left cheek that made her stumble backward. From the first attack, Astrid realized the poor girl did not know how to fight. It did not make sense to make her fight an experienced warrior. The candidate attacked again, delivering blows right and left with all her might but with little accuracy. The warrior blocked several blows and then delivered a kick to the stomach which left the girl breathless, and she fell to the ground.

Astrid wanted to go and help her and took a step forward, but two of the warriors held her back. They made signs that she could not intervene. She had to return to her place.

The candidate caught her breath and got up. She tried to hit the warrior with everything she had, but no matter how much she tried, she could not and always ended up on the ground. But she never stayed down. Every time she was knocked down by her rival she got back up, sore, and attacked again as if nothing could keep her down. Where she got her rage to get back up again and bear such a beating, Astrid did not know. At last, with a left hook, the warrior knocked the candidate down. The girl had suffered a terrible beating.

The warrior moved away and Belona gave her verdict. She showed the palm of her open hand and held it out to the side, arm parallel to the ground. She moved it dramatically slightly up and then down and finally palm up. The warriors began to applaud hard. Two warriors wearing white bracelets, whom Astrid guessed were healers, came and took the unconscious girl away.

They called the second candidate. This one was from Erenal, because there was no need to find anyone from among the warriors to translate. She told her story as the Nocean girl had done before, and once she finished Belona said a few words. Astrid noticed that the last thing Belona said was a question, but she did not know what it was or the answer. The girl was in her mid-twenties, and she was to fight the same muscular warrior. The fight was different though. The candidate attacked three or four times, and it was obvious she did not know how to fight either. At the fourth blow of the warrior, the candidate stayed on the ground, crying, and did not keep attacking.

Belona acknowledged the fight as done, and her downward palm indicated that the candidate had not passed the test. The warriors intoned a solemn, sad chant of farewell. Two warriors led her away.

The next candidate was the Masig. Astrid guessed she would be interesting, and she was right. She told her story, which a Masig warrior translated into Erenalian, and when Belona asked the question, the answer was different from the others'. Astrid soon realized why and what the question was about. A new warrior entered the rectangle and the muscular one left. The new warrior was not very tall but she was wirier, with brown hair and brown eyes. She seemed to move well. She handed over her weapons.

The officers gave both fighters a knife. They stood in front of each other. The Masig stepped forward and delivered slashes right and left, seeking to cut the warrior, who nimbly avoided the attacks. The Masig knew how to fight with a knife. She attacked and withdrew, unable to reach the warrior, who dodged skillfully. Astrid knew that in the prairies, all the children were taught to use the knife so they could defend themselves from predators, animal or human. The warrior blocked the next attacks with her knife and lunged to attack. The Masig was not as skillful and had trouble defending herself. But she did not give up and attacked with big leaps before rolling on the ground, which surprised the warrior.

Belona stopped the fight. She had seen enough. It was clear the Masig would be a good warrior. Her palm was upward, and all the warriors cheered the candidate who would be joining them.

The process was repeated with the next candidates. Unfortunately, they were not as lucky. Four in a row received the palm down, and Astrid felt awful for them. But the next one, the other Nocean who also fought with a knife, did pass the test, which cheered the audience. The next one also passed. Although she underwent a beating fighting unarmed, she never gave up. They had to stop the fight because she was badly beaten. Astrid realized that even if they did not know how to fight, Belona accepted them if they did not give up and showed they had a fighting spirit.

The next candidate did know how to fight. Astrid guessed she was some mercenary soldier. She was strong and disfigured by scars. She was from Rogdon, Julia seemed to understand. She asked for a sword. This was getting interesting. Another warrior was called to fight with a sword. She had long brown hair and was also quite strong, but not as much as the muscular one. They were both given long swords, the kind the warriors used, which were not very long but just right to be considered long swords. They were double-edged, so they were pretty heavy.

The fight began, and the candidate quickly made it obvious that she knew how to use a sword. She attacked with a combination of blows, cuts, and thrusts which had undoubtedly been taught to her as a soldier. That woman had served in the army, and one that used swords, which were not all. The sisterhood warrior also knew how to use the sword and was very skilled. She blocked, deflected, and countered with measured thrusts and cuts, and her footwork was agile and swift. It was an interesting fight. It was clear that the soldier knew how to use the sword and the warrior, who was better than her, let her show off.

Belona stopped the fight and accepted the candidate, who left the quadrangle with cheers and applause from the warriors. The remaining candidates each had their opportunity but did not pass the test. Finally, it was Astrid's turn. She was the last, and she had the feeling this had been on purpose. They called her name, and she walked to the center of the quadrangle nonchalantly. The officer called Julia, who came out of the audience and stood beside Astrid, who smiled at her.

"I'll translate," whispered Julia.

"Thank you."

"Tell us your story. Why are you here?" Belona asked.

Astrid nodded and told her story again as she had done at the gate the day before. Julia translated every word. Astrid spoke with serenity, trying to sound as sincere and at the same time as desperate about her future as she could. Once she finished her tale, Belona spoke to Victoria and Diana for a moment, then addressed Astrid.

"We're familiar with your sister Valeria's story," she said, "General Augustus is a personal friend of mine. Your sister helped us with Zangria, then she refused to continue helping us. She fled when she was locked up. Are you going to do the same?"

"No, ma'am, I've come to stay."

"She's Norghanian, we shouldn't admit her. The war is about to begin," said Victoria.

"Norghanian, betrayer of her own, and seeing what her sister did… I don't think it's worth the risk..." Diana said.

Astrid saw they were not going to accept her, so she played her trump card.

"You should accept me. You have no one with my fighting skills."

"You think so?" Belona said.

"I can defeat any of your warriors," Astrid said in an icy tone.

Julia looked at Astrid to make sure she wanted her to translate that. Astrid nodded. "Translate." Julia swallowed and relayed her words.

Belona threw her head back.

"She says it with conviction, it's not bravado," she commented to Victoria and Diana.

"I don't believe it," Victoria said. "The Norghanian Rangers are good, but not so good as to defeat our best warriors."

"I am a Ranger Specialist with several specializations. I'm not just a regular Ranger."

"That's interesting," Belona commented. "If you're so good, with your multiple specializations, I want to see that."

"Can I do the test?"

"You can, but it won't be a regular test, it will be an advanced one. And I won't promise that I'll accept you, even if you pass. Although I don't believe you will."

"Even so, I'd like to take the test."

"Fine, I'll give you a chance." Belona was thoughtful for a moment.

Astrid waited. Julia, beside her, looked frightened.

"Everything'll be all right," Astrid whispered.

"Very well, you'll have to defeat five of my warriors. You've already seen three of them: Camila in unarmed fighting, Fulgora in short weapons' fighting, Edesia in the sword fight. And the last two will be Diana and Victoria."

A murmur rose among the warriors, who seemed impressed.

"Do you still want to do the test?" Belona asked her.

"Absolutely," Astrid said determinedly.

"Very well, you are granted the chance."

The warriors began to applaud hard. They were going to enjoy a good show, a good fight, and there was nothing a sisterhood warrior liked more.

Astrid took a deep breath. It was not going to be easy. She did not have her Ranger gear. Some poisons would have come in handy in this situation. Still, she would make it. She had to. She would show them she was the best warrior and would earn their trust. This was the only way.

Chapter 38

The first fight against Camila, in unarmed combat, was one that could quickly turn bad if the muscular warrior laid hands on her. So the strategy she would follow was to hit and move back, not letting herself be grabbed or caught. Camila was almost twice as big as her, but the highest and strongest towers had a weak point, and Astrid knew this.

"Ready?" Julia translated, standing right behind her.

"Ready," Astrid confirmed, looking at her opponent three paces away.

"Go ahead." Belona signaled for the fight to begin.

Astrid clenched her hands tightly, flexed her legs, one forward and the other back, and balanced her body. Camila, seeing that Astrid was not attacking, moved forward and delivered a right punch, seeking to hit Astrid in the nose. With great agility and reflexes, Astrid retreated half a pace, letting the fist pass by in front of her face and then delivered a side kick to Camila's left knee, which she had forward. The warrior grunted with pain and delivered a combined attack of left punch and forward kick. Astrid moved with speed and good enough balance for the attack to hit nothing but air. Camila found herself off position, with Astrid at her left. She went to turn and received another strong side kick in the left knee. She grunted with pain again and attacked, enraged, with two cross punches from right and left, followed by a right hook. Astrid simply stepped back with lightning-fast agility so that all the attacks were a handspan short. Then she leaped forward with her right leg extended and hit Camila in the face. The warrior bore the blow. She tried to counterattack and received a third side kick in the knee. This time the knee gave, and the muscular warrior fell to the ground.

Astrid watched her from two paces away. The warrior tried to get back to her feet, but her knee would not hold her weight and she fell down. She stayed sitting on the ground. She managed to get up again and tried to make a go at Astrid, but she was limping horribly. Astrid slid to one side and made as if to hit the other knee without actually doing so. Camila raised her hands and shook her head toward Belona.

"Winner, Astrid!" Belona cried.

The next fight was against Fulgora and would be a fight with short weapons. She was not worried about this style of fighting. No matter how good her opponent might be, knives were Astrid's strongest point. It was not that she believed herself to be the best, because Viggo would make her sweat, and there was always someone better than oneself. Astrid never forgot this, but she doubted such a person was here. There were good warriors here, but not exceptional ones. In any case, she decided not to be overconfident and probe her opponent without trusting her.

"I demand a fight with two knives," Astrid said.

"I accept," Fulgora said.

"Fine, go ahead," Belona signaled them to begin.

Astrid and Fulgora probed each other, both with their knives held in front, bodies bent forward and balanced. Astrid delivered a couple of cuts to gauge Fulgora's reflexes and defense. She moved and defended herself well. And the fight began. Fulgora attacked fast and was well balanced. Both fighters' knives clashed, and the sound of metal against metal echoed throughout the quadrangle. Their cuts and thrusts were fast and the blocks and deflections even more so. Fulgora fought well and her technique was good. Unfortunately, as Astrid had thought, she wasn't better than someone like herself or Viggo. She let the warrior try her best offensive combinations and deflected or blocked them all. She decided it was time to end the fight, and with a swift movement she made one of Fulgora's knives fly out of her hand. The warrior stepped back, and Astrid waited to see whether she was willing to keep fighting or not. Fulgora wanted to keep fighting, she refused to look foolish in front of everyone watching. She continued attacking with one knife, but Astrid contained the attack easily since she had both her knives. She waited for the right moment, and when she attacked, she disarmed Fulgora again. Her second knife flew out of her hand and fell to the ground.

"Winner, Astrid!" Belona called before anything worse could happen.

The warriors watching the fight were upset with the results and began to express it with boos at Astrid.

The next fight was against Edesia and would be a sword fight. Julia brought water to Astrid. It was cold and she was not sweating, but even so, she needed to hydrate. All exercise, particularly if it was intense and required focus drained the body, and sustenance was necessary.

Edesia stood in position with a long sword in her hand.

"Ask Belona if I can fight with two knives. My skill with the sword is zero."

"Of course," the leader replied, "but you'll be at a clear disadvantage. A sword's reach is three times that of a knife."

"Even so, I prefer knives."

"Very well, granted."

Edesia nodded at her with a salute and the fight began. The sword truly had an advantage over the knives—that was obvious from the first moment. The warrior delivered two well-executed cuts and a strike and Astrid had to take two leaps backward to get out of range of the sword. But Astrid had been expecting this. The trick was in measuring the distances correctly, and in the fact that she had two weapons and her opponent only one. Edesia took one step forward and delivered a thrust straight to Astrid's stomach. She deflected the sword with her left knife and then moved forward, delivering a cut with the right which nearly reached the warrior's face. Edesia reacted skillfully and withdrew while she countered, which forced Astrid to defend herself. The warrior tried several feints to trick her into attacking the legs so she could go for the head, but Astrid read her perfectly and refused to fall in her trap. She decided to attack, and with a swift diagonal slide to Edesia's left, she delivered a cut to her ribs. The warrior had to block with her sword from the right and did so in a bad position, with the sword downward, protecting her whole ribcage. That was what Astrid was looking for. With another swift slide, she stood behind the warrior and delivered a cut with her left knife. Edesia tried to turn, but her position was awkward and she could not turn in time. Astrid caught her and cut into her reinforced armor. The warrior finished turning and delivered a cut to her rival's head. Astrid crouched with tremendous agility, and while the blade brushed the top of her head she delivered two cross cuts to the warrior's legs. She did so by measuring, over the leather skirt, without slashing Edesia's thighs or knees, which she could have easily done.

Belona stopped the fight.

"Winner, Astrid!" she proclaimed.

Edesia nodded, acknowledging her defeat, and withdrew.

The warriors in the audience were no longer booing. Astrid's demonstrations were spectacular, and they realized that. Applause began to be heard, with some cheers in Astrid's favor.

She was allowed to rest a while, and Astrid drank more water and ate some nuts with honey someone brought her. While she was resting, she saw Diana entering the long rectangle. All the warriors began to applaud and praise her name at the top of their voices, expressing their hope that she would win and teach a lesson to the Norghanian. The warriors adored her, that was obvious.

"This part of the test will be with a bow," Belona called. "I'm sure a Ranger has perfect mastery with the bow."

"Yes, I've mastered the bow," Astrid confirmed.

"Very well, this is going to be interesting, I have always believed that Diana can defeat a Ranger, and now is the time to prove it," Belona said.

They stood at the left side of the rectangle, and all the other warriors cleared out of the right side. They set up two targets three hundred paces away, which a warrior counted.

"Each archer will have three shots. The results of the three shots will be added in the end."

Astrid was brought a composite bow. She checked it with expert hands and eyes.

"I don't like it, it's badly balanced and is poorly tensed," she rejected it.

Diana eyed her with an amused grin.

"Bring her one of mine," she said.

A warrior brought Astrid one of Diana's bows. It was obviously a work of art, she could tell just by looking at it. She inspected it and nodded.

"A magnificent bow," she said.

"Thanks, it's from my own collection. It cost me a good bit of gold," Diana told her.

"Ready," Astrid said, nocking an arrow.

"Very well. Our guest will go first." Diana yielded the turn to

Astrid.

Astrid concentrated, measured the strength of the wind and the likely deviation, and released. She did so three times in a row almost without stopping to aim. The three arrows hit the bull's eye.

"I was expecting nothing less," Diana said and aimed and released. She took three shots, stopping to aim at each one. She hit the bull's eyes too.

"Move the targets back to four hundred paces," Belona said.

"Four hundred and fifty," Astrid asked.

Diana looked at Astrid and then nodded in agreement.

The targets were set at four hundred and fifty paces.

Astrid released and once again hit the targets in the bull's eye.

Diana released and two hit the bull's eye. The last one deviated slightly, although it was accepted as good.

"I request that the targets be set at six hundred paces," Astrid said.

The warriors were whispering. That distance was unthinkable, even for experts, and you had to use long bows and special arrows.

Diana agreed.

"I think it's fair," she said, but she was looking doubtful.

The targets were set, and the two contestants were brought long bows and quivers with long arrows. They both checked the bows and arrows and accepted them as good.

"Good luck to both, the distance is tremendous," Belona told them.

The two archers released their long bows. They did so slowly, measuring the shot carefully, as well as the distance and wind. This was a sniper's shot. Astrid knew she could do it; after all, she was a Sniper. She released confidently and with determination. She did not miss. She made three bull's eyes. Then Diana released but only hit one bull's eye. The other two deviated slightly.

"I declare Astrid the winner!" Belona proclaimed.

"I've never seen anyone release like you," Diana told her, admitting she had been surpassed.

"I'm a Sniper."

"That explains it," Diana smiled.

The warriors applauded and cheered both competitors who had granted them such an impressive show. They were enjoying themselves immensely.

The final fight arrived. Victoria approached the center of the quadrangle, and Astrid guessed by the way she moved that she was going to be a tough rival. But she had not yet met anyone she could not defeat. She would have to see whether Victoria was capable of beating her. She hoped not.

"Last duel. I understand you'll want to use knives, right?"

"Yes, ma'am."

"You won't be able to do anything with knives against my broadsword," Victoria warned her. There was no bravado or superiority in her tone, only knowledge of swordsmanship.

"I'll just have to try," Astrid replied.

"Very well, as you please," Victoria drew the broadsword she carried at her back. It was huge. She also carried a long sword and a short one at her waist.

Astrid sighed. She hoped Victoria would not be able to wield that broadsword for long and that its extreme weight would slow her down. Although for some reason she had a feeling this was not going to be the case.

The fight began, and Astrid kept her distance from the broadsword, which was almost as long as she was. Victoria launched a couple of thrusts right and left using the weapon with both hands, and she did so with speed and agility. The only advantage Astrid saw was that if Victoria used the weapon with both hands the reach was somewhat less, although still big. Astrid was moving around Victoria in a circle and changing direction to gauge her reaction time and weak point. Victoria was right-handed and drove the broadsword with the right hand rather than the left. Her weak point was the left side, and Astrid made a couple of attempts of approximation, but she had to withdraw because the thrusts of the great weapon were powerful and swift. It was not a good idea to block a broadsword with knives, because she could lose them and even damage them.

Seeing that her opponent had the advantage, Astrid decided that the best strategy was the counterattack, so she did not attack first but waited for Victoria to do so. The warrior launched several attacks, first with flat thrusts, then in a diagonal, moving straight at her. She was good. Great coordination, strength in her arms, good technique with the sword, and skilled footwork, although not excellent. Astrid avoided them without trying to block, using fleeting and measured side movements. Victoria used strong attacks, and this time she did so with a vertical thrust. Astrid saw her chance. Victoria was advancing as the broadsword was falling down, seeking to split her rival in two. Astrid spun round and slid forward. The broadsword brushed her back and only met the ground. Astrid had advanced and had Victoria a handspan away. The warrior started raising the broadsword, but Astrid delivered a blow with the pommel of her left knife to the temple of her rival.

Victoria was stunned. Astrid seized the chance, and hitting with both pommels on Victoria's hands, she forced her to drop her weapon. The broadsword fell to the ground with a metallic sound on the tiles. Victoria recovered from the blow and drew her sword.

Astrid looked at her. She knew she was not going to give up, so she would also have to defeat her with the sword. Victoria attacked, and in a moment Astrid saw that she was even better than Edesia. The thrusts and blows she delivered used great technique, although her footwork was still slow. That, coupled with the fact that now she could block the attacks with her knives, gave Astrid confidence. She blocked the thrusts with her two knives, and the lunges she dodged by shifting her body. But the combined attacks and feints Victoria delivered were dangerous, hard to block and avoid. She nearly got Astrid on two occasions, and Astrid knew a third would be the definite one and she did not want it to happen. So she risked it, because 'without risk there is no victory'.

She moved back so a feint would not reach her, then leapt with her right leg stretched out in front. Taken by surprise, Victoria turned so the kick would not reach her, but in turning she lost her position. Astrid touched down and immediately rolled on the ground because she knew a side cut was coming. It was the most adequate attack from that position. She was right. The lunge brushed her head but missed. Astrid attacked Victoria's ankles with a sweeping kick. She did not manage to knock her down but made her lose balance and stumble. Astrid did not miss her chance; she jumped at her again with her leg stretched out in front, and this time she hit Victoria in the chest and knocked her down. Before she could get back up, Astrid had her knife at the warrior's throat.

"Winner, Astrid!" Belona cried.

Both contenders rose amid applause and cheering from the

warriors who had enjoyed a spectacular show.

Victoria nodded at Astrid, acknowledging defeat.

"An excellent show!" Belona told them. Then she addressed all the warriors. "This is what you must all aspire to. To be great warriors like them!" The warriors reacted to their leader's words with more applause and cries of excitement. "Follow their example!"

"The cries went on, and Belona addressed Astrid.

"You have surpassed all my warriors. Therefore," she showed her the palm of her hand up.

The warriors applauded the decision.

"Thank you, ma'am."

"Now that you have passed the test, follow me inside," Belona told her. "Julia, you come too, to translate."

"Yes, my lady."

They went into the keep, and Belona led them to a large hall where the rest of the contestants who had passed the test were waiting with the warriors who acted as translators.

"It's time for you to take your oath."

Astrid stood with the other contestants.

"Belonging to the sisterhood is not obligatory, but it is for life. If you agree to become a member and take the oath, you will be with us for the rest of your lives. Think well before you take the oath, because afterward you won't be able to change it. If you enter the sisterhood, you will obey our laws and our leaders. Our sisterhood fights for women and for our kingdom, Erenal. These are our only rules. We will do whatever is possible to help women and Erenal," Belona told them.

For a while they were left alone so they could meditate about what it meant to enter the sisterhood. Astrid liked the sisterhood. The thing was that she could not stay. She had other goals in life. She felt bad for having to lie and deceive, but she was a spy after all, and lies and deceit were part of her profession. She only hoped they would not contaminate her too much.

"Have you made your decision?" Belona asked when she came back with Victoria and Diana.

The contestants nodded after the warriors who acted as translators had relayed it in their own languages.

"Very well, show me your palms."

They all showed them to her.

"Palm up, you accept to enter the sisterhood. Palm down, you refuse, you do not wish to enter, and you may leave," Belona told them. She stood before the first contestant, one of the Noceans. Her palm was up. Belona took a knife out and made a cut on the palm. The Nocean closed her hand.

"By my honor and my life, I swear to serve the Fighters of the New Sun until my death. If you accept, open your hand." The Nocean girl opened her palm, "Welcome," Belona smiled.

She repeated the oath with the rest, and they all accepted to belong to the sisterhood. Astrid was the last one, and she accepted, opening her hand.

"Welcome. You are truly exceptional, and you'll be very good for us," Belona told her.

"Thank you, ma'am."

After the oath, they were taken to a dining hall, also on the ground floor of the keep, and were given a celebration meal. The food was exquisite, and there was plenty. They were even given wine and beer. The leaders of the sisterhood presided over the table, and the new warriors with their translators sat at a long table and were served delicious dishes. The conversation was entertaining and they were all very happy, all except Astrid, who needed to find the Gauntlet and did not see it anywhere.

When the meal ended, Belona showed them the lower rooms of the great keep, and then she took them to the first floor where she showed them the library with tomes of history, of Erenal and other nations; books about the art of the sword; the bow; and war tactics. The library was considerably large, and it was filled with military books and tomes about the use of weapons. Astrid liked it, but she found it odd that they only had these types of books.

Belona took them to another hall to show them something that left their jaws hanging.

"This is our collection of weapons, which rivals that of King Dasleo himself," she said proudly.

In a huge hall, four cabinets that covered the walls from side to side and stood over six feet tall exhibited an infinitude of weapons. There were swords, knives, axes, pikes, halberds, bows, crossbows, and many other weapons, all of great quality. There was not a single one that was plain or of little value. All the new warriors were staring at the collection with wide eyes.

"Here you find kings' weapons, some legendary. Famous weapons from various kingdoms. Even weapons that have killed mythological creatures, or so the legends say," Belona smiled.

When she heard this, Astrid started searching the shelves looking for the Gauntlet. She saw it among several similar pieces, like spiked gloves, only this one was gold and unmistakable. She snorted. There it was. Right in front of her.

"Do you like these weapons?" Belona asked Astrid.

"I love them."

"I thought you'd like this hall. It's the favorite of all of us here in the sisterhood."

"Can we use these weapons?"

"I am afraid not. These are priceless weapons, and we cannot risk losing them. They are my personal collection."

"I understand."

"Yet, someone with your skills and experience might be worthy of one of them. I believe you'll manage to make me give you one for your services," Belona said with a wink.

Astrid smiled. Unfortunately, she had no time to earn the Gauntlet. She would have to go with Plan B, stealing it. She only needed an opportunity, a small distraction to carry out the theft. Attempting it with so many warriors in the keep was risky, even for her. She decided not to rush, although she was greatly tempted. She would wait for her chance.

A week later, while she was practicing in the main quadrangle with the most expert warriors, Astrid's chance presented itself. Belona came out of the keep and called for a meeting. In a moment, four hundred warriors were lined up before their leader, who was accompanied by Victoria and Diana.

"King Dasleo has ordered me to join him. The war begins, and a great battle is being prepared on the plains. All the rank warriors will come with me to the capital to join the King's army. Those warriors without rank may watch the battle but not take part in it. I recommend that you do watch. You can learn a lot being on the site of a battle."

Astrid looked at Julia, and she touched her wrist to indicate she had no rank. Although she had been there for a long time, since she was no good with weapons, they used her for other tasks and she had no fighting rank. Astrid, being a newbie, did not either, although she could fight better than anyone. She could not take part in the battle, but she was given the chance she had been waiting for.

"For King Dasleo and for Erenal!" Belona cried.

All the warriors repeated the cry at once.

"For the Fighters of the New Sun!"

The warriors shouted at the top of their voices.

"For the Fighters of the New Sun!"

The following morning, three hundred and fifty warriors left for the front, leaving fifty in the fortress.

"Would you like to go and see the battle?" Julia asked Astrid as the warriors marched on.

"Yes, of course. But if you don't mind, we'll go tomorrow at first light. I want to sleep well tonight to be rested and able to watch the whole battle."

"Of course, no problem."

The following morning, Julia and Astrid left the fortress to go and witness the great battle. In Astrid's rucksack was an object of great power, one that could kill dragons.

Chapter 39

When things got complicated, sometimes they got really complicated. Viggo was looking at five regiments of a thousand soldiers each belonging to the Zangrian Army, maneuvering outside the city of Somonor. It would not have been very significant, save for two reasons: first, they were all heading south, accompanied by a long convoy of carts and wagons with supplies of all kinds. This could only mean they were headed to the border with Erenal. And second, that all those soldiers were traveling under the many-times-decorated General Zorlten, who had Sansen's Knife in his possession.

From his horse, hiding among the trees of the fir forest, Viggo was able to see the General among twenty captains he was talking to. The General was a man in his fifties, with well-trimmed white hair and a short beard. Like all Zangrians, he was short and wide at the shoulder and, from what Viggo had seen, he kept fit for his age. There was no trace of the obesity so common among nobles and soldiers used to the good life brought by having a good position and success in the court or on the battlefield.

Things were complicated, but that was not going to stop Viggo from getting the Knife. A difficult situation like that only drove him to face it with more enthusiasm. If he had to get through a whole army, no problem, it would not be the first time. Besides, the Zangrians might be tough, skilled fighters, but they were not the most intelligent by far. They were honestly a little dull, so he would manage. He only needed an opportunity, so he would wait for one to appear.

Milton clicked his beak in his cage that was hanging from the saddle on the horse.

"And what's wrong with you now?"

The owl hooted.

"You can't be hungry, I gave you my dried meat and you gulped it all down. You're as much of a glutton as Gerd."

Milton replied with more clicking.

"I'm not letting you out. I know you, and you won't want to come back in."

Milton's reply was to hoot again, loudly.

"Shut up, half the army will hear you."

Since Milton would not shut up, Viggo gave him more meat, and the owl gulped it down. He also tried to peck Viggo with his sharp beak and scratch his hand with his claws.

"You're so charming. I'm going to adopt you, then you'll see."

General Zorlten's army moved for days to the southeast. Viggo was following the great caravan of soldiers and carts, always at a good distance to not be discovered. Since they were heading southeast, he had to veer southwest. He did not like it much, because soon he found they were entering the Thousand Lakes. The place was beautiful with all those immense blue lakes surrounded by greenery and forests. There were thousands of them, and it was one of the wonders of Tremia. The problem was that it was very well watched by Zangrian patrols at the north half and by patrols from Erenal at the south half. He would have to avoid not only the patrols, on foot or mounted, but also soldiers in boats, which were everywhere on the many large lakes.

"This is becoming more and more fun."

Milton hooted.

"Don't make a sound, or I'll hand you to the enemy and they'll cut off your wings for spying."

The owl clicked loudly.

"I bet you don't understand a word I'm saying, you rodent with wings. The thing is you like to peck and scratch, and you seize any opportunity."

Milton hooted repeatedly.

Viggo had been going close to the Zangrian camp to study the way they set it up, the guard shifts and changes, the outer patrols, and the best path to follow in order to reach General Zorlten's tent. He had to admit that the Zangrians were not clumsy regarding everything military, but they were not outstanding either. This gave him a chance he was going to take. Unfortunately, he could not spy too long, because the patrols were diligent and timely and he ran the risk of being found.

Every morning at dawn, the Zangrians broke camp. They sent mounted patrols first in the four directions, and the ones that went southeast were doubled. Viggo had to go west and wait until the army set out.

That morning he had met an added difficulty. When he was retreating to the lakes, he had encountered a Zangrian control post, which meant they were nearing the border.

"Stop! Who goes there?" an officer of the control post had shouted at him, or so Viggo had guessed, because he did not understand the man's words. He was good at killing—talking not so much, and foreign languages not at all. Five Zangrian soldiers were with the officer, all carrying shields and spears and wearing the garish yellow and black, as Viggo considered the bright colors.

Viggo looked at the officer. The morons had set up the control post between two lakes so there was not much space to pass. Besides, they had set up removable stakes so that no one could gallop across in either direction.

"Identify yourself!" the officer shouted.

Since Viggo was uniformed like a Zangrian soldier, they had to be puzzled seeing him on his own. The mounted patrols were typically made up of four Zangrian riders. He thought about attacking them, but it would be too much noise for nothing and he would risk being discovered by another Zangrian patrol. So he opted for the strategy he liked the least: strategic retreat, because he was never going to admit it was plain flight.

He spurred his horse and galloped away to the north. Milton protested at being jolted. Viggo heard the shouts of the officers behind him and looked back. The control guards were running to their horses to pursue him. Viggo led his horse at a gallop, skirting a large lake, and then veered west. He did not want to encounter another control post, so he headed for a forest he saw a little to the north. The four soldiers chasing after him saw him enter the woods and went in after Viggo without a second thought.

It was a beech wood, and there was a lot of shrubbery. They found Viggo's horse with the protesting Milton in a clearing. The four Zangrians looked around without finding Viggo. They dismounted and, armed with their spears and shield, they began the search around the horse and the hooting Milton.

Viggo came out from behind a nearby shrub and hit one of the soldiers in the back of the neck with a thick branch. There was a loud *crack* when the branch broke, and the Zangrian fell to the ground, unconscious. Viggo continued running and attacked the next soldier as the man was turning to face him. As he ran toward the soldier he bent over and picked up a stone the size of a peach from the ground, throwing it hard and accurately at the soldier's forehead. There was a *bonk* when the stone hit the man's forehead and helmet, and the Zangrian's head was thrown backward. Viggo reached him and knocked him out with two punches.

The other two soldiers ran to spear Viggo, but unfortunately for them they were strong but not very fast due to their short legs, combined with the weight of their robust torsos and big heads. Viggo went around a tree quickly and nimbly while the soldiers pursued him with shouts which Viggo assumed meant 'stop' and 'don't run' but that was exactly what Viggo wanted. It took him no time to get well ahead of them through trees and shrubbery and then hide among the foliage. When they lost sight of him, the Zangrian soldiers moved warily with their spears and shields ready. They looked like two turtles out of the water. The terrain did not help either, since the shrubs were taller than they were, meaning they barely saw anything ahead of them.

Viggo moved at a crouch through the shrubs like a cheetah in the jungle and went around the soldiers' backs. He approached with absolute stealth. He was at home in the middle of the forest, like a cat playing with a mouse, and the poor Zangrians did not stand a chance here in the thicket.

He hit the first one in the back of the neck with the pommel of his knife. He had to do it twice to knock him unconscious, and as he was falling on his face Viggo vanished again in the shrubs. The remaining soldier came over to his fallen partner and said something to him. Viggo appeared behind him and also left him unconscious with a couple of blows to the nape.

"Sorry to be so blunt, but I can't waste the few Summer Slumber knives I have left on you. They're for more complicated missions."

He went back to where his horse was waiting and Milton was still making a racket.

"You can shut up now, I've dealt with them. I don't need you drawing any more attention."

Milton became quiet, which left Viggo perplexed.

"Did you by any chance understand me?"

The owl clicked his beak.

"I bet not."

Milton hooted.

Viggo continued his way south and went straight to the control post he had encountered. He spurred his horse to a full gallop and charged. There was only the officer on one side and two soldiers on the other at the post. When they saw him charging at them, they started to shout. Milton took courage and hooted as if he were chanting an attack. Viggo led his mount straight at the captain, who was between the lake shore and the cavalry stakes.

"We'll just get through, don't worry," he whispered in the horse's ear.

The officer drew his sword while the soldiers leaving their side of the post ran to the other to help him. Viggo charged at the officer who stepped backward with a yell, pushed by the horse. Viggo delivered a kick in the face to finish him. They fled south at full tilt while Milton hooted in triumph.

Three days later, Viggo was checking out the war camp of General Zorlten, a hundred paces from the border with Erenal. The General's five thousand soldiers had set up camp and began the preparations for war. It appeared they were the first group out of all the armies that would participate in the great war. Carefully, Viggo tried to find out where the army of Erenal was camped. He did not go too close, because he knew he was crossing the border and the Erenalians would have sentinels and archers posted all along the imaginary line that separated the two kingdoms for over two leagues both to the east and west. He did not see the rival army, which puzzled him. If the Zangrians were beginning to arrive at the border with their armies, the Erenalians should be doing the same in case the Zangrians invaded them, but he saw no sign of the Erenal Army.

From what he had marked on his map, the large plains spreading beyond the border were the Plains of Erenalia. He decided not to set foot in them: there was too much risk of being seen. There was not a single tree or bush to hide behind in that immense clearing. But he did think it was a great field for a battle. Surely Zangria and Erenal had faced each other on these plains on more than one occasion.

This war was something entirely secondary in his mind; his goal was Sansen's Knife. He waited for the next two nights to get closer to Zorlten's war camp, watching everything that went on and how they were organized.

After spying on the camp for two more days and familiarizing himself with the Zangrian military methodology and their organization, he infiltrated the camp on the third evening. He was wearing the uniform of a Zangrian soldier, with shield and spear, and he walked hunched over to look shorter. He had managed to come up with a walk and posture that allowed him to pass for a Zangrian.

He stopped every time he encountered soldiers, whether on duty or on patrol. He would bow his head and grunt as way of greeting if they came too close. The bad-tempered grunt worked well—almost all of these ugly, short soldiers had a bad temper, and grunts and ill manners were common among them. This came in handy, since he did not have to speak a language he did not know.

Walking through a camp with about a thousand tents in yellow and black, with hundreds of fires in front of them and soldiers everywhere, should have been an unthinkable idea, yet Viggo moved through the camp with total ease. His cool and collected persona helped him in these kinds of situations. He never got nervous or panicked. He moved nimbly from one half-hidden position to another. With each measured, calculated advance, he came closer to the large tent that belonged to General Zorlten. The light from the innumerable torches and fires did not reach the floor in between tents, piles of crates, supply carts, and other large objects, which is where Viggo was going to pass.

The truth was that nobles and generals had a bad habit of choosing the largest and most ostentatious tents for themselves. For an Assassin, that was as good as a sign that read: *I'm here, come and kill me.* They should have known that the best strategy was to sleep in a regular tent so it would be impossible to know where the General was among the thousand identical tents. In fact, using this tactic and changing tents every night at least would make it very difficult. Sleeping in the largest and most elegant tent was pompous and unintelligent. But as Viggo liked to think, "the stupidity of some is the fortune of others." He smiled and changed positions again.

He already had the General's tent in sight. The problem was that it was surrounded by a ring of guards that encircled the tents belonging to the General's trusted officers and more guards. So how did you get through a closed line of guards? Simple—you did it by creating a distraction and moving fast. Viggo waited between two tents for the right moment. He saw the opportunity and acted. He threw the tips of two Earth Arrows at the fire in front of part of the safety line. The tips exploded when they hit the flames, causing two loud bursts and a cloud of dust and earth.

The ring of guards, caught by surprise, ran to find out what had caused the commotion. Viggo seized that moment to slip away swiftly and vanish among the officers' tents. He moved low, avoiding the guards in front of the tents. He had to draw on his patience until he found a path that led to the back of the General's tent.

He left the spear and shield on the ground. They were cumbersome. First he got rid of two guards in front of the officers' tents, strangling them from behind until they fell unconscious from lack of oxygen. They were strong but, being short, surprising them from behind with a suffocating grip and immobilizing them was easier than doing the same to a huge Norghanian. And it was more efficient than having to hit them twice or three times on the head. Viggo hid the bodies between the tents.

Two guards were standing at the back of the General's tent. Viggo drew two of his glass-tipped knives and, coming out between two tents, he threw them with both hands at once. The guards did not even see the throw, and both knives hit them in the neck. The tips broke, and the Summer Slumber put the two Zangrians to sleep. Viggo ran to the tent and cut the lining carefully and silently.

He opened the tent and looked inside. It was an elegant, sober military tent. A large table with maps was positioned beside the entrance. Several armchairs and a round table with drinks were to one side. An armory and another table were on the other side. The general had to be asleep in an inner chamber with canvas walls where Viggo heard snoring. He went in and headed to the bed, where he found Zorlten fast asleep. Viggo smiled—he had him.

He searched everywhere among the General's belongings to see whether he carried the knife on him. If that was the case, he could simply grab it without needing to wake him up, which would be less trouble for him. But he did not find it. Then he noticed a coffer, locked with a key, to one side by the General's dress armor. He smiled—it had to be there. He took out his lock picks and carefully picked the lock. He opened the coffer with the General's snores sounding behind him. Half the coffer was filled with gold coins, a lot of gold coins, while the other half contained important-looking documents, all rolled up. And he saw two beautiful knives. His eyes went to them at once, they were so exquisite. One was gold and the other silver, and they both shone brightly in the light of the moon. It had to be the gold one, but just in case he took both. Better to make sure. He also took a good amount of gold, which he put in his belt.

He closed the coffer.

And the alarm rang through the camp.

Viggo could not believe his bad luck. He almost had the knife and the alarm had sounded. He slipped out of the General's bedroom as Zorlten was beginning to wake up. If the General found Viggo there, he would be in serious trouble. The alarm horns continued to ring. Viggo made his way to the rent he had made at the back of the tent just as the General was getting up and beginning to put on his armor. He called for his escort with a shout.

Viggo left the tent at a crouch as the escort was entering the front. He passed the unconscious bodies of the guards and recovered his spear and shield. He pretended to be another guard running with the others because of the alarm until he was at a safe distance, near enough to the forest that he could run inside fast and vanish. Once in the forest, he watched the developments without being seen.

Two new Zangrian armies were approaching. Viggo watched them arrive and maneuver. The first army went east of the already-set-up camp, and the second one went to the west. Each army had five thousand Zangrian soldiers, just like General Zorlten's. Between the three camps, there were already fifteen thousand soldiers there.

He spent the night watching from the safety of the forest trees. He wanted to gather as much information as he could. The new camps finished setting up at dawn, and in the light of day Viggo was able to identify the two generals who had just arrived. He smiled—he knew them both. The life the Panthers led drove them to have illustrious acquaintances in rival nations.

The first of the generals he recognized, and who had camped on the east of General Zorlten, was General Zotomer. Viggo remembered the conversation he had shared with the General in the dungeons of the royal castle. How things had changed with the new shift in events. Zotomer had asked for his help in contacting some 'friends' to obtain his freedom with gold or some other exchange. Viggo would have liked to help him but he had more urgent matters to attend to at the time, such as his own leader being locked up a few cells below. In an interesting turn of events, Zotomer, who was now free, had become an ally of Thoran's, the same man who had locked him up when he believed the Zangrians were behind the murder attempts on him and his bride. In all likelihood, both Zotomer and his monarch, King Caron, could not be too happy with Thoran. And yet, they had allied themselves with King Thoran against a common enemy: the Kingdom of Erenal and King Dasleo.

Viggo smiled and thought for a moment about how complicated the political situation was, and the alliances. How easy it would be, considering how much they all hated one another, to get them to shift from allies to enemies with various betrayals. If it were up to him, he would betray them all and stab them in the back mercilessly. Although, undoubtedly there would be many varied repercussions, almost all of them bad. Luckily, he did not have to make this kind of decision, they had Egil for that. The know-it-all would manage to find the best political option for them, and he was glad it was Egil and not him who had to think it all through and calculate it all.

If recognizing General Zotomer was curious, identifying the second general was even more interesting. It was none other than an old acquaintance, General Zorberg. Viggo remembered how Zorberg had made an alliance with Arnold, Egil's brother, when he was the King of the West and had fought with his Zangrian soldiers beside the Nobles of the Western League against Thoran and the Nobles of the East. He also remembered that when Arnold had died from poisoning, Zorberg did not want to support Egil as the new King of the West and had left the battlefield with his troops.

"Well, well, well, Tremia is a small world after all. Here we have one Zangrian General whose throat I'd like to cut," he muttered to himself under his breath.

But, before doing something like that, he had to consult Egil. You never knew whether killing a general would be beneficial or not, especially one who had already allied himself with the West against Thoran and who now, unless things changed dramatically, was once again an ally of Thoran and Norghana, since King Caron was forming an alliance against Erenal and its allies.

"What a complicated dilemma. I'd better ask Egil," he whispered and then headed to the heart of the forest. He went to where he had hidden his horse. Since he moved the horse to a different location every day, he had trouble remembering where he had left him. Viggo found him tethered to a tree. He rummaged in his saddlebag and sat on the ground.

Milton hooted.

"Don't bother me now, I'm writing a message to Egil."

Upon hearing Egil's name, Milton hooted louder.

"Yeah, yeah, I know you like him and you don't like me. Shut up and let me write." He organized his ideas in his head and then wrote them into short direct sentences to inform Egil of everything he had seen. The last sentence was simply "Instructions?" He rolled up his message and put it in a small container, then he took Milton out of his cage. The owl pecked and scratched at Viggo pitilessly with his claws.

"Bloody scrawny, flying rodent!" he cried while he cursed and Milton attacked him. He managed to tether the container with the message to Milton's right leg. Then he moved away so the owl would stop attacking him. The owl flew to a branch above the horse and perched there, staring at Viggo defiantly. He seemed about to lunge at Viggo and take his eyes out at any moment.

"Message! Egil!" he ordered Milton forcibly.

Milton shook his wings hard and tucked them. He did not move.

"Message! Egil!" Viggo repeated, knowing perfectly well that the owl understood the order. He had been trained by the Rangers and could understand a series of specific commands, one of which was 'message'.

"Take the message to Egil, you brainless chicken!" Viggo said, pointing his finger at him.

Milton lunged at Viggo, who covered his face with his arms. But Milton did not attack him, hooting as he passed over Viggo's head and flew off.

"I'm roasting him. I swear, one day I'll roast him."

Chapter 40

Viggo had no doubt that what was brewing here would be a great battle, one that would be remembered. King Caron had just arrived with fifteen thousand Zangrian soldiers and had taken position in the Zangrian war camp. In all, with the five thousand soldiers of General Zotomer, the five thousand of General Zorlten, and the five thousand of General Zorberg, they formed an army of thirty thousand Zangrian soldiers. They were a sea of yellow and black with their Zangrian banners, now all they needed was the order to advance to battle.

Viggo had the feeling that both the Irinel army and the Norghanian one were heading here right at this moment, and that was why the Zangrians had advanced their position. It did not make sense to march north when the Norghanian forces would be on their way, including his friends. That evening he had a special visit in the forest where he was hiding from the Zangrian forces. Milton appeared, flying in circles above Viggo's head.

"I see you, flying rodent, come down and give me the message."

Milton flew around him a couple times and then settled on a branch.

Viggo went to him, cursing under his breath.

"Let me see that message," he said and tried to grab it from the owl's leg.

Milton pecked his hand and scratched him with his claws.

"You twisted, brainless bird!" Viggo had to withdraw his hand.

Milton hooted loudly.

"Give me Egil's message, or I'll cut your wings," Viggo threatened the bird.

Milton gave two hops to the right of the branch and then two other hops to the left.

Viggo raised his arms to the heavens and ranted a while longer. It took him a dozen attempts and several scratches before Milton let him take the message. Viggo read attentively.

"Interesting… our Egil is planning something…. As you wish, wise-guy, I'll do what you say." He looked at Milton. "See? I was right, we'll meet here."

A couple of days later, the first troops from the Norghanian Army began to arrive. Viggo smiled. Here came the fearsome Norghanians to battle. Things were going to get interesting fast. What surprised him was that it was not the fearsome armies of King Thoran. It was not the Thunder Army, or the Snow Army, or the Blizzard Army—it was the Nobles of the West with their men of arms.

They arrived at the Zangrian camp, and several officers came out to welcome them with a hundred soldiers. After the welcomes and formal greetings, the troops of the West obtained permission from the Zangrians and began to prepare their war camp. They did not take long to set up their tents in blue and black, forming a large, compact rectangle. Viggo counted about ten thousand soldiers, although many of them were not even soldiers but people of the West who had been recruited as militia. He saw Duke Erikson and his forces, busy with preparations. The Duke seemed to be in command of all the troops. He also saw Duke Svensen, who was already setting up his tents. Count Malason and his people were busy with weapons and shields. He also saw Count Bjorn and Count Axel, whose soldiers were in charge of the food and water wagons. The forces of Count Harald and several lesser lords started to raise a palisade to the south with anti-cavalry stakes.

"There's the whole Western league. Only their leader's missing, our beloved know-it-all…" Viggo reflected.

Milton clicked his beak.

"Don't complain, at least I'm talking to you."

Thoran was sending the Nobles of the West first, and with all certainty they would be the first to be sent against the enemy forces to be massacred. Viggo knew it, and so did each and every one of those setting up camp at that moment.

A couple of days later, horns and trumpets rang out. Viggo found a position to watch what went on. From the west there appeared a huge army in green and white. These were the forces of the Kingdom of Irinel. Judging from the direction they came from, they must have descended from the northeast, skirting the Thousand Lakes to then enter them, following a western course. They must have done it at the level of the border with Erenal to come this way now.

As they approached, Viggo had no doubt they were soldiers of Irinel. They were unmistakable, almost all with red hair in various shades and covered in freckles. They were thin and not as strong or tall as the Norghanians, and they had a look of lively intelligence. They wore medium chainmail armor and a helmet without a visor. As weapons they carried a spear and tear-shaped shield, both of steel, and on their backs they carried javelins which they used as a throwing weapon. He noticed there were a large number of soldiers who only carried javelins, as if they were archers. The uniform and the shield were painted green and white in equal parts, the colors of the Kingdom of Irinel. Their coat of arms was the white, six-headed flower of the kingdom.

Viggo saw them advance and stop to the left of the Norghanian camp. As was protocol, several Zangrian officers with a hundred soldiers went out to welcome them. Once they had obtained Zangrian permission, the Irinel troops began to prepare the war camp. Viggo couldn't see who was in command of the green and white army. He certainly did not see the Druid Queen or her father or brother, which did not surprise him either. Kings always arrived after their armies, once the area was controlled and safe. After all, they were in Zangrian territory, and caution was a must.

Having a front-row seat when the armies arrived gave Viggo a certain thrill. He had finished his main mission, and now all he had to do was wait for the rest of the Panthers. He wondered whether they had all been successful, especially Ingrid. He was hoping it was so. Yes, for sure, they had to have succeeded just like he had. He was looking forward to seeing them all, especially Ingrid—he was dying to hold her in his arms and kiss her. They would soon be together, he was absolutely certain.

The following morning brought new horns and trumpets of warning, which meant more armies were approaching. Viggo was breakfasting with a hare he had caught, three quarters for himself and a quarter for Milton. He stood up and peeked out of the first line of forest trees to see who was arriving. There must have been several armies, because the ground shook under the footsteps of what he calculated must be tens of thousands of heavy soldiers. Not only was the ground shaking as if there was a small earthquake, but the noise was growing louder as well.

He recognized them as soon as he saw the first lines of the arriving soldiers. They were the Norghanian armies. First came the Thunder Army. They were unmistakable because of their size. They were Norghanian assault soldiers, big and strong, true northern warriors. They wore winged helmets over long hair and golden beards. The Thunder Army consisted of the tallest, strongest, and toughest Norghana had. They wore full scaled armor, carried round wooden shields reinforced with steel, and they fought with axes, a short one they carried at their waist and another large double-headed weapon they carried on their backs. Over their ample torsos they each wore a red breastplate with white diagonal streaks. General Rangulself was leading them. He had four thousand soldiers.

"Here they come, 'those who clear the way for the rest to follow,'" He recited their motto to Milton.

The owl hooted, victorious.

They headed to the Norghanian camp already set up by the Nobles of the West and began to prepare one right beside them. Very close.

"Well, it looks like they want to be the first, along the Nobles of the West. Let's see what Thoran has to say about this."

Milton looked in every direction, turning his large eyes.

After the Thunder Army came the Snow Army, another four thousand soldiers led by General Olagson. They also wore winged helmets and scaled armor. They were known as the best heavy infantry on the continent, and they fought with swords and round wooden shields. They carried a short axe as a second weapon. Their function was to finish off the enemy once the Thunder Army had opened the way.

"These fight well, although in my opinion the best are the Invincibles," Viggo said to Milton.

The owl hopped a couple of paces on the branch.

Finally, the Blizzard Army appeared. They wore light armor with breastplates decorated with horizontal streaks in red and white. It was the least renowned of the three armies but necessary to stand up to the enemy troops. It was formed by light scouting cavalry, archers to punish the enemy infantry from a distance, and lancers on foot to stand up to the cavalry. They also consisted of four thousand soldiers, led by General Odir.

"I don't like this army as much, they're a bit soft," Viggo told Milton, who did not miss a detail from his perch on the branch.

The Snow Army set up its camp behind the Thunder Army. The Blizzard Army set up camp behind the Nobles of the West, who eyed them warily.

Viggo waited impatiently for his friends to show up, but they did not. He had to resign himself and enjoy Milton's company, who was less quarrelsome than usual. It must have been due to all the soldiers of different armies camped further south.

"Don't leave this forest, you could get shot by an arrow," Viggo warned the owl in a serious tone.

Milton hooted.

Viggo did not know whether it was a 'yes', a 'no', or 'I don't understand', but he took it as good sign. He had already warned the owl.

About mid-morning the following day, the horns and trumpets rang again. Viggo hastened to watch who was coming. It was the Invincibles of the Ice. These soldiers were not as big or strong as those of the Thunder or Snow Armies, but they were more agile and weathered, and above all they were incredibly skilled with the sword. They were dressed entirely in white: winged helmet, breastplate, and cloak, even their shields. Only the chainmail under their clothes was metal colored, but it was barely visible.

"I like this group. They're the best infantry in all of Tremia. They use the sword and the shield. For them the axe is the weapon of the clumsy," he told Milton, who was looking everywhere.

If the Invincibles were arriving, it meant that King Thoran, his brother Orten, Count Volgren, and the other Nobles of the East must be coming shortly after. Viggo was not wrong. Once the four thousand Invincibles had passed, he saw them. They were in the middle of a column, well protected by the Royal Guard under Commander Ellingsen and the Royal Rangers led by Raner, the First Ranger. He saw them advance with their haughty manners.

"Here comes our wonderful king with his friends."

Milton hooted.

Viggo was only half-interested in this. He wanted to know whether his friends were with the group. He had to wait a while until he finally saw them, bringing up the rear of the never-ending armed column—his beloved Ingrid, as well as Nilsa, Gerd, Lasgol, and Egil. He felt an immense joy and nearly started jumping, shouting, and waving at them. But that would most surely end with him riddled through with arrows, so he had to bite his lip to contain himself. He realized Astrid was missing. Where was she? He remembered that her mission was taking her to Erenal, and in that case she would be trapped behind enemy lines, the same as what had happened to him. Perhaps Egil had told her not to cross and to wait on the other side in case of what might happen. He hoped she would be all right. Yes, Astrid knew how to handle herself perfectly well.

After the retinue, Viggo saw a group of Rangers. Thoran was also sending the Rangers to fight in the great battle. Among the first group he could see Captain Fantastic and Luca. This was going to get ugly for everyone, the Rangers included.

A special retinue of the Zangrian Army came out to welcome the King of Norghana, the three Zangrian Generals among them. King Caron did not show himself for the moment. Thoran acknowledged the courteous reception and then ordered their camp to be set up.

The Invincibles created a camp behind the Snow Army's. In the middle they set up the great tents for the King, his brother, and the Nobles of the East. The Royal Guard and the Royal Rangers situated themselves to protect them.

"It's time to go and see our friends," he told Milton.

The owl hooted happily.

"Get in the cage," Viggo told the owl, showing it to him.

Milton clicked his beak and showed Vigo his claws.

"You're the most horrendous owl in all of Tremia."

Chapter 41

Astrid had been watching the troops of Erenal set up their war camp for days. General Augustus, whom King Dasleo had commanded to lead his army, had arrived first with his legion made up of six thousand infantry soldiers and three hundred riders of light cavalry. From what Astrid knew, the legions of Erenal were famous for their war formations, unique in all of Tremia. Also for how well organized and directed they were. They were extremely efficient and Astrid, who was watching them practice formations, had proof.

"They look good, don't they?" Julia, who did not leave her side, said.

"They do indeed."

"That's because they are. Those formations they're practicing will grant them victory in battle."

"That's their reputation," Astrid admitted. "I like their dress and armor."

"That's how the glorious legions of Erenal are equipped," Julia said.

The infantry soldiers wore chainmail armor over green woolen tunics that ended in a skirt with leather protection. Over the breastplate they wore flexible plated armor that covered them from the shoulders to the waist to give better protection. The helmet was square and open, leaving the face uncovered. They also carried a square half-shield, slightly oval. Astrid thought they were very well protected. They carried two javelins, one heavy-looking like a spear in one hand, and a lighter throwing javelin on their backs. From their waists hung the well-known Erenal swords which were double-edged and wide but short, and a dirk. The only part that looked less protected was from the waist down, but they covered it with the shield.

"I prefer my knives, but I have to admit they're armed and protected for conquest."

"The legion prepares and equips them for victory. That's why they rarely lose a battle," Julia said proudly.

Astrid noticed that the officers wore a similar armor, more robust and bright, and that the difference was in the fact that they did not carry either javelin or shield. They also wore a large plumage topping their helmets which differentiated them from the plain soldiers who had nothing on top of theirs. The generals, on the other hand, wore bright plated armor. In fact, it looked like silver, over a deep-red toga and a helmet with feathers like a fan. They were unmistakable.

The second legion arrived three days later with General Militius in command, a reputed general in Erenal. His forces were also made up of six thousand infantry soldiers and three hundred riders, which seemed to be the composition of a legion in Erenal. They camped beside General Augustus' legion.

Astrid and Julia moved closer to watch the legion arrive and set up camp.

"Do you think they can take on the Zangrians?" Astrid asked.

"Without a doubt. They've already beaten them at several important battles. The legions of Erenal will come out victorious once again, I'm sure of that."

"What do you think about the Norghanian forces? They're more powerful than the Zangrians."

"The Norghanians are big and strong, but skill means more than strength. When they face the legion, they will learn that the hard way," Julia said with a triumphant smile.

"You might be right."

"I am, you'll see," Julia said firmly.

Two days later, the third legion arrived, led by General Primus with the same number of soldiers as the two before. They had set up camp beside the other two legions. The sum of the three consisted of almost twenty thousand soldiers. A force not too excessive in number, although fearsome because of the reputation they had and what Astrid observed as they practiced.

"The Erenalian generals are famous for their advanced military strategies, the formations they use and their martial skill and intelligence in battle. We're renowned and feared," Julia was telling her as they watched the third legion arrive.

"I've heard that the study of the art of war is King Dasleo's favorite subject. Is that true?" Astrid asked.

"It is. The King has been studying the art of war since his childhood, it's one of his favorites."

"It's good to study war, seeing how events have been developing in these later times."

"Our dear monarch of Erenal is also the benefactor of the Great Library of Bintantium. At the Library there are Master Archivists of War, scholars devoted night and day to the study and advancement of the military arts."

"That's a good philosophy." Astrid believed that if you wanted to win in the art of war, you had to know it thoroughly. Dasleo, his Generals, and their Master Archivists, knew war to perfection because they studied it. That was going to greatly complicate Thoran's and his allies' lives.

"In spite of this, our monarch isn't a warrior king. He's not a conqueror of kingdoms. He's a lover of arts and culture. He has made our nation the envy of neighboring kingdoms regarding knowledge, science, art, and culture."

"That honors him, more so considering the constant wars with Zangria and other kingdoms, as is the case now."

"Erenal is a great kingdom and its monarch an exceptional figure. Besides, he's very beloved by his people," said Julia.

The following day, they heard the news that King Dasleo had already left Erenalia, capital of the kingdom of Erenal, and that he was expected to arrive shortly. He did so a day later, leading his own legion of six thousand infantry units and three hundred cavalry, plus five thousand militia men. Nilsa and Julia were there to see him arrive. It was an amazing spectacle. He arrived with full honors, and trumpets and drums welcomed him.

"Here comes our glorious monarch!" Julia was beside herself with joy.

"Not a very discreet arrival..." Astrid commented. She preferred a stealthier approach.

"Why should it be? Let everyone know that King Dasleo has arrived with his legion, ready to deliver death to the enemy."

"Okay, putting it that way..."

"Let Erenal's enemies quake because Dasleo's legions will trample them."

They enjoyed the parade and the majestic arrival of Dasleo, whom his troops acclaimed with admiration and love. Very different from the feelings Thoran generated among his troops, that was for sure. But, from what she had been told at the beginning of her mission, it was expected that the combined forces of Zangria, Norghana, and Irinel would be about eighty thousand soldiers. She wondered how many forces Dasleo and his allies could muster. It was one of the reasons she was still on the Erenalian side and had not crossed the border to the other side and her comrades. She was dying to see Lasgol, to see and hold and kiss him, but she would have to wait a little longer. She had been communicating with Egil by owl, and he had asked her to spy on Dasleo's forces and his allies. He needed to know what allies Dasleo had gained, how many soldiers and what kind. So Astrid was waiting patiently while she gathered all this information. Her belonging to the order of the Fighters for the New Sun gave her the perfect cover. No one doubted her loyalty dressed in that tunic, and no one suspected that she was in truth a Norghanian spy. If they did, she would be a dead woman.

The first to appear were the allies of the east, of the Kingdom of Moontian. She watched the soldiers, and they surprised her as much as she had expected. The first thing she noticed when she first saw them was that they looked bloated, their whole bodies, even the faces. She found it most strange. They were of average height but tended toward the short side compared to a Norghanian, but their bloated bodies gave the impression of being very strong. She noticed that there was muscle in their arms and legs, besides the bloating. They wore golden breastplates, vambraces, greaves, and a skirt of metallic plates, also golden, that reached to their knees. They also wore a flat, square helmet without a visor so their beautiful eyes of different shades of pink could be seen. From what Astrid knew, they wore their heads clean shaven, although she could not see due to the helmets. In one hand they carried large rectangular shields that covered them from neck to ankle, and in the other hand they carried overwhelming picks and thick hammers, which they wielded as if they were Norghanian war axes.

Astrid understood what Lasgol had told them about the mountain people now that she saw them. They were a people born from the depths of their mountains. The war picks and hammers proved it.

And most of all, they were exotic and striking. They were unmistakable, and watching them left one reflecting on how their existence was possible.

"They're amazing, aren't they?" Julia asked as she came running to watch the arrival of the new army.

"They are, I'd never seen anything like them," Astrid had to admit.

"I was so looking forward to seeing them," Julia said, thrilled. "I've heard so many things about them, and they're so unique."

At the head of her armies came Queen Niria herself, of shocking beauty. Astrid got closer to see her better and had to admit she was one of the most beautiful and exotic women she had ever seen. It did not surprise her—she had a reputation of being very beautiful. She was accompanied by a dozen women, also remarkably pretty. One thing that surprised Astrid was that the women looked very much like the men but were less bloated. Instead, they seemed to have very curvy bodies. She had to admit they were beautiful and delicate in their appearance. Their skin was a pale violet, and their pink eyes and lips stood out on faces full of beautiful features.

The first ally of Erenal, the Kingdom of Moontian, was considered a young kingdom, which until recently had been nothing more than a few tribes that inhabited some mountains and the areas around them. But lately they were gaining strength thanks to the two gold mines, the largest in Tremia, in the depths of their mountains. The kingdom was east of Erenal, right below the kingdom of Irinel, with which it had already had border and territorial trouble. They were very similar to those of Zangria and Erenal, therefore it was logical that if Irinel supported Zangria, Moontian would support Erenal. Their fates ran parallel, but for Erenal, Moontian's support was important for two reasons. The second one was that this kingdom had the support of the Confederation of the City States of the East. This was because of the gold, of course. The cities wanted to be included in the gold trade Moontian had as raw materials in its kingdom.

"How many are there?" Julia asked.

"I've counted about twenty thousand soldiers, all infantry."

"True, they don't have cavalry," Julia commented, surprised.

"I don't see archers or javelin throwers either…"

"Or lancers. They don't seem to have any long-distance weapons.

That's surprising. But, it seems clear to me that those infantry soldiers are going to break a lot of heads with their heavy picks and hammers."

"That's for sure!" Julia laughed.

Moontian's armies set up camp beside the Army of Erenal. King Dasleo and his generals came out in person to welcome Queen Niria. They exchanged formal greetings and showed themselves to be most respectful and kind.

Suddenly, as if not wanting to be considered lesser for arriving late, the second ally of Erenal appeared. It was none other than a City State of the Confederation of Free City States of the East. Astrid did not know which one it was and had to ask.

"It's the City State of Yort, on the East Coast," Julia told her.

"Oh, what do you know about them?" Astrid had no knowledge of this city state.

"That they're very, very rich. They say the streets are paved in gold," Julia smiled.

"You can't be serious."

"No but it's almost true," Julia laughed again. "They're one of the richest city states in the East. Maritime commerce is their strong point, and they like gold a lot. It is said that too much."

"And who doesn't?"

"But they do more than anyone else. They're always trading in gold, that's why they're Moontian's allies."

"Because of the mines…"

"Exactly, gossip says that life is worth nothing in Yort, only gold. Also that they even buy the souls of their rivals with gold..."

"I'm not sure I'm going to like that city."

"If you have gold or want to trade for it, it's the best place in all of Tremia, or so they say."

They watched the army of the city of Yort, which was not as big as those of their allies. Astrid counted fifteen thousand soldiers. She was surprised by how different this army was from those she was used to. The soldiers were dressed in strange clothes. They wore silver breastplates, and under it loose blouses in yellow and blue that made their arms look bulging. The pantaloons were also the same color and came down to the knees. Blue stockings covered them from the knee down. They carried large pikes in their hands.

"Those soldiers are quite different and dress funny," Astrid commented.

"Yes, that kind of attire is used in only a couple of the city states of the east. They believe themselves modern and advanced, elegant and superior."

"They're wearing colored stockings…."

"They are," Julia shrugged.

"And what's that large pike they're armed with?"

That's a halberd. They're huge. They're like a large pike, but evolved. If you look carefully, they end in a pike tip, but they've added the head of an axe and a pike on either side."

"Yeah, now that I see them closer…"

"It's very good against the cavalry, but also against the infantry due to its length and because it can stab or cut."

"Very interesting."

At that moment, Astrid saw something that drew her attention even more. Behind the halberdiers, who were two thirds of the forces, came the archers, who dressed similarly with bulging blouses and pantaloons of strident colors and did not wear breastplates. But that was not the most outstanding thing. What made her jaw drop was the fact that they did not use bows, they carried huge crossbows. Astrid had always wanted to see a crossbow—well, shoot one.

"They carry crossbows!" she cried, unable to hide her excitement.

"Yes, it's a very special weapon. Only the City States of the East have them."

"I'd love to be able to try one."

"I'm not sure they'd let you, but you'll be able to see how they practice, I'm sure."

"This city has a funny army, halberdiers and crossbowmen."

"Yes, but they're very well equipped and paid. The soldiers of the city of Yort are professionals. It's their trade, and they're paid good gold for it."

"You mean more professional than a soldier of the Erenalian legion?"

"A lot more. And not only that, in the city state, professional soldiers are considered higher status. Only noble families are above them. They are very well respected."

"That city has an interesting civic organization. The soldiers in other kingdoms are not usually the best. Although they are paid, usually poorly, they're not very professional mostly."

"That's why these are so well known," Julia said.

The following day, the last allies of Erenal arrived. They were none other than the Coporneans. This was a curious race from the Island of Coporne, in the Central Sea which divided the North and South of Tremia. With the passing of the centuries, they had taken over all the islands in the Central Sea, and from there they controlled all the maritime trade. They had the reputation of being a race of sea pirates.

"Look at the Coporneans, they're joining the war," Julia said. "I had my doubts about their coming."

"Aren't the Coporneans of Erenal and the City States rivals?" Astrid was under that impression.

"And of the Nocean Empire. The Central Sea is very important, and their control of the maritime trade brings a lot of riches."

"Then why are they joining for war? What interest do they have?"

"Good question. From the rumors, King Dasleo has offered them a beneficial alliance. He'll give up control of the Central Sea and pay a trading fee for the Erenalian ships that trade in the Central Sea."

"Oh, then it's a commercial deal. They're here for money."

"For money and control. If Dasleo pays them a commercial fee in the Central Sea, they also secure control of said sea. Maritime skirmishes between Erenalian triremes and Coporneans happen often."

"Aren't the Coporneans really pirates?"

Julia laughed.

"Yes, indeed, many consider them pirates. And of course, that's their strong point."

Astrid looked at the Copornean soldiers. They had white skin, although suntanned by the good weather of their region. They were of average height and complexion, with fine faces, brown eyes, long chestnut-brown hair, and beards. They used bronze-colored armor with breastplates, vambraces, and greaves in the same color. They wore a simple helmet which also left their eyes and nose visible. They were armed with short swords and bows. Astrid had the impression that they were indeed trireme pirates. Only they were on firm land instead of at sea. They were led by about twenty officers, who by rank had to be captains.

"I count ten thousand, you?" Astrid asked Julia.

"Yes, about that number."

"Do you believe they'll fight with honor?"

"That's a lot to expect from the Coporneans."

"Will they betray Erenal?"

Julia shrugged.

"I guess that as the battle goes and whoever has the best chances to win emerges, the Coporneans might change sides."

"In that case, it'll be best that King Dasleo keeps his eyes wide open."

"He will, don't worry," Julia said. "He knows these pirates very well."

"If I'm not wrong, these are all the forces of Erenal and its allies," Astrid said.

"Yes, they're all these."

"Let's see, Dasleo has thirty thousand soldiers. Moontian has brought twenty thousand. Yort has come with fifteen thousand more. And last of all, Coporne has sent ten thousand pirates. That makes a total of seventy-five thousand soldiers. A considerable force."

"Impressive, in my opinion," Julia commented proudly.

"I think the battle that's coming will make history."

"One of the biggest the continent has seen in a very long time, that's for sure."

"We'd better get ready," Astrid said, watching the armies carefully.

"Do you think it'll start soon?"

"I'm afraid so. They'll finish planning their strategies and preparations, and then the great battle will begin. It's going to be an epic, heartbreaking battle."

Chapter 42

The Panthers had just finished preparing their war camp. The Rangers were camped at the rear. Raner had set up a command tent in the middle of all the Rangers' tents and had summoned them.

"The Royal Eagles, at your command," Ingrid saluted as she entered the tent.

"Come in, we need to coordinate," said Raner, who had a map of the region spread out on a rustic trestle table.

Nilsa, Egil, Lasgol, and Gerd followed Ingrid into the tent.

Well, I'm glad to see Nilsa and Ingrid are back. When did you arrive?" Raner asked as soon as he saw them.

"I joined our forces on the outskirts of Norghania, sir," Ingrid replied. "I couldn't get there in time to leave with everyone."

"I arrived a day ago, sir," said Nilsa.

"I'm glad to see you're well and with us. We're going to need you. I've been so busy with all the preparations for the war that I haven't been able to greet all the Rangers as they arrived."

"We're at our leaders' and the Rangers' disposal," said Ingrid.

"We're always ready," Nilsa added.

"Gerd, Lasgol, and Egil returned in time to leave with us for the front, and they've already informed me of their missions. How did yours go?"

"I managed to obtain the Dragon-killer, sir," Ingrid said proudly.

"That's excellent news."

"I also managed to obtain Antior's Beam, sir."

"The javelin? That's really good news!"

"It wasn't easy ...." Nilsa started to say.

"I can imagine. Gondabar will be very happy. With Gerd's axe, Egil's spear, and Lasgol's bow, we now have five weapons to kill the dragon with. You've achieved a remarkable feat. This gives us a chance!"

"First we must study the four new weapons, sir," Egil said. "We believe they're the ones we're looking for, but we're not entirely sure yet. Besides, even if they are the legendary weapons we were looking for, we don't know whether their power is the same as

Aodh's Bow. We already have evidence that it can kill a dragon."

"A lesser dragon…" Lasgol specified.

"There's a difference," Egil said with a smile.

"But we do believe they'll be able to kill Dergha-Sho-Blaska, won't they?" Raner asked in an almost desperate tone.

"Yes, we hope they can, or at least that they'll help us defeat him," said Egil.

"Good, then what I understand is that we have four new weapons we need to study to verify if they have the power that lets them penetrate a dragon's defenses. Is that right?"

"That's right, sir," Egil said.

"Very well. Who can study them? Someone we trust, I mean. I'd rather the Ice Magi did not intervene. Since Maldreck is their leader they have become very secretive and reluctant to cooperate, unless it's the King himself who gives the order."

"Given that Maldreck is their leader, this behavior is only a reflection of his personality," Nilsa said.

"And his greed," Ingrid added.

"We'd better leave Maldreck out of this. He'd try to take the weapons from us to control their power," said Lasgol.

"The best ones to analyze the power of these weapons are Enduald and Galdason. They're at the Shelter and are entirely trustworthy, sir," Egil said.

"Good, that's a very good idea. It's decided then, they'll be the ones to study them."

"We'll have to wait for the victory so we can go to the Shelter," said Ingrid.

"Unfortunately, King Thoran wants all the Rangers who can fight here. We can't ignore a direct order from the King. He's ordered me to make sure the Royal Eagles are close in case he needs you, which reminds me, there are two missing. Where are Astrid and Viggo?"

"They haven't arrived at the war camp yet, sir," Egil said. "But they're not far. Viggo will join us at any moment now, and Astrid has infiltrated the Erenalian forces."

"Infiltrated? In Erenal's war camp?"

"Yes, sir. She'll report on the enemy troops and any suspicious or dangerous movement she detects."

"In that case, it's better that she doesn't come back. I want her reporting."

"She has the Gauntlet."

Raner was thoughtful.

"Even so, she's more valuable as a spy right now. Have her inform us of any unusual movement of the enemy."

"We'll let her know, sir," Egil said.

Lasgol was not happy with that at all. If she was discovered, she would be sent to prison, or something worse. They might even hang her for spying on the enemy. He knew this was one of her Specializations, the one he valued most in her. But it was so risky that Lasgol could not help fearing for her.

"The few spies we have are having a lot of trouble infiltrating," Raner said. "One or two have been captured…"

The more Lasgol heard, the more he hated what he was hearing. He knew Astrid was an extraordinary spy, but even she might be found out and captured on the wrong side of the war.

"Sir, Nilsa should report what she witnessed in the desert," Egil said, "it's important."

"Go ahead, Nilsa, I'm listening." Raner focused his attention on her.

"Yes, sir, I'll tell you how it went, with as much detail as I can remember." Nilsa then told him what had happened. She had already gone over it for her friends, but she had not had time to report to the leaders because of the armies marching out of Norghania in such a hurry.

Once she had finished, Raner remained thinking with a serious look on his face.

"This is both important and extraordinary. I'll inform Gondabar immediately, as well as the rest of the Rangers' leaders."

"Yes, sir."

"So, the Noceans were defeated in the battle?"

"Yes, although they fought with courage and their sorcerers managed to kill thousands of creatures."

Raner sighed.

"We're going to need magic against those creatures, and our magi aren't the most receptive… we'll have to think about how to present the matter to them. To them and to Thoran, considering how it went the last time we tried telling him of the importance of this matter …"

"Perhaps a better stratagem would be to focus on the reptilian creatures and not on the dragons," Egil suggested.

"Good idea, that's the way to approach it… none of the dragons took part in the battle?" Raner asked as an afterthought.

"None, sir. That's what we all find so disturbing," Nilsa replied.

"They have to be planning something else," said Lasgol, who had the clear feeling this was the case.

"Something very relevant if none were present," Egil added, supporting the idea.

"But they don't have the Pearls, right? You've hidden them well, that's what you told me," Raner fixed Lasgol with his gaze.

"They don't have the Pearls. I managed to find a container so they won't be detected, and they're in a deep, secret place."

"That eases my mind. Whatever they're planning, at least they don't have the power of the Pearls to do it. Let's hope they won't be able to follow through with their plan without the Objects of Power. Or at least hopefully it will delay them enough to find out what they're planning."

"Let's hope so," Lasgol said, nodding.

Raner was thoughtful again.

"I'll report everything to our people. We must concentrate on the great battle before us and the ensuing war. The King wants you close, so don't leave the war camp. I'll free you of your duties as Royal Rangers so you can move about freely, but don't leave, the King might call you at any moment."

"Yes, sir. We'll stay close, sir." Ingrid nodded.

"Very good. If Astrid reports, bring me the information at once."

"Yes, sir," Egil promised.

"One last thing before you leave. Lasgol, the king has lifted your punishment due to the war. You are a Royal Eagle again," Gondabar informed him.

"Yes, sir," Lasgol agreed and looked at his friends. They were smiling at the good news.

The Panthers went back to the tent they shared in the part of the camp reserved for the Rangers. Most of their comrades were on watch duty or scouting, so the area was deserted. They had been assigned a large tent since they were the King's Royal Eagles, and this granted them some privacy and space to think and plot. Gerd and

Nilsa were playing with Argi, the giant wolf puppy from the Frozen Territories Gerd had adopted. Ingrid was examining the Dragon-killer with bright eyes.

"The pearls are safe in the Gray Chasm, right?" Ingrid asked.

"Yes, Camu helped me hide them there," confirmed Lasgol.

"Great, they won't find them there."

"That's the idea," Lasgol wished.

"And how come Aibin hasn't accompanied you here?" Egil asked Nilsa.

The question took Nilsa by surprise and she blushed.

"He helped me back to the Pearl and then he continued his training path in the deserts. He must first tour the west side of the Nocean Empire before heading north. He promised me that he would reach Norghana… and that he would come to greet… us… on behalf of his father.

"A boy who does his duty," Egil nodded his approval.

"Yes, he does... and he is honorable..." Nilsa blushed even more.

Ingrid noticed, but she didn't say anything. She sat down to examine the Dragon-killer.

"The more I look at it, the more I'm convinced it's the true Dragon-killer."

"Let's hope that's true," Lasgol replied, smiling.

Aodh's Bow, Rogdon's Spear, Antior's Beam, and Gim's Double Death, all gold-colored, were being kept in an armory. They looked like a king's plunder from war and conquest.

Argi was racing around the tent with Nilsa and Gerd. His tongue was lolling out, and it was obvious he was having a blast.

"He's adorable," Nilsa said, smiling.

"Isn't he?" Gerd agreed, drooling at seeing the wolf pup so happy after all he had been through. It had not been easy looking after him and bringing him back from the Frozen Territories, but he had managed to do so, and he was delighted with the little one.

"What do you mean 'adorable'? It's another beast, as if we didn't have enough already," a voice said from the entrance.

"Viggo! You're here!" Ingrid cried, leaving the sword on the floor and lunging at him to kiss and hug him.

"The numbskull is back," Nilsa said.

They all stood up and hastened to greet him. But they had to wait until Ingrid finished covering him in kisses, which took some time.

"I'm so relieved you're okay," she said once she had finished showing him how happy she was to see him.

"You're as ravishing as always, my blonde warrior," Viggo said, winking at her as she let him go.

"You always arrive at the right moment," Gerd said with a smile from ear to ear.

"You didn't think I was going to miss the battle of the century, did you? Bards need feats to sing about in this epic battle. That's what I'm here for," Viggo said, beaming.

"It's obvious that wandering around hasn't blown the wind out of your sails," Nilsa told him.

"The wind has done nothing to my sails, but I see it's burnt your skin, quite a lot. You look like you were grilled."

"That's what happens when you travel the deserts," replied Nilsa, who was tan and had dozens of burns on her body.

Lasgol and Egil greeted Viggo affectionately.

"Did everything go well?" Lasgol asked.

"Of course everything went well. If they give a mission to the best Assassin in Tremia, how do you think the mission is going to go?"

"Here we go…" Nilsa covered her ears.

Don't be so vain," Ingrid chided.

"Did you get Sansen's Knife then?" Egil asked him.

"Of course. And I didn't even have to kill the Zangrian general who had it."

Lasgol, Ingrid, and Egil exchanged surprised and relieved glances.

"You have to tell us everything you've done," Ingrid said.

"Yeah, especially about the Zangrian general. Let me remind you they're our allies now," Egil said.

"Yeah, as if that mattered at all. Allies today, enemies tomorrow, and the next day neither one nor the other, then back again."

"Well, there's some truth in what you're saying," said Egil.

"I'm always right."

"Very well, let's sit down and you can tell us everything," said Gerd.

Viggo told them all his adventures in his particular way, complete with exaggerated, scathing comments.

"It's a good thing you didn't kill him, or we would've had a real mess on our hands," Ingrid said.

"His camp is right there," Nilsa said, pointing her finger.

"Yeah, I'd know it with my eyes closed."

"Can we see the Knife?" Gerd asked.

"Of course. Here it is." Viggo reached in his rucksack and handed Gerd the two knives. "It's the gold one, but since there were two, I brought both."

"Well, don't let the Zangrians see you with them," said Nilsa.

The knives were passed around.

"We need Enduald and Galdason, but seeing that all the weapons are the color of gold," Lasgol said, indicating the other weapons in the armory, "I'd lean toward the gold one."

The others nodded.

"Well, tell me, what have I missed?" Viggo wanted to know." Apart from the fact that the giant has adopted a mutt."

"He's no mutt, he's a giant white wolf," Gerd replied, picking Argi up in his arms.

"He looks like a mutt to me."

"You'll see when he grows up… you'll get what you deserve then."

"And what about the bug and the kitty, where are they?"

"A little farther North. We decided not to bring them to the war camp," Lasgol replied, "but they're alert and waiting."

"Are we going to have problems?" Viggo asked, raising an eyebrow and looking at Egil.

"Many, and very interesting," Egil replied with a smile.

"In that case, I'll have to repair my equipment and get more poisons."

"That's a good idea," Egil told him.

"You're expecting that much trouble?" Gerd asked him.

"Unfortunately, yes."

"With so many kingdoms and armies here, the opposite would be strange," said Ingrid.

"That's true, things are going to get complicated," Gerd said, realizing.

"Irrefutable, my dear friend," Egil winked at him.

Chapter 43

Lasgol and Egil left the camp and headed for the woods a little to the north. They were stopped by two patrols of Rangers, but when they recognized the Panthers they let them pass without asking questions. They entered the forest where they knew Ona and Camu were hiding. They found them beside a stream.

"How are you?" Lasgol asked them as soon as they reached them.

We much good, Camu messaged.

Ona chirped once and came over to Lasgol, rubbing her head against him. Then she did the same with Egil.

"Ona, good," Egil said, stroking the snow panther's beautiful fur.

Everything good here.

"Wonderful. We have a mission for you. Well, for you, Camu," Egil said.

Ona whimpered.

You can't come, Ona, but we'll be back soon, Lasgol transmitted to her.

The panther lay down and whimpered, and Lasgol stroked her.

What be mission?

'Spying. You like the idea?" Egil asked him.

I much good spy.

"Of course, how could it be any other way…" Lasgol said, rolling his eyes.

Egil smiled.

"I need to get to a tent of the Nobles of the West in their camp without being seen. I have to speak to them, but we don't want Thoran and the Nobles of the East to know about my conversations or dealings with my Nobles."

Not difficult.

"Not for you, but for us it's a little more complicated."

"Can you make the two of us vanish?" Lasgol asked him.

I can. Much powerful.

"Yeah, you always say that. But can you?"

I can, sure.

"Very well. We'll wait for nightfall, then we'll go down. We have an important meeting to attend," Egil said.

At midnight, protected by Camu's Extended Invisibility Camouflage skill, they slipped into the camp of the Nobles of the West. The guards could not see them, so they could slip in quite easily. They were careful not to make noise and were careful about where they placed their feet so as not to leave suspicious prints, but otherwise they had no problems. Camu's skill was a true blessing for situations like this one. They reached the command tent. There were two sentinels at the entrance and people inside, judging by the shadows thrown by the oil lamps.

Since they did not want to be seen and also so no one would make any movement that might draw attention, they moved to the side of the tent where there were no guards. Egil slit the canvas with his knife and motioned Lasgol to follow him into the tent. Camu remained outside, invisible, and Lasgol and Egil became visible the moment they left his magical range and entered the tent.

"Welcome, we were waiting for you," Duke Erikson greeted them.

"Thank you, Lords of the West," Egil replied courteously. Inside the command tent were Dukes Svensen and Erikson, Counts Malason, Bjorn, Axel, Harald, Egil's cousin Lars, and several lesser lords of the west, practically all the Lords who made up the Western league.

"The honor is ours, King of the West," Duke Svensen saluted Egil. "Curious way of accessing our tent."

"You can never be too cautious when the enemy has eyes and ears everywhere," Egil replied with a smile.

"Lasgol, I'm glad to see you again," Count Malason greeted Lasgol fondly.

"My pleasure too, sir," Lasgol returned the greeting respectfully, but he was glad to see the Count, and it made him think of Martha and the bear-like Ulf. At once he felt a terrible yearning. As soon as he could, he would have to go to Skad and visit them. He had been too busy lately.

"Cousin Lars, I'm pleased to see you," Egil said to his cousin.

"Greetings, Cousin Egil. I'm glad to see you in good health," Lars replied with a slight bow.

"If you will grant me a moment, I'd like to greet you all properly. I believe the occasion calls for it, and I could not forgive myself for not doing so," Egil said.

"Of course, you are our lord and the King of the West," Duke Svensen said.

One by one, Egil greeted and shook hands with all the men in the tent. He greeted them with respect, calling them by their given name, since he knew them all. Not only them, but their family history and everything they had done for the West. Many of them had fought with and supported his father, and others had done the same for his brothers. He thanked each and every one personally and from the heart. Once he finished, he addressed them all.

"It's an honor to be here today with you in this tent. I want to thank you for your support today and all these tough years we've had to live through."

"Our King has our absolute support, now and forever," Duke Erikson said.

"And your king appreciates it, more so in this hour when the future looks so dark. But, before we continue with this meeting, are we safe?" Egil asked.

"We are, Sire. The sentinels at the perimeter are all trustworthy. No one will see us or listen to us in here," Duke Erikson assured him.

"And all of us here in this tent are loyal to the West and our King," Duke Svensen said.

"Thoran's order has just arrived. We must get ready to go into battle in three days," Count Malason said.

"Thoran is sending us against the enemy armies first. He's doing it without giving us any backup," said Bjorn.

"He's sending us to certain death. We have no way out," Axel joined him.

"We all know that. He's been waiting for an opportunity ever since the Civil War," Harald added.

"We're all aware of this move," said Svensen. "The King of the West is also aware of it."

"I am," Egil nodded. "I knew this day would come, I've known it for a long time. But not everything is lost. That's why I've come today to speak to you."

"It isn't? The moment he gives the order to attack, we'll all die, or at least most of us will," said Bjorn.

"We should try and escape now, while we still have the chance,"

Axel said.

"If we tried to escape now, he'd hunt us and hang us all," said Harald.

"No one's going to try to escape," Duke Erikson ordered. "Death before dishonor."

"At this point, the situation we're now in seems desperate," said Svensen. "But we're not dead yet."

"Let our King of the West speak," Count Malason said.

"Thank you. It's true that the situation looks desperate for the West, but we have to understand that not everything is lost. Thoran is risking everything in his war, especially in this battle. He's made alliances with Irinel and Zangria, and he believes that with them, he'll defeat not only Erenal but also the Western League and will weaken Zangria, all in a master move."

"Right now it looks as if he's going to succeed," said Lars.

A faint smile appeared on Egil's face.

"It's one thing to consider what the outcome might look like before the battle, and a very different one to see the actual outcome. Thoran doesn't hold all the cards. There are too many critical factors which might not go as he believes they will. In fact, I'd bet that not everything's going to come out as he and his brother have planned."

"How is our Lord so sure?" Axel asked.

"First off, because he's underestimated Erenal and her allies. They'll put up a resistance that Thoran and his allies aren't expecting."

"We all know the worth of the Erenalian legions," said Duke Erikson, "no doubt Thoran does too."

"Yes, but they only fear the Erenalian legions, and that's where they're wrong."

"Who else should they fear?" Bjorn asked.

Egil thought for a moment.

"I have information about the enemy forces. Dasleo has thirty thousand soldiers in his legions. Queen Niria has come with twenty thousand soldiers from Moontian. The City State of Yort has sent fifteen thousand professional soldiers, and finally, Coporne has sent ten thousand pirates. That makes up a combined force of seventy-five thousand."

"And they're sending us first and without protection against all of them," said Axel.

"The Plains of Erenalia will drink up our blood first," Harald said gloomily.

Voices of concern and protest rose in the tent. They were all aware that they were being sent to certain death against such impressive forces.

Egil raised his hand so they would stop talking.

"Silence, everyone!" Duke Erikson ordered.

There was silence, and Egil explained his statement.

"I am the King of the West. It's my responsibility to watch over the well-being of the West, of our people, each of your well-being. I will not let you be massacred in that great battle three days from now."

"My lord won't be able to prevent it…" Bjorn contradicted him.

"Remember that everyone thought I wouldn't survive after the death of my father and brothers. No one thought I'd manage to survive being an Olafstone, and yet here I am. I live, and I plan on living for a long time. Even more, I intend to reign in Norghana. And for that to occur, I can't let you be annihilated on that battlefield three days from now. I won't let that happen."

"You have a plan, Sire?" Duke Svensen asked, hopeful.

"I'm working on one. I won't lie to you, it's not fully completed and it might go wrong in some aspects. There's no easy solution to this complicated, critical situation. But, we still have three days, and I'll work to have it all thought out. I'll find a way to save the West, to save you," Egil said, convinced.

Lasgol, beside him, was feeling awful for his friend. The pressure and responsibility he had taken on were colossal. Egil was a master strategist, a man with a privileged mind for planning and solving problems of great complexity, but even for Egil this situation might prove too much. Lasgol was not sure his friend would manage to find a way out. They could all die, including Egil. In the political game, winners did not forgive the losers.

"If our King is confident of finding a way out, I am too. He will," Duke Erikson said supportively, bowing his head before Egil with respect.

"My sword is yours, Sire. I'll do whatever you command," Count Malason followed. "I trust my King."

"I can but trust in my King. My blood is yours," Harald said and bowed his head.

"I'll follow you to the death, Sire," Bjorn said, also bowing. "West or death!"

"For my honor and that of the West, for our blood, I'll follow you!" Axel said, bowing his head.

One by one, all the Nobles and Lords of the West paid homage to Egil and deposited their lives in the hands of their Lord, the King of the West.

"You honor me greatly," Egil said with his hand to his heart. "A king could not have better Nobles on his side. I'll send you my instructions. I beg you not to question them and to do exactly as I tell you, without deviation. If you improvise, if you try anything different, we'll all die. I can promise that."

"We'll follow our King's orders without hesitation and without the slightest deviation," Duke Erikson promised.

"Thank you all for your loyalty and honor. They're invaluable," Egil said, feeling moved, but he held firm.

"Loyalty and honor can only be earned with blood and sweat. Our King earned them a long time ago. Today we merely show him so," Count Malason said.

Lasgol could feel the strength and emotion of the moment. All these nobles, honorable and loyal, were putting their faith in their king's hands. He was awed.

"Tell Camu that we're coming out and need him to cover us," Egil whispered to Lasgol.

Camu, get ready, we're coming out.

I ready.

Egil took his leave, and he and Lasgol left the tent. As soon as they came out, they vanished. Camu was right there. They felt around until they found him, then stood on either side of him.

Let's go back to the forest, Lasgol transmitted to him.

The three left the camp without anyone seeing them.

Chapter 44

Preparations for the battle of the century picked up speed the following day. Every war camp was boiling with activity. From the distance they looked like anthills where the queens had sent all their ants to work, and these were running back and forth doing a variety of tasks.

The frenetic activity in the war camps contrasted with the watch missions assigned to the Rangers. Their goal was to have the whole border under surveillance. They had been placed so as to make it impossible for an enemy force to cross the border, whether on foot, horse, or boat through the lakes, including any spies or informants. In fact, the Rangers had not been informed of enemy movement but had captured a number of spies with traps and Elemental Arrows, and killed three who were escaping along the plains with snipers. Molak had hunted the last one at night, with a shot beyond six hundred paces and with almost no visibility. Raner had congratulated him personally.

Lasgol was growing increasingly worried about Astrid. If *they* were hunting down spies, their enemies were no doubt doing the same. He feared she would be caught and hanged, or that she would be brought down as she tried to come back, as Molak had done with the last enemy spy. The war was ruthless, and more so when it was about spying and betrayals.

Horns and trumpets rang out again. The Panthers went to see who was coming. Based on how prolonged the announcement was, it had to be someone important. And indeed it was. Accompanied by over a thousand soldiers of Irinel as his protection detail, King Kendryk was arriving, accompanied by his son Prince Kylian and Heulyn the Druid Queen.

The Panthers watched the arrival of the retinue.

"Don't you find it strange that the Druid Queen should accompany her father and brother?" Nilsa asked with a raised eyebrow.

"To a wedding or a funeral, not really. To a war, yeah, a little," said Ingrid.

"Queen Heulyn was looking after her mother. She must be feeling better," Gerd guessed.

"Knowing her like we do, I bet my pay that she's here against her father's will," said Viggo.

"And you'd win," Nilsa said.

"Thoran isn't going to want her here, that's for sure," said Ingrid. "She's an important distraction at a critical moment for his aspirations."

"Her husband and father are risking their lives in this war, as well as their kingdoms. I guess that's why she's here," argued Lasgol.

"Irrefutable, my dear friend," Egil confirmed with a smile. "There's too much at stake for the Druid Queen to stay home idly while Norghana and Irinel risk everything."

"Look on the bright side. Thoran will soon be going crazy, and we'll witness it," Viggo said, laughing.

"Don't forget the Queen might demand that we protect her," Gerd said.

"Oh yes, that too," Viggo realized, and his good humor vanished.

"Whichever it is, if Kendryk is here already, we'd better get ready for the battle," Ingrid said.

"The battle is inevitable," Egil said in a troubled tone. "Besides, it's going to be a fierce one. Thousands of soldiers are going to die, many thousands, unfortunately. The fate of several kingdoms is at stake, and this is how those fates are forged."

"On the battlefield," said Ingrid.

"And off of it," Egil said in a mysterious tone.

The retinue passed before them, and they all recognized a rider who came behind the Druid Queen. She was a beauty.

"Valeria doesn't leave the Queen for a moment," Nilsa commented.

"She's her bodyguard and person of trust," Ingrid replied.

"Where one goes, the other one follows," said Viggo. "It's a pity Astrid's not back yet from the other side, she'd be delighted to see Valeria again," he smiled at Lasgol.

"Valeria might have important information," Lasgol ventured.

"Yeah, but she might not want to give it to us. She might even give us false information to throw us off," Ingrid said.

"She's been good to us, we have no reason to distrust her," said Nilsa defensively.

"She also hasn't given us any reason to trust her. Better not trust her at all," Ingrid said firmly.

"I agree with my blonde warrior," Viggo said, nodding.

They watched the retinue being welcomed with all due honors by the Zangrians. Then they headed to the camp of the Kingdom of Irinel. However, the Druid Queen and Valeria continued to the Norghanian camp and entered King Thoran's tent. They waited to hear the enraged shouts of Thoran but, to their surprise, they heard nothing, which puzzled them even more.

That night, Egil and Lasgol left the camp again on a spying mission. The Ranger sentinels let them pass at the control posts around the war camps. They joined Camu and Ona in the Northern forest.

Spy mission? Camu asked, thrilled.

"Yes, Camu, tonight we have a spying mission. An important one."

I ready. I much good spying.

"Let's just let it be."

Ona whimpered.

Sorry, beautiful, you can't come.

The poor snow panther resigned herself.

"For this mission, I need to go alone," Egil suddenly said to Lasgol.

Lasgol froze.

"You don't want me to go with you?"

"Sorry, my friend, it's better that I go alone."

"It's not that you suddenly don't trust me?" Lasgol was having trouble accepting Egil's request. They were good friends, the best, and now this looked like a lack of trust.

"Of course not. If there's anyone I trust in the world, that's you," Egil said firmly, and he sounded honest, but at the same time he sounded sad.

Lasgol swallowed hard and reflected. There had to be an important reason why Egil did not want him to accompany his friend. He had to accept it and trust Egil.

"All right. If you don't think I should come with you, I won't."

Egil put his hand on Lasgol's shoulder and looked him in the eye.

"I swear that if I could I'd let you come with me, but I can't. I have to go alone, it's imperative."

"And if something happens to you? What are we going to do?"

"Nothing will happen to me, Camu will hide me. No one will know what is going on, I'll be in and out."

"Are you going to the Western Camp again?"

"No. And please don't ask me where I'm going, it's better if you don't know, for your safety and the safety of all."

"Fine, I won't ask, and I'll let you do whatever you have to do. You always have a master plan, and I know it usually requires covert, secret, dangerous actions."

"That's usually the case, yes."

"Just make sure you're not caught."

"I'll make sure, don't worry."

I bring Egil sound and safe.

"Thanks, Camu," said Egil, smiling.

"Make sure that if things go wrong, you get him out of there," Lasgol told Camu.

No problem. I bring Egil sound.

"Very well. In that case, good luck!" Lasgol offered his hand to Egil, who shook it firmly.

"Do you trust me?" Egil asked him.

"I trust you," Lasgol replied.

A moment later, Egil and Camu left, leaving Lasgol petting Ona and feeling a little low-spirited. He would have rather accompanied Egil in whatever he was going to attempt, which he was sure was going to be dangerous.

A while later, Lasgol returned to the Rangers' camp. He was thinking about what had happened and knew his friends would want to know about it. He was also thinking about Astrid, hoping she would be all right. The latest news said she was okay, and she had passed on to them all the information about the enemy forces, so he was feeling somewhat easier, but not too much. He had been going to tell Egil to ask Astrid to come back and join them all on this side.

If he did it, Astrid would not listen. She would continue spying for Egil.

"Hello, handsome. Long time no see," a voice Lasgol immediately recognized said.

He turned around and saw Valeria smiling at him. She looked very pretty, more than ever, and that was difficult.

"Valeria, what a surprise."

"Yes, I was actually waiting for you, to surprise you."

"Waiting? For me?"

"Of course," she smiled and flicked her blonde hair with an unobtrusive, well-learned movement.

"Why's that?"

"Because it always cheers my heart to see you," she smiled coquettishly.

"You know Astrid's not here and that's why you're saying all these things, right?"

Valeria winked at him.

"Of course I know. I've been watching from a distance. Viggo's already seen me, he's always alert."

"Even if she's not here, that doesn't change things. I still love her."

Valeria mimicked an arrow piercing her heart.

"You can't blame me for trying," she replied with a saintly expression on her face.

"Yes, I can. You give me a hard time."

"It's what you deserve for picking her instead of me."

Lasgol shrugged.

"That's how love works. We don't choose, our heart chooses."

Valeria's eyes opened wide, and then she made a lovestruck face.

"You're truly a gem, you know that?"

"Absolutely not."

"I hope there's another life, so we can find each other and fix what has gone south in this life and end up together."

"That's a lot to hope for," Lasgol replied with a smile. "Why is the Queen here?"

"Good way to change the subject. The Queen has decided that her presence here on the battlefield was necessary."

"And is her mother better?"

"Not really. Druid healers are looking after her, but they don't know whether they'll manage to save her."

"I'm sorry to hear that. So the Queen decided to come regardless?"

"She's a determined woman, and her priorities are very clear. Her place is here, she has too much at risk."

"Does her father, King Kendryk, approve of this?"

"No, he doesn't. They've been arguing the whole way from Irinel to here. But Heulyn and her father rarely agree on anything. They've been arguing her whole life."

"Yes, it was him who ordered us to kidnap her from the Druids, I remember."

"And made her marry Thoran to form this alliance we seem to enjoy now. The Queen doesn't want her father and husband to ruin everything after all she's had to go through."

"Oh… I see, she's here to make sure they win."

"That's right. She's not going to throw away all the sacrifices she's made to become Queen of Norghana. If she has to lead Thoran's and Kendryk's armies herself, she will."

"I believe she's capable of such."

"Yes, that and a lot more."

"I hope we come out victorious in this whole situation."

"You're hoping for a lot, but you've always been an optimist with a good heart," Valeria said affectionately.

"It's no good to be pessimistic."

"Some say that pessimism helps people live longer."

"Do you believe that?"

Valeria shrugged and smiled.

"No, but you should always be alert to everything."

"I agree with you on that. Now that we have this chance to talk, I want to ask you a favor."

"The great Lasgol of the Royal Eagles wants to ask *me* a favor? Has the world turned inside out all of a sudden?"

Lasgol bowed his head.

"Yes, do it for me, if you care about me at all."

Valeria tilted her head and looked at Lasgol. Then she heaved a deep sigh.

"For you, I'll try. Tell me, what do you need?"

"You have privileged information. Let me know if you see things turning against us."

"You're asking for a lot. That might be considered treason. The Druid Queen wouldn't forgive me."

"Only if the situation is insurmountable."

Valeria was quiet for a moment, thinking.

"For you, I'll try, but I can't promise anything."

"Thanks, that's all I'm asking."

"I guess we'll see each other after the great battle. Or in the next life," Valeria said with a wink. Then she threw him a kiss, and with a swift turn, she left.

Lasgol thought he would have no more surprises that night, but he was wrong. When he was already close to this tent, a figure enveloped in a white, hooded cloak called him.

"Lasgol, come over." The figure was right at the edge of the Rangers' camp, as if he did not want to come in. Lasgol narrowed his eyes and saw that it was Maldreck. He was not surprised to see him. He knew that King Thoran would bring his Ice Magi for the battle. On the other hand, the fact that he was here, looking for Lasgol, was not good. What did the leader of the Ice Magi want from him at this hour? It could not be anything good, that was sure. Being Maldreck, and considering what had happened in Rogdon with the container, this meant trouble. He did not want things to affect his friends, so he went over to where the Mage was.

"What does the leader of the Ice Magi want from this Ranger?"

"I see you don't beat around the bush, I like that. Beating around bushes is a waste of time, and we both know what side we're on."

"On the side of the King, and Norghana," Lasgol replied.

"Yes, sure, of course," Maldreck smiled, and Lasgol realized it was a false smile. Maldreck was only on his own side.

"What do you want?"

"I want to know two things that intrigue me greatly. One, where did you hide the container Mirkos the Erudite gave you? And the other, how you defeated my Ice Mage."

Lasgol narrowed his eyes and meditated on his answer.

"Mirkos' container is unimportant."

"Oh no it isn't, don't try to fool me."

"It's only a container."

"It wouldn't be by any chance for the Pearls of Power, which you say you no longer have with you?"

"No, it's not for them. The monster swallowed the pearls, or the river did. I don't know what happened to them."

"You're a bad liar, Lasgol. We both know that you're using that container to hide the pearls. Those pearls are mine, and I want them back."

"I'm telling you the truth. I don't know where those pearls you're talking about are."

"Tell me the truth! Tell me where they are! Give them to me!" Maldreck shouted at him furiously.

Lasgol shrugged.

"I don't have them, and I don't fear you."

"Well, you should!" Maldreck threatened him with his finger.

"I'll answer your second question. I defeated your mage with my own magic."

"Your magic can't compare to that of an Ice Mage. You're a simple apprentice with barely any power."

"You might be reading my aura wrong. If I was in your place, I'd measure it again."

"You whippersnapper, vain and insufferable fool! You'll pay for this!"

"The great Ice Mage had better measure his words, or else he'll end up like his pupil," Lasgol said threateningly.

Maldreck was dumbfounded. He could not believe anyone would threaten him, least of all when it came to magic. He turned bright red with rage, raising his staff as if to cast a spell. At that moment, Nilsa came out of the tent with her bow in her hand.

"Everything all right, Lasgol?"

"Everything is fine, Mage Hunter, thank you," Lasgol said, choosing his words deliberately.

Maldreck soon realized he would have to fight not only Lasgol but his friends as well, and that made him think twice. He lowered the staff.

"This doesn't end here," he threatened Lasgol.

"Yeah, yeah, I guess not."

Maldreck left with a look of rage on his face.

Nilsa made a signal to Lasgol, and he replied with another that everything was okay. Then he remained thoughtful. Things were getting complicated. Too complicated.

Chapter 45

King Caron of Zangria had called for a final meeting before the beginning of the great battle. Surrounded by strong safety measures, King Thoran of Norghana and his retinue, and King Kendryk of Irinel and his own, had arrived at the war tent. The arrival and entry to the tent had been tense, and both monarchs and their generals had passed through the Zangrian war camp, which had made them quite nervous. Being in Zangrian territory, Caron had the right and the obligation to organize the offensive and, as was normal in this kind of circumstance, he would do so from his own war tent. Thoran and Kendryk could not refuse to attend if they wanted the alliance to continue. They had not refused, and so here they were, tense and wary.

King Caron's war tent was huge and watched over by more than a thousand soldiers. Since they were in the middle of their own army, they did not fear murder attempts or betrayals. From the side of King Caron, Generals Zotomer, Zorlten, and Zorberg were by his side, since they led the armies of the Kingdom of Zangria. They were all wearing their best dress armor, like King Caron, who shone in gold and silver and was visible from a league away. He might be short, but he made himself stand out.

When they arrived, the Zangrian generals saluted King Thoran and his retinue, which was made up of his brother Orten and several important Nobles of the East: Count Volgren, Duke Uldritch, and Duke Oslevan. No Noble of the West had been invited. But the three generals leading the Norghanian armies had come as well: Rangulself, Olagson, and Odir. The last to enter were First Ranger Raner and Ellington, Commander of the Guard. They were all dressed in their best attire with colorful armor, although the Norghanians were not as bright as the Zangrians. They stood to one side of the tent.

A moment later, King Kendryk of Irinel arrived with his son Prince Kylian, First General of all the Irinelian armies, as well as Reagan and two other generals. They were all dressed in green and white and wore elegant dress armor with green cloaks featuring the white flower of the realm. They saluted respectfully and stood at the other corner of the tent, forming a triangle with the other two groups. In the center was the large oak table with all the maps of the area and the armies' camps, both their own and those of the enemy.

To everyone's surprise, a moment later the Druid Queen came in. After saluting King Caron and his generals, she greeted her father and brother. King Kendryk's eyes were burning—it was evident he did not want her to be there. Kylian, on the other hand, smiled at her. After that, Heulyn turned to greet her husband, Thoran, and stood beside him. Thoran was looking at her, unable to believe she was there. He was dumbfounded, not knowing how to react. It was obvious he did not want Heulyn to be there beside him. The Druid Queen had received the refusal of her husband and father to attend that military meeting, but despite their commands, she had come. There was too much at stake for her not to be there.

"Thank you all for coming," King Caron greeted them. For his size, his voice was deep and strong.

"The honor is ours," King Kendryk said.

"It's time to act and finish off Erenal and her allies," Thoran said.

Caron nodded.

"Before we start discussing the strategic details of the battle, I would request that anyone here who is not in a military position kindly leave the tent. What we are going to discuss here is only for the ears of those who command our armies."

"That is a wise and cautious decision," Kendryk agreed.

Several of the Nobles of the East in Thoran's retinue left the tent, as well as all the servants and valets. Once all those who had no military responsibilities left, the gazes of the three kings turned to Heulyn.

"Your Majesty, if I'm not mistaken, you have no military responsibilities…" Caron said respectfully but clearly inviting her to leave.

Heulyn lifted her chin proudly.

"I am Queen of Norghana and Princess of Irinel. I have every right to be here."

King Caron looked at Thoran and then at Kendryk to see whether he was offending them. But by the looks of both kings he concluded that was not the case. They did not want the Druid Queen there either.

"Leave the tent, my wife. This meeting is only for generals and commanders in chief of the armies, their kings," Thoran told her with contained rage.

"I am Queen of Norghana," Heulyn insisted adamantly.

"The Queen, my dear wife, does not have a military position. I beg you to obey and oblige our host."

Orten grabbed Heulyn's arm to make her leave.

"King Kendryk? You're not going to support me either?" Heulyn asked her father.

"I'm sorry, Queen of Norghana, but this is not your place," her father replied with authority and anger.

Heulyn shook Orten's hold on her arm and headed to the entrance.

"My husband and father have humiliated me today. One day they will regret it." With these words, that sounded like a curse on the two kings, Heulyn left the war tent with lightning in her eyes.

"I am sorry for this embarrassing situation. My wife still doesn't understand the responsibilities of her new position as Queen of Norghana," Thoran apologized with clenched fists, enraged.

"It's understandable. Besides, with her character..." King Caron said with a condescending smile.

"She will learn her place," her father King Kendryk promised. "It's a matter of maturity, she only needs time."

"And being shown her place," Caron insisted.

"That will be done, I swear, my lords," Thoran replied, and by his angry tone it was obvious he was absolutely embarrassed by his wife's behavior, although he was trying not to show it.

"Very well. Let's continue with the battle plan for tomorrow," King Caron said.

"How many soldiers do Dasleo and his allies have?" Kendryk asked.

"According to our spies, abut sixty thousand in all," Caron said.

"My spies have informed me that Dasleo has thirty thousand soldiers in his legions. Moontian has brought twenty thousand soldiers. Yort has fifteen thousand more, and the Coporneans have ten thousand pirates. A total of seventy-five thousand soldiers," Thoran corrected him.

"Are those numbers correct?" Kendryk asked. "We were also estimating about sixty thousand soldiers."

Thoran looked at Raner to confirm the information.

The leader of the Rangers nodded. They had Astrid's reports, which were much more exact.

"My numbers are correct," Thoran said.

"In that case, we must devise a new strategy to face those forces," Caron said, looking at his generals, who nodded.

The three monarchs, supported by their generals, argued all night about the best strategy and course of military action. They placed and moved wooden pieces on the great map of the Erenalian Plains. The pieces represented the different armies of each kingdom that would take part in the battle. The generals and strategists suggested attack and defense tactics according to what they expected might happen during the battle.

As expected, there was no consensus for a long time. They studied strategies in case of possible attacks and how the different armies would retreat if needed. Infinite different scenarios were proposed. Little by little, the most likely scenarios became relevant and the most unlikely were dismissed. They continued discussing until they reached some agreement. It was not easy because, although they were all after the same goal in that tent—victory at the battlefield—they did not all share the same thoughts on how to obtain said victory and the cost in lives that each kingdom would suffer. They all wanted to come out victorious but not weakened. Winning the battle would be meaningless if they lost almost all their armed forces, since whoever suffered that misfortune would be left at the mercy of the other winners.

The meeting lasted until midnight, when at last the three kings reached an agreement that satisfied everyone and at the same time would grant them victory. Thoran and his legation left first, and after a moment Kendryk left with his. Everything had been settled for the great battle, one that would mark the history of Tremia.

The order to march into battle came at dawn in all the war camps on the Zangrian side of the border. It was followed by countless trumpets and battle horns. All the armies of Zangria, Norghana, and Irinel set out to take their places at the battlefield. They had been preparing for two days, so when dawn came, all the camps knew what was going to happen and were ready.

The soldiers finished dressing and donning their armor, then armed themselves and stood in line in their regiments, awaiting the final orders from the officers. The same preparation was repeated throughout the three war camps. The officers ordered their soldiers to get in line, and they obeyed without wasting a moment. There were troubled and anguished faces among the soldiers. Many had not slept at all the night before in anticipation of what was going to take place. They were all aware that fighting, blood, suffering, and death awaited them. Those who survived this latest threat would be the most fortunate.

"It looks like the moment has come," Ingrid said to her friends in the tent they all shared.

"It was expected," Egil nodded.

"What do we have to do?" Gerd asked.

"Try not to get killed and kill lots of enemies, that's the short answer," Viggo replied, smiling eagerly, impatient for action.

"We'll follow Raner's orders, as we're expected to," said Nilsa.

"Camu and Ona are close by, and they have their instructions about what they have to do," Lasgol commented.

"We'll adjust according to how the battle develops," Egil told them.

"How can it develop? We win and they lose, that's the only development," Viggo said, absolutely certain.

"Don't be so optimistic. The others are also skilled fighters, and experienced from what I heard," Ingrid told him.

Raner's voice reached, them loud and clear.

"All Rangers, to me!"

The Panthers left their tent and joined the rest of Rangers standing in line before Raner. Molak and Luca saw them and waved at them. The Panthers returned the wave with smiles. They also saw other familiar faces who they waved to. Since the Rangers were always on missions, it was difficult to meet often. A war was not exactly the best circumstance for meeting again, but there they were, almost all the Rangers, although some were still on missions at the border and would not take part in the fight directly.

"Listen to me carefully! The King has ordered his Rangers to defend His Majesty's position!"

"Well, well, isn't our dear king brave. And here I was thinking he was going to lead his troops to set an example…" Viggo commented with sarcasm.

Ingrid elbowed him in the ribs.

"Don't be a numbskull… they're going to hear you…"

"As if they aren't thinking the same thing. Do you really believe they're stupid?" He said, looking at his friends and acquaintances in the Rangers.

"Shut up and listen to Raner."

"We'll defend the King's position from any attack, especially from the enemy magi!" the First Ranger ordered.

"I'll deal with that," Nilsa said excitedly.

"I'll help you," said Molak. "My bow has three times the reach of an enemy spell, nothing like being a Sniper."

"Then stay beside me," Nilsa smiled.

Viggo started messing with Captain Fantastic but Ingrid elbowed him again. The situation was too dangerous: there was no time for nonsense.

Lasgol whispered to Egil.

"Is everything going well?"

"That's a question I can't answer yet. We'll have to see how events develop on the battlefield."

"Doesn't sound too promising…" Lasgol replied,

"That's because it's not really promising at all. Our odds—ours, not Thoran's—are few. But let's not lose hope."

Lasgol sighed.

"I'm not losing faith. Let me know what you want me to do when the time comes."

"Don't worry, I'll let you know," Egil said with a wink.

"Everyone, follow me in line. We march to battle!" Raner ordered.

The alliance of the kingdoms of Zangria, Norghana, and Irinel started out toward the battle. The scouts went first to make sure there were no traps on the battlefield. They checked the land almost to the enemy war camps and made sure the troops' advance was safe. They returned to report and the armies moved on.

The positioning strategy of each army at the start of the battle had been one of the most difficult subjects to agree upon. King Caron demanded the honor of fighting Dasleo's legions, which would be placed in the middle in all certainty. He hated the legions of Erenal above all else. It had taken a long time to persuade him it was better that he deal with the right flank and leave the center to the Norghanian infantry, which was the most powerful in Tremia. Thoran and Kendryk had insisted. In the end, Caron had yielded the center to Norghana reluctantly.

The first to stand on the battlefield were the Western Nobles, with ten thousand soldiers and the militia dressed in blue and black. They were led by Dukes Svensen and Erikson, Counts Malason, Bjorn, Axel, Harald, and several lesser lords of the West. They were all tense, not only the soldiers but the nobles as well. They stood and awaited orders.

The next to position themselves were the Norghanian Thunder Army, consisting of huge soldiers with red breastplates decorated with white diagonal streaks led by General Rangulself. They stood just to the right of the Western forces. Behind them, as was usual, stood the Snow Army with its heavy infantry wearing white breastplates under the command of General Olagson. General Odir's soldiers, the Blizzard Army, positioned themselves to the right of the Snow Army. The Invincibles of the Ice, the most fearsome infantry on the continent, stood behind the Snow Army. Every army had four thousand units.

Thoran, his brother Orten, and their nobles stood behind their armies. The Rangers were between the monarch and the armies. The Royal Guard was behind and at the King's sides to protect him. In all, Norghana had brought a force of little over twenty-six thousand. They stood in the center like a sea of red and white waves.

The Panthers had the Norghanian armies in front and Thoran behind with the Eastern Nobles. Raner was with them, leading them.

"Line up and maintain the position."

"Wonderful, we're in the middle. We'll have the best views," Viggo joked.

"The center is the most important part in any battle," Ingrid told him.

"Then it makes sense that we're here. Who better than us to keep it safe?" Viggo said, puffing up his chest.

"Wait till you see the enemy forces, you might not be so cocky," Nilsa retorted, getting more and more nervous.

"I have the feeling this is going to be a horror nightmare," Gerd said.

"Everyone, stay calm. Everything will be all right as long as we stay together," Lasgol said cheerfully.

"Together and as one, we'll make it," Egil joined him.

Nerves began to affect everyone. The battle was inevitable, and they all knew there would be pain and death.

King Caron's Zangrian armies moved next. They stood on the right flank of the Norghanian forces. Generals Zotomer, Zorlten, and Zorberg, each one leading a force of five thousand infantry soldiers, stood at the front. The fifteen thousand soldiers took their place behind, with their monarch at the rear. The Zangrian Army, a total of thirty thousand soldiers, filled the right side of the battlefield like a swarm of wasps in yellow and black.

The forces of Irinel stood on the left flank in their green-and-white colors. King Kendryk had brought a large army of thirty thousand Irinelian soldiers: infantry and javelin throwers of great skill. Prince Kylian led them. They lined up with the infantry in the first rows and the javelin throwers behind.

"I don't see the Druid Queen, do you?" Nilsa said.

"No, she's not with Norghana or Irinel," Ingrid replied.

"That's odd, I thought she wanted to be here today," said Nilsa.

"That's what she had to have come for," said Gerd.

"They must have stopped her," Viggo guessed. "Thoran and Kendryk are not the type to take kindly to being contradicted, and that's the Queen's specialty."

"It is significant, indeed," said Egil thoughtfully.

The Panthers were watching the allied forces all around them. It was an ocean of soldiers in red-and-white, yellow-and-black, and green-and-white colors, a colossal armed force of over eighty-five thousand units, ready and prepared to defeat the enemy. The horns and trumpets rang, proclaiming that the armies were all in battle position.

Suddenly new horns and trumpets, accompanied by war drums, were heard to the south, on the other side of the plains. The enemy armies were beginning to take their places on the battlefield.

"Beware, here they come," Nilsa warned them as she stood on tiptoe to take in everything.

"Let's see what they look like," Viggo said nonchalantly.

"Indeed," Ingrid agreed, not so confidently.

The first to appear were Dasleo's legions. They moved in perfect formation, all their soldiers marching at the same pace, shields and javelins in hand. Four legions that were clearly distinct, forming perfect squares with the cavalry behind them. They were led by Generals Augustus, Militius, and Primus. The last legion was led by King Dasleo himself. In all there were twenty-five thousand legionnaires, and just watching how they were formed and the way they advanced revealed how good they were as soldiers. They stood in the center, facing the Norghanian forces, two thousand paces separating them.

The trumpets, horns, and drums continued ringing, and on the left flank of Dasleo and his legions stood the soldiers of the City State of Yort: halberdiers and crossbow archers, with colorful, bulging clothing, a force of fifteen thousand professional soldiers as colorful as they were feared.

"Look, they have crossbows!" Nilsa was excited.

"And enormous pikes with axe heads," said Gerd, interested.

Then, another army appeared on the battlefield and stood beside that of the city of Yort. They were the pirates of the Island of Coporne in their bronze-colored armor, with breastplates, vambraces, and grieves the same shade and armed with swords and short bows. They stood without any order, combining with the Yort army to face the Zangrian army in front.

"Well, I'd say this balances the forces," Viggo commented.

"Twenty-five thousand in that flank," said Lasgol.

"There are thirty thousand Zangrians," Gerd said in a hopeful tone.

"Yeah, but they're very short. They don't count as full soldiers, three quarters at the most," Viggo joked.

"Stop saying nonsense. The forces are balanced on that flank," Ingrid scolded.

Finally, the forces of Queen Niria of Moontian came to stand on Dasleo's right flank in front of the forces of Irinel. The Queen had brought twenty thousand soldiers with violet skin and pink eyes, armed with war picks and hammers, ready to squash anyone who dared stand in front of them.

"The Moontians have placed themselves in front of Irinel," said Nilsa.

"They must have planned it that way. There's a strong rivalry between Irinel and Moontian," Egil said. "Territorial disputes. There's an undeclared war between them."

"Oh, interesting, so the violet chubbies are going to take on the skinny redheads. That'll be worth seeing. My money is on the violet ones. Only a real brute comes to war with picks and hammers."

"The Irinelian soldiers are also very skilled. Their javelins are fearsome," said Lasgol.

"We'll soon find out," Ingrid commented.

All the horns, trumpets, and drums stopped suddenly, and a grave silence took over the battlefield. It was the silence before battle, the calm before the storm.

The Panthers took a deep breath, trying to release all the tension from their bodies and minds.

The battle was about to begin.

Chapter 46

The silence was broken by Thoran's order, given at the top of his voice.

"Attack, for Norghana! Death to the enemy!"

The Norghanians replied as one voice, thousands of throats crying for victory.

"For Norghana! Death to the enemy!"

Caron gave the order to the Zangrian armies.

"For Zangria! Death to Erenal and her allies!"

His soldiers shouted too, thousands of voices crying: "Death to Erenal! Death to the enemy!"

Kendryk gave the order to his troops.

"For Irinel! To victory!"

Thousands of soldiers in green-and-white shouted too.

"For Irinel! To victory!!"

The horns and trumpets called to march with their powerful sounds. The enormous armies of Norghana, Zangria, and Irinel started moving toward the enemy, who remained still, waiting. With every step of the eighty-five thousand soldiers of the alliance, the ground shook. The noise they made was such that it felt like an earthquake. The sound was a mixture of sharp blows hitting the ground, combined with the metallic jingling of the thousands of suits of armor and weapons the soldiers wore and carried. It was a chilling sound, as if a large tsunami of earth and steel were rising under their feet.

After the armies, their monarchs, nobles, and personal retinues followed at a prudent distance. The Panthers went after the Norghanian army with the rest of the Rangers around them and Raner in command. They were followed by Thoran, Orten, and the Eastern Nobles, protected by the Royal Guard.

The soldiers moved onto the field like an unstoppable sea of killer ants. They came within a thousand paces of the armies of Erenal and her allies, and the order came to stop. The generals called it, and it was passed down to the officers and soldiers. Trumpets and horns rang out the order to halt. The three armies stopped as one and waited in formation.

"Why the heck are we stopping in the middle of an advance?" Viggo asked, frowning.

"We're waiting to see what the enemy forces do," Ingrid told him.

"We seem to be going cautiously…" Gerd commented.

"We should attack them straight on with all our forces and finish this once and for all," Viggo said impatiently.

"That wouldn't be smart at all and actually very reckless," Egil corrected him. "We could fall into a trap they've prepared for us."

"Besides, their magi and archers would shred us if we advanced directly and without protection," Lasgol added.

Viggo made a face but did not say anything else. He knew his friends were right and he was wrong.

Suddenly, the horns, trumpets, and war drums started ringing on the enemy side. The four armies started moving. If the advance of the armies of Zangria, Norghana, and Irinel had made a tremendous thundering noise, that of their enemies equaled it. The armies of Erenal, Moontian, Yort, and Coporne moved as one, and again it was like an earthquake, this time from the south. The armies advanced among calls for battle, and there were shouts and war songs in different languages.

The allied armies of Erenal moved five hundred paces, then stopped another five hundred paces away from the Norghanian forces and her allies. The horns, trumpets, and drums went silent. The chilling atmosphere reigned over the plain once more, which was now crowded with soldiers. There were over a hundred and sixty thousand soldiers on the great plain belonging to the various kingdoms, and they were watching and measuring each other. The generals were ready to give the order to fight, the foreboding silence of foretold deaths hovering over the battlefield.

Who would be the first to attack seemed a matter of strategy, and cold blood.

Thoran was unable to hold back, and his hate-filled shout gave way to fighting.

"Kill them all! Death to all our enemies!"

The generals hastened to give the order to their troops, and the positioning and maneuvering of the formations began on both sides.

The Nobles of the West began to move forward onto the legions of Erenal. They did this in rows, without good order and with an unsteady rhythm, since there were a lot of militiamen among them who tried to follow the soldiers as best they could. The Thunder Army followed a moment later, leaving some distance. They were much more coordinated, forming a solid block of infantry which could knock down any wall or enemy formation they encountered. They made way for the Snow Army, which started following them, also in a compact formation. In front of them, the legions of the Erenalian army started to maneuver, their generals in the lead. They formed four elongated rectangles with the soldiers at arm's length and in perfect order. After them came the light cavalry.

On the Zangrian side, their armies began to move, forming three rectangles each led by one of their generals and the last, a little further back, led by King Caron himself. They maneuvered into place and started moving toward the enemy forces waiting for them. The Copornean pirates were shouting bravado and victory cries while they made provoking gestures and signs. Then, the professional forces of the city of Yort waited in formation with the halberdiers, their weapons ready, and the archers with their crossbows.

King Kendryk's Irinelian forces began to move forward, also in compact groups. His soldiers marked their pace with war songs of Irinel featuring lively heroic melodies. They marched with their tear-shaped shields in front and spears and javelins ready. They were advancing at a good rhythm and singing as if the victory were guaranteed. Prince Kylian led them, and they were advancing toward the forces of Moontian. The soldiers of the mountains waited without moving, striking their shields with their picks and hammers while they shouted at the top of their voices, taunting the soldiers of Irinel.

Three hundred and fifty paces between both hosts, fighting began. The archers of both sides began to release on the enemy. The armies of the north were received with a volley of arrows from the armies of central Tremia. The order was almost simultaneous from the armies of both sides.

"Shields up!"

"Archers forward!"

"Advance!"

"Defending positions!"

The armies of the north were moving forward under a rain of thousands of arrows. Luckily for them, the enemy armies did not have too many archers.

"Do we release?" Nilsa asked, seeing arrows flying about.

"We wait for Raner's order," Ingrid told her.

"If we don't release, we're going to be riddled with holes," Viggo protested.

"They don't have too many archers," Lasgol said, "actually quite few."

"The legions of Erenal only have a few hundred archers in each legion. The Moontians are pretty much the same, and it's the same with the pirates. The only ones with a real archery force are the Yorts," Egil said.

"So, why don't they shoot?" Nilsa asked, straining her neck to see better.

"Crossbows have a much shorter reach than our bows," Egil told her. "They're a lot more powerful, capable of piercing through armor, but they deviate off course a lot from a distance. They'll wait until they have the enemy at a hundred paces before releasing."

"Wow, that's good to know," said Ingrid.

"Rangers, release at the enemy!" Raner's order was heard when they were two hundred and fifty paces away.

"At last!" said Viggo.

Hundreds of arrows flew from among the Rangers, who were releasing with their composite bows, long bows, and a few sniper ones.

The Rangers released, and the archers of the Blizzard Army released as well. Arrows rained over the legions of Erenal. Then suddenly, at an order from their generals, the four legions took on an advanced battle formation. The soldiers of the first rows kept their slightly convex rectangular shields in front of them to stop the arrows directed at them. The soldiers in the back rows raised their shields and held them above their heads, covering themselves and the soldiers on the first rows. They formed a shell of shields over the legions and the arrows hit the shields without reaching the soldiers under them.

"What's that formation?" Ingrid asked, surprised.

"They've covered themselves on all sides with their shields," Nilsa said.

"I believe they call it the tortoise formation, since it resembles the shell of one, covering them completely," Egil explained. "They use it against arrows and javelins, as well as against rocks in sieges. We won't be able to hit them with our arrows as long as they maintain it."

"I can only see a roof of shields and a wall of shields under the roof. Who do I shoot at?" Gerd asked, puzzled.

"This isn't good news," said Lasgol as he kept releasing.

"I'm beginning to understand the reputation of these legions," Ingrid commented.

On the Zangrian side, the soldiers were moving directly to face the Copornean pirates and Yort's halberdiers. Two of the four Zangrian armies attacked the forces of the city of Yort. The other two attacked the Copornean pirate forces. They were received by the pirates' arrows, and when they were about to reach the halberdiers of Yort, the soldiers with crossbows began to release in between their comrades with great skill. The Zangrian soldiers had to protect themselves behind their metallic rectangular shields, and even so, the arrows reached them and they started to suffer casualties. The advance continued, but the pace decreased.

Dasleo remained in the rear with his magi and personal guard. The Yorts and the Coporneans did not appear to have sent their magi to fight. It was not strange. Magi were valuable resources, and as a rule they only fought beside their monarchs. They were not loaned to other kingdoms to fight their wars. They were too valuable to lose in the wars of others.

On the left side of the battle, the army of Irinel was advancing on Moontian at a fast pace synced to the songs of war. The first lines of Irinel came within twenty paces from the first line of the mountains forces, and at an order of their generals, they stopped. The whole army of Irinel stopped as one, maintaining distance between the soldiers. The singing changed—now they were singing something more pressing and shrill. Moontian's archers were releasing at the Irinel troops, causing casualties, but there were not enough of them to decide the battle, and the Irinelians protected themselves with their tear-shaped shields.

The Moontian soldiers, who were waiting for the clash of weapons, were puzzled. Why had Irinel stopped advancing? They found out a moment later. Thousands of javelins flew from the green-and-white ranks to fall on the Moontian soldiers. Many of the javelins reached the mountain infantry, causing death and serious wounds. After the first wave of javelins came a second, and it was followed by a third wave in rapid succession. The Moontian generals realized they were being destroyed with short-distance throws. They gave the order to advance their troops. The Irinelians would defeat them with that tactic.

In the center of the battle, the army of the Western League was taking cover from the legions' arrows, which did not fall in large quantities, so they were able to move forward. A little further back, the Thunder Army came, determined to cut the legions of Erenal in two. The Snow Army would come after the Thunder and was on their heels. The Blizzard Army was releasing against the four legions to keep them busy and controlled, who were maintaining their tortoise formation and therefore could not move forward. The generals of the Norghanian armies led their soldiers closer to the legions.

"We're at magi distance, watch out, everyone," Nilsa warned.

"Magi? What magi do Erenal have?" Gerd asked, concerned.

"Elemental Magi and also Healers, similar to the Rogdonian Magi," Egil explained. "Astrid has confirmed that Dasleo counts on at least six powerful Elemental Magi who serve him."

"Then we're balanced," Lasgol commented as he saw the Ice Magi advancing, surrounded by the Invincibles of the Ice to stand at spell-casting distance.

"Here come our own," said Ingrid when she saw them.

"Maintain the position and release! Cover the Ice Magi!" came Raner's order.

The Rangers released at the legions.

Maldreck and his five Ice Magi began casting spells against the legions of Erenal. They all had two protective spheres covering them. Lasgol recognized them. The first one was a translucent sphere of anti-magic energy. The second one was solid and frozen against physical attacks. Maintaining both spheres consumed their energy, even more if they had to strengthen them, but without them a mage could die from an arrow or an enemy spell, so they were essential. Lasgol had his own *Woodland Protection*, which was similar to the protective sphere against physical attacks, and Camu had an anti-magic dome which was similar to the anti-magic sphere of the Magi, only much more powerful.

A winter storm of large proportions began to form over one of the legions. Threatening, dark clouds appeared over the soldiers, and from them came the storm with terrible lightning and thunder while the temperature started falling dramatically. Freezing hurricane winds came down from the storm to whip at the legionnaires. Over another legion, a dark compact cloud, almost black but surrounded with ice like the ceiling of a frozen cavern, took shape. Huge, heavy stalactites started falling from it, striking the soldiers with terrible force and squashing them under the shields that protected them. The Ice Magi continued conjuring, moving their staves and chanting words of power. The ground under another of the legions began to cover with gray frost. A moment later, hundreds of stalagmites of sharp ice emerged from the frozen substance with great force, killing the soldiers, who had no defense against an attack from the ground. Over the fourth legion, the Ice Magi cast a spell that froze the ground at the feet of the soldiers and then caused ice to climb up to their knees. The soldiers were frozen, stuck to the tundra floor, unable to move. They tried to pull their feet free, but it was impossible.

On the right side of the battle, hostilities were intensifying. The halberdiers stood firm with their halberds forward while thousands of arrows flew from behind them to reach the Zangrian soldiers who advanced, protected by their shields and their short stature, which helped them take cover behind them. They tried to break the resistance of the halberdiers, who without a shield, were keeping them at bay with their long weapons while the archers with crossbows killed them. The Zangrians were not managing to break the system of the Yort soldiers and were suffering many casualties. The Zangrian spears were a lot shorter than the halberds and the Yort soldiers' arm span.

The pirates assaulted the first ranks of the two Zangrian armies at sword-stroke distance with assault cries. They leapt and hit Zangrians who were bearing the chaotic and disproportionate attack of the pirates and their deafening cries behind their shields. The sound of metal on metal was dulled by their war shouts. The Zangrian soldiers were surprised by the drive and chaos of the pirate attack, and the first lines fell. The Zangrian generals noticed and ordered the formation of a wall of shields to repel the attack. It worked. The pirates struck with their swords, but all they encountered were the shields of the Zangrians who stayed close together, shoulder to shoulder, protected by their shields. The Zangrians began to push back using their spears from behind their protection.

On the left side, the battle took on a strange appearance. The infantry of Irinel was holding its position and throwing javelin after javelin against the Moontian infantry, which was moving in to crush them with their hammers. A large group of Druids, unmistakable with their dark-green hooded cloaks; the tattoos on their arms, face, and legs; and their long staves with runes, marched through the ranks of Irinel until they stood two hundred paces away from the Moontians. There were more than thirty of them, and they began to cast a spell on the first lines of Moontian soldiers. Suddenly, huge roots emerged from the ground and trapped the soldiers of the enemy army. A moment later, the roots began to crush their prey with tremendous strength, breaking their bones. The Druids continued casting, raising their staves above their heads, and giant poisonous plants which released spores of poison and acid appeared in between the soldiers. These were accompanied by enormous carnivorous plants, which began to emerge at different points between the puzzled soldiers. The plants attacked and ate the soldiers, as if the plants were huge dragon snouts. The Moontian soldiers fought desperately against the plants, hitting them with their war picks and hammers, which were not effective against that type of enemy. Bewilderment took over the first ranks of the army of Queen Niria. Hundreds of giant, carnivorous, poisonous, spiked-rooted plants appeared, creating chaos everywhere.

In the center of the battle, the magi of Erenal reacted at the sight of their legions suffering casualties. Six magi appeared among the soldiers of the legions and started conjuring. They were unmistakable since they carried a long staff with a gem at the top and wore a long, white toga with a representation of the four elements in the middle of their chest: a sun for fire, a sea for water, a mountain for earth, and wind for air, all of them inside a golden circle. They had conjured the two protective spheres: the anti-magic which was translucent and the sphere that offered physical protection the color of solidified lava. The magi knew they would have to fight the Ice Magi, so they all used the most harmful element to them: fire.

"Get ready!" Lasgol warned, knowing what was going to happen next.

"Release at the magi!" shouted Nilsa.

"Are we within their range?" asked Gerd.

"We aren't, but our forces are," said Egil, pointing at the armies in front of them.

Suddenly, five balls of fire were created by the Elemental Magi of Erenal. The flames were a considerable size, and with a movement of their staves, they sent them against the Norghanian troops. The first ball hit the front lines of the Western League soldiers. It was going to burn them to ashes. The other balls passed above their heads and headed toward the different Norghanian armies. The ball that impacted against the first lines of the Western Army did not burst. The soldiers, who were hiding behind their shields, saw how the ball hit the first line but did not explode. On the contrary, it was going out. That was not the case with the others. One of the balls impacted in the middle of the Thunder Army and exploded, burning hundreds of soldiers and catching just as many on fire. The cries of pain and horror rose to the skies. The next ball of fire reached the Snow Army, killing another hundred soldiers and making a hundred more run around, covered in flames. The next two caught the Blizzard

Army and the Invincibles of the Ice, with similar results. A moment later, another five balls of fire reached the Ice Magi, but their defenses held.

"Everyone, release at the Elemental Magi!" Raner's order came. "Only the Magi!"

Hundreds of Rangers' arrows fell on the Magi of Erenal. That did not stop them from sending five other balls of fire against the Norghanian forces, which struck the soldiers, delivering death and destruction among the Norghanians. All except one, the ball that hit the forces of the Western League. This one, like the first, did not manage to burst. The Ice Magi intensified their attack against the legions of Erenal as well, delivering as much death and destruction as their rivals. The soldiers of Erenal died, frozen, crushed by blocks of ice or skewered by sharp, solid ice stakes.

On the right side, the Zangrian troops were in trouble. The professional soldiers of the City State of Yort were causing many casualties among the Zangrian soldiers, who could not break their formation of halberdiers combined with the crossbow archers. The pirates, on the other hand, were slowly being whittled down. The Zangrian troops, more organized and compact, were finishing off the pirates who had initially surprised them with their wild, chaotic assault.

King Caron, seeing the Yorts defeating his troops, decided to send his five Magi to solve the situation. There was no doubt they were Zangrian Magi by their physical build, since they were as short and wide-shouldered as their fellow soldiers. The difference lay in their attire, also in yellow and black, but they wore long, heavy robes instead of armor. They carried in their hand, staves with gems at their tips. The five Magi stood two hundred paces away from the first enemy lines and started to cast a spell.

In front of the halberdiers, on the ground, a whirlwind formed which raised a dust cloud and attracted every nearby rock, big and small, to its center. A hundred paces to their right, another whirlwind formed that attracted all the metal in the area. Pieces of iron and copper headed to the center, but as the spell increased in intensity, it began to pull in the weapons and armor of the fighters, both

Zangrian and Yorts. Swords, halberds, shields, and helmets flew into the whirlwind, attracted as if by a giant magnet. The soldiers had to hold onto their comrades to avoid being dragged in too. The pieces of armor flew into the whirlwind and ended up in its center.

The five Zangrian Magi began to crouch and rise with their staves in front of them, as if they were lifting something. They continued casting and making a lifting movement. Suddenly, a huge stone elemental emerged from the first whirlwind. It was a being made up of stones and magic, shaped like a human and at least twenty-one feet tall and nine wide. It was all stone—the head, torso, arms, and legs—and rock combined to give it a human shape. A moment later, a metal elemental emerged from the other whirlwind. If the first one was made up completely of stone, this one was made up of metal. Also humanoid, it was as tall and large as the first one.

The Zangrian Magi sent their creatures against the army of Yort.

"What the heck are those?" Viggo asked when he saw them.

"They're elementals, one of stone and another of metal," Egil explained. "They've summoned them. The Zangrian Magi are Summoning Magi."

"Summoning?" Ingrid said.

"They can summon different types of creatures to fight for them. These are elemental. These Magi are intelligent. A flesh summoning would've fallen, riddled by the arrows from the crossbows, but creatures of stone and steel can't be harmed with regular weapons."

Egil was not wrong. The crossbow archers released against the two huge creatures, but their arrows did not penetrate their bodies of stone and metal. The halberdiers tried to stop the advance of the two beings which approached them with great strides, but the soldiers' attacks had no effect on the feet and ankles of rock and metal. The creatures started to crush the soldiers of Yort with powerful steps and hit them with their arms and the stumps they had for hands. The soldiers were thrown in the air by the strength of the two creatures.

On the right flank where the Druids were winning the battle for Irinel, there appeared among the soldiers of Moontian half a dozen magi in pink robes with the silhouette of a mountain inside a square in the middle of their chest. They started to cast a spell, moving their staves that each ended in a brown-colored gem. They did this in unison, as if reciting the same spell. Suddenly, the soldiers of Irinel felt the ground under their feet quaking all around them. A terrible noise began to emerge from the ground they were stepping on. Before the horrified soldiers, the ground opened in large cracks, and a tremendous earthquake destroyed the hosts of Irinel. Soldiers and Druids fell to the ground, unable to keep their balance because of the terrible tremors and the movement of the earth's plates. Many fell inside the numerous, fathomless cracks, abysses that led to an endless darkness, or the earth movements the magic quake was creating. Panic took over the soldiers of Irinel. The earth was swallowing them as if it were a live monster with a thousand mouths open to devour them. This was no earthquake, it was powerful Earth Magic, and it was swallowing them.

The soldiers of Moontian did not move. They let the powerful magic of the Earth Magi deal with their enemies. Prince Kylian ordered his troops to retreat. They had to get away from the range of the terrible earthquake which the enemy Magi were creating. The soldiers tried to withdraw, but many were not able to and fell in the abyss. The Druids, unable to concentrate and conjure in the midst of such a devastating earthquake and the noise it made, retreated at a run.

The soldiers of Norghana were now attacking the center with all their force. The Ice Magi and the Rangers were attacking the Magi from Erenal without pause, focusing only on them, and the Magi were having serious trouble to maintain their defenses. This prevented them from attacking the troops. Nilsa and the other Mage Hunters were using distracting arrows that caused great impacts and loud noises to prevent the enemy Magi from concentrating properly. At the same time, Molak and the other Snipers were releasing against the defenses of the Magi, with powerful sniper shots that snapped pieces off their solid-lava shields. The rest of the Rangers were releasing with Elemental Arrows, seeking to either stop the Magi from casting or hoping to pierce their protective spheres designed to protect them from physical attacks. The Magi of Erenal defended themselves as best they could but were unable to concentrate under the combined attack of the Ice Magi and Rangers.

The Western League Nobles were now fighting the first ranks of one of the legions of Erenal, and they were not managing to break the closed formation the legion defended itself with. The Thunder Army attacked another of the legions, charging with all their might, in a wedged formation as usual. The huge Norghanians struck the shields of the legions' soldiers with their two-headed axes, and they did it with so much force and power that they managed to create a dent and eventually split one of the legions in half. They went in, delivering tremendous two-handed axe blows and knocking down anything that got in their way. The Snow Army followed them and attacked another of the legions. They encountered an ironclad defensive formation and had to work really hard. The Norghanians used sword and axes to try and open up a breach, and the legion repelled them with javelins and short swords. The fight became fierce between the legion and the Snow Army, neither seeming to have the upper hand. The last of the Erenal legions maneuvered to go and help the other three but were met with an unpleasant surprise: the Invincibles of the Ice. They moved toward the legion, and with their coldness and skill with the sword, they attacked the legion formation.

"What do you think, Egil?" Lasgol asked his friend as he released at one of the Magi from Erenal, trying to pierce through the man's already weakened defenses.

"The Western Nobles won't be able to defeat that legion, but they're not suffering too many casualties since the legion has the order to defend, not attack. The Thunder Army is destroying the legion it's fighting, and the Snow Army is beginning to breach a little but is suffering many casualties. The Invincibles are making a large breach and destroying their legion.

"That's pretty good, isn't it?" Nilsa said, evaluating the situation.

"Not too bad," Ingrid corrected her.

"We have to finish off the Magi. Then Erenal will be ours," Viggo said. "I'm all for going in myself and doing it with my knives."

"No! Don't move!" Lasgol shouted at him.

Viggo and Ingrid turned in surprise at the shout.

"What's up?" Gerd asked, raising an eyebrow.

Lasgol looked at his friend, and Egil nodded.

"We have to stay here together," Egil said. "Look."

Nilsa, Ingrid, Gerd, and Viggo looked at Egil.

"What does that mean?" Ingrid asked him.

Egil pointed at the side of Irinel. Beside Prince Kylian a hooded rider had appeared, unrecognizable because he or she wore a scarf that covered both mouth and nose.

"Who's that rider?" Ingrid asked.

"It's the Druid Queen," said Egil.

"The Druid Queen? What's she doing dressed like that? She's unrecognizable," said Nilsa.

"There's an important reason for that," Egil replied.

The Druid Queen said something to her brother, and Kylian waved a red flag.

"What does the red flag mean?" Ingrid asked.

Egil did not reply and pointed at King Caron of Zangria on his horse. They all followed his finger to where he was pointing.

King Caron waved a red flag too, and Generals Zotomer, Zorlten, and Zorberg waved red flags.

"Egil, what's going on?" Nilsa asked nervously.

"What does that mean?" Gerd asked, his voice laced with fear.

Egil pointed again, this time toward the center.

Duke Erikson and Duke Svensen waved red flags.

"It means the real battle begins now," Egil told them.

At the total astonishment of his friends, all the armies with red flags maneuvered, turning to face the forces of Norghana.

Chapter 47

The Zangrian armies maneuvered on the right flank. They all retreated as one, moving away from the armies of Yort and the pirates of Coporne they had defeated. The Zangrian Magi let the two large Elementals keep attacking while the army retreated. Once they were two hundred paces from Yort and the Copornean pirates, the armies led by Generals Zotomer, Zorlten, and Zorberg turned toward the Norghanian troops.

At an order from their generals, they moved onto the Blizzard Army and the Invincibles of the Ice who were fighting the legions of Erenal. They caught them by surprise, attacking their flank. The Norghanian solders could not believe what was happening—their allies were attacking them while they were fighting hard against the legions.

"Treachery!" cried General Odir of the Blizzard Army.

His archers stopped releasing against the Magi of Erenal and started releasing against the Zangrian soldiers to protect their own as they turned to face the new attack. The light cavalry and the lancers had to intervene to rescue the infantry.

The Invincibles saw the Zangrian attacking them and with a cold calm maneuvered to change the formation. They took on an L shape to defend themselves from the legion of Erenal in front and the Zangrian forces on their right flank. It was a weak formation, but they had no choice since they were facing two forces at once. Invincibles and Zangrians exchanged blows, and soldiers began to fall on both sides. The Invincibles continued fighting with their usual coldness and efficiency.

The legion of Erenal took advantage of the Zangrian attack and stepped back. Their general ordered them to compact their ranks. They had lost a large number of soldiers against the Invincibles. They formed a compact square and withdrew to see what was going on.

On the left flank, Prince Kylian was ordering the Irinelian troops to retreat, leaving the fight against the troops of Moontian. He established a wide line with the Druids and the javelin throwers he had left to prevent the Magi of Moontian from closing in to attack and ordered the rest of the infantry to regroup.

King Kendryk was shouting at his children. The three on horseback were having a bitter argument.

"Kylian, what do you think you're doing? Keep attacking Moontian!" King Kendryk shouted at the Prince.

"Attacking Moontian has become too costly and doesn't favor our kingdom's interests," Kylian replied in a calm tone.

"I am your father, the King of Irinel! Do as I say! Attack Moontian!"

"My sister has a better proposal," Kylian replied.

"Your sister? What proposal? What are you talking about?"

"We're going to attack Thoran," Heulyn said.

"What are you talking about? Have you lost your mind? That's absolutely crazy!"

"It's not, my dear Father, it's the best strategy, given our situation," Heulyn told him.

"We can't attack Norghana! They're our allies, we signed an alliance!"

"Correction, Father. *You* signed an alliance with Thoran. Kylian and I haven't signed anything."

"You're the Queen of Norghana! You can't go against your husband!"

"I am the Queen of Norghana, yes, and I want the North for myself! And of course I can go against that brainless brute of a husband!" Heulyn looked at her brother. "Give the order, Kylian."

Kylian nodded. He turned and ordered his infantry to attack the Norghanian forces.

"Attack the Thunder Army and the Snow Army!" he ordered his generals.

"No! You fool!" his father yelled. "Generals don't follow that order! Attack Moontian!"

The generals looked at the King and then the Prince, undecided.

"I'm the Commander in Chief of the Army. You'll obey me!" Kylian told the generals.

"I'm the King of Irinel, obey me!" Kendryk shouted.

"Today is your last day as King. Today, you'll abdicate in favor of your son," Heulyn told him.

"That's high treason! Take the Prince and Princess!"

At that moment, four Druids appeared and cast a spell with their staves. From the ground under the King's mount emerged creepers and twisted roots which rose quickly, growing uncontrollably and capturing the King on his horse. Kendryk and his horse were completely immobilized, trapped in the creepers. His wide-open eyes and his unhinged jaw were the only things he could move.

"Generals, obey my brother's orders. He's the new King of Irinel."

The generals looked at one another, then at Kendryk trapped in the creepers, and they nodded.

"Yes, my Lord and Lady," one of the generals said and went to execute the orders.

"You ungrateful brats! I gave you everything!" Kendryk yelled at them.

"You've also treated us as if we were nothing but your pawns, at your disposal for your political games," Kylian replied.

"Did you forget that you had me kidnapped when all I wanted was to go on my way among the Druids?" Heulyn recriminated him with acrimony.

"I am your father! You must obey me!"

"We have already, against our will," Heulyn said. "Did you not make me marry that human scum that is my current husband? Do you know what I've had to put up with? Do you know what you've done? You sold me like a slave to a degenerate. You've insulted me irreparably. I will forever be tainted. I will never go back to being who I used to be because of what you've done."

"It's for the good of Irinel!"

"And for the good of Irinel, your rule ends today," Heulyn said.

"You can't do this to me!"

"You have cursed yourself. I warned you at the war tent where you humiliated me for the last time, you and that swine called my husband. 'My husband and my father have humiliated me today. One day they will regret it,'" Heulyn repeated the curse. "Today is that day."

The forces of Moontian, seeing the Army of Irinel pull back and start attacking the Norghanian army, withdrew as well. Queen Niria was watching the shifting tide on the battlefield and was waiting before making a decision about her next actions. Events had changed very unexpectedly.

The forces of Irinel attacked the Armies of Thunder and Snow. General Rangulself of the Thunder Army noticed the change immediately and gave the order to retreat. They had practically annihilated one of the legions of the army of Erenal, and the attack on his left flank forced the General to stop.

"Square wall of shields!" he ordered his soldiers.

They withdrew at once and formed the square of shields.

"Left flank, hold on!" he shouted while the soldiers of Irinel crashed against that flank hard.

General Olagson, who was also defeating another legion of Erenal, found himself with the same problem. The forces of Irinel were upon him, and he could not finish destroying the legion of Erenal as it was retreating.

"Attention! Wall of shields!" he ordered.

His soldiers stopped attacking the first rows of the legion and withdrew to form the square of shields.

"We defend our position!" he ordered.

The soldiers of Irinel attacked them on the left flank and the rear with tremendous force.

All of Thoran's forces were being attacked by his allies, so the Norghanian armies were maneuvering to defend themselves and repel them.

Thoran was watching what was happening, wide-eyed.

"It can't be… this can't be happening."

"We've been betrayed, Brother!" Orten was yelling at him desperately. "It's a bloody betrayal!"

"Treachery, my lord!" Count Volgren was shouting, and the other Nobles of the East joined him.

Thoran was watching the battlefield, absolutely outraged. He could not understand or accept what was happening.

"I've been betrayed…"

"Irinel and Zangria have betrayed us!" Orten yelled.

Thoran looked at King Caron and saw him ordering his troops to attack the Norghanians. Then he looked at Irinel and saw Kylian sending his troops against the Norghanian armies. Then he understood—he had fallen into a trap. Caron would rather see Norghana fall than take the risk with Erenal and had made a deal with Irinel to destroy him.

"Bloody traitors! You'll pay with your lives for this!"

Orten noticed something else.

"It has to be Heulyn, Kylian can't have acted alone! That Druid Witch wants Norghana for herself! She's betrayed you!"

Thoran eyes opened wide.

"Yes, it has to have been her. Brother, my wife has betrayed us with that swine of Caron. I swear to the Ice Gods, they'll pay with their blood! I'll kill them all!"

"Protect the King!" Orten shouted.

The Royal Guard surrounded the monarch.

Seeing what was happening, Maldreck and his ice Magi withdrew until they were beside the King and the Nobles of the East.

"Magi, protect me!" Thoran ordered them.

"I can't believe this is happening," said Nilsa as she watched the battle with large eyes.

"By now, I'll believe anything," Viggo smiled.

"Thoran has been betrayed, in the middle of the battle." Ingrid was finding it hard to swallow.

"What do we do now?" Gerd asked, puzzled.

"Let's keep calm," Lasgol told them.

"And follow orders," added Egil.

"The orders of…?" Nilsa wanted to know.

"Raner's for now. I'll let you know when we need to act," Egil said.

They all nodded.

"Rangers! Protect the King!" Raner's order came loud and clear. "Let no enemy reach the King!"

The Rangers ran to surround King Thoran and form up with the Royal Guard. The Panthers remained together.

"Shoot at the soldiers of Zangria or Irinel if they come near!" Raner ordered.

All the fighting was concentrated in the center of the battlefield where the Norghanian armies were. The armies of Thunder, Snow, and Blizzard were defending themselves as best as they could from the Zangrian and Irinelian forces. The defensive squares they had formed were holding, and being tough Norghanian soldiers, it was difficult to defeat them. The Invincibles were killing Zangrians right and left; more than defending themselves, they seem to be on the offensive.

The only ones barely fighting and who were withdrawing carefully to the north were the forces of the Nobles of the Western League. They were being attacked by the forces of Erenal, but they defended themselves without attacking as they retreated. From the distance it looked like a strategic withdrawal, but in reality, they were not actually fighting, instead escaping the mess and leaving space for the soldiers of Irinel to reach the other Norghanian armies more easily.

At that moment of the fight, King Dasleo sent messengers to Queen Niria with new instructions. The armies of Yort and the pirates of Coporne had been defeated and the survivors were regrouping, but the forces of Moontian were strong, and Dasleo still had two full legions.

In a combined attack, Dasleo and Niria sent their remaining armies against the Norghanians. Two legions of Dasleo and two other Moontian armies attacked the four Norghanian armies, who were holding up in the middle of the battle, fighting against the troops of Irinel and Zangria.

The fighting turned fierce. The Norghanian soldiers were surrounded from the south, east, and west. They could only escape north, which was where the Western troops were withdrawing. They were being attacked by the forces of four kingdoms, and the Norghanian soldiers were defending themselves with everything they had. But the legions' sheer size advantage was soon evident. The Norghanian soldiers were fighting proudly, killing right and left, but there were too many enemies.

The first lines of the shield squares began to fall. The fallen soldiers were replaced by comrades from inside the square, which took their place and went on fighting. Unfortunately for the Norghanians, they were also falling under the tremendous pressure of all the armies they were fighting against. The light cavalry of the Blizzard Army was massacred by the legions' cavalry. The archers released continuously, but a sea of enemies surrounded them. The javelins of the soldiers of Irinel were wreaking havoc within the defensive squares. The war picks and hammers of the Moontian infantry were destroying the wooden shields of the Norghanians.

The Norghanian generals saw they were lost.

"Retreat in formation!" Rangulself ordered.

"Retreat, maintain the pace and the formation!" ordered Olagson.

"Retreat to the north!" Odir ordered.

The three armies began to withdraw, trying to minimize their casualties, which were growing at every turn. The Invincibles found themselves alone in a sea of enemies and also began to withdraw.

"The battle is lost, Brother!" Orten told Thoran.

"Bloody traitors! I'll gut and quarter them all!" Thoran yelled beside himself.

"Your Majesty, we have to flee, the enemy is getting closer," Count Volgren warned him.

"My guard, to me!" called Thoran.

Commander Ellingsen and the Royal Guard mounted.

"We're withdrawing!" Thoran ordered and galloped away at top speed. His brother followed, and then the Nobles of the East and the Royal Guard.

"Look how brave our monarch is. He runs away as fast as he can while his armies fight for their lives," Viggo commented sarcastically.

"His Ice Magi are also quite brave," Nilsa commented a moment later as the Magi, finding themselves alone without their king, also fled, riding at full gallop.

"I don't think they're going to stop until they arrive in Norghania," Gerd said, seeing them leave.

"What should we do?" Ingrid asked Egil.

"We wait for our people," Egil replied with a look of mystery.

"By ours you mean…"

"The West, of course," Egil said.

Lasgol looked at Raner, who was not sure what course to follow. The battle was lost—the King, his Nobles, and Magi had fled, and the armies were in retreat. Lasgol went over to the First Ranger.

"Sir, we should protect the retreat of our troops," he suggested.

"I can't believe they just fled like that…" Raner was nonplussed.

"We have to help our people, sir," Lasgol insisted.

"Yes, you're right. We must help our armies. Rangers, cover the retreat! Release at the enemy!"

The Rangers obeyed and started releasing at all the soldiers trying to finish off the Norghanian troops, whatever kingdom they were from. They released repeatedly while the Norghanian armies retreated from the battlefield, very depleted, with the exception of the Western troops, who had suffered few losses.

"Keep releasing! Aid them in their retreat!" Raner shouted.

The Rangers did not stop releasing against the enemy forces, which consisted of thousands of soldiers from four different kingdoms.

The army of Western Nobles reached the Rangers, followed by the other four armies which were retreating as fast as they could. At that moment, something interesting happened. The Zangrian forces and those of Erenal met in their pursuit of the Norghanians, and the same happened with the forces of Irinel and those of Moontian.

And the battle took another unexpected turn.

One which, although it was not likely, was expected.

King Caron decided to attack King Dasleo's legions, and Queen Niria ordered the attack on the forces of Irinel. The four kingdoms started fighting among themselves, which allowed the Norghanian forces to flee north.

The Norghanian armies, horribly weakened, hastened their flight to the Norghanian war camp to regroup.

"Everyone, to the war camp!" Raner ordered the Rangers.

The escape was now on in earnest, almost a race.

Lasgol looked one last time at the battlefield. There were casualties of the four different kingdoms by the thousand, strewn throughout the plain. The Zangrian armies were pressing the legions of Erenal, and their Magi were beginning to fight against one another. They were very even.

The same was happening with the forces of Irinel and the armies of Moontian. They were fighting with hate and spite, but they were even in strength. The Druids and the Earth Magi were trying to tip the scales of the battle.

Lasgol saw the thousands of dead and those who were still

standing and fighting and he felt a terrible sadness, an empty void. So much death and suffering, for the greed of their monarchs. There was no need for that slaughter, for all that needless suffering. No kingdom had come out victorious, and the rivalries and hatred had increased and would last for generations, which was the worst thing. A great hopelessness overwhelmed him. All their efforts, their good intentions, for what? For everything to end like that, in a great battlefield with many thousands of casualties? Was that what they were always going to achieve, no matter how hard they tried to do the right thing?

He shook his head. He wanted to get rid of the unpleasant aftertaste and the defeatist ideas filling his head. And then he saw someone running like a spark toward him. He narrowed his eyes and realized who it was.

"Astrid!"

"Lasgol, at last!"

They clung to each other and kissed passionately.

"You're okay, I'm so glad!" Lasgol told her. He had been very worried about her.

"Hey, you two, we have to leave, now!" Ingrid urged them.

"Yeah, let's go," Astrid said, and they ran after the group.

The rest of the Panthers greeted Astrid at a run while they all sprinted to the war camp.

Chapter 48

The armies had regrouped in the Norghanian war camp. They were healing all the wounded they could and sending off the brave soldiers whose wounds could not be healed and over which death hovered like a vulture waiting for their last breath, with honor. The cries of suffering and pain and the blood and death spread throughout the camp.

Raner was organizing the Rangers. They had to get out of there as soon as possible. They were in Zangrian territory, and King Caron had just betrayed them. There was no trace of King Thoran, his Nobles, or his Magi. They must have fled north, toward Norghana.

General Rangulself was talking to General Olagson about the best route to take to leave Zangrian land as fast as they could. General Odir was gathering supplies for the return, urging his soldiers with shouts. The Zangrian soldiers could appear at any moment. The Invincibles were licking their wounds. Of the four armies, the Invincibles were those with the least casualties. They still had two thousand, five hundred units. The Thunder Army and the Snow Army had been reduced to half with only two thousand survivors. The Blizzard Army only had a thousand soldiers left.

A little to one side, keeping their distance, were the nine thousand men of the Western League who had suffered the least losses in the battle. They were breaking camp and preparing to go back. The Nobles of the West with Erikson and Svensen in the lead kept their eyes on the king's armies, as well as on Egil.

Raner organized the Rangers to keep watch around the armies in case they were attacked by any of the other kingdoms. He also sent scouts to secure a way back to Norghana, through the Thousand Lakes to the west. They had to go up toward Norghana but not through Zangrian territory. He sent Luca to search for traces of King Thoran's group.

Luca returned just as the Norghanian armies were starting out.

"They've ridden to the west," he informed.

"Good, it's the less dangerous escape route," Raner commented.

"Did you see anything else?" Egil asked Luca.

"They've split up. The Ice Magi haven't followed the King."

"They must have lost them," Ingrid said.

"The Ice Magi are incapable of following the trail of a skunk in heat," Nilsa said.

"And there's another thing… more serious…" Luca said.

"What's that?" Raner asked him.

"There's evidence of fighting and blood, right on the way out of Zangrian territory."

"That's not good news," the First Ranger was concerned.

"Several riders managed to continue north, but there were casualties, quite a few," said Luca.

"An ambush?" Raner asked.

"I'm afraid so, sir. A strong force came out of the trees and attacked them."

"Did you see bodies?" Raner wanted to know.

"No, sir. They've been taken, but from the footprints on the ground, the fallen were from the Royal Guard."

"That was an ambush. They were waiting for them, they knew they'd be fleeing that way," Raner guessed.

"Do you know whether the King escaped?"

Luca shook his head.

"I couldn't tell."

Raner took a deep breath.

"Let's hope he managed to."

"We should get going," Molak warned suddenly. "They're coming."

"Zangrians?"

"Yes, it seems the battle's over. Erenal is retreating with what's left of the legions, and the rest of their allies are doing the same."

"Then Irinel must have withdrawn too," Raner guessed.

"We'd better make sure," Lasgol said, "I'll go and check."

"I'll come with you," said Astrid.

"Hurry up, time is of the essence," Ingrid told them.

Lasgol looked at Egil and his friend nodded. Lasgol noticed that Egil did not seem in much of a hurry.

Lasgol and Astrid went into the forest to the northeast. As soon as they did, Lasgol received the message.

Be here.

Lasgol stopped.

"Camu and Ona are here," he told Astrid.

The two appeared a little further north and came over.

"Camu! Ona! You're so handsome!" Astrid said as she hastened to pet them both.

I handsome. Ona too, Camu messaged to her.

"Yes, without a doubt."

I much good battle.

"What does he mean?" Astrid asked,

"He's been protecting the first ranks of the Western League Army with his anti-magic dome."

I stop balls of fire.

"Wow, that's quite impressive."

Much impressive. Magi of Fire no can burn us.

Ona whimpered.

"Egil was right about the Erenalian Magi. He placed you at the right spot to save the Western soldiers. They would've been charred alive if Camu hadn't been there."

"Very well done, Camu."

"Let's go, we have to see what the forces of Irinel are doing."

The four went on at a run toward the east, to the war camp of Irinel where their forces were regrouping.

"There they are," Lasgol said, lying low.

They all stopped and watched.

Kylian and Heulyn were talking while their generals were regrouping the troops. They were healing the wounded. A dozen Druids were helping with the healing. The army of Irinel still had over fifteen-thousand-foot soldiers, ready to fight.

"I wonder whether they'll go home through the north or come through Norghana," said Lasgol.

"You say this because of the Druid Queen?" Astrid asked.

"Yeah, because of her."

"I doubt he'll yield his throne."

"It's Thoran's for as long as he lives," said Lasgol.

At that moment, from among the trees a hooded figure armed with a bow appeared.

Astrid and Lasgol turned toward her and aimed their bows.

The figure pushed back the hood. A blonde mane of hair and large blue eyes proclaimed who she was.

"Valeria," said Lasgol.

"What do you want?" Astrid said coldly.

Valeria smiled.

"I have only one moment, Lasgol. That which you asked me about, I'm confirming now." And with these words, she turned and left.

Astrid looked at Lasgol.

"What was that about?"

"We have to warn Egil."

Lasgol was telling Egil what had happened while the Norghanian armies were starting out toward Norghana, taking their wounded with them while the dead were left behind.

The Western Army remained behind, awaiting instructions.

First Ranger Raner approached Egil and Lasgol.

"We must return to Norghana," he told them. "We don't know what's happened to the King, but we must operate under the assumption that he got away."

"We'd like to search a little more about the possible whereabouts of the King, if you please," Egil asked Raner.

"You think he might not have managed to escape?" Raner asked worried.

"I have a hunch about that, yes," Egil said.

Raner looked at the Panthers.

"Fine, you have my permission. Find out everything you can and come back fast to report. Don't get caught."

"We won't, sir," Egil promised.

Raner left with Molak, Luca, and other Rangers, who had remained in the rear.

Once alone, Egil went over to the Western Army as they waited. He spoke in whispers to the Nobles. They nodded and left.

The war camp was deserted. Only the dead remained.

"And now what? Another battle or betrayal?" said Viggo with sarcasm.

"Now, we have a meeting to attend," said Egil.

"Here?" Ingrid said, surprised.

Egil pointed behind him toward Zangria.

The others did not know what to say.

It was midnight when the meeting took place. In the middle of the forest beside a lake in the shape of a half moon, Egil was waiting with an oil lamp in one hand. From the forest, a figure appeared, accompanied by six bodyguards.

"Good evening, Egil," the Druid Queen greeted him as she pushed back her hood, revealing her face.

"My lady," Egil replied courteously.

"I did not know I had someone so important among my Royal Eagles. You should have told me."

"I'm not someone important, just a Ranger," Egil replied modestly. "There was nothing to say."

"Intelligent and reserved, those are good qualities. You are the King of the West, and you lead the nobles of the Western League."

"I am a son of the West and of Norghana."

"When we negotiated this alliance, I did not know it was you who was behind the West. I thought it was Erikson or Svensen. I did not find out until just recently. You hid it very well."

"In the game of treason, it's more prudent not to show oneself."

"That's true. How did you know I would accept?"

"I didn't. I hoped King Caron would be persuasive."

"And I was, wasn't I, dear Druid Queen?" a voice with a strong accent said in Norghanian.

King Caron of Zangria appeared, accompanied by General Zorberg. Behind them were a dozen soldiers, two of which had a prisoner, hand-tied and gagged.

"Most persuasive and convincing."

"As Egil was with General Zorberg, and then with me," King Caron admitted.

"I did my best," admitted Egil.

Good evening, my intelligent allies," Caron greeted them.

"Your Majesty," Egil bowed.

"King Caron," Heulyn bowed as well.

"Bring him," the King said to his soldiers. "Leave him in the middle."

The soldiers left the prisoner in the center of the three speakers. It was none other than Thoran himself. His hands were tied behind his back, and he had been beaten.

"My beloved husband, what happened to you? You look awful," Heulyn said in a voice filled with sarcasm.

"He tried to escape, just as you said he would," Caron said. "And the way Egil calculated he would escape. We had a pretty ambush prepared for him. Several, in fact. We caught Thoran, and Orten, and the rest of the nobles fled. His guard, unfortunately, was eliminated, they almost all fell. We let a few wounded go, Ellingsen among them."

"It was the best route to return to Norghana," Egil said modestly. "I gave you three possible ways of escape just in case."

"It's a joy when a plan as elaborate as ours," Caron indicated Heulyn, Egil, and himself, "within another elaborate plan, that of Kendryk's, Thoran, and mine, turns out so well," he admitted.

Thoran struggled on the ground and tried to insult them, but the gag prevented him.

"Now that Thoran has fallen, and Kendryk too, because I guess Kylian will reign in Irinel…"

"He will," his sister confirmed.

"… Good. and I guess one of you will reign in Norghana…"

"I will reign," said Heulyn determinedly.

"That's inconsequential to me," said Caron. "We wanted Thoran, and we have him. Besides, Norghana is weakened once again, which is something that's good for me," Caron said with a grin. "I can't have two strong neighbors, one to the north and the other to the south. It's bad for my people's health. Now both Norghana and Erenal are weakened, whereas I haven't lost too many forces. It's been a very satisfactory battle. Besides, Irinel now has additional trouble with Moontian, so they'll be dealing with constant skirmishes and even a war after what's happened here today. Queen Niria won't be able to help the King of Erenal, which once again benefits me. With the added bonus of witnessing the fall of two of the most important, vain kings, which is something you don't see every day. I think everything has turned out very well."

"For Zangria and her King, without a doubt," said Heulyn.

"What do you want me to do with him?" Caron asked, indicating

Thoran kneeling on the ground.

"He could've killed me when he took the throne after Uthar's death. I won't kill him here today," Egil said firmly.

King Caron nodded.

"Very well. I respect your wish."

A snort of relief emerged from either side of the gag.

"I do want him killed. I need him dead in order to reign!" the Druid Queen said." I demand his head."

A look of horror appeared on Thoran's face.

"Dead or in prison," Caron corrected her. "You could be the Regent while your husband rots in my royal dungeons."

"It will be easier for me to reign if he's dead," Heulyn said.

"Probably, but I'm not going to kill him. I'd rather have him in my dungeons. Whether the King of the West or the Druid Queen reigns in Norghana, it's a problem for both if Thoran continues alive, so I'm keeping him, to exert a little pressure to ensure a prosperous relationship in the future," Caron smiled.

"That sounds like blackmail," said Heulyn.

"That's exactly what it is. If my wishes are not granted, I can free him and make your life quite complicated," Caron threatened. "Take him," he told his soldiers, who grabbed Thoran and dragged him away.

"And now, I must return to my duties. It's been a pleasure to deal with such intelligent and skillful people," the King of Zangria said and left.

Egil, Heulyn, and her bodyguards were left alone in the clearing.

A tense silence fell on them.

Chapter 49

"It seems everything has gone as planned, except that I wanted Thoran dead," the Druid Queen said.

"Considering the difficulty of the plan and the innumerable uncertainties, the result has been very satisfactory," Egil replied.

"Yes, and now there's only a small stumbling block before I can reign in Norghana."

"I understand that you're referring to me."

"Yes, I am. I can't let the King of the West live when he wants to take my throne, as you can understand."

The bodyguards pushed back their hoods, and Egil saw five Druids and Valeria.

"I don't see Aidan with the Druids you've brought to kill me. Why not?"

"Aidan didn't want to be a part of my ascent to power. He did not agree with betraying my father or with killing you. I had to put him in prison. I don't like the weak of heart who are always looking for a balance between forces. Sometimes some forces are unstoppable," she said, indicating herself.

"I'm sorry to hear that. He's a good man."

"So are you, but you must die so I can reign. I won't let the Western League take the throne from me. Kill him!" she ordered, pointing her finger at Egil.

Valeria raised her bow and aimed at Egil.

The five Druids began to cast a spell on Egil, who remained still, looking at the Queen.

The Druids finished casting their spell on Egil. The first of the Druids sent a dozen stakes straight at his body. The second Druid made a thick oak trunk appear out of thin air, which he dropped on Egil to crush him. The third made three wolves appear that lunged at Egil. The fourth called upon a bear that delivered two blows with its claws to disembowel him, and the fifth threw a thick branch with a sharp tip straight at him, designed to run him through.

All the spells died when they hit the anti-magic dome surrounding Egil. The animals vanished upon touching the barrier. The missiles and tree did too. They hit the dome, there was a flash of silver, and the spells died.

Beside Egil, Camu, in his invisible state, had canceled all their spells.

Before Valeria could release her arrow, an Elemental Earth Arrow hit her in the middle of her forehead. The tip broke on impact, and as her head was thrown backward the burst of earth, smoke, dust, and a stunning substance enveloped her face. Nilsa had taken her from a distance of two hundred paces, high up in one of the trees.

"Treachery! What's this? Kill them!" the Queen shouted.

From the thicket behind the Queen, two dozen soldiers of Irinel came out armed with shields and javelins. They were the Queen's guard.

The first to fall were the Druids. Five arrows from the forest hit them. They were Elemental Earth Arrows, which left them stunned and confused. They did not even see where they had come from, since the Panthers were all hiding in the forest. These five arrows were followed by five subsequent Air Arrows, and the discharges knocked them out.

The Queen's guard went straight for Egil, who was still in the same place, not moving. From Egil's side flew three Fire Arrows, which hit the first soldiers and upon detonation burst into flames and made the soldiers throw themselves on the ground and roll over to put out the flames on their clothes. The next soldiers came three paces away from Egil and threw their javelins at him.

"You're dead!" the Druid Queen cried triumphantly.

The javelins were heading straight at Egil's chest, but they hit something before reaching him and dropped to the ground. The soldiers gaped in disbelief. Stepping forward, Lasgol appeared, covered in his *Woodland Protection.* Camu had kept him invisible. Lasgol used his *Multiple Shot* skill and knocked down the three soldiers with one shot.

Five more arrows came from different parts of the forest and knocked down five other soldiers running toward Lasgol and Egil. Lasgol handed his bow to Egil and grabbed Aodh's Bow from his back. They both released at once against two other soldiers.

"Finish them! Eliminate all!" the Queen yelled furiously.

At that instant, from one side of the forest Astrid appeared with her knives in her hands and lunged at three soldiers at lightning speed. From the other side of the forest came Viggo, also at top speed, and with a leap he lunged at four enemies. The soldiers, taken by surprise by the lightning-fast attacks, were knocked down.

Gerd appeared a moment later with knife and axe, accompanied by Ona, and he went to help Lasgol and Egil who were still releasing. He went toward the soldiers and attacked them. Ona followed suit and fell on the Irinelians.

Nilsa was releasing over and over with her anti-mage arrows, which burst against the Druids as they were trying to get up from the ground and attack again. She stunned them, preventing them from concentrating enough to conjure. On her own she was able to keep them under control. Every time one of them recovered, she stunned him again with an arrow to the torso or the head.

Valeria recovered and stood in front of the Queen, covering her with her body.

"Behind me, my Queen," she said.

Heulyn got behind Valeria.

"Kill Egil!" she ordered her.

"Yes, my lady." Valeria aimed at Egil.

She was hit full in the chest with an Air Arrow. Valeria began to convulse and fell to the ground. From the bushes came Ingrid, aiming at the Druid Queen.

Astrid and Viggo dealt with the seven soldiers they had fallen upon in the blink of an eye. They were no rivals for them. With accurate cuts, the Assassins poisoned them, leaving their legs and arms half-paralyzed, unable to continue fighting. They finished the soldiers off a moment later.

Gerd took care of several soldiers with tremendous blows, making their shields fly off in the air. Ona knocked down soldiers with her powerful leaps to then finish them on the ground.

And suddenly, no one was left beside the Queen, who was still standing in the forest clearing.

"Curse you! You're my servants! You have to serve me! I'm your Queen!"

The Panthers surrounded the Druid Queen.

Ingrid, who was aiming at her heart, said, "I'm afraid that's not true anymore."

"We serve the true King of Norghana," Nilsa said.

"The one who must reign by right of succession," Astrid added.

"Our friend," said Lasgol.

"Who deserves to be King and will do a great job," said Gerd.

"To sum up, the little wise-guy who's played you all," said Viggo.

The Druid Queen, finding herself surrounded and defeated, broke down and fell on her knees.

"Don't kill me, I beg you!"

"Yeah, sure, you say that now. Like you didn't want to kill all of us," Viggo replied.

"You're a risk to me," said Egil.

"I won't be! I'll go back to Irinel with my brother!"

"Yeah, so that you can come back with your brother's army to claim the throne of Norghana," Astrid said.

"I won't! I'll stay in Irinel! In my own land!"

Egil looked into her eyes.

"I don't believe you, your greed and ambition are insatiable. You'd try and get the throne of Norghana again, and that throne is mine."

"Don't kill me!"

Egil made a sign to Astrid. The Assassin showed him her two knives. Egil shook his head and Astrid nodded. She took out a scarf, poured a substance on it, and put it over the Druid Queen's mouth and nose. She dropped, unconscious, on the ground.

"This has been most entertaining," Viggo said, smiling.

I cancel magic, Camu messaged to all very proudly.

"You did great," Lasgol congratulated him.

"Without you, my plan wouldn't have worked," Egil admitted.

"Which of your plans are you referring to?" Gerd asked with a smile.

"Several, in fact," Egil smiled as well.

I much good spy, Camu messaged.

"Astrid, you can retire, your post has been covered," Viggo joked.

Astrid smiled.

"Camu is extraordinary in many aspects."

I much extraordinary, yes.

"And he seems to have Viggo's ego sometimes," Nilsa said, laughing.

"So, what are we going to do with her?" Lasgol asked Egil.

Egil sighed.

"Kill her and end the problem," Viggo suggested.

"We can't kill her in cold blood," Nilsa refused.

"She attacked us first, hoping to kill us. It's within our rights," Ingrid stated.

"I wouldn't feel good killing her in cold blood..." Gerd admitted.

"I'm with Gerd, I can't see us killing her either," Lasgol said.

Egil raised his hands.

"We must look forward, to the future, to what's best for Norghana. Killing her now will free us of a direct enemy. But there would be repercussions. Irinel, her brother Kylian, would never forget us and would make us pay. We don't need to have Irinel as an enemy, not now that Norghana is so weakened."

"Then what do we do with her?" Lasgol asked.

"I've been thinking about it for days, what to do at this point... and believe me, in many of the scenarios that went through my mind, we never got to this point."

"We died before," Gerd said.

Egil smiled.

"Let's leave it at 'we failed before getting here.'"

"So, what should we do?" Lasgol asked him.

"The best move I see for now is not to kill her, but to deliver her to Queen Niria of Moontian instead. Irinel and Moontian are rivals and are practically at war, more so after this battle, where they were both on opposite sides. We deliver the Druid Queen to the Queen of Moontian, and that way Irinel won't be able to attack Moontian without risking them killing their Princess. At the same time, we agree with Queen Niria to keep her hostage and convince Irinel not to attack Norghana. As long as the Druid Queen is in the hands of Moontian, her brother Kylian won't attack either Moontian or Norghana."

"I have to say that when you get diabolical, you excel at it," Viggo said with a slap on Egil's back.

"This would never have occurred to me in a thousand years, but I think it's a wonderful way out," Ingrid said.

"We get rid of her, she's imprisoned in the depths of the mountains, and we make sure that Irinel doesn't attack us... I think it's fantastic," said Nilsa.

"A marvelous strategy," Lasgol nodded.

"Thank you... for not killing her..." said a voice coming to.

The Panthers turned with their weapons ready.

Valeria had woken up and was getting to her feet with difficulty.

"Let me help you," Nilsa said, helping her to stand.

"You had to hit me in the middle of my forehead?" she protested, feeling the lump she had there.

"That way it was more convincing," Nilsa apologized.

"Thanks for the warning. You've saved my life," Egil said gratefully with a bow.

"Yeah, we're really grateful," said Lasgol.

"I owed it to you, for letting me live when you could've punished my betrayal with death. Now we're even," she said as she held her head in her hands in obvious pain.

"Yes, we're even. The past is buried," Egil said.

"It appears I'm out of a job," Valeria said, looking at the Druid Queen unconscious on the ground.

"Maybe you need a new one," Egil offered her.

"What would the new job be?" Valeria asked, raising an eyebrow.

"Spying for the new King of Norghana," Egil said as he jabbed his own chest with his thumb.

"Sounds good. What would I have to do?"

"Considering that no one knows that you've helped us, I want you to go to Irinel and tell Kylian what's happened here and his sister's fate. I also want you to let me know of any movement of Irinel that's against the interests of Norghana."

Valeria thought for a long moment.

"Agreed. You've just found yourself a spy for your cause."

Egil offered her his hand, and she shook it.

"If you do it well, who knows, you might end up being one of us," Egil offered.

"That would be great."

"No way!" Astrid protested.

Valeria smiled.

"Go, be convincing," Egil told Valeria.

"I will be."

Valeria nodded at each one, as if returning the favor received by the Panthers, and then she left.

"Who'd have thought that the little blonde would come through," Viggo commented with sarcasm.

"I knew she wouldn't betray us," said Gerd. "She has a good heart, as hard to believe as it is."

"She surprised me, in a good way," Ingrid admitted. "If it weren't for her, Egil would've fallen into an ambush and died."

"Now she's one of us," said Lasgol.

"Not entirely," Astrid specified, frowning.

"And what do we do now?" Gerd asked.

"Now we return to Norghana and take the throne," Egil said with absolute conviction.

Chapter 50

The morning brought snow and cold winds from the north. The sky was covered with dark clouds that threatened a coming storm. Egil breathed in the cold, wintry air and felt better. It smelled of winter, of Norghana. He rode to the south gate of the great walled city of Norghania, capital of Norghana. He found the gates shut with the soldiers of the four armies inside and crowding the battlements.

He sighed. He looked back and saw Dukes Erikson and Svensen, Counts Malason, Bjorn, Axel, Harald, and the rest of the nobles and lords of the West and a host of nearly fifteen thousand soldiers belonging to their duchies and counties. While the four armies had gone to take shelter in the capital to recover from the defeat at the battlefield, the Western Nobles had gone back to their domains and had recruited everyone who could wield a weapon. Egil had asked them to do so when they had parted ways in Zangria. They had the opportunity of recovering the crown for the West, and they were not going to lose it.

Egil greeted his Nobles with a bow, and they returned the greeting. He knew that these nobles and their troops would follow him to the death, and he could not be prouder. He reflected on the situation. There were only two options: a peaceful one, with less probabilities of success, in which they gave him the crown; and a violent option where he would have to lay siege to the city and take it by force with his troops. They would soon know which of them would occur. In any case, they had come this far, and now they had to finish what they had started.

The city behind the tall walls of Norghanian rock rose imposingly. The falling snow and the winter weather did nothing but add character to this city which represented the soul of the realm.

Egil made a signal, and the Western Nobles took their places behind him. They moved forward until they were six hundred paces from the walls.

They stopped.

They waited.

The gates of the city opened and about twenty riders came out.

Egil and the Western Nobles waited for the riders to approach. Once they were close enough, Egil recognized them. They were Count Volgren, the most powerful Noble of the East, and with him were Generals Rangulself, Olagson, and Odir. The rest were escort soldiers.

"Good day, Lords of the West," Count Volgren greeted them courteously but with a serious look on his face.

"Good day to you, Count," Egil returned the greeting with a slight bow of his head.

"Will it be a good day, or will we have bloodshed?" General Odir of the Blizzard Army asked.

"Odir, control yourself, please," Count Volgren told him.

"You'd better," Duke Erikson advised him in a hard tone.

Odir was about to say something, but General Olagson grabbed him by the arm.

"The situation is tense enough already, there's no need to increase hostilities," Count Volgren said.

"Very true. The best we can do in this situation is to keep calm," Egil said in a friendly tone. "We're all aware of what's at stake and how volatile the situation is."

"Yes, we are," General Rangulself of the Thunder Army agreed.

"In that case, we'd better speak clearly," Duke Svensen suggested.

"What do the Western Nobles want?" Volgren asked.

"To restore the legitimate King to the throne of Norghana," said Erikson.

"Egil Olafstone," added Svensen.

"Norghana already has a King and Queen," said Volgren. "The throne is theirs."

"Thoran has fallen. So has the Druid Queen. They will not be coming back to Norghana," Erikson informed them.

Volgren wrinkled his nose and then exchanged glances with his generals.

"What certainty do we have that it is indeed true?" Rangulself asked.

"Thoran and his brother are in the dungeons of King Caron in Zangria. Heulyn is in a prison of Queen Niria's in the mountains of Moontian," Egil informed them.

"Have they been captured? Are we sure of that? There's been no demand for ransom," said Volgren.

"And there never will be. They'll never get out of where they are now," Egil said firmly.

The three generals looked at one another with contradictory expressions.

"You already knew about Thoran's situation. Commander Ellingsen informed you of the ambush they suffered," Egil said.

"True, that is the case."

"And we have just informed you of what has happened to the Queen," Egil continued.

"The fact that the King and Queen are not present doesn't mean they're no longer the King and Queen," said Volgren. "We'll negotiate their liberation, pay whatever amount of gold is asked, and bring them back."

"Only we're not going to do that," Erikson corrected him.

"We won't negotiate their ransom because we're going to crown a new King, the legitimate King," said Svensen.

"Thoran is the legitimate King, whether he's in prison or not," Volgren insisted.

"We have an army that says otherwise," Erikson threatened him.

The generals became uneasy and wriggled in their saddles.

Egil raised his hand to calm things down.

"We've already been through a civil war with my father and brothers. I'd rather avoid another one if possible. The East is never going to acknowledge me as King of Norghana, and the West is never going to acknowledge Thoran as such. This leads us inexorably to armed confrontation and to further weaken an already weakened kingdom, especially after the recent defeat."

"You may leave in peace. There's no need for any bloodshed," Volgren proposed.

"But I can't do that," Egil shook his head. "I can't do it because of them," he said with a wave of his hand at the fifteen thousand soldiers of the West. "I can't do it because of my nobles, I can't do it because of my late family, and I can't do it because of me. I am going to be King, by right, by blood, and by strength. You may accept it and prevent another war, or you may refuse and die. It's in your hands."

"You bring strong words," Volgren said with a grim look on his face.

"The words of a King," Egil relied in a dry tone.

"The army doesn't enter into disputes of succession or about the crown," said General Rangulself.

"We serve the King, the one on the throne," Olagson said.

"And we kill whoever intends to take it," Odir added.

"That's the question. I'm not taking the throne from anyone, I'm going to take it because it's vacant," Egil said.

"That's a subjective way of interpreting what's happening here," Volgren replied.

"No, it isn't. There's no one sitting on the throne, and there isn't going to be anyone because the King and Queen are in enemy hands, enemies who won't return them for any amount of gold. They have no descendants, therefore the throne is deserted."

The generals looked at one another again. This explanation had befuddled them.

"Don't listen to those twisted words," Volgren said. "We'll pay the ransom and get the King and Queen back."

"And if they don't agree to the payment? Then what? Someone from the East will take the crown? Thoran's second cousins? That won't happen. The West won't allow it. Never," Erikson said.

Before Volgren could reply, Egil spoke.

"You have three days to talk it through and reach a decision. We'll camp here. If in three days, at dawn, these gates open and I'm hailed as the new monarch, there will be no bloodshed. If the gates remain shut, we'll lay siege to the city, and we'll take it. You four won't live to tell the tale, because it will have been in your hands to prevent it by crowning the true King."

Volgren and the other three generals were quiet.

Rangulself spoke after a moment.

"You'll have your answer in three days, Egil Olafstone."

The riders turned and returned to the city.

"What do you think they'll decide?" Erikson asked Egil.

"The Nobles of the East will refuse, they won't accept," said Svensen.

"The final decision will depend on the generals," said Egil. "They lead the armies, and it'll be them and their troops who will do the fighting and dying."

"I hope they make the right decision."

"So do I, but we'll see," Egil said, glancing at the great walls.

It was the wee hours of the third day, and come dawn Egil would have his answer. While the forces of the West camped and watched in front of the city, Astrid and Viggo were entering the rooms of Queen Heulyn through the secret passage the Queen had used to go in and out with the Druids and which they knew of. They moved with absolute stealth and, covered by the shadows, searched the rooms. They were deserted. They went on and searched that whole wing of the royal castle. They found no guards. The Irinelians had left with the Queen, and the Norghanians were too worried with the force outside the walls to patrol an area that was now uninhabited.

They made sure the area was clear and then went back for the rest of the Panthers who were waiting in the passage. Ingrid, Nilsa, Gerd, and Lasgol entered the castle. They were all wearing black clothes and cloaks and a scarf that covered their mouth and nose. Only their eyes were visible.

"Clear," Viggo whispered.

"We'll deal with it, you wait here," Viggo said.

"Okay."

Camu, Ona, are you here with us? Lasgol asked them.

We here, rearguard.

Very well.

Astrid and Viggo vanished, each going down a different corridor. The rest waited for their comrades to return. They did after a good while.

"Very well, all clear," Viggo said.

"You'll find a few unconscious guards we had to deal with," Astrid warned them.

"Everyone ready?" Viggo asked.

"Ready," Ingrid nodded.

"Well, let's go then," said Astrid.

All the Panthers left the room, crouching and in silence.

Viggo put the knife on Count Volgren's throat. At the touch of the cold steel on his skin, he opened his eyes. He saw the Assassin over him on the bed and panic overwhelmed him.

"Don't kill me!"

"Shut up and listen, because you're risking your life."

"Yes… I'm listening, but don't kill me."

"The truth is that I'd rather kill you, but I've been told to only give you a message, which is a shame."

"What… message?"

"At dawn, you'll get together with all the Nobles of the East in the castle, the three generals, and the Ice Magi, and you'll tell them all that the best thing for Norghana is to avoid bloodshed and let Egil become King."

"I…. no…"

"You may choose. You either do this, or I'll slit your throat. I have to insist that I prefer the latter."

Count Volgren did not want to accept—it showed in his eyes that he was resisting the idea. He did not want to give the throne to Egil.

"Tomorrow…"

"One more thing. If you accept and don't follow through, I'll come back, and when I do, there will be no chatter. I'll slit you throat, end of business."

"No…"

"Besides, I'll tell you a secret. I can kill you in your sleep whenever I want, like tonight."

"All… right… Egil… will reign…"

"That's the way I like it. Don't disappoint me," Viggo threatened as he leapt to his feet and left through the door.

At that same instant, the rest of the Panthers were delivering the same message to half a dozen Nobles of the East, the most important ones, in their rooms. Egil had decided to make sure there would not be another blood bath between the East and West. This was ending at dawn, and it was going to end without any more deaths.

Once their mission had ended, the Panthers left the castle through the secret passage and waited for dawn.

Chapter 51

Dawn arrived on the morning of the third day. The hosts of the West prepared for battle. The Nobles rode with Egil in the lead and covered the six hundred paces, as they had done three days before.

The gates remained shut.

They waited.

"They're not giving us the throne," Duke Svensen told Egil.

"We'll have to take it," Duke Erikson said.

"Let's wait a little longer," pleaded Count Malason.

Egil nodded at the Count's plea.

"We'll wait, there's always time for fighting."

At mid-morning, when the hopes of the West were beginning to vanish, the gates opened suddenly. Count Volgren, the three generals, and their escort came out of the city on horseback.

"Let's see what their answer is," said Erikson.

"Let's hope they decide with their heads," Malason said.

The group reached them and stopped.

"Good day, Lords of the West," the Count greeted them.

"Count, Generals," Egil greeted them with a slight bow of the head.

"We have confirmed that the King and Queen are in enemy hands, as you informed us," Count Volgren said. "We have also confirmed that no ransoms will be asked for their release."

"Which leads us to the war with Zangria and Moontian," General Olagson said.

"Not necessarily," Egil corrected him.

"Why not?" General Odir asked upset.

"There won't be war with Zangria and Moontian if I'm crowned King," Egil said.

"How can you guarantee such a statement?" Rangulself asked.

"Because he plotted the capture of the King and Queen, just like the betrayal of Zangria and Irinel," Count Volgren said.

Egil neither admitted nor denied it.

"What's the answer? The time I gave you is over," Egil demanded in a firm tone.

The generals and Volgren exchanged glances.

"In the absence of a king, the generals of the Norghanian armies do not take sides one way or another in the fight for the succession and the throne. It's a political matter, not a military one," General Rangulself said. "We will stay on the sidelines. We'll serve the king, be he the old one or the new."

"Do the other two generals confirm this?" Egil asked.

"We do," said Olagson. "We don't need another war that will bleed us out until we're dry. We've already suffered enough casualties."

Odir nodded reluctantly.

"Then we have the Nobles of the East and the Invincibles who serve them," Egil looked at Volgren.

The Count heaved a deep sigh.

"Without the support of the armies, and with the very persuasive night visit early this morning, the Nobles of the East will not offer any resistance. We only ask for one condition in exchange."

"I'm listening," said Egil.

"There will be no retaliation against the Nobles of the East," Volgren asked. "The nobles who have supported Thoran will not be killed, or imprisoned, or punished personally or economically. We will be allowed to return to our domains without prejudice, and alive."

"No way!" Svensen protested. "They'll suffer, just like we've suffered under Thoran."

"The punishment must be equal to what we received!" Erikson declared.

Egil raised his hand to calm them down.

"As you see, my Nobles don't agree to these terms. But, I'll grant you what you ask to avoid greater evils. Put it in writing, and I'll sign it."

Erikson and Svensen were about to protest, but Egil motioned them to be silent.

"This isn't a time for revenge," he told them. "It's time to come to the throne."

The two Nobles understood and nodded.

"Very well. I'll write the terms for your signature. The throne is yours, Egil Olafstone," Volgren said in a defeated tone.

"We'll prepare the entrance of the new King," said General

Rangulself.

The group returned to the city.

The Nobles of the West were looking at one another, unable to believe they had achieved victory without any bloodshed.

"Did we make it?" Erikson asked with wide eyes.

"It looks that way," Egil replied with a triumphant gleam in his eyes.

"I can't believe it," Svensen said.

"After all this time…" said Malason.

At noon, the armies of the three generals came out of the city, whose gates remained open. Rangulself with the Thunder Army stood on the right of the great gate. Olagson and the Snow Army stood on the left, Odir and the Blizzard Army also on the right, after the Thunder Army. Then came the Invincibles of the Ice, with Olagson in command, and they stood on the left in front of the Snow Army. They formed a corridor between the four armies toward the gate so Egil and the forces of the West could enter to receive homage.

"The armies have come out of the city," Erikson said, still not fully believing it.

"They're handing it to us," said Svensen, having trouble believing it too.

"They're doing it to avoid more bloodshed," said Malason.

The rest of the Nobles and Lords of the West started to cheer and acclaim Egil and the West. Their joy was unbelievable. Only a few days before they were all going to die on the front lines of battle, sacrificed by a king who wanted them dead. Now they were going to enter the capital triumphantly and crown a new King—Egil, the King of the West.

"For the West!" they cheered, raising their weapons.

"For the throne! For the new King!" they shouted at the top of their voices.

"For the King of the West!" they cheered.

"For Egil, King of Norghana!" cried fifteen thousand voices, and their shouts were heard leagues away.

Egil gave the order, and they went forward. He was in the lead, surrounded by Dukes Svensen and Erikson, Counts Malason, Bjorn, Axel, Harald, the rest of the Lords, and the fifteen thousand soldiers of the West who all wore blue and black and formed a long line ten units wide. They arrived where the four armies were formed and went along the corridor they had made for them. Egil nodded at Count Volgren, who returned the nod, bowing his head and not lifting it in a show of respect. Egil saluted Generals Rangulself, Olagson, and Odir the same way, and they also bowed their heads.

Egil and his forces crossed the gates of the city. Word of what was happening had spread throughout the city, and its inhabitants, fearful, were looking out of windows and doors without daring to come out in the streets. They had already lived through a civil war, and the winner this time was of the West, so they were afraid of retaliation, although this time there would be none. Egil was not going to punish the people for the mistakes of their government. Only the leaders were responsible.

They went up the main avenue, and as they passed by and the citizens saw there was nothing to fear, they started flooding out into the streets. By the time they reached the royal castle, a large crowd was watching the forces of the West as they passed by. The gates of the castle, like those of the walls, were open, and the soldiers and the diminished Royal Guard were lined up in the inner courtyard in front of the entrance to the main building. Beside the Tower of the Magi, Maldreck and his Ice Magi were lined up. At the other tower, the Rangers' Tower, Gondabar, Raner, and the Rangers who were at the castle were also lined up.

Egil and the Western forces entered and occupied the whole bailey. The rest of his forces remained outside the castle, waiting. There was not room for all of them inside.

Egil stopped before the few remaining Royal Guards, led by Ellingsen, who had an arm and a leg in splinters.

"Commander Ellingsen," Egil nodded at him.

"My Lord," Ellingsen replied, bowing his head.

"I'm glad you did not die."

"Thank you, my Lord."

"I understand you are aware of the situation."

"Yes, my Lord."

"Do you wish to remain in your post, or would you prefer to be replaced?"

Ellingsen looked at the Nobles of the West, then at Egil.

"I serve the King of Norghana and the Kingdom. I will serve you," he said and got down on one knee with a grimace of pain.

"I accept your loyalty," Egil said and motioned him to get up.

The Nobles of the West were whispering, worried. Ellingsen was a lesser noble of the East. Giving him the leadership of the King's Guard was dangerous. Egil looked at them and made a gesture that meant he understood their concern.

"I know what I'm doing," he assured them.

Egil led his horse to the Tower of the Magi. The Nobles and a few hundred soldiers followed him.

"Maldreck," Egil said without formalities.

"My Lord," Maldreck made a bow.

"I am? Am I your Lord?"

"Of course, Your Majesty."

"Do you swear fealty?"

"Of course, my Lord." Maldreck got down on one knee, and when he did the other five Ice Magi did the same.

"I hope you will serve me with loyalty and honor."

"So we shall," Maldreck said.

Egil nodded, although he knew the venomous snake only served himself and his own interests. It was not the time to deal with Maldreck's hidden treachery, and he needed the Ice Magi.

The last stop was before the Tower of the Rangers.

"Gondabar, Raner, I'm pleased to see you," Egil said.

"And we're happy to see you. Forgive me, to see our Lord," Gondabar corrected himself.

Egil smiled.

"I need your loyalty. I don't demand it, but I need the Rangers with me to be able to reign."

Gondabar sighed. "The Rangers serve the King and Norghana. If Egil Olafstone is the new King, we'll serve him with honor and loyalty," Gondabar promised.

"Raner?"

The First Ranger nodded.

"I'll serve you with honor and loyalty," he said and dropped to one knee.

Then Gondabar did the same with difficulty, leaning on his staff. The rest of the Rangers followed their leaders' example.

"Thank you all," Egil said.

Satisfied, Egil dismounted, and with him all the Nobles of the West. He headed for the Throne Hall. The Royal Guard made a corridor, and Ellingsen accompanied him. Raner joined him and also accompanied Egil.

They entered the Throne Hall and walked down the large corridor. The hall was empty with the exception of six figures standing beside the throne. Ingrid, Nilsa, Astrid, Lasgol, Gerd, and Viggo were waiting with big smiles on their faces. Egil walked toward them, unable to stop smiling.

Egil reached his friends and nodded at each one of them.

"Thank you, for everything," he told them with his hand on his heart. "I'd never have done this without you."

"Yes you would, but it would've cost you a bit more," Gerd replied with a huge smile.

"It's been a pleasure and an honor," Lasgol said, also smiling and moved.

"Today is a great day for all of Norghana," Nilsa said with great happiness.

"Today, at last, Norghana has her true King—noble, fair, honest, and honorable," Astrid said proudly.

"A King in his own right, by blood, who will rule with honor, intelligence, and wisdom," Ingrid said seriously.

"I'm going to keep calling you names, you know that, right? Even if you're king and all," Viggo told him.

Egil smiled.

"I'll grant you that boon, it'll be my first mandate."

"Your Majesty," Ingrid said, indicating the throne.

Egil heaved a deep sigh and, lifting his head, he sat in the throne.

Everyone in the hall, which was now crowded by the Royal Guard, the Royal Rangers, the Nobles of the West, and their soldiers, went down on one knee.

Lasgol stood up and at the top of his voice called, "Long live Egil Olafstone, King of Norghana!"

"Long live King Egil Olafstone!" everyone cried.

Egil, his eyes moist with emotion, thought of his father, his brothers, their sacrifice, everything they had fought for and died, and which he had achieved at last.

"For you, Father, and for you, brothers, the crown of Norghana returns to our family, the Olafstones."

The adventure continues in the next book of the saga:

Deep Threat (Path of the Ranger, Book 19)

Acknowledgements

I'm lucky enough to have very good friends and a wonderful family, and it's thanks to them that this book is now a reality. I can't express the incredible help they have given me during this epic journey.

I wish to thank my great friend Guiller C. for all his support, tireless encouragement and invaluable advice. This saga, not just this book, would never have come to exist without him.

Mon, master-strategist and exceptional plot-twister. Apart from acting as editor and always having a whip ready for deadlines to be met. A million thanks.

To Luis R. for helping me with the re-writes and for all the hours we spent talking about the books and how to make them more enjoyable for the readers.

Roser M., for all the readings, comments, criticisms, for what she has taught me and all her help in a thousand and one ways. And in addition, for being delightful.

The Bro, who as he always does, has supported me and helped me in his very own way.

Guiller B, for all your great advice, ideas, help and, above all, support.

My parents, who are the best in the world and have helped and supported me unbelievably in this, as in all my projects.

Olaya Martínez, for being an exceptional editor, a tireless worker, a great professional and above all for her encouragement and hope. And for everything she has taught me along the way.

Sarima, for being an artist with exquisite taste, and for drawing like an angel.

Special thanks to my wonderful collaborators: Christy Cox, Mallory Brandon Bingham and Peter Gauld for caring so much about my books and for always going above and beyond. Thank you so very much.

To my latest collaborator James Bryan, thank you for your splendid work on the books and your excellent input.

And finally: thank you very much, reader, for supporting this author. I hope you've enjoyed it; if so I'd appreciate it if you could write a comment and recommend it to your family and friends.

Thank you very much, and with warmest regards.

Pedro

Note from the author:

I really hope you enjoyed my book. If you did, I would appreciate it if you could write a quick review. It helps me tremendously as it is one of the main factors readers consider when buying a book. As an Indie author I really need of your support.

Just go to Amazon end enter a review.

Thank you so very much.

Pedro.

Author

Pedro Urvi

I would love to hear from you.
You can find me at:
Mail: pedrourvi@hotmail.com
Twitter: https://twitter.com/PedroUrvi
Facebook: https://www.facebook.com/PedroUrviAuthor/
My Website: http://pedrourvi.com

Join my mailing list to receive the latest news about my books:

Mailing List:
http://pedrourvi.com/mailing-list/

Thank you for reading my books!

Made in United States
Troutdale, OR
06/04/2024